P9-BXX-093

"COMPELLING."
– The New York Times

"HILARIOUS!"
– People

"MIGHTY IMPRESSIVE!"
– Newsday (N.Y.)

"WONDERFUL!"
– Publishers Weekly

"ELEGANTLY WRITTEN,"
– Los Angeles Times

"SHARP AND FUNNY,"
– The Washington Post Book World

"EXCITING!"
– The Denver Post

"FRESH, NEW AND DIFFERENT."
– Tony Hillerman

"SUSPENSEFUL,"
– Miami Herald

THE SUN RISES ON ANOTHER BLOCKBUSTER
FLORIDA CRIME NOVEL!

THE CRITICS LOVE
FLORIDA STRAITS,
THE EXPLOSIVE BEST SELLER BY
LAURENCE SHAMES

"Resounding with great Noo Yawk dialogue and packed
with bad guys in shiny blue suits and good guys in pink
bikini briefs, *Florida Straits* is a wacky caper too won-
dafaull fa woids."
—*People*

"Sharp and funny . . . a comic suspense novel where the
comic and the suspenseful are beautifully merged. . . .
Shames shows a fine deft touch throughout . . . funky,
funny characters that will have you hooked on the
whole ride."
—*The Washington Post Book World*

"The plot line flows like a strong ocean current, and
Shames's quirky Key West denizens clash wonderfully
with the insulated and seamy lives of the mobsters."
—*Publishers Weekly*

"Funny, elegantly written, and hip . . . a nifty new
crime novel!"
—*Los Angeles Times*

"I can't remember when I've had more laughs at the
Mafia's expense. The funniest part is that *Florida
Straits* for all its zaniness provides a truer picture of
mob life than all the recent spate of as-told-to exposé
books put together."
—Peter Maas

PLEASE TURN THE PAGE FOR MORE
EXTRAORDINARY PRAISE . . .

Florida

A NOVEL

A DELL BOOK

Straits

Laurence Shames

Published by
Dell Publishing
a division of
Bantam Doubleday Dell Publishing Group, Inc.
1540 Broadway
New York, New York 10036

This book is a work of fiction. Names, characters, places, and inci-
dents are either products of the author's imagination or are used fic-
titiously. Any resemblance to actual events or locales or persons,
living or dead, is entirely coincidental.

ISBN: 0-440-21511-0

Reprinted by arrangement with Simon & Schuster Inc.

Printed in the United States of America

Published simultaneously in Canada

July 1993

10 9 8 7 6 5 4 3 2 1

RAD

For my sister Germaine,
And in memory of my brother Neil Marc
[1955–1956],
whom I never knew but often miss,
And of Phil Landeck, rare man, rare friend.
So Phil, when will we drink the '82s?

Acknowledgments

Deep thanks to my editor, Chuck Adams,
and my agent, Stuart Krichevsky.
More stalwart and congenial allies
a fellow never had.

Part I

1

People go to Key West for lots of different reasons. Joey Goldman went there to be a gangster.

His best friend Sal Giordano tried to talk him out of it. "Fuck is down there for you?"

They were sitting in a green vinyl booth in Perretti's luncheonette on Astoria Boulevard in Queens. It was January. Outside, torn newspapers were stuck in dirty ice at the bottom of dented wire garbage cans. People walked past holding their hats, their coat collars pulled up to their ears. Skinny dogs squatted on the pavement and steam came out from under them. Joey turned the question around. "Fuck is there for me up here?"

"Up here?" Sal seemed dumbfounded by the remark and gestured toward the grimy window as if pointing out what was obviously paradise. "Up here? Up here is everything, Joey. Up here you got friends, you know the ropes. You need money, you know

13

where to get it. You want sausage, calamari, braciole, you know where to find it, eh? Down there? Down there it's like a little pissant desert island."

"Sounds good to me," Joey said, but Sal kept right on going.

He rubbed a thick hand over his blue-black jowls, then counted on his fingers the things that would be lacking. "There's no unions. There's no casinos. There's nothin' to fence, 'cause the spicks already stole it all. Drugs? You don't wanna fuck with drugs, Joey. The Colombians'll whack your ass. So fuck is in Key West? Fucking palm trees. Fucking coconuts. Joey, listen, you feeling down, you want a vacation, take a vacation. I'll front ya the cash if ya need it. But don't move there. I'm telling you, it is not for you."

"I'm not feeling down," Joey said. "I feel terrific. And I like palm trees." He took a sip of his espresso and his dark blue eyes went out of focus, like he was already picturing the beach, the green water, the curled shrimps with their heads buried in cocktail sauce. "I like to be warm, Sal. I hate the fucking cold. All winter, that coughing, blowing your nose, your feet all frozen. Fingers like you can't even hold the god-damn steering wheel—"

"Joey," Sal cut in, "I don't like freezing my ass off any more than the next guy. But I'm not asking for the weather report. I'm asking what you're gonna *do* down there."

"I'm gonna, like, take over."

Joey was twenty-seven, something below average height, and had almost finished the eleventh grade. He'd had two jobs in his life, neither for very long, none since his mother died and he cut out any pretense of being a citizen. Once he sold shoes, but quit because he didn't care for the sour smell of feet and the crusty feel of second-day Ban-Lon socks. The other time he was a greeter-seater at a seafood joint in Sheepshead Bay, but quit when he realized it made as much sense to do absolutely nothing as to show fat families to their tables on Sunday afternoons.

"Take over *what*, Joey? This is what I'm asking you."

"I guess I won't know that till I get there, will I, Sal?"

Sal picked up his little espresso spoon and frowned at it. He was four years older than Joey and had long ago started being a kind of older brother to him, mainly because Joey's own brother—half brother, really—didn't seem to want the job.

It was a complicated situation. Joey's mother had been Jewish, but they lived in an Italian neighborhood. Everybody knew who Joey's father was, but only certain people were allowed to say so, because Vincente Delgatto was a powerful man with a proper Sicilian wife and a legitimate black-eyed heir. Joey's mother, a slender redhead, had been a beautician at the neighborhood funeral home and had met Joey's father during a period of local unrest, when he'd been something of a regular there. Theirs was said to have been an affair of unusual intensity—though people may have said that simply because of the unusual intensity of Thelma Goldman's gaze. She had turquoise eyes that were always stretched open under thin arched brows, and when she looked at someone, she seemed to be not just seeing that person but fixing him in some idealized, final form.

This could be disconcerting, and some people thought Thelma Goldman was a little crazy. Sometimes, it was true, she did unkind things without meaning to. When Joey was ten, eleven, she made him wear a suit on Jewish holidays, which was confusing to Joey because he didn't feel the least bit Jewish, he felt Sicilian like his friends. Also, the suit always got him beat up. As far as Sal could remember, Jewish holidays were the only times Joey got into fights, and he always lost. That's when Sal started looking out for him. He felt sorry for the runty kid with the knees scraped out of his suit pants and snotty blood coming out of his nose.

"You talk to your old man about this, Joey?"

It was a question Sal hated to ask, because he knew it would make Joey mad. Not that Joey had much of a temper. He didn't. This was one of his worst professional shortcomings. Some guys had a great gift for getting mad; they'd get mad over anything and could instantly puff up into a terrifying display. Joey only got mad when he was mad, and there were only a few topics that got him going. His father was one of them. "Fuck for?" he answered.

"Maybe he's got something for you. Something worth staying for."

"All of a sudden?" Joey said. He splayed his hands out on the Formica table and examined them. "All of a sudden he's gonna gimme something good? Come on, Sal, you know the kinda bullshit work I get. Errand boy. Gofer. Maybe now and then I get to hold a bagga money and pass it to the next jerk down the line. Let's not kid ourselves. I know where I stand. My old man's gonna be *consigliere* any day, my half brother Gino struts around like he's God's fucking gift, and I'm a mutt who's never even gonna get a button."

"Cut it out with that mutt stuff," Sal scolded. "No one gives a shit about that but you."

"Why should they?" Joey said. "But Sal, it's facts. I'm not full Italian, I can't get made. Simple as that."

"O.K. But Joey, you know and I know that plenty of guys make damn good livings without a button."

This was the wrong thing to say. Joey leaned forward over his wrists and blanched between the eyebrows. "Right, Sal, and that's exactly my fucking point. Am I one of those guys? Not hardly. Doesn't that tell you something? I got a father who's a big shot, a brother who thinks he's a big shot, and I gotta scrape for nickels and dimes? Who's lookin' out for little Joey, huh?"

Sal sipped espresso and tried a different tack. "It ever dawn on you that maybe the old man's tryin' to protect you?"

The question made Joey swallow. He didn't try to answer it. "Sal, listen," he said. "My mind's made up. It's not like I'm storming off in a huff. I've thought it over. A lot. I stay around here, I can't be anything but like a third-string guy. I go someplace new, O.K., maybe I fall on my face, but at least I take my shot."

A bus went by outside, belching black steam and rattling the front window of Perretti's. Sal narrowed his eyes and tried to picture the far end of the New Jersey Turnpike and the long road that came after it. All he could conjure up was a vague idea of Trenton, followed by an endlessness of dashed lines snaking away to nowhere. Suddenly it felt to him like *he* was the one going far away from everything he knew. The thought scared him like a shriek in the night. He reached across the table, grabbed Joey by the back of the neck, and pulled his face close.

the bank, everyone's always saying how they're gonna move out on the Island. The girls from school, they all think they're going to L.A. It's like a safety valve, all this talk about leaving. But no one does it."

"And why don't they?" Joey said. He sat up higher in bed and gestured with his coffee mug. "One reason. They don't have the balls."

"Don't curse, Joey. It's common."

"Balls is a curse? Balls is a part of the body."

Sandra had put on her big square glasses. She let them slide forward on her narrow upturning nose and stared him down in the mirror.

"Awright," he resumed. "Nerve. They don't have the nerve. They'll bitch and moan all right, because that's easy. But will they change things?"

"Not everyone *can* change things." Sandra had had good evidence of this. Her father was a longshoreman and a drunk who would now and then stop drinking and start crying. Her mother was a loud and flamboyant complainer who would quite regularly pack up the kids, run away to the Poconos or Montauk, and come back forty-eight hours and half a carton of Newports later with nothing settled. Sandra could still remember the red wool coat her mother always bundled her into on these strange excursions. It had big square black buttons that Sandra toyed with in the car. "Besides," she continued, "change means *change,* Joey. It doesn't just mean going somewhere else."

But Joey was not to be deflected. "Yeah, people'll look around and say, 'Look at this crummy apartment I live in. It's got one stupid window that looks out at an airshaft. It's got one radiator that hisses like a mother and drips rusty water onna floor. It's so small my girlfriend can hardly fit her behind between the bed and the mirror.' Am I right, Sandra, am I right?"

"Look," she said, "the apartment's a dump. Who's arguing? You wanna move to Park Avenue, I'm ready. But Joey, people don't turn their whole lives upside down because they have a small bedroom."

"Maybe they should. It isn't like their lives are so terrific right side up."

Sandra was putting on lipstick. She tried to talk and got some on her teeth. "Joey," she finally said, "maybe life isn't supposed to be terrific."

"No? Then what's it supposed to be?"

"You know. Like O.K., organized, decent. Regular."

Joey put his coffee mug on the nightstand, sat up in bed, and hugged his knees. "Nah," he said at last. "Just decent? Just regular? Nah, I can't buy that. Besides, Sandra, can we be a little honest here? I don't believe that's really what you want either. Because if it was, you'd be a jackass to be with me, and I don't think you're a jackass. I'm never gonna be a working stiff, you know that. A regular guy hoping for a ten-dollar raise? I'd slit my goddamn wrists. I gotta do things the way I gotta do 'em."

"That's fine for you, Joey. But what about me?" Sandra turned to face him. She had thin bluish skin that flushed salmon pink in the cold, the heat, or the wind, and now a rise in blood pressure was making her cheeks gleam through her makeup. "I realize this is hard for you to grasp, but I feel pretty good about things the way they are. I don't mind it here. And I like my job."

"So you'll get another job," he said. "They have banks in Florida."

There was a certain expression, not severe, exactly,

but immovable, that came onto Sandra's face at moments when she realized that a double helping of practicality was required of her. "You sure it's that easy?" she said.

Joey wasn't sure, it showed in his face. Sandra pressed her advantage. She squared her shoulders and straightened the placket of her blouse. "Besides, I like being able to say, 'I'm your Anchor banker.' I like the sound of it. I like the prestige."

"What prestige? Sandra, you're a teller at a drive-up window in Rego Park."

"And what the hell is wrong with that?"

Joey held up his hands as if fending off a punch. "Nothing's wrong with it. It's terrific. It's great. But don't make it sound, ya know, like I'm asking you to throw away a career in high finance."

"No," Sandra said, "all you're asking me to do is throw away the only job I've got, leave my friends, drop out of accounting class for like the third time already. And I'm supposed to do all this just because you've got something to prove to your father and brother?"

Joey let his hands fall so that they slapped against his thighs. He pushed a noisy breath past his gums and shook his head. "First of all, Sandra, he's my half brother. Second of all, this has nothing to do with them."

Sandra crossed her arms and leaned back against the dresser. Her mouth curled into what would have been a smirk except that her light eyes softened at the same time. "Joey, I thought we were being honest here. Let's face it—everything you do has to do with them."

Joey pursed his lips and looked down at the creases

in the blanket, the way they fanned out, then flattened. He reached for his coffee mug and took a few seconds to hide his face in it and think. But Sandra went on before he'd come up with anything to say.

"Listen, Joey, I'm late. I'll think about it."

She slipped into a fuzzy white cardigan and sidled around the bed to give Joey a kiss. She was in the doorway when she turned and spoke again. "Joey, lemme ask you something. I know better than to look for any promises from you. O.K. But you're asking me to drop everything and move to Florida. Will you at least admit that that's like a serious thing to ask somebody to do?"

Joey absently smoothed the creases in the blanket. For a moment it seemed harder to answer the question than it would be to sit there sipping coffee until Sandra left, then quietly pack a bag and go away without her. Then he pictured the empty front seat of his car. "Yeah," he said softly.

"Yeah what?" Sandra pressed.

Joey looked down at his feet under the blue blanket. The radiator started to hiss and a drop of rusty water plopped into the pie plate that Sandra had put underneath the valve. "Yeah, it's like serious."

3

On the long ride south on Interstate 95, Joey Goldman's 1973 Eldorado convertible burned five quarts
of oil, drank up two hundred and thirty gallons of gas,
and blew a right rear tire next to a water tank that
said Lumberton, N.C. While putting on the spare,
Joey tore a fingernail and spent the rest of the day
trying to nibble it back into shape. It was the sort of
thing you could do on cruise control.

When Sandra saw her first palm tree, she started
to laugh. It was all by itself in front of some rest rooms
in a turnoff just north of the Florida border, like
Georgia was telling the world that it had palm trees
too.

"What's so funny?" Joey asked her.

"Tropicana," Sandra said. "It looks like the girl on
the orange juice."

South of Jacksonville, they stopped at a Waffle
House for sausage and eggs, and Sandra changed into

a pair of turquoise shorts and white sandals with flowers on the insteps. Joey rolled up his sleeves, undid the second button of his shirt, and told himself he would never again remove the sunglasses that Sal Giordano had given him as a going-away gift. He loved them. They had dark blue lenses that gave everything the velvety look of the half hour after sunset; the black plastic earpieces slid through his hair with a feeling smooth as sex. At Vero Beach he pulled off onto the shoulder and took the Caddy's top down. This required some wrestling because the frame was rusty and the electric system hadn't worked in years. "January eleventh," Joey said. "Seventy-six degrees. Sandra, did I tell ya this was gonna be great?"

They spent that night south of Miami so they could drive the Keys in daylight. Their motel room had a smell that would always be with them from then on, but which they would hardly ever notice again, it was so much a part of south Florida. The smell was a sort of far-off mildew mixed with salt, mixed with iodine, mixed with oysters choking on mud, mixed with a very fine dust of limestone that was always dissolving in the breeze. Rounding off the aroma was a hint of toasted sawdust, as if the termites cooked the wood as they ate it.

Joey and Sandra made love amid that Florida smell, then they listened for a few minutes to the locusts and the distant traffic, then Sandra started to cry.

"Hey?" said Joey. He touched her shoulder under the damp sheet.

"It's O.K.," she said. "It's O.K." She nuzzled her face into her pillow. "But Joey, aren't you even a little afraid we just won't like it here?"

He raised himself up on an elbow and breathed

deeply of the dust, mold, and strange flowers closed up for the night. He'd never really thought about it quite that way. He'd decided he would like it, he didn't have to think about it. He was going someplace warm, to do some business, establish himself, launch an enterprise. The place had to be suitable, but beyond that? Did Al Capone like Chicago? Did Meyer Lansky like Las Vegas?

"It's gonna be fine," he said. "Terrific." He turned over and groped around in the dark to make sure his sunglasses were on the nightstand next to him. Then he fell asleep with just the haziest misgivings barely beginning to scratch at his brain.

"Islamorada," Joey said, pointing out the open window of the Cadillac at many millions of dollars' worth of gleaming boats. "That's where the President goes fishing. Also my Uncle Tony. He went fishing there once. Brought back this big stuffed thing, this fish with like a spike kinda nose. But the guy didn't stuff it right. Still smelled like fish. Then it rotted. Right up onna wall. Got all soft and started to drip. Uncle Tony was pissed."

Sandra rubbed sunblock on her pale arms and looked out at the bait shops and the seashell stores. Then she started smearing up her legs, and by the time she looked out the window again, the shops were gone, the palm trees were gone, everything was gone. "Joey," she said, "there's no land there." She grabbed her armrest.

"Ain't that something?" Joey said. "Yup. The Keys. Unbelievable. You ever hear of this guy—what was his name? Flagler. Right. This guy could organize. You see that other bridge over there?"

He pointed to an arc up on trestles that ran parallel to U.S. 1. Pelicans were perching on it, scratching their bellies with their beaks. Black kids were fishing, dropping hand lines into the shallow green water where the Gulf of Mexico met the Florida Straits.

"That was Flagler's railroad. Now get this, Sandra. Guy buys up all this land, dirt cheap 'cause you can't get to it. So he builds a railroad, which makes the land very valuable. He builds hotels, and he charges whatever he likes 'cause he's the only guy who's got 'em. It's like total control, and it's legal. Flagler needs cash, he sells a swamp somewhere for a few million. *Oh, it's underwater? The land's onna bottom. Trust me.* He puts up dog tracks, amusement parks. This guy had all the leverage. A genius."

Sandra looked over at the railroad trestle. "But Joey, there's big holes in it. I mean, places where it just stops."

And it was true that large stretches of shining water and empty sky could be seen through Henry Flagler's railroad.

"Yup. That was the only problem. Hurricanes. Some trains blew inna water and it wasn't fun anymore, I guess. Well, you can't buy off a hurricane. At least this way boats can get through." He adjusted his sunglasses, wiggled the plastic earpieces through his hair.

Sandra watched him out of the corner of her eye. Joey was not usually so chatty, almost never before noon. Most days he woke up grumpy, his mood as rough as his morning stubble. Sandra wasn't crazy about that, but at least she was used to it.

"You say you've never been here before?"

Joey was too wrapped up in the scenery to notice

that the question had a suspicious edge to it. True, there were things he didn't tell Sandra, though they were not the sort of things a girlfriend needed to get jealous about, just things it was better she didn't know. But he'd never been to the Keys before, and he said so.

"You seem to know a lot about the place."

He let go of the steering wheel and shrugged. "I know people who've been here."

"Like your Uncle Tony."

"Yeah, Uncle Tony. And my mother."

Sandra paused. She seemed surprised—not that Joey's mother had been to the Keys but that Joey mentioned it. His mother had been dead six years. Sandra had never met the woman, and Joey never talked about her if he could help it. Three, four times a year, she came up in conversation, usually around some holiday, when everyone was feeling lousy anyway. Not that Joey hadn't loved his mother. That was just it. He had, Sandra knew that. But Joey was not one of those people who managed to pull some sweet juice out of being sad. For him, to linger on a sad thing that couldn't be fixed was as pointless as sticking your finger in your eye.

"When was your mother down here?" Sandra ventured.

Joey looked away from her, out the window at the pelicans, and waited to see if he'd get the usual knot in his belly and if it would clamp his mouth. It didn't happen. Maybe it was the sunshine, maybe just being away from Queens. "I think she was here a few times," he said.

Sandra stayed still and quiet.

"I never really got the story straight," Joey continued. "And of course I'm never gonna hear it from my old man. But as well as I make out, what happened was like, if my father had business in Miami or Tampa or even Havana in the old days, he'd arrange for my mother to come down, and they'd have a few days together. You know. Some lobsters, some champagne, some dancing, some jazz, some walks onna beach. Pretty romantic, I guess. Then he'd go back to the wife and baby Gino, and my mother would ride home on a separate train."

He squeezed the steering wheel, pursed his lips, and tugged on an earlobe. "Fucking sordid, isn't it?"

"If they cared for each other . . ." Sandra began. But then, as though the notion didn't convince her, she let it trail off through the open roof. Joey flashed her a bent look that seemed to say, *Thanks for trying*, but the notion didn't persuade him either. He blew out a long breath, turned on the radio, and listened to static for a while.

"Reception sucks down here," he said.

It took Seven-Mile Bridge to pull him out of his sulk.

"Now *this* is really something, Sandra. Seven miles, nothing but water. How'd they do it? Like hammer some stakes innee ocean? I mean, this whole road is just like. . . like if they had a pier at Coney Island that ran practically to Sandy Hook. I mean, *look* at this!"

Sandra held on to her armrest and squirmed, as if trying to find a shady place in the roofless car. Pelicans scudded by, big and slow as clouds, and terns dove underneath the trestles. Joey clicked on the cruise control and half stood in the driver's seat to get a better view of the green water dotted with clumps of dusty mangrove and splotched with reddish patches

"It's only the passenger side. The glass didn't even fall out. It's just, ya know, smashed. Looks kinda like a spiderweb. Sit up. I brought coffee."

Joey groped for his sunglasses on the night table. He slid them on, then opened his eyes. The tinted lenses didn't blot out the fuzzy dots of mold where the ceiling met the walls.

Sandra had brought with her a copy of the Key West *Citizen*, already folded to the real estate ads.

"Expensive," she said, bouncing the eraser end of her pencil off her lower lip.

"So what else is new?" said Joey. He had around nine thousand dollars cash with him, which was all the money he had in the world. No bank accounts, no social security, nothing written down. But, he told himself, capital was not the key to his business, vision was, and vision he had. He didn't have the details worked out, that much was true, and in fact his plans had gaps as yawning as those in Henry Flagler's railroad. Still, in his mind he could see the grand sweep, the structure. He'd lay the groundwork himself. It would be tough making the connections, mapping out the turf, but it had to be done. That would take a month or two. After that, his boys would handle things. Of course, he didn't know exactly who these boys would be. But they had to be out there, they always were. Street guys, soldiers, guys who maybe had a little gambling action, a string of girls, some pull with the restaurants, but who needed someone a little savvier, who thought a little bigger, to get things organized. That's what Joey would do: organize. And once things were set up, he'd live the genteel and quiet life of a Boss. Guys would come to him, say Hello, Joey—no, make that Hello, Mr. Goldman.

He'd gesture them into a chair, and they'd be flattered to be asked to sit. Then, discreetly but not without a certain ceremony, they'd hand over money. This part Joey could see quite clearly: Sometimes the money would be in neat white envelopes, other times in rumpled paper bags. The transactions would take place at a spotless glass table, under a palm tree, by a swimming pool.

"Sandra, these places have pools?"

"Yeah, Joey." She narrowed her light green eyes and gave a sigh that was midway between exasperated and amused. "For thirty-five hundred a month, you get a pool."

"*Marrone*," said Joey. "These are houses?"

"Yeah. There's also condos, but they seem to rent by the week. About fifteen hundred."

Joey hid his face in his Styrofoam coffee cup. "Well, it'll be no problem once I get things going."

"Right," said Sandra, "but it's a little bit of a problem right now. I'll call a broker."

"Yeah, call a broker," Joey said. He knew how these things worked. He wiggled the earpieces of his shades and spoke in a worldly tone. "The prices they print, Sandra, they never expect to get 'em. We'll make 'em an offer."

"Your offer's been refused," the broker said, hanging up the phone. "Sorry." He had a gray crew cut, capped teeth, one small diamond earring, and an almost priestly air of truly wanting to help. He'd shown them four houses and three condos. They'd all been too expensive, and not one owner seemed willing to negotiate. Now Joey and Sandra were back at the real estate office, sitting on aluminum chairs while the broker riffled through his box of properties. "You have to understand," he said. "It's season. The town is really full just now."

Joey pulled on his lip. "We seen seven empty places in an hour," he said. "How full can it be?"

The broker just smiled. "If a pool is a priority for you, maybe you should consider a compound. There's a nice little two-bedroom cottage available on Packer Street. Eighteen hundred a month."

"What's a compound?" Sandra asked, and in the question was a note of dread. She was trying to choke down panic, a fear that she'd made a terrible mistake in quitting Anchor Bank, a terrible mistake in coming to Florida, and could easily make the worst one yet in picking a place to live. *Compound.* The word sounded military, or southern. Would it be Quonset huts and navy brats, or tar paper shacks with doorless refrigerators and hound dogs in the yard?

"Oh," said the broker, "it's very Key West. A compound is a cluster of small houses, fenced off from the street, usually built around a pool and Jacuzzi and barbecue that everybody shares."

"Doesn't sound very private," Joey said. He didn't much like the idea of the neighbors standing around roasting wienies when the boys came to deliver cash. But of course this first place was just temporary. Once the enterprise got rolling, they'd move to one of the rambling, hedged-in establishments in the pricey corner of town.

"You give up some privacy," the broker conceded. "But less than you might think. How long you been in Key West?"

"One day," Sandra said, a little sheepishly. She seemed to understand already that Key West was one of those places where people, for lack of much else to say, bragged about how long they'd been there. You couldn't get much lower on the social ladder than one day.

"Well, you know," the broker said gently, "one of the things you'll discover is that no one really cares what anybody else does down here. The island's too small and the weather's too hot to get bothered. Believe me, a more tolerant town you're never going to find."

"Doesn't look like much from outside," Joey said. He was standing under a scorching sun in a narrow gravel driveway, between a rank of plastic garbage cans and a row of rusty mailboxes with names scrawled on pieces of adhesive tape.

"That's the whole idea," said the broker. "Laid back. Unpretentious. Very Key West. But watch."

He punched in a combination and pushed open a wooden door cut into the grape-stake fence. Instantly the temperature dropped five degrees and the baked, dusty smell of the street disappeared. The compound was a small private jungle of palms and ferns, jasmine bushes and banana trees, bougainvillea and hibiscus. Right in the middle, like the old village well, was a big sunken hot tub, and to the left of it was a free-form pool ringed with pale blue tile. A man was standing waist-deep in the water. He had his elbows propped on the edge and was reading a paperback. In front of him were three cans of Bud in foam rubber sleeves and an ashtray full of butts.

" 'Lo, Steve," the broker said to him. "Whatcha reading?"

Steve turned the book over, as if he had to look at

the cover to remind himself. "Nazis," he said. "Buzz bombs."

"Ah," said the broker. "Well, this is Joey and Sandra. They'd like to see the place."

"Help yourselves," said Steve. Then he smiled. "If you're interested, we'll talk. This is where I do most of my business." Then he smiled. He never smiled while he was talking, only after. You could count the beat, waiting for the teeth to come out from under the wiry red mustache.

The house was small but bright and airy. Sisal rugs. Ceiling fans. A Florida room with louvered windows. Bad paintings of seashells and water birds.

"And it's got an outdoor shower," said the broker.

"I usually shower inside," said Joey. "I'm funny that way. Whaddya think, Sandra?"

Her answer was without excitement but very definite. "It's by far the best for the money. I think we should take it."

"You think he'll come down on the rent?" Joey asked the broker.

The broker shrugged. "Compounds cater to, well, it's a special market. Ask him."

Outside, Steve had lit another cigarette and moved on to the next beer down the line. "How d'ya like it?" he asked. Then he smiled.

"It's charming," Sandra said.

"Yeah," said Joey; "lotta charm. Very Key West. But about the rent . . ." He paused, hoping Steve would take over. Steve just sipped some beer. "I mean, it's a little small."

"Cozy," Steve said. "But you've got the grounds and the pool. And we've got a nice group of folks here. Over there"—he turned and pointed to a trellised cottage half hidden by vines—"that's where Peter and Claude live. They're bartenders. Work nights at a place called Cheeks. Over here"—he gestured toward a bungalow tucked away behind the hot tub—"that's Wendy and Marsha's place. They have an antique store. And back there"—he did a little pirouette—"that's Luke and Lucy. He's a reggae musician and she's a mailman. Nice people. Considerate."

It was only at this point, when Steve was maneuvering around the swimming pool, that Joey realized he was naked. Dwarfed by his big, stretched belly, his submerged private parts looked like baby birds left home in a nest beneath an overhanging cliff. Of buttocks he had virtually none.

"And whadda you guys do?" Steve asked. Then he smiled.

Joey hesitated. This was not a question that was asked among his circle of acquaintances, nor was he accustomed to chatting with naked guys in mixed company. "Well," he said, "Sandra here is in banking. And me, well, I do this and that."

"This and that," Steve said. "Well, that's what most people do down here. You'll fit right in. Anyway, you wanna think it over, think it over. This is where I'll be."

Sandra tugged at Joey's sleeve.

"Excuse us a minute," said Joey, and they retreated to a shady alcove in back of the gas grill. Joey took off his sunglasses and put them on again.

"I don't know about this, Sandra. I came here to be a businessman, not a goddamn nudist. I mean, you gonna get naked with these people?"

"Me?" said Sandra. As if by reflex, she reached up

toward the high collar of her blouse. "Joey, I'm the original prude, you know that. I blush if someone sees my slip. But if other people wanna take their clothes off, I got no problem with that."

"I dunno," said Joey. "And I'm not crazy about the idea of living with a Fed right here."

"Who's a Fed?"

"What's 'er name? Lucy."

"Joey, she's a mailman."

"A Fed's a Fed. You think they don't all work together? They all wanna know your business. Right away it's the IRS, the FBI."

"Joey, admit it. You're just uptight about the naked part."

He languidly dug a toe into the compound's white gravel. "Awright, I admit it. I didn't bring you down here to hang around a bunch of guys with their dicks out. Am I weird? No, I'm not weird. Sandra, this is a weird town."

"You're the one who wanted to come here," she said. "I was perfectly happy to stay in Queens. Say what you want about Queens, Joey, at least people don't go around with nothing on."

Joey raised his hands up around his temples. It was a gesture of surrender but also a warning that he didn't want to hear any more. "So, Sandra, you're telling me you wanna live in this freakin' nudist camp?"

"I'm telling you we haven't seen anything better we can afford. I'm telling you I don't wanna go back to some depressing motel that stinks of mildew. And I'm telling you that if we don't make a decision, I'm gonna scream."

Joey tapped his foot; the gravel dust did not come off his black loafer. Then he walked back to the pool.

"So, Steve," he said. "We're innerested. But eighteen hundred—it's a little steep for us. Take fifteen."

Steve looked at the broker. The broker looked at Steve.

"Fifteen if it's year-round," said the naked landlord. "If you'll sign a full-year lease."

"Deal," said Joey. He felt like he'd gotten away with something, and it cheered him up. Three hundred bucks off just for signing a stupid piece of paper.

"I'll get the lease," Steve said, but Joey stopped him with a gesture before he could wade to the stairs. Underwater was bad enough. He wasn't ready for full frontal in the glaring light of day.

"We'll go get our car and stuff," said Joey. "We'll sign the papers after."

5

On a breezy morning at the end of January, Joey Goldman stood in front of his bathroom mirror and tried to figure out how best to display his sunglasses on those rare occasions when he wasn't actually wearing them. Some guys, he'd noticed, hooked them around their second shirt button, and let them hang straight down. This was stylish, Joey thought, but maybe, well, a little feminine. Of course, he could simply drop them in his breast pocket, but then they were invisible, he got no benefit at all. Maybe the suave compromise was to put them in the pocket, but with an earpiece looped outside.

Joey spent about ten minutes on this problem, and told himself he wasn't killing time, he was working on his image, which after all was an important aspect of his business. He wasn't hiding out inside the compound, inside the cottage, behind the bathroom door. Or maybe he was. Had he ever in his life had a more frustrating few weeks? He couldn't say for sure.

He hadn't made a nickel, and it was a damn good thing Sandra had right away found a job. Seems there was a shortage of bank tellers in south Florida, and considering what they were paid, that was not surprising. Her salary at Keys Marine was just enough to halve the pace at which they were going broke.

Meanwhile Joey had a lot of time to himself, to think, to organize, to set things up. But all he'd really accomplished was laying down the base coat for a glorious tan. That, and meeting the neighbors.

The neighbors were very Key West, and Joey, who was not, had a tough time figuring out how he was supposed to feel about them. Take Peter and Claude. They couldn't have been nicer or more welcoming, but they were, after all, queer. Claude was blond, very tall and thin, and walked like he was modeling mink coats. Peter had bleached his hair but kept his eyebrows dark, as if trying unsuccessfully to look sinister. They worked late, and would emerge from their cottage around two P.M., wearing sarongs. They'd offer Joey herb tea and cookies that didn't snap, they bent: Key West was a humid place. Then they'd ask him questions about the theater, the opera, downtown clubs, stuff like that. Questions about New York, but not the New York Joey knew. Joey couldn't deny that he appreciated the company, the chitchat, but he also couldn't deny that there was something faggoty about herb tea, about a drink where you could see the bottom of the cup. He couldn't tell if he was pretending to like Peter and Claude but didn't, or pretending not to but did.

With Wendy and Marsha, it was the opposite. They

were cordial enough, but Joey had the distinct impression they didn't like him. They made him feel like he was intruding from a distance. They had a cat they took for walks, and they held each other's arms while they walked it. They always seemed to be deep in conversation on deep subjects—art, politics, whatever. Wendy, or maybe it was Marsha, had the hairiest legs Joey had ever seen, legs with ringlets. His eyes were drawn to them as to the stump of a missing arm, and this made conversation awkward.

With Luke the reggae musician, conversation was awkward for a different reason. Luke didn't talk. He lived with a Walkman clipped onto the waistband of his shorts, and would sometimes sit for hours with his feet dangling in the pool and his eyes narrowed in concentration. When Lucy the mailman came home from work, she'd plop down next to him on the cool tiles, still wearing her post office shorts, slate blue with a navy stripe at the side. Lucy was extremely beautiful, for a Fed, with huge dark eyes widely spaced and skin as even and inviting as the morning's first cup of creamy coffee. But even this caused Joey some unease because he hadn't been raised to find black women, or letter carriers, attractive.

So the compound, all in all, was diverting, a relatively inexpensive form of foreign travel. But Joey hadn't come to Florida in search of the exotic, he'd come to make his fortune, and the fact was that three weeks into his new life, he was no closer to a payday than on the morning he'd bolted Queens. Not that he'd been lazy. No. Especially in the first ten days, two weeks, he'd been enterprising as hell. He'd really put himself out there. But nothing had worked. He'd been laughed at, kissed off, insulted, threatened, and if he hadn't caught a beating, that was only because of his well-developed feel for the moment when he should back off and scram.

First, there was the disaster of the numbers game, what the Cubans call *bolita*. It was a nice little operation, pegged to the track at Hialeah but locally run, and Joey didn't see why he shouldn't have a piece of it. He wasn't looking to muscle in, and he wasn't looking for a handout. He wanted a partnership, and he'd give value for his cut. Numbers was something he knew; he knew it big-city style. So he'd bring some sophistication to the racket, expand it up the Keys. It would be good for everybody. More cash flow for the Cubans, and for Joey a natural recruiting pool for some solid soldiers.

So he went to a café on Virginia Street, sat down at the counter near a fan whose grille was matted with streamers of greasy dust, and ordered up a Cuban sandwich. He watched the *patrón* slap it together; it wasn't pretty. Fatty pork. Some kind of gray lunch meat with big globs of lard stuck in it. Limp onions sodden with oil. Thick smears of warm, off-color mayonnaise on both sides of the spongy bread. Joey started feeling queasy before he'd had a bite. From his Sicilian father he'd inherited a certain finickiness about all foods not invented, cooked, and served by Italians; from his Jewish mother he'd acquired the phobic belief that anything not kept tightly wrapped in the refrigerator, then overcooked would instantly turn to poison. But Joey had a job to do. He started the sandwich.

"I wanna buy some *bolita* numbers," he said softly to the *patrón*.

The man was overweight, unshaven, his teeth

looked soft, and one of his shirttails was hanging out.
But stupid he was not. He looked at the gringo suf-
fering through his lunch. The gringo wore a stiff white
shirt like no one wore in Key West, except maybe to
a wedding, and he carried his sunglasses like a cop
who was trying not to look like one. "We no sell numbers here."

Joey gave him a knowing wink. "Come on. This is
my neighborhood now. I'm right around the corner.
You're telling me I gotta go all the way to where I
useta live to buy my numbers?"

"Where you use to live, my friend?"

Joey stifled a belch. "Bertha Street." That was near
where Sandra worked.

"Ees not so far, my friend. You like the *bolita,* you
buy your numbers there."

A week and four nauseating lunches later, Joey had
acquired enough credibility to be allowed to buy some
losing numbers, and to meet the *bolita* runner for
Virginia Street. His name was Hector. Hector was six-
teen, didn't walk right, was cross-eyed behind thick
glasses, and went to Catholic school. Joey decided he
wouldn't recruit him as one of his boys, just use him
for one little errand.

"Hector," he said, "hold out your hands. Here's
twenty dollars. That's for you. Here's a hundred dollars. That's for your boss. Give it to him and tell him
to arrange a meeting between me and *his* boss. Tell
him a gentleman with friends in New York would like
to discuss some business with him. You got that,
Hector?"

Next day, Hector told him that Señor Carlos would
see him at four o'clock at a laundromat on White
Street. This allowed Joey to get up from the lunch

counter without having to finish his glistening pile of greasy fried bananas.

He pulled up in the Eldorado and saw three men sitting on mesh beach chairs under an awning, playing dominoes on a cardboard box. "I'm looking for Carlos."

The men stood up, and the one in the middle, who was a head shorter and fifty pounds lighter than either of the other two, said, "I'm Carlos." He was clean-shaven and very wiry, with black hair swept straight back. He'd been born in Florida, went to college for a year, and had no accent except when he wanted one. He wore frameless glasses that gave him the nervously studious look of an early Bolshevik. "Nice car." He lifted his chin toward the smashed windshield.

"Coconut," said Joey.

"Happens a lot down here," said Carlos. "Makes you look like a local."

Joey was duly flattered. Newcomers to Key West always liked to be taken for locals. This changed after they'd met a few.

"Come on," said Carlos, "we'll talk in the back."

He led the way through the laundromat. It was full of old Cuban ladies in black dresses and had the yeasty smell of warm lint. A girl in tight jeans seemed to be having a nervous breakdown on the pay phone. Carlos's men filed behind Joey, giving him the uneasy feeling that someone was about to step on his heel. He felt his shoulders hunching up as if in preparation for the blow.

At the back of the laundromat, a vacant doorframe gave onto a garden. A big four-sided picnic table had been built around a lime tree, and on this table was a basket, a basket big as a tire, filled with unidentifiable fruits. Carlos motioned Joey into a chair, and he himself sat on a picnic bench. His two huge and hairy men perched on the table on either side of the gigantic fruit bowl; the effect was of a still life by a painter who had lost his mind.

"So, Mr. . . ."

"Goldman. Joey Goldman."

"Yes. Mr. Goldman. What can I do for you?"

"I admire your operation," Joey said.

Carlos looked utterly bored by the compliment and made no answer. One of his men picked up a fruit that resembled *Sputnik* and started peeling it with a knife considerably larger than was strictly necessary for the job.

"I'd like to work with you," Joey continued.

Carlos frowned. "You Jewish?"

"Half. You got a problem with that?" Vague memories of disastrous Yom Kippur fistfights cropped up not in Joey's mind but in his stomach.

"Me?" said Carlos. "Not at all. You know what the Puerto Ricans call the Cubans? *Los judiós del Caribe.* They call us that because they're jealous. Because we work hard. We know how to do business. Whadda they know how to do? Cook beans and talk about pussy. Me, I have no problem with Jews. I just like to know who I'm dealing with."

"I'm also half Sicilian," Joey said.

"Ah," said Carlos. He balanced his chin on his knuckles; the pose made him look more than ever like an earnest, aging student. "Half Sicilian. Friends in New York. Cadillac. Goes around flashing hundred-dollar bills. So what are you trying to tell me, Mr. Goldman? Are you telling me things are so bad up north that the Mafia has to send a guy all the way down here to fuck with my little *bolita* game?"

Carlos's goon had finished peeling his fruit and was sucking out the flesh. It had slimy seeds in it, and the goon started spitting them out closer to Joey's black loafers than seemed respectful.

"Did I say anybody sent me?" Joey said. "All I said is I got friends up there."

"Well, good for you," said Carlos, and without raising his voice a single decibel he managed a crescendo of irritation. "I got friends too. I got friends in Miami and I got friends in Havana and I got friends in city hall. And in case you haven't looked at a road map lately, those places are all a lot closer to where you're sitting than fucking New York is."

The spray of slimy seeds came closer to Joey's feet, so close that he couldn't help examining them. They consisted of tiny black pits surrounded by globes of yellowish ooze. He slid his shoes back a couple of inches and didn't realize until later that by that small retreat he had in effect surrendered.

"Carlos, I been looking at road maps plenty. But listen, I'm coming to you like a gentleman, to see if we can work together. You got no reason to get mad."

"That's where you're wrong. I do have a reason. You cost me a hundred twenty dollars already. Fredo, give the man his hundred twenty dollars."

The goon who was not sucking fruit lumbered down from the picnic table and approached Joey. He reached deep into his pants pocket, seemed to be scratching his gonads, then produced a pair of bills.

Joey waved them away. "Hey look, I don't want that money back. That was an investment."

"You don't understand," said Carlos. He shook his

head sadly at the ignorance of outsiders. "It's a cultural thing. You don't give my people money. To give people money, that's an honor. You haven't earned that honor, Mr. Goldman. I give them money. And I never take anything away from my people. Never. So you know what that means? It means that money you spread around so you could look like a big shot, with your fucking Cadillac, your New York plates, that was my money. And now I got a reason to be mad at you."

"Carlos, listen . . ."

"Fredo, give 'im the fucking money."

The goon approached, a hideous, blubbery smile on his face. He reached out his fat fingers and put the bills in Joey's shirt pocket, the same pocket as his sunglasses. The gesture was actually rather gentle, yet it felt to Joey that talons had snapped out and were clawing at his heart.

"There," said Carlos. "That's what you've cost me, just by coming down here. So do yourself a favor and don't ever cost me one more dollar. You got that, Mr. Goldman?"

6

Joey had not been able to remember the retreat through the laundromat. The first thing he recalled was standing on the sidewalk, watching the low red sunlight bounce off his smashed windshield and throw rainbows onto the Caddy's old upholstery. He reached for his sunglasses, and when he pulled them out of his shirt pocket, the hundred and twenty dollars fell onto the street. He hesitated a moment, thinking that it would be a suave gesture to let the money lie there. Then he bent down and plucked the bills off the hot asphalt, hoping no one would notice.

Back at the compound, he'd made a rum and tonic, sat down with it near the pool, and noted in himself a dangerous desire. It was the desire just to sit there and do nothing. When things went badly, it made sitting near water with a cocktail seem absolutely heavenly, saner than any possible action. Then, too, there was the tropical thing. Up north people kept busy to keep warm, kept moving so as not to get trampled. Here it was pleasantest to stay still. This was not something you decided but something you realized through your pores. The air was the same temperature as your skin. It felt good. Soft breezes whispered of the timeless appeal of being a lazy bum.

The only problem was the money.

That, and the way Sandra looked when she got home from work—pale, dressed in long-sleeved business blouses that were too warm, her light eyes tired behind the big square glasses, her fingertips gray-green from counting out fresh twenties. He'd greet her, tan, in a bathing suit, and after hello there'd be a pregnant silence. Problem was, anything Sandra said—What's new? How was your day?—sounded to Joey like a reproach. Not that Sandra meant it that way. She'd sit down on the edge of Joey's lounge chair and pull her skirt primly over her knees. She'd take deep breaths of the jasmine and frangipani, getting the stale aftertaste of air-conditioning out of her lungs, and she'd try to make civil conversation. Joey, like a sulky teenager whose true frustration is that he has nothing to hide, would seem to be hiding behind one-word answers. His day was fine. Nothing was new.

The thing was, Joey would have liked to talk to her, but where he was from, there were a lot of things you just didn't discuss with your girlfriend. *What's new? Well, I tried to take over the numbers racket today. How was your day? Lousy—a three-hundred-pound Cuban spit fruit on my shoe.* No, this was not stuff you told your girlfriend, only your pals. But that assumed you had pals, and who were Joey's buddy-boys down here? Peter and Claude? So Joey mostly kept mum. As soon as he could, he moved the conversation away from himself.

"Sandra," he'd say, "those clothes, they're too hot. You must be like sweltering. Why don't you buy yourself some new ones?"

By reflex, Sandra would run her hand along the fabric of her skirt. "This is O.K. for now. After I get a few paychecks, maybe I'll go shopping."

"And then we gotta get you tan."

Sandra gave a little laugh. "Never happen." Then she looked down at the still blue water of the swimming pool, looked at it as if it were a thousand miles away instead of at her feet. "I wouldn't mind some time to lay around, though."

There it was, thought Joey. Not an accusation, not even a complaint. Just the truth. Joey was not holding up his end, and he knew it.

So, a couple of evenings after his meeting with Carlos, he went downtown to look into the pimping business.

He wasn't going to be a pimp. He had standards about that kind of thing—though it was true that, under the pressures of idleness and exile, he could already feel his standards beginning to erode. Still, pimps (by which Joey meant New York pimps) were an unseemly and amateurish lot. They took drugs and wore idiotic hats, they squandered assets and drowned themselves in after-shave, their business acumen was in their dicks and they had no feel for detail work. They badly needed organization, and that's where Joey would come in—as a sort of pimp's pimp, to discipline them like they disciplined the women. It could be a good thing for everybody, Joey thought. Territory could be fairly assigned. Arguments and slashings could be kept to a minimum. Everyone would earn more and the public would be guaranteed a quality product.

Assuming, of course, that Key West had pimps.

So Joey went down to Duval Street to interview some whores. But they weren't where he expected them to be. Key West, being a place that is literally on the edge, out of sight of neighbors and off limits to embarrassment, is a town where people go to misbehave, a tax haven for the libido. The misbehavior, or attempted misbehavior, is focused near the harbor: the edge of the edge. That's where the tourist bars are, where college students hurtle out of Sloppy Joe's, bravely trying to reach the curb before they barf, where bad music from weather-warped guitars spills through the glassless windows of Rick's, The Bull, and Margaritaville. By all logic, that's where the hookers should have been, ambushing sports made frisky by tequila.

But the streetwalkers had apparently been moved out of there, in deference, no doubt, to the more sedate visitors off the second-rate cruise ships and the occasional parents who had read the wrong brochure and brought their kids along. So Joey cruised Duval toward its quiet end, the ocean side, where souvenir shops closed at six P.M., where people sat on rocking chairs on the porches of guesthouses, and where on nights of south wind you could hear water splashing on the rocks. It seemed a strange place to look for hookers, but that was where they were.

There weren't many of them. On his first cruise down the street, in fact, Joey spotted exactly one. She was so skinny that the tendons in back of her knees stuck out like bridge cables, and from the way she walked, jittery and woozy at the same time, Joey decided she was probably too strung out to talk to. So he parked the car, sat down on the seawall, watched the pelicans move in and out of the glow of lamps on the pier, and waited. The air smelled of iodine and wet stone. Joey, to his surprise, became more rather than less patient the longer he sat, and he dimly realized how thin the line could be between waiting for something and waiting for nothing.

After twenty minutes or so, a tall redhead came sashaying down the street. Her wig was done up in a modified beehive, her short skirt followed the curve of her hips like the skin on a banana, and her big earrings glinted under the streetlamps. There was professionalism and even grandeur in her slightly knock-kneed gait. Joey approached her.

"Wanna party, handsome?" she asked him. The voice was breathy and suitably lewd, and it issued forth from a full, bowed mouth to which a purplish lipstick had been applied with a surprising degree of measure and restraint.

"I wanna talk," said Joey. "Buy you a drink?"

"For starters," cooed the hooker. She had a beauty mark stenciled onto her right cheek, and her eyebrows were tweezed into a steep arc that suggested constant astonishment.

"Where do you like?"

By way of answer, she took Joey's elbow and led him down Duval Street. They walked in silence for a block and a half, and Joey tried not to notice that he was greatly enjoying the rub of her bust against his arm. She was wearing a magenta brocade blouse that fit like a corset and gave her a cleavage like a baby's ass. Also, she smelled good; her perfume was citrusy and clean. She had style, Joey decided. And poise. In New York she'd be at least a two-hundred-dollar piece.

She maneuvered him into a place called Working-man's Tropic. Dim, without music, it was not a tourist joint. At one end, two guys were shooting pool in a golden cone of light. The bar itself was dark wood bristling with beer spigots. Here and there, unkempt ferns dangled from the ceiling. Joey and the hooker sat down at a wicker table, under a plant. Leaves trailed down and tickled Joey's neck.

A waiter came over and the hooker ordered a Kir Royale. Joey asked for a scotch.

"You have great-color eyes," she said to him, clink-ing glasses. "Almost like Liz Taylor. I've always thought bedroom eyes should be dark brown. But that dreamy violet—I'll have to reconsider." She lapped her drink. "So what would you like to talk about?"

"I wanna talk about what you do."

She scanned his face for a moment, and then a look of deep concern crossed her features. *Poor puppy*, the look said. *Can't function? Just want to hear?* Then the kind look was replaced by a mock scolding one and accompanied by a wag of the finger. "I never tell tales on other clients," she said.

"No, no, no," said Joey. "You don't understand. I don't mean *what* you do, I mean how you do it."

The hooker giggled, rounded her shoulders to show off her collarbones, and managed a serpentine squirm in her chair. "That's an art, baby. That's not some-thing that can be explained over one drink."

Joey took the hand that was cold from holding his glass and ran it through his hair. "Look. . .what's your name?"

"Vicki," said the hooker, managing to make the word sound like some forbidden body part.

"Look, Vicki, we don't seem to be connecting here. What I'm talking about is the business side. You see?"

Vicki's mouth came out of its bowed smile, collapsed for a moment into a confused pout, then hardened to a thin line; her tweezed eyebrows fell from their inquisitive arc to parallel the narrowed lips. "No," she said, "I don't see."

At that moment there came an unfortunate ebb in the noise level of the bar, and when Joey spoke again it seemed as if he was addressing the room at large.

"What I'm asking," he said, "to put it simply, is, well, do you have, you know, a pimp?"

"A pimp?" said Vicki, not softly.

The pool players put down their cues. Guys at the bar pricked up their ears.

"A pimp? What're you, crazy? You little piece of shit, what do you think I am? You think I'm a common whore, you little limp-dick shitass?"

Joey reached a conciliatory hand toward Vicki's wrist, but she yanked her arm away. Then she stood up, knocking over her chair and spilling the remains of her Kir. "I'm an artist, you little scumbag. You heartless, gutless, sexless. . .oh sweet Jesus, how I hate people like you."

A thick blue vein was standing out on Vicki's neck, and her lips were quivering in the effort to shape more words. None came, only a ferocious exhalation that seemed to rattle her teeth. Finally, with a green flame of loathing in her eyes, she reached into her blouse, pulled out a tit, and threw it at Joey. It was made of hard rubber, and it hurt his ribs as it bounced off them. The tit landed on the table, wobbled a moment like a twirled coin, and came to rest nipple side up. The red-tinted nub stared at Joey like a blind but accusing eye.

"*Marrone,*" he said.

The bouncer had arrived. He had a shaved head that was a smaller outcropping of his neck, a single sapphire earring, and he cleaved to the notion that the regular customer was always right and the first-time visitor always wrong. He lifted Joey out of his chair with such deftness that Joey almost didn't notice he'd been levitated.

"Hey, bubba," he said, casting a sad glance at the ersatz bosom on the table, "can't you see you're upsetting the lady?" His face was close to Joey's and his breath smelled of nachos.

"Little misunderstanding is all," said Joey. His arms were pinned to his sides.

"It happens," said the bouncer, and he gave Joey a sympathetic squeeze that made him burp up some scotch. "So why don't you just apologize, then go away and never come back."

Joey looked across the table at Vicki, half of whose bosom was still heaving with rage. Apologize? Apologize in public? Apologize in public to a transvestite whore? He, the son, albeit illegitimate, of Vincente Delgatto? In New York this would never happen. But this was not New York, and it had gotten through to Joey that not one person in Workingman's Tropic was on his side. In a flash of pained and utter befuddlement, he was not even sure that *he* was on his side. "I'm sorry, Vicki," he managed to say.

The bouncer eased his grip and Joey filled his lungs.

Vicki straightened her wig, stuck out her chin, and mustered as much dignity as her empty bra cup allowed. "I accept," she said regally. "But only because you've got such pretty eyes. You little douchebag."

7

So all in all, it had not been going well for Joey, and as he sat poolside in his shaving robe and sunglasses, he pondered the narrowing range of his options. The bitch of it was that at every moment it seemed to him that he was very close to getting something started. All it took was for the first piece of the puzzle to fall into place. An income opportunity—*any* income opportunity—would allow him to go out and hire some muscle, and he'd be set. Or if he could somehow get some muscle behind him, the income opportunities would create themselves.

But how did you start? And how low could you go? Already Joey had faked car trouble on U.S. 1 so he could flag down a supermarket truck and propose to the driver that maybe a few hundred pounds of sirloin steak should fall out the back; the teamster had answered by producing a crowbar from under the driver's seat. Next, Joey had casually broached the question of insurance with the proprietor of a local surf-and-turf emporium; the restaurateur said he would check his policy and came back from the kitchen whispering to a pair of slathering Dobermans with stud collars. No one in Key West seemed the slightest bit afraid of Joey, and he found this disconcerting. It made him secretly suspect that even in New York no one had been afraid of him, only of the yeggs he ran with.

"Sandra," he asked one night in bed, "do you think I'm like, what's the word, intimidating?"

Sandra Dugan was not a woman of wide sexual experience, but the most basic of intuitions told her that if you cared about a guy, you didn't giggle at him when you were between the sheets. Instead, she seriously appraised his face. It was boyish, no getting around it. The blue eyes were lacking in threat, the half-curly hair was lamblike in spite of Joey's efforts to keep it slick and tough. Only the cleft in the chin suggested the possibility of violence, and the cleft in the chin was barely visible. "No, Joey," she said, "I wouldn't call you intimidating." Then, to soften the blow, she asked a somewhat disingenuous question. "But why would you wanna be?"

Joey measured his need to talk against the tenets of his code. He couldn't say he wanted to look scary so he could shake guys down. "Ya know," he said, "just so I could, like, persuade people to do things for me."

"People do what they want," said Sandra. "You want people to do things for you, Joey, you have to make them want to."

But what Joey wanted was for people to hand him large amounts of cash. This didn't happen by making nice. It happened by ... well, Joey was close to admitting he didn't know how it happened. And in the meantime here he was, snuggled up in the sack, helplessly going broke. In the meantime he was feeling more guilty every day that Sandra was earning and he was not. No, he had to keep pushing.

But why? Where was the justice in it, the sense? Joey thought about Steve. *He* didn't push. All he did was stand bare-assed in the pool all day. And, unlikely as it seemed, Steve was in his quiet way a big shot. He owned the compound. He was a landlord in a town where rents were through the roof. How had it happened? Did he start off rich, or once do something very smart? Joey had to admit he didn't have a clue how most people made their livings, couldn't figure the logic that made the legitimate world keep turning. If he could figure it out ... well, hell, he had his own angles to worry about.

And there were plenty of them he hadn't looked into yet. There was bed linen for the hotels and table linen for the restaurants. There was construction, union or otherwise. There was garbage. He just had to keep up his initiative. He'd get some sleep, drink some coffee, catch some sun; then, when he was feeling rested and looking prosperous, he'd drag his desperate ass downtown and try again.

Cliff, the daytime bartender at the Eclipse Saloon, smiled weakly and stifled a yawn. This was the sleepy time, coming up on four P.M. The lunch rush was over, the waitresses were smoking and yakking across the empty dining room as they filled the ketchup bottles and topped off the saltshakers for dinner. The bar was vacant except for a couple of lushes who'd been there since breakfast and the occasional regular who stopped by for one pop and some air-conditioning. Late afternoon was also when the dullest strangers wandered in, baffled tourists traveling alone, salesmen who needed a quick belt before opening the swatch book one more time. They always wanted to talk, these solitary ones. They talked about ex-wives, their time in the navy, the clogs in their fuel injectors. They talked about autumn in New England, winter in the Rockies, springtime in Amarillo, about everyplace they ever remembered being happy, but not happy enough to stay there. Now here was a guy who wanted to talk about garbage.

"So how does it work down here?" Joey asked, nursing his tequila. "Is it city, or private, or what?"

"You pay the city," said Cliff, "and the city contracts it out."

"Ah," said Joey. Cliff didn't want to sound bored, and Joey didn't want to sound disappointed. But if garbage money went right to the town, hell, that was like socialism. How could you skim if the checks got mailed straight to city hall, if there were no private carters to squeeze? It killed initiative. "And there's no one who's, like, independent?"

The bartender caught himself yawning and pretended instead to be swallowing a sneeze. "I think the problem is using the dump. We've got this huge landfill here. People call it Mount Trashmore . . ."

Across the U-shaped bar, a white-haired gent was gesturing for a cocktail, and Cliff took the opportunity to escape.

In a moment he returned, and his manner toward Joey had become just slightly deferential. "Bert would like to buy you a drink," he said, nodding toward the old man. "And if you have a minute, he'd like to talk with you."

Now, the Eclipse Saloon was a serious drinking establishment, the edge of whose bar was heavily padded with vinyl-covered foam rubber so customers could rest their elbows or their heads for long periods of time. Joey suddenly felt his arms sinking helplessly deeper into the upholstery, and he realized that his strength was being sapped by an idiotic gratitude that had put a lump in his throat. For weeks he'd been pushing, pushing, pushing. He'd thrust himself on people, taken the lead in every encounter. Everybody had either shied away or been ready to fight. This—O.K., it was a tiny thing, a free drink, but except for the occasional cup of herb tea, it was absolutely the first time in Florida that anyone had done anything for him.

He nodded a thank-you and the old gent waved him over.

He had white hair that in recent years had taken on a tinge of bronzy yellow, yellow like the color of nicotine. He was lean and tall, but with the stretched-out droop of someone who used to be taller. His eyes were black, deep-set, and just a little too close together around a bent and monumental nose.

"Hello, Joey," he said. "Siddown."

The recognition should have made him very edgy, but Joey was so hard up for company that he barely let himself be bothered. "How you know my name?"

"This is a small town, Joey. Guy shows up, drives around in an El D with a New York tag, starts asking about *bolita*, starts talking to truckers, it gets noticed, people talk. And me, I'm a guy people talk to. No particular reason. Except I'm around, I'm available, I listen."

There was something strange about Bert's voice, something that Joey could not immediately place. Then he realized what it was. Bert sounded normal to him. "You from New York?"

"Yeah. Brooklyn. President Street."

"Whaddya know. Me, I'm from—"

"Astoria," Bert put in. "Right around Crescent Street."

Joey gave an uneasy little laugh. "You tryin' to make me, like, paranoid?"

"Joey," said the old man. He leaned back on his stool to give his young companion a chance to see him whole. "You really don't remember me? I guess I've really fucking aged."

Joey scanned the old man's long and loose-skinned face, and meanwhile Bert went on. "And if ya don't mind my saying so as an old family friend"—he pointed to the earpiece of Joey's sunglasses looped over his shirt pocket—"carrying your glasses that way, it makes you look like a pimp."

"Yeah?"

"Yeah," said Bert. "And speaking of which, if you're gonna pimp, try females. You might do better."

"You know about that." It wasn't a question, and Joey no longer sounded surprised.

"Small town, Joey. Very small town. But hey, that goes for every town. New York's the same. Joey, your father's a friend a mine, a business friend. And I knew your mother. A lovely woman. Plus which, I knew you, Joey, when you were a little kid. Four, five years old. Too little to remember, I guess. I useta see you inna park. You had the curliest hair of any kid there. You don't remember?"

The old man's lips were full and always moving,

as if his teeth didn't set too comfortably in his gums. His ears were close to his head but big and soft, with fleshy lobes. His shirt was immaculate, with a pattern of white diamonds embossed on a white background, the starched wings of the collar as straight and even as the tail fins of a plane. "Bert," said Joey. "Bert." He screwed his face into deep-memory mode; then it unwound into a tentative smile. "Bert the Shirt?"

The old man give a quick and furtive glance around the virtually empty bar. *"Piano, piano,* Joey. That's not a name I'm known by anymore. It's just Bert d'Ambrosia, retiree."

"Bert," Joey repeated, like the name tasted good in his mouth. "Sure I remember. My mother liked you. Said you were a gentleman. And you always had hard candies in your pocket." Then Joey's face darkened and by primitive reflex he recoiled. "But hey, I thought you were dead."

"I was," said the old man casually, pulling the cherry out of his whiskey sour and nuzzling the fruit off its stem. Taking his time, he licked the froth from his lips and smiled.

Old people took a grim delight in talking about their ailments and operations, about their arteries hardening and their brains softening, their ankles swelling and their field of vision shrinking. In Florida these small epics of collapse and decay had become both an art form and a competitive sport, and Bert the Shirt d'Ambrosia had polished his delivery to the point where he was seldom beaten in the ghoulish contests. He had the best material, after all. Arthritis, phlebitis, prostate trouble, even cancer—these things couldn't hold a candle to a guy who'd actually died.

"Yeah, Joey, I was fucking dead. Scientifically, electronically dead. *Morto, capeesh?* Yeah. This was about eight years ago.

"You remember what the papers called the I-Beam Trial? Big-ass fucking trial. RICO. Construction racketeering, shit like that? They pulled in everybody. All the families. Some guys they booked, some guys they just subpoenaed. Big publicity splash. Well, a few guys didn't wanna go to court, remember? They faked angina, fainting spells, whatever.

"Me," Bert went on, "I went. I wasn't indicted. They were just yankin' my chain. I figured fuck 'em, they wanna put me on the stand, I can take the heat. Big mistake, Joey. I get to court, there's a million reporters on the steps, the prosecutors are in their best suits, cameras are in my face. I start not feeling good. I get clammy, my arms start to tingle. I get this tightness in my chest, and all I can think of is that it's like a fucking meatball rolling toward my heart. I'm thinking, Shirt, you asshole, all those big-ass steaks, all that booze, all those cigarettes, all that tension—now you're gonna die right here on the six o'clock news.

"I can hardly talk. I whisper to my lawyer, 'Hey, Bruce, I think I'm havin' a heart attack.' He laughs. He thinks I'm fuckin' around. 'Hey, that wasn't the plan,' he says. 'You wanted to appear.' Then he notices I'm turning blue.

"So now I'm on a stretcher, they're carrying me back down the courthouse steps. My eyes are closed, and I can still see flashbulbs going off. And it dawns on me, the one good thing about dying. I went to court to play the big man, show everybody I wasn't afraid. Now I couldn't give a fuck what anybody thought. They wanna think I'm a common criminal,

they wanna think I'm a coward, fuck does it matter?
You live, you die. I should care what these assholes
thinka me?

"By the time they get me to the ambulance, I'm
pretty out of it. I hear the siren, but it seems like
really far away. I know I'm movin', but it's like bein'
on a boat more than drivin' downa street. They stick
this oxygen mask over my face, and the oxygen has
like a blue smell, an electric smell. It makes me
think of when I was a little kid and went to Rockaway and there was a big-ass summer thunderstorm.
The air smelled like that after lotsa lightning. I
thinka that, my mother onna beach with me, and I
start to cry.

"They told me after, I was unconscious by the time
we got to St. Vincent's. They put me on a whaddyacallit, a monitor, were rolling me through the hall, and
that was that."

"That was what?" Joey asked, his elbows deep in
the padded bar, his drink getting watery in front of
him.

"*It*," said Bert. "That was *it*. I died."

"Unbefuckinglievable," said Joey.

"Yup. They told me after, I was dead for like forty
seconds. They jump-started me with this cattle prod
kinda thing. I twitched like a goddamn spastic, then
I started breathing again.

"So anyway, I stood inna hospital three weeks. They
hadda check for brain damage, shit like that. When
ya die, ya know, it affects the mind sometimes. And
I'll tell ya something weird. The only parta my brain
that was affected? I can't carry a tune no more. I can't
even sing Happy fucking Birthday. And I useta love
to sing.

"So I did some thinking. I decided I wanted out. Yeah, outta the family. I mean, enough was enough. My nerves were shot. So when I got home, I went right to the top, right to Scalera. Joey, that man was a prince. He invited me to his house. I took a copy of my EKG with me.

"So he gives me a glass of anisette, and he says, 'Shirt, what's on your mind?'

"So I unroll the paper on his dining room table and I say, 'Frankie, you know what this is?'

"He looks at it, it's like a graph, ya know, and he says, 'Looks like the fuckin' stock market.'

"I say, 'No, Frank, it's my life. And you see this flat part over here? This is where I died.'

"And he says, 'Jeez, Bert, I'm sorry.'

"So I says, 'Don't be sorry, I'm O.K. now. But Frank, the way I look at it, I've given my life for this thing of ours. I was solid and loyal to the end.'

" 'I knew you would be, Bert,' he says. 'But what are you getting at?'

" 'Frank,' I say, 'I feel like I deserve something for dying.'

"Now, this makes Scalera a little nervous because, as fine a human being as he was, he didn't like to part with money. He was a little, ya know, cheap, let's face it. So he says, 'Whaddya want, Bert?' but his voice isn't quite as friendly as before.

" 'All I want is to be allowed to walk away,' I tell him. 'I want your blessing to retire.'

"So now he's relieved that I'm not asking for cash. But he's still nervous because what if it gets around that it's O.K. to quit, and good earners start walking away? 'Jeez, Bert,' he says, 'I'd like to say yes, but it'd be, like, a precedent. I mean, O.K., you're a special case, you died. But what if the next guy says to me, Hey, I got shot, or, Hey, I got my knees smashed in. I mean, where would I draw the line?'

"Well," Bert continued, "to me it's pretty obvious where he should draw the line: death. When a guy dies, he can quit. How much clearer could it be? But hey, he's the Boss. I'm not gonna argue. I just wait.

"So he asks me, 'Where you wanna retire to?'

" 'The Florida Keys,' I tell him right away. I mean, I been thinkin' about it the whole time I was inna hospital.

" 'Hm,' he says, 'that sounds nice,' and it was almost like the Godfather was envious of me. You know why, Joey? 'Cause I was ready to walk away, ready to leave everything behind. That's the only thing people really envy. Remember that, kid. 'Well, Bert, I'll tell you what,' he says. 'We can't call it retirement. But you go to Florida with my blessing, and we'll say you're my eyes and ears down there. We need information, contacts, we'll call on you. How's that?'

" 'Frankie,' I say, 'that's great. God bless you.' So here it is eight years later, Joey, and here I am." Bert lifted his hands and his eyes toward the ceiling, but whether he was thanking heaven for his resurrection or simply locating himself in space it was impossible to tell. "Six years ago I had a triple bypass, and today I feel as good as an old fart can expect to feel."

Joey took a sip of his tequila. "Unbefuckinglievable, Bert. Afuckingmazing. So have they called on you?"

The old mafioso leaned closer and Joey caught a whiff of his bay rum after-shave above the booze-and-washrag smell of the bar. "Joey," he whispered, "this is why I wanted to talk to you. This is what I'm trying to tell you. There's been nothing for them to call on me *about*. In the early years, yeah, every three, four months they'd ask me to check up on something, but it was usually something in Miami. These New York guys, ya know, they got no sense of geography. I'd say to them, 'How the fuck should I know what goes on in Miami? Miami is as far from here as Brooklyn is from Baltimore.'

" 'Oh yeah?' they'd say. 'Where's Baltimore?'

"But Joey, since Scalera got whacked, I hardly get called at all. Once in a great while maybe. But our friends are just not active down here, Joey. This is what I'm telling you. And why aren't they? 'Cause there's a whole different mix of people down here— Cubans, military, treasure hunters, smugglers—and a whole different set of scams. Your father knows that, Joey. Your brother Gino should know it."

"I'm not working for my father," Joey said. "And I'm not working for Gino. I'm here on my own."

Bert sucked down the last of his whiskey sour and considered. "On your own? This I didn't realize." He cocked his head, pursed his loose lips, then blew some air between them. "On your own. O.K., Joey, you got balls, you got ambition, I respect that. But Joey, what you're trying to do—you don't just show up some-place and act like you're a goddamn franchise, like you're opening a branch office of the Mob. Whaddya think, it's like fucking McDonald's? Maybe you can sell the same hamburger on every street corner in America. With scams it's different. You wanna operate here, you gotta come up with something local. Ya know, a scam that fits the climate."

Now, three or four times in a person's life, probably not more, something is said that really makes a dif-ference. The moment, the source, and the need to hear that thing all line up perfectly, and the comment ends up seeming not only like the listener's own thought but his destiny. Joey drained his glass and ran a hand through his hair. "You're right, Bert," he said. "I know you're right. But what should the angle be?"

The old man looked down at his watch. "Holy shit," he said. "I gotta go. I got some guys coming over to play gin rummy."

He reached down under his barstool as if retrieving a hat, and came up with a dog. It was a chihuahua with a wet black nose, bulging glassy eyes, and quivering whiskers, and it fit in the palm of Bert's fleshy hand.

"That dog was there the whole time?" Joey asked.

"Yeah," said Bert, and he stared at the animal's glassy eyes. "I hate this fucking dog." Then he addressed the dog directly. "I hate ya." He turned his glance back to Joey. "I gotta take him with me everywhere, or he shits onna floor. For spite. It's not even my dog. It's my wife's dog."

"So why doesn't your wife take care of him?"

"She's dead."

"Ah jeez, Bert, I'm sorry."

"Old news. She's been dead five years. And it was like her deathbed wish. *Bert, promise me you'll take care of Don Giovanni.*"

"Don Giovanni?" Joey said, looking dubiously at the quaking little creature.

"Yeah. Ya know, like the opera. My wife loved the opera. A very cultured woman, my wife." Then he said to the chihuahua, "Our Carla, our dear sweet pain inna neck, Carla, wasn't she cultured?" And to Joey: "But the fucking dog, I hate the fucking dog. Cliff, put this on my tab." And he got up slowly.

8

Joey pushed open the door to the compound and breathed deeply of the jasmine and the lime. He was feeling optimistic and benign. One of the ladies was poaching in the hot tub, only her dark coarse hair visible above the roiling water. "How's it feel in there, Marsha?" Joey asked.

"Feels great. But I'm Wendy."

Inside their cottage, Sandra was standing in the kitchen, watching fish fillets defrost. She was just out of the shower and had a towel, turban style, on her head. She wore a short pink robe, and rivulets of water still gleamed on her pale legs.

"Hello, baby," Joey said. "You look sexy."

"Hi, Joey." Sandra made it a point not to echo his buoyant tone. "You sound happy. Been drinking?"

"Come on, I had two drinks. But that's not why I'm happy. I met a guy, a guy from New York. Knows my

71

old man. Isn't that a pisser? We had a nice talk. It was like neighborhood."

"Good," said Sandra. "I'm glad you had a pleasant afternoon." She looked at the fish, laid out on a warped wooden cutting board. Frozen, the fillets had been silvery and smooth. As they melted, they turned bluish and flakes bent back like small barbs.

"Sandra, hey, you like it better when I'm in a lousy mood and just mope around?"

"No, Joey, of course not. It's just—"

"Just what?"

"Joey, listen. I don't mind that you're not bringing in any money right now. I really don't."

"I think you do," he said.

"Maybe I do," she admitted. "To tell you the truth, I'm not sure if I do or if I don't. But Joey, that's not the point. It's not like you're a freeloader. It's not like you're lazy. I know you're not. You're out there putting in time, putting in trouble. I know that. But Joey, here's the thing. You don't wanna tell me the details of what you're trying to do, fair enough, I don't need to know. But isn't it getting pretty obvious that it isn't any easier to do things your way than it is to make an honest living? So why not use that energy—"

"Oh Christ, Sandra, we're gonna start in on this again?"

"Yeah, Joey, we are." Sandra crossed her arms and pressed them against her midriff. Her face, already flushed from the shower, turned a shade pinker under the unsteady fluorescent light. "Joey, I'm not sure I really understand why you came down here, but I'll tell you why I did. I came down here because I love you. That's the only reason. Not to get a tan. Not to wear sunglasses. Not because I was unhappy in

Queens. To be with you. I thought you really wanted to change things around and you had to go far away to do it."

Joey examined his shoes. Sandra went on.

"The things you were doing in New York—look, I'm not stupid, Joey. But O.K., that was New York. That was your family, those were our friends. Fine. No one ever seemed to get in trouble, and if people got hurt, they weren't the people we knew. I'm not saying I liked it, but I could live with it."

Joey looked at the linoleum floor, at the ancient oily dust that stuck to the base of the refrigerator and hung down like a filthy beard. "So live with it and stop bitching."

Sandra undid her turban and draped the towel over the back of a chair. "Joey, that's what I'm saying. I'm not sure I can live with it down here. Down here I can't make excuses for you. I can't say you were born into it, I can't say it's what all your buddies do. Down here you got a choice, Joey, don'tcha see that? And as far as I can tell, you're choosing the exact same stuff you were doing in Queens."

"Oh yeah?" said Joey. He put his hands on his hips and tried to muster a tone of righteous indignation. "And just how sure are you about that?"

Sandra picked up the cutting board and spilled off some gray water that had come out of the fish. "I'm *not* sure," she admitted. "How should I be sure? You don't talk to me. And I'd love to be wrong, believe me. But Joey, how does it look? Does it look like you're joining the Florida work force? No, it looks like you're hanging around waiting to win the lottery. And now you tell me you meet a guy from New York. He knows your father.

We know what that means. It's just like the old neighborhood—"

"But Sandra," Joey cut in, "you're missing the whole point, which you woulda got if you let me talk insteada jumping down my throat before I'm even inside the goddamn door. The guy's from New York, yeah. And if you must know, he's family, that's true. But the point is that even *he* says you can't run a New York–style business down here, ya gotta go with the local style. Now, coming from him, I believe it. I mean, the man is a professional. So that's why I'm happy, Sandra. It's like a new idea, like a light bulb lighting up. And I have this feeling that this guy Bert and I are gonna do some things together."

"Legal things, Joey?"

Joey widened his dark blue eyes. "Now it's gotta be legal? A minute ago it just had to be different from New York. For Chrissake, Sandra, quit while you're ahead."

She looked at the fillets on the cutting board. They were still oozing gray water and had taken on the glazed translucence of someone's eyeballs when they have a cold. "That fish looks lousy."

"Yeah, it does," said Joey. He approached it as though it might be carrying a grave disease and gave it a clinical poke with his index finger. "Feels all mushy." He sniffed at his hand. "Doesn't smell terrific either. Could be like spoiled."

He went to the sink and started washing up with dish soap. He was fastidious about his hands, Joey was, aside from being finicky about his food.

Sandra sighed and ran her fingers through her short blond hair. "What's gonna be with you, Joey? Well, come on, let's go out. I get paid tomorrow."

9

Bert the Shirt d'Ambrosia did not look terrific in his Bermuda shorts. Loose skin gathered around his knobby knees as at the neck of a Chinese dog, and on his right thigh, clearly visible through the sparse white hair, was the scooped-out pink scar of an old gunshot wound. His dark nylon socks ended three inches above his ankles, and the brown mesh shoes made his feet look bigger than they really were. But the old mobster was saved from dowdiness by the splendor of his blue silk shirt. It had horn buttons and the shimmer of the tall sky just after sunset. There was navy piping around the collar and a monogram on the chest pocket.

"Boo," said Joey Goldman.

Bert looked up in no great hurry. He was sitting at a poolside table at the Paradiso condominium, playing solitaire under a steel umbrella. "Was a time," he said, "you couldn'ta got the jump on me like that.

Now? What the fuck. I'm just an old guy playing cards."

"You got a watchdog," Joey said. Don Giovanni, his wet nose twitching, cowered beneath the old man's chair.

"Fucking dog isn't worth shit. But siddown, Joey. I'm glad you came by."

The younger man pulled up a white wrought-iron chair and eased himself into it. "Nice place." The Paradiso had three pink towers that bristled with balconies and framed a big pool and a pair of tennis courts; the Atlantic Ocean was across the street. Through Joey's tinted lenses, the water was a milky green not much darker than the color of celery.

"It's not too bad," Bert said. "They don't have bocce, that's the only thing."

"Well," said Joey, and he left it at that. The old man turned up an ace, waved it in the air, and kissed it. "Bert, I was thinking about what you said the other day."

Bert cocked his head but said nothing. He was at the age when things he'd said forty years before left a more reliable track than things he said five minutes ago. Fortunately, he'd developed the knack of looking sage while waiting to be reminded what he'd been so wise about.

"Ya know," Joey went on, "about how ya gotta come up with, like, a Florida caper, something that makes sense for where we're at."

"Not where we're at. Where *you're* at." The Shirt put a black seven on a red eight.

"Whatever," Joey said. "Anyway, it makes a lotta sense. Except . . . except. Except, Bert, I can't for the life a me figure out what the angle oughta be. The last two nights, I couldn't sleep. I got outta bed and went outside. It's like three inna morning, and I'm sitting under a palm tree like a fucking lunatic, telling myself, Think Florida, *think Florida.* But I just come up with stupid fucking things. Suntan lotion. Baby alligators. This kid I knew in like second grade—he had a pencil sharpener that looked like an orange. Said Florida on it. So how the fuck am I supposed to make a living off of baby alligators and stupid-ass souvenirs? Bert, I'll be honest with ya. I'm balancing neatly onna ballsa my ass down here. I ain't made a nickel. My girlfriend's getting fed up and I can't say I blame 'er. I gotta get something started or I'm in deep shit."

Bert reached out and placed a cool hand on top of the younger man's. "Joey," he said. "Joey. Listen to yourself. You're saying, *Think Florida,* but listen how nervous you sound, how wound up. That's not Florida. That's not tropical. To be that worried, that's still New York."

"O.K., Bert, I know it is. But what can I say. I am that worried. I ain't slept. Coupla days ago I hadda pay the February rent. I reach into the drawer to get the cash, I count up what I got, and I say, Where the fuck is my money going? It's not like I'm being a big shot. It just goes." He yanked off his sunglasses and showed Bert his eyes. They were owlish to begin with, because he left his shades on when he sat in the sun. But now the pale circles had turned a nubbly yellow, and the bloodshot whites made his deep blue irises look almost grapy.

"Awright, Joey, you're under some strain. I can see that. So let's go back to basics. Look over that way, past the gates. Whaddya see?"

Joey put his sunglasses on again, twisted himself in

his chair, and peered past the pool, the tennis courts, the hibiscus hedge. "A road."

"Then what?"

"The beach."

"Then what?"

"Water," he said. "I see water."

"Good, Joey. Now doesn't that make you feel calm, all that nice cool green water? Doesn't it calm you down?"

"The truth, Bert? Fuck no. Not at all. I'm like itchy all over. What would make me feel calm is if I knew what the hell I was doing down here, if I thought I was heading for a payday."

"Kid," said Bert, with the sad patience of a junior high school teacher. "You're not paying attention. This is what I'm telling you. A payday would make you calm, maybe you oughta look to the water for a payday. That's where the money comes from down here. Always has. Always will."

Joey stared off at the shallow green ocean, but the ocean didn't talk to him. He pulled at his chin, he squirmed in his seat. Bert kept playing solitaire.

"Look what passes for old money down here," the retired gangster continued. "The Bergens. The Clevelands. You've hearda those families, right? How you think they got rich? They were pirates. Yeah. Legal pirates. There's a reef around five miles out from here. The water in between, it's called the Florida Straits. Now, ships useta all the time run up onna reef and sink. These families that are so rich now? They lived in shacks by the water. Shacks! They peed innee ocean. They didn't even have glass inna windows.

"But they were smart. They built lookout towers. A ship goes down, boom, they jump in their boats and row out the Straits. They rowed out there in squalls, in hurricanes. And the law of the sea says the first guy who gets there, it's his boat. He owns whatever's on there—silver, jewelry, cash, whatever. Course, sometimes it helped to have a shotgun, to prove you were there first. So these snooty families that get hospital wings named after them, they started, like, as hijackers."

Joey was still staring at the water; his hairline was crawling. "So, Bert, you're telling me I should get a fucking rowboat and wait for a shipwreck?"

"Nah, forget about it," said the older man. "This was a hundred years ago. These days, there's treasure salvors, it's big business. There's this one guy, Clem Sanders—"

"Bert," Joey blurted, "so what are you telling me? I'm like dyin' heah."

"What am I telling you?" Bert repeated. "Joey, I'm sevenny-tree years old, I been dead, I hafta all the time know what I'm saying? I'm just thinkin' out loud, like trying to clue you in on the local traditions. 'Cause they matter, Joey. Remember that. Local traditions. They matter in New York, they matter here. Where's the goddamn dog?"

Bert reached down underneath his chair, stretched his fingers toward the quivering chihuahua, and looked skyward to check the position of the sun. Then he stood up halfway with the chair lifted against his shrunken backside and moved a foot or so around the table. "You're a pain innee ass," he said to the dog. Then, to Joey: "I gotta keep him in the shade or he like dries out. He went inta convulsions once. Almost popped his eyes right out of his head. Fuck you laughing at?"

"Bert," Joey said, "you weigh like a hundred seventy pounds and the dog like weighs four ounces. Wouldn't it be easier to move the dog?"

"Dog don't wanna move. Dog don't wanna do nothing but shit onna floor and now and then jerk off on a table leg. Mind your fucking business."

"I ain't got no business. That's why I'm here."

"Right," said Bert. "So think about water. This is what I'm telling you. This Clem Sanders guy, this treasure guy, he goes around telling people that a whole third of all the gold and silver and jewels that's ever been mined has ended up at the bottom of the sea."

"A third of everything?" said Joey. " 'Zat true?"

Bert turned his palms up and shrugged. "How the fuck should I know if it's true? I only know this guy says it." He put a red three on a black four.

Joey went back to staring at the green water and listened to the dry rustle of the palms. "So Bert," he began, trying to keep his tone businesslike and to choke back the rising wave of panic, the unspeakable fear that he might go broke, come up with no ideas, and return, ashamed, to Queens. "I don't know what I'm gonna do. But let's say I come up with a way to pull some bucks outta the ocean. We gonna be partners, or what?"

Bert pursed his full and restless lips, turned over his last card, and, stymied, gathered up his losing hand. "Kid," he said, "it's nice of you to ask. But I'm through. Me, I'm all talk and no action, and I like it that way. It's real easy. And I'll tell ya something, Joey. The longer you stay in Florida, the more you appreciate what's easy."

10

It was unusual for anyone to knock at the gate of the compound, since half of Key West knew the combination to the lock. But several days after Joey's visit to the Paradiso, at about ten-thirty in the morning, there was a rapping at the wooden door. Steve the naked landlord was already in the pool with his beers and his ashtray in front of him, his paperback spread open on the damp tiles. Peter and Claude, the bartending blonds, were having breakfast in their sarongs. So Joey straightened his sunglasses and went to the gate.

It was Bert the Shirt. He was wearing a salmon-colored pullover of the finest Egyptian cotton, with a mesh of subtly contrasting buff at the collar and sleeves, and he had Don Giovanni cradled in the crook of his arm. "Joey, there's something I gotta talk to you about. Got a minute?"

"Bert," said Joey, surprised and grateful to be visited, "I got nothing but time. Come on in." For a fleeting moment he was embarrassed about receiving a guest in his bathrobe and slippers, and about the naked body in the pool and the pretty men in their pink and turquoise silks. But the feeling passed. This was the Keys; this was home now. It was the land of take-it-or-leave-it and no apologies. "Did I tell you I lived here?"

"Carlos did," said Bert, walking slowly along the gravel path between the jasmine and the banana plants. "The *bolita* guy. He had you followed. You didn't know that?"

Rather than admit it, Joey changed the subject. "I didn't know you talked to Carlos."

"Carlos talks to me," the older man corrected. He stopped walking and gave Joey a soft little slap on the cheek, a mix of affection, scolding, and warning. "Joey, I'm telling you to relax down here, but that doesn't mean you shouldn't pay attention, eh?"

"Yeah, Bert. You're right. Bert, this is Steve. Steve, this is Bert, an old family friend."

"Morning," Steve said. Then he smiled. Sunlight glinted off his moist freckled forehead and red mustache.

"Whatcha reading?" Bert asked.

Steve turned the paperback over and looked at the cover to remind himself. "Japs," he said. "Submarines." Then he smiled.

Joey led the way into the cottage and motioned Bert onto a settee in the Florida room. Shafts of sunlight sliced in through the louvered windows and threw stripes across the sisal rug. "Coffee, Bert?"

"No, Joey, no thanks. Siddown. This is kinda serious. Joey, you been in touch with your old man since you left?"

Joey was halfway into his chair when he became certain that Bert was about to tell him his father was dead. Icicles scratched at the inside of his chest, and his forehead started instantly to pound. Bert read his face.

"Joey, no, it's nothing like that. He's O.K., he's fine. But tell me, you been in touch with him?"

Joey sprang back from his flash of guilt and grief with a moment of bravado. "Shit, Bert, I left New York to get away from him."

"Come on, Joey. No bullshit now. Just yes or no. You been in touch with him or not?"

Joey was stung by the older man's sternness, and there was a note almost of whining in his answer. "No, Bert, I haven't. I swear. Fuck is this about?"

Bert leaned forward, put his dog down on the rug, and dropped his voice to a raspy whisper. "A coupla guys come to see me last night," he said. "Guys based in Miami. They weren't in a good mood. In fact, they were ready to whack somebody. Joey, tree million bucks in Colombian emeralds has been lifted off of Charlie Ponte's crew, and it was pretty definitely an inside job. People get dead over that kinda thing."

"Three million bucks," said Joey. His own stash had dipped below four thousand, and the poorer he got, the more big numbers impressed him. "Jesus. But wait a second, Bert. If it was Charlie Ponte's crew, I don't see what it's gotta do with my old man."

Bert the Shirt sat back slowly and seemed unwilling or unable to talk until his shoulder blades had made secure contact with the cushion. "Probably not your father directly. But maybe some of his boys. Joey, it's this same old problem with drugs. Biggest fucking mistake our people ever made was not making a clear policy and sticking to it. Either dominate the business or don't fuck with it."

Bert paused to lick his teeth. Outside, palms rustled and water splashed. The air smelled of iodine and limes.

"But anyway," the old man continued, "Charlie Ponte's crew, they're inna coke trade. They're not supposed to be, it's unofficial, but they are—it's like an open secret. Your father's people, supposedly they're not. But no offense, Joey, your father's crew has this like superior attitude—"

"I hear ya," Joey cut in. "I ain't offended, believe me."

"Yeah, well, to them," Bert went on, "it's like the guys that are in drugs are outlaws, outsiders. They don't respect 'em, they think of 'em as fair game, like as if they weren't friends of ours.

"So, what happens with Charlie Ponte is this. He's expecting a two-million-dollar shipment from the Colombians, and the shipment is seized by the Feds. Charlie doesn't even get a look at it. So now he's pissed. He's got dealers without product, his business is disrupted. But the Colombians, they're so fucking rich it's unbelievable. Their attitude is like, 'Oh well, that shipment was only a few million. Kiss it goodbye.' The main thing to them is to keep the account active. So they want Charlie to be happy. So they say to him, 'Look, you were expecting two million in product, we'll give ya tree million in emeralds. Keep it as collateral, sell it off, it's up to you.' It's like a token of goodwill."

"Some token," Joey said.

"Yeah, right," Bert said. "But these guys, the money they have, it's like you or me giving a guy a buck to park the car. So anyway, Charlie gets his emeralds. Or supposedly he does. They get dropped someplace in Coconut Grove—I don't know where, and I don't wanna know. But a safe place, a place that's been used before, and only the Colombians and Charlie Ponte's guys know about it. And that's where they disappear from."

Joey tugged at an earlobe, then raked the back of his hand across his unshaven face. Tiny squiggles of limestone dust floated in the slashed light of the louvered windows. "Bert," he said, "maybe I'm a little slow, but I still don't see where this has to do with my father."

Bert leaned over to check on the dog, and moved it out of a stripe of sun into a stripe of shade. "Joey, there were a coupla low-level guys who were like floating between the two crews. They'd commute between Miami and New York, they'd do little errands for Ponte, little jobs for your old man. They were lookin' to get made, and they were very ambitious. They found out more than they needed to know about the drop in Coconut Grove. They ain't floatin' no more, Joey. They're lookin' at coral. Up close. And they ain't got no snorkels."

"Jesus," said Joey, and in spite of himself he almost smiled. Not that he was happy about guys getting clipped; it was just exhilarating to be near some action again, to be getting information. "So you're saying these guys brought in other guys in my father's crew?"

Bert shrugged. "These guys were angling for a button, Joey. A tree-million-dollar score earns a guy some points. But of course, scoring it from another family was not too bright."

"Maybe the spicks welshed. Maybe they took the stones back. Maybe they were never delivered."

"Could be," said Bert. "But that isn't the Colombians' style. Why would they bother?"

Bert slowly crossed his legs and drummed his fingers lightly on the arm of the settee. For the first time, he seemed to be looking around at Joey's cottage, at the bad paintings of birds and shells, the haphazard furniture made tolerable and even likable by the fact that it was rented and not owned. "Not a bad little place," he said without enthusiasm.

Joey gave a modest nod. "Well, it ain't the Paradiso. But it's fine until I really get on my feet." He shot the older man a wry glance, which was as close as he would come to admitting that that might be never.

Then there was a pause. If Joey had been watching closely, he would have noticed that Bert the Shirt was momentarily exhausted and was marshaling his strength. But Joey wasn't watching closely, he was slipping back into his obsession with figuring how to pull a living out of Florida. "And that reminds me. I was thinkin', Bert, about what you said the other day, ya know, about money comin' outta the water? If that's the way people get rich down here—"

Joey suddenly fell silent because the Shirt had put a hand to his chin and started wagging his head as if in deep sorrow or disbelief.

"Wha', Bert?"

The old mafioso looked down and spoke to his chihuahua. "This kid, Giovanni. Is he very brave, very stupid, or does he just not listen?"

The younger man only crinkled his forehead.

"I mean," Bert said to him, "what have I been telling you heah? Your father's crew is suspected of stealing tree million dollars from our own people. Two guys have already been clipped. A coupla very nasty *paisans* show up in Key West. Joey, why d'ya think they came heah?"

Joey just sat.

The Shirt addressed his dog. "This kid, Giovanni, he's a nice kid, but he's an asshole." Then he glared at Joey. "Asshole, they were looking for you."

"Me?"

"Joey, use your fucking head. You just happen to be about twelve hundred miles closer than anyone else to where the emeralds were. And you just happened to move down here right around the time this whole thing had to get planned. How does it look?"

Joey rubbed his stubbly chin and admitted to himself that it did not look great. "But shit, Bert, I was always the last to know what my father's crew was up to even when I was living right there. Why d'ya think I ain't there no more?"

"Why should Charlie Ponte believe that? Joey, you know how these people think. Always look for the blood ties first. You're still your father's son. Maybe you don't feel like you are. Maybe you don't have his name. But everybody knows it, just like everybody knows Charlie Ponte sells dope. So, Joey, I'm telling you like a father, watch your ass. These guys will probably come back, and they are very pissed. If I didn't stand up for you, they woulda been here last night. Just to talk. Probably. But it would not have been pleasant."

"You stood up for me, Bert?" A sublime and unbounded gratitude made the hair lift on the back of Joey's neck.

Bert looked at the rug, at his quailing dog.

"What did you tell 'em?" Joey asked.

"Never mind what I tol' 'em."

"Hey," said Joey, "I wanna know." He squeezed the arms of his chair and puffed up within himself, opening the passageways like a young man does, the better to absorb a compliment from a respected elder.

"Forget about it," Bert advised.

"Come on," Joey insisted. "I wanna know."

"Awright," said Bert. "I told 'em you were too much of a loser to be involved in anything that big."

"Thanks, Bert. Thanks a lot."

"Sorry, kid. You asked. Besides, it was the best thing to say at the time. On that you hafta trust me."

11

"Joey, will you think about it at least?"

Sandra held an enormous fish sandwich in both hands and had a glass of beer in front of her. They were sitting at the Eclipse Saloon, in a booth under a big stuffed marlin and a faded photograph of a novelist who used to be world-famous in that bar and regularly got stewed there. A loop of fried onion was dangling from the underside of Sandra's roll and, fish-like, she approached from below to snag it between her teeth. "I mean," she said, "it's not like it's a regular job. All you do is talk to people, schmooze 'em up. You work outside. It's straight commission. You don't really have a boss."

"That part's bullshit," said Joey. He absently dredged a french fry through a puddle of ketchup. "There's always a boss. I'd still be depending on some suit to hand me a paycheck."

"Joey, what can I say? Life is bosses. That's how it

works. Your pals from New York—don't they have bosses? Your buddy Sal, he has a boss. Your brother Gino has a boss."

"At least their bosses aren't citizens," Joey said, but the argument sounded thin even to him. His resistance was fading, diminishing in direct proportion to his bankroll, and in proportion, as well, to his growing if still unadmitted awareness that it was no easier to launch a criminal career than any other kind, only more dangerous.

Then, too, as jobs went, what Sandra was suggesting didn't really sound so awful. OPC, it was called— Off-Property Contact. What it meant was that he would hang out on a corner of Duval Street, buttonhole tourists as they drifted past, and try to persuade them to take a tour of a time-share resort. If they took the tour, Joey got forty bucks a couple, and that was the end of it. Didn't matter if they bought, didn't matter if they'd never buy in a million years. His job was only to talk them past the door. The fellow who had the job now was this guy named Zack, the husband of Claire, who was one of Sandra's fellow tellers, and supposedly he was pulling in eight hundred bucks a week. A real go-getter, this Zack. He'd just passed his real estate test and was ready to move inside, to sell. No doubt Sandra, whose circuits were wired between the opposing poles of practicality and dreaming, imagined that Joey would get on that same track.

"Joey, you'd be great at it," she coaxed. "It's exactly what you like to do. Don't be pigheaded just because it happens to be legal. It's a hustle."

Joey wavered. The last thing he had in mind was an ongoing entanglement with the world of pay stubs

and file cabinets, sales meetings and company picnics. But as a temporary thing, very temporary, well,
maybe he could salt away a few dollars while plan-
ning his next moves. "I don't know, Sandra, standing
there all day, having to be nice to these jerks—"

Sandra played her trump card. "Who says you have
to be nice? That isn't how this guy Zack makes his
eight hundred a week. He browbeats. He needles.
Joey, the idea isn't to be nice, the idea is to capture
these people. You use anything that works. Guilt.
Jokes. Fibs. Crazy promises. It's a con, Joey. It's a
game."

"And it's legal?"

"And it's legal. It's real estate. Joey, think of it as a
legal way of taking hostages."

Across the street from the Eclipse Saloon was a
bank, and in front of the bank was a sign that blinked
out the time and the temperature. Other places,
those thermometer signs tended to exert the morbid
fascination of an accident scene: How bad was it?
you asked yourself as you drove by. Would it hit one
hundred in July? In January, would the frigid numbers skid through zero into the awful minus? In Key
West it was different. There was something smug
about the temperature sign. It made you feel like
knocking wood, as if you'd caught yourself gloating
about your own good fortune. In the daytime the
sign always seemed to read eighty-two degrees,
though on occasion the mercury would plummet to
seventy-eight or a heat wave would raise it to a
steamy eighty-four. When the sun went down, the
temperature went down with it, and just as gently.
By full darkness the reading had settled into the

middle seventies, and there it stayed until after midnight. By dawn it was just cool enough so that, many mornings, you woke up with a dim but pleasurable recollection of having groped for a cool sheet to pull under your chin.

When Sandra and Joey emerged onto the sidewalk, the sign said seventy-six degrees and a moon just shy of full was throwing a cool white light that broke into red and blue fragments in the smashed glass of the Eldorado's windshield.

"Beautiful out," said Sandra.

"Drive to the beach?" said Joey.

The Caddy's top had not been up in weeks, and the open car held the smell of sunshine and limestone dust. Through what was left of the muffler, baritone pops issued forth, steady as the beating of a drum. Joey slipped through the narrow residential streets and onto A1A, the fabled road that traces out the very rim of Florida, separating land from water with a line hardly more substantial than a layer of skin. He drove past the Paradiso condominium, almost to the airport, then pulled off the pavement on the ocean side and pointed the car toward Cuba.

Sandra slid closer and put her hand on Joey's knee. The feel of it made him realize that they hadn't touched much lately. "It's been tough for you, huh?" he said. "With the move and me not earning and all?"

"A little. I'm O.K."

For a while they sat in silence. Traffic zipped by behind them, and ahead moonlight played on the shallow water, tracing a rippled white line from the horizon to the seawall in front of them.

"You know what I love about moonlight on water?"

Sandra said. "No matter where you are, it points right to you, like the moon knows you're watching and is picking you out for something, something special."

"Yeah, but it points to everybody," Joey said.

"O.K., O.K., but I don't have to think about that. I just see it pointing to us. Look. Right at us."

Joey put his arm around her. Sandra usually wore clothes that puffed her up—fuzzy sweaters with big outlines, blouses with built-in shoulders—and after almost four years, Joey was still sometimes surprised to feel her narrow bones and thin skin in his hands. He squeezed the small knob at the top of her arm, rubbed the spare flesh between shoulder and elbow. "Sandra," he said softly, "what if I just can't do it?"

"Do what?"

"This job." He took his arm away, put both hands on the steering wheel, and looked absently at his zeroed-out speedometer. "I mean, Sandra, I think I'm pretty bright. I got confidence. But I also got this lousy feeling, it makes me mad, like there's all kindsa things that everybody else knows and I don't. Dumb stuff. Filling out forms. What ya say onna telephone. When ya use a paper clip and when ya use a staple. I mean, these stupid little things that people know if they have a job. Me, I've never done that. To me it's like a big mystery."

"You're a little scared, Joey. That's O.K."

The word was like a lance, and after the flash of pain and the squelched rage of denying it was so, there was relief. Joey stared out across the flat and moon-shot water of the Florida Straits and let out a long breath that whistled slightly between his teeth.

"You can do it, Joey," Sandra said. "I know you can. Things are gonna get better for us."

12

Zack Davidson was thirty-two, had sandy-brown hair, hazel eyes widely spaced, horn-rim glasses held on with an elegant elastic cord, and Joey Goldman hated him on sight. He hated the way his hair fell onto his forehead in a seemingly casual yet perfect arc, like a spent wave crawling up a beach. He hated the confident pinkness of his knit shirt, the perfect way the ribbed cuff neither hung loose nor pinched his arm. He hated the cheap but perfect cotton belt holding up his khaki shorts, and the conceited inexpensiveness of his Timex watch. Everything about him said yacht club, golf course, prep school, WASP, and gave Joey a feeling in his gut as if a hot fist were yanking at the inside of his navel. It didn't help at all that Zack had right away gone into the question of Joey's sunglasses.

"Eye contact is real important," he was saying.

"Tough shit," said Joey. "The glasses stay."

He said it as if throwing a punch, and like a punch,

the remark caused the receiving party to pause and reconsider who he was dealing with. Zack put down the pencil he'd been twirling and stared at Joey across the narrow desk. They were sitting in the downtown office of Parrot Beach Interval Ownership Associates, next to a scale model of the development. Immaculate under Plexiglas, the model featured pastel duplexes with dainty shutters, feathery plastic palms, Barbiesque figures on tiny lounge chairs around a pool whose water was made of blue Saran Wrap. A toy boat was pulled up on a real sand beach.

"Joey," Zack said at last, "you got a lousy fucking attitude. I like that in a person. Shows spirit. But you have to make it work for you, not against you. I can train you or I can train the next hard-on down the line. So you want this fucking job, or what?"

Now it was Joey's turn to ponder. He hadn't expected to hear such blithe obscenities from Zack Davidson's well-formed lips. Then again, all of this was new to him, he had no idea what to expect. Stalling for time, he studied the miniature development, the tiny hedges, the teensy people. He found it spooky. Life sometimes seemed small enough without suggesting that you could boil it down, stick it under glass, and take the whole thing in in a single look.

"Yeah," said Joey, "I want the job, but I ain't gonna let the job make me crazy."

"Good answer," said Zack. "So what you do, you put your craziness *into* the job. You see what I'm saying?"

Joey didn't.

"Best OPC we ever had," Zack continued, "was a total lunatic. His name was Whistling Freddie. Failed comedian. He'd stand on the corner on a washtub, whistling Mozart. When people stopped to listen, he'd start talking at them like the guy in the Fed Ex commercials. Then he'd go into impersonations, foreign accents, dick jokes. By the time he got around to selling the tour, people were helpless. People can't say no when they're laughing. Remember when you were a kid, somebody tickled you and it took all your strength away? Same thing. And you know where Whistling Freddie is now? In the Virgin Islands, on top of a hill, on three acres of his very own."

Zack ended with an emphatic nod, and it very faintly dawned on Joey that he had no idea if he should believe a single word. It was all so neat with Zack. You cursed, he cursed; suddenly you're on the same side. You mention craziness, he jumps in and makes it sound like craziness makes you rich. What if it was all bullshit? Then again, what if it wasn't? What if having a straight job meant that you unleashed your rotten attitude, gave vent to your personality defects, made an ass of yourself in public, and the upshot of all this legitimate embarrassment was that you ended up a substantial property owner with money in the bank?

"Look," Zack resumed, "this business is about one thing and one thing only. Human nature. It's all a question of reading people. Who's our best prospective customer? We have two. A dumb guy who thinks he's smart, and a cheapskate who thinks he's a sport. Why? Because the dumb guy who thinks he's smart figures, Hey, why should I spend a hundred fifty bucks a night in a hotel when I can spend thirty thousand on a time-share and save money? The cheapskate who thinks he's a sport, he wants to let people know he's a player, he's in the market to buy, but the thought of a three-hundred-thousand-dollar house makes his bowels loosen. So O.K., how do we recognize these people?"

Joey just sat. He knew how to recognize a debtor who couldn't meet his vig payments, he knew how to recognize a contractor eager to kiss up to a union. He didn't know how to recognize a likely hostage for a time-share tour.

Zack bounced the eraser end of his pencil against his clipboard. "I'll give it to you in two dirty words," he said. "Social class. What kind of tourist we get down here, Joey? On the one hand, we get a lot of southern, blue-collar, white-trash, flag-waving, Bible-thumping, football-crazy, redneck slobs. No value judgment implied. They drive down in the ol' RV and park near a pier so they don't have to walk too far to sit on a milk crate and go fishing all day. When you see 'em downtown, they always have a lot of writing on their clothes and there's usually something weird about their socks. These are not our people, Joey. This isn't snobbery, you understand. It's just that we want our owners to be happy, and folks like this are never truly content unless they're in a truck.

"At the other extreme," Zack continued, "we get a few very rich people down here. New Yorkers. Bostonians. People who own large pieces of downtown Toronto. They've already done St. Barth's, Mustique bores them, now they're slumming closer to home. They wear pastels. They weigh, on average, sixty pounds less than the poor people. The women are flat-chested, the men have no behinds, but they look good in their clothes. These are not our customers either. The rich are squeamish about time-sharing. It nauseates them to think, the week before, someone with less money was sitting on their toilet.

"No," said Zack, standing up next to the Parrot Beach model and gazing down like a god at a fresh-imagined world, "our buyer is somewhere in between. We want the guy who's like fifty-five, on his second or third wife. He's a dry cleaner, a sales manager, he's making like sixty, seventy grand, and he thinks he's upper crust because he has expensive golf clubs and a Ralph Lauren shirt. He acts like he doesn't give a shit about the gifts you get for taking the tour, but if you look closely, you can see him toting it up: meal voucher, forty dollars; passes to the Treasure Museum—"

"Treasure Museum?" Joey cut in.

"Yeah, the Clem Sanders Treasure Museum. Clem's a salvor. Fucking rich by now—he's one of the partners in the property. Anyway, the passes are worth twelve bucks, so that makes fifty-two. Tour takes two hours, that works out to twenty-six bucks an hour: *Is my time worth more or less than twenty-six bucks an hour?* That's our boy, Joey. He's got some money in the bank, he'll go the extra twenty dollars a week to rent a T-Bird instead of a compact, but he can't stop wondering if his life is worth twenty-six bucks an hour. You get it?"

Joey sat there. He was dazed. He wasn't sure if he got it or not. It seemed to him that only when he entered the Parrot Beach office had he truly left Queens. Before that, he was carrying his neighbor-hood around with him, as if he had taken the little stash of things he knew about and packed it in the car along with his black loafers and alpaca cardigans. Now all of a sudden he'd been plunked down in a vast new borough, the neighborhood of American salesmanship. It was a different place.

"So you gonna, like, try me out?" The question was a little weak, almost as if Joey was hoping Zack would say no.

"No tryout, Joey. You want the job, you got the job. Around here it's sink or swim. You fuck up, we won't have to fire you. You'll make no money, feel like a horse's ass, get disgusted with the whole thing, and stop showing up. Here." Zack bent down, opened a desk drawer, and threw a pink shirt at Joey. "This is what you wear."

He caught the shirt by reflex, but then looked down at it as though it were a thing unclean. It was the color of cotton candy and had the same ribbed cuffs that looked so annoyingly perfect on Zack Davidson's well-tanned and lightly freckled arms. "Shit," he said, "I gotta dress up like some wimpy-looking prissy-ass WASP?" Then it occurred to him that maybe he'd gotten a little too personal. "No offense."

"What offense?" said Zack, resuming his chair and leaning it back on its hind legs. "You think I'm a WASP? That's a crack-up. I'm a Jew, man, Litvak trash from Newark, New Jersey, the lowest of the low. They fucked our name up at Ellis Island. Should've been Davidovich, something like that. But Joey, remember. Social class. Appearances. Reading people. Study up, my friend. It's gonna be the key to your success in this business."

13

Getting Sal Giordano on the telephone was not a simple process. He was paranoid about wiretaps and refused to have a phone at his apartment. You could leave a coded message for him at Perretti's luncheonette on Astoria Boulevard, and if you got lucky he might even be there when you called. But he wouldn't actually talk on the old rotary pay phone in the green-painted alcove at the end of Perretti's counter, because that phone could be tapped as well. The most Sal would do was say hello, give a few one-word answers, and arrange a conversation on a different phone. To be safe, however, this other phone had to be away from the immediate neighborhood and couldn't be used too often. This meant there had to be several choices. So Sal had to figure out which phone he wanted to use that day, how long it would take him to reach it, given traffic and weather, and then hope the box hadn't been vandalized by the time he got there. Crime paid, but convenient it was not.

On an afternoon toward the middle of February, after trying morning and evening, from home and from downtown, for several days, Joey finally managed to connect with his old friend. "Sal!"

"Joey!" said the gruff, familiar voice. "Where are you, man?"

"Key West, like I said I would be." For Sal, the question had been first and foremost a part of his routine security check on telephones, and so the next and more radical part of Joey's answer did not immediately sink in. "In a deli next to where I work. Where're you?"

"Me?" Sal said. "Inna parking lot of the Airline Diner, out near La Guardia. 'Scuse me if I gotta yell. Lotta fuckin' planes going by. Hey, wait a second. Did you say where you work?"

"You picked up on that, huh?" said Joey. "Unbefuckinglievable, huh? Yeah, I got a job."

"Doing what?" Sal yelled, above the whine of a landing jet.

"Real estate. Sort of. I stand onna corner and con people into going to look at these condos. Time-snare, they call it. Starting to make a little bit of money."

"Joey, that's great," Sal said, and though he meant it, he could not keep out of his voice some of the same doubt and sourness that had crept in when his younger pal had first said he was heading south. It had to do with watching someone you care about go someplace you know that you will never follow. "So you haven't taken over the rackets yet?"

Joey laughed into the phone. "Hey, I tried. Fact, I got some stories, Sal, you'll shit. Probably I'll try again sometime. But ya know, what I was tryin' to do, it was too much too soon. The rules down here, the traditions, everything's different. Up north the money comes outta the street, down here it comes outta the water."

"Fuck does that mean?" shouted Sal Giordano.

"That's what I gotta figure out before I try again," said Joey. "And inna meantime I'm hooking tourists for forty bucks a couple. How are things up there?"

Sal hesitated as a plane screamed past. "Up here it's like eighteen degrees, old ladies are falling down onnee ice, and I'm freezing my nuts off."

"I'm not asking for the weather report, Sal. How're things?"

Sal hesitated again, though this time there was no airplane. "Not great, Joey. It's a very tense time up here. Very tense."

"The cops?"

"Nah, not the cops. Cops are pretty much leaving us alone. It's among our own people. There's a lotta mistrust, lotta bad feeling. Some guys have been disappearing. People are talking like maybe there's gonna be war."

" 'Zis about Charlie Ponte's emeralds?"

"Fuck you know about that?" Sal asked, and even though he was talking to his adopted kid brother, the former runt who never won a fight and was never entrusted with any but the dullest and most trivial errands, such was the mood of wariness among members of the Queens and Brooklyn Mafia families that he could not quite squelch a note of suspicion. "You know more than you did when you was up here."

"I got a friend down here," Joey said. It sounded

like, and was, a boast. "You remember a guy named Bert the Shirt?"

"Sure I do," said Sal, above the jet noise. "Good man. But wait, ain't he the guy that dropped dead onna courthouse steps?"

"Yup. He kicked the bucket. But they brought him back, and the Pope let him retire. People still look to him on Florida business, though."

"Joey," said Sal, "do yourself a favor—don't get curious about this. It's bad, I'm telling you. Your old man, they finally made him *consigliere*, but it's not like they're doing him a favor, the way things are. Everyone's like getting ready for a siege. Practically every day there's sit-downs, everybody plotting, trying to figure out who's with who. Your brother Gino, he's tryin' so hard to look brave it's ridiculous. It's a fucking mess."

"So Sal, get away, take a vacation. Come down here and relax awhile. You'll love it. You're like the only person I miss from the whole fucking city."

"*Marrone*, Joey. Think. With what's going on, it would only be like the stupidest thing in the world to suddenly show up in Florida. Besides, it wouldn't be doing you any favor to show these guys you're buddy-buddy with the family. That's just asking for trouble."

Joey frowned at the coin box and tugged at the collar of his pink shirt. "You're right, Sal, I guess you're right. Maybe not now. It's just that I'd like to see ya sometime."

"Sometime. I'll get down there sometime." Sal said it like he didn't believe it would ever happen. A jet seemed to be revving up next to the phone booth. "So listen," he screamed, "you stay outta trouble down there. You got any messages you want me to take to anyone? Your old man? Your brother?"

Joey looked out the window of his phone booth, at the life of a Key West deli. A guy with a shaved head was making conch salad sandwiches. A girl with her boobs hanging out of an undershirt was sucking mango juice through a straw. Outside, it was eighty-two degrees, people were not worrying about tapped telephones or about being murdered by their colleagues, and Joey was suddenly very grateful to be right where he was, doing just what he was doing, nothing more and nothing less. "No, Sal," he said. "No messages. No messages for anybody."

14

"Hi, folks, how ya doin'? . . . Beautiful day, huh? . . .
Y' enjoying Fantasy Island? . . . Great. Where ya from?
. . . Minnesota, whaddya know. Me, I never been to
Minnesota, but hey, there's lotsa places I never been.
Minnesota, that's where the Packers play, right? Nah,
wait a minute, what's wrong with me, that's Wiscon-
sin, that's the other side of the lake or whatever it is
they got up there. Minnesota, that's the Vikings. . . .
Whassat, you hate football? Me too, to tell ya the
truth. Silly game, ain't it? Buncha big galunks breakin'
each other's legs. Hey, who wantsta wear helmets and
shoulder pads and get flattened by three-hundred-
pound galunks when you can wear practically nothing,
lay under a palm tree, and get flattened by a pitch-
erful of margaritas, eh? Speakin' of margaritas, how'd
ya like to take a look at the most beautiful resort in
Key West? Sand beach, pool, balconies, the works.
Tour takes about ninety minutes. . . . Whassat? You're

meeting friends in an hour? Great. Bring 'em along. Come back here with 'em, take the tour, and you'll all go out for dinner on me.... That's right. Forty-dollar meal voucher. Per couple. Good at twenty-five of Key West's finest restaurants. Conch chowder, key lime pie. So you'll come back?... Great, I'll be here. You see this little square of sidewalk? You'll recognize it? It's got a crack over here, a curb over there? Awright. This is where I'll be...."

Joey slid off his sunglasses, wiped his forehead, and watched the Minnesotans recede into the crush of Duval Street. They'd be back, of that he had no doubt. Not that they'd take the tour. No. They'd be back because tourists who walked Duval Street in one direction always walked it in the other. It was that, or swim to the motel. Sometimes people bantered on the return trip, pretending they were still considering. Sometimes they crossed the street a half block away to avoid a second pitch. Now and then they got hostile. People reacted in different ways to being charmed. Human nature.

Take the Minnesotans. Joey, as per Zack's advice, was studying up, trying to read them. They'd seemed perfect prospects. Fifty or so, wedding rings, family types, normal. The woman wore green pants with an elastic waistband whose puckers quickly stretched to accommodate her fallen bottom; the man had a fishing hat with a trout fly in the band. Joey, who had no wife, no children, belonged to no church, no civic associations, had never been farther inland than downtown Philadelphia, had never caught a fish, and had been part of the legitimate economy for nine days now, tried to imagine their life. The wife, he gathered from a certain softness around her mouth, didn't work, and probably felt a little bad about it, now that all four kids were gone. The husband was an assistant vice president in... in... What the hell did people do in Minnesota? What did they have up there, cows? O.K., a place that made cheese, something like that. So of course he liked to fish, to get away from the cheese smell. The wife, well, she mostly liked to do stuff at home, stuff with thread, that's where she really felt confident. Joey wanted to think that after they'd walked away, she said to her husband, *What a nice young man. It must be hard just to talk to strangers like that.* But the husband, he'd want to show that he was the worldly one, he knew what was what. *Once they get you inside, it's hard sell, Martha. Real hard sell. This fella Bill, he was once in Puerto Rico, and one of these fellas got him to go inside, and four hours later...*

"Hey, New York, how ya doin'? Your friends are gonna hate ya when they see that tan, ya know. But that's why you're here, right? So your friends'll hate ya? Looks good. Use that sunblock, though, don't be a wise guy. What parta New York ya from?"

The fellow in the Yankees baseball cap just kept walking, urged along by his ladyfriend, who was tugging at his elbow. Across Duval Street, shadows were lengthening in front of T-shirt shops and narrow stores selling frozen yogurt. The first early drunks were starting to bob and weave, and the steady hum of noise was occasionally punctuated by a tattooed grotesque in a sleeveless leather shirt going by on a Harley.

"Hello, folks, you enjoying our beautiful weather today? What are you, Japanese, Hawaiian, what?"

"Hello, folks, how's Key West treatin' ya today?

Hey, that is a fabulous hat you have. How they get all that fruit to stay in there like that?"

"Hello, folks, great afternoon, huh? You been puttin' your time in onna beach, I see. Those blisters'll be gone in a coupla days, don't worry. But hey, since you're outta commission anyway, how'd ya like ta see the Clem Sanders Treasure Museum . . ."

"Hello, folks. Hey, what's with the crutches? . . ."

"Hello, folks, awesome weather, huh? Hey, you really go to Harvard, or you just wear the sweatshirt?"

"Hello, folks, gorgeous day, isn't it?"

"Yes, ittis," said a small, white-haired lady in crisp khaki pants. She put a lot of bite into her *t*'s, and Joey was so surprised that someone actually answered him that he found himself leaning forward on the sidewalk, his arm stuck out in a hooking gesture, his smile frozen, momentarily unable to speak.

"Ittis, indeed," said the husband. He was a silver and pink old fellow who didn't seem to like the sun. He wore a Sherlock Holmes cap with one brim for his forehead and another for his neck, and his plaid shirt was neatly buttoned at the wrists.

Joey knew immediately that these were people who would take the tour and would never in a thousand lifetimes buy a time-share at Parrot Beach. But that was not his problem. They wanted the meal ticket. They wanted something to do. Probably more than anything, they wanted to sit down.

"Where you folks from?"

"Ottawa," said the lady. She bit the *t*'s.

"Zat in England?"

They thought Joey was kidding. They laughed politely. Joey felt suddenly the way he sometimes used to feel when trying to get a girl to go to bed with him.

All parties wanted the same result, for all intents and purposes the matter was settled. Yet there were certain forms and rituals that needed to be adhered to, still the awkward business of maneuvering her into the bedroom or onto the couch. So Joey spieled, and the nice old couple from Ottawa played along. A Harley-Davidson roared by, trailing a string of mopeds like a goose with goslings. Sunlight flashed off the tin roofs of downtown Key West. Finally, when all the ceremonies had been observed, Joey led the nice couple up the path to the Parrot Beach office. They would sign the guest book. They would admire the scale model. They would ride the shuttle bus to the property, sip fresh-squeezed orange juice, let themselves be hammered for a while by the sales staff, and Joey Goldman would get his forty bucks, forked over from the mysterious coffers of the legitimate world.

Returning to his post, he resolved to put the commission toward a pair of tennis shoes. The black loafers he was wearing were stylish but wrong. They let too much heat come up through the sidewalk and their thin soles passed along the pebbled texture of the concrete. He figured he'd keep this job at least a few more weeks, till he found the right way back to his true calling. This was temporary, very temporary, but for as long as it lasted he might as well be comfortable.

15

In the last week of February Joey made four hundred and eighty dollars and decided to celebrate by inviting Bert the Shirt over for filet mignon and a couple bottles of Valpolicella. It was time, he felt, that Bert and Sandra met. It was time he learned to use the gas grill at the compound. It was time, maybe, to get on terms with such basic social ceremonies as having a friend to the house on Saturday night.

Sandra bought a new blouse for the occasion. It was thin white cotton stamped with small pink birds, and it hung on the back of a chair while Sandra brushed on her eyeshadow and dabbed on her lipstick. She was beginning to have what was, for her, a tan. On her face and shoulders, orange-pink dots were strewn across her blue-white skin, gradually coloring her in the way a comic strip is colored in. The resulting blush made her light eyes seem a crisper green, green like a vegetable with crunch, and her short hair closer to silver than to yellow. "You know," she said, lifting a bra strap to better examine her tan lines in the mirror, "sometimes I think I'm the only person in this town who wears a bra."

Joey had a quick flash of Vicki, and banished the image.

He regarded Sandra's chaste white appliance, with its rim of dainty lace, its girding of clasps and elastic. "Well, you don't have to wear one," he said, feeling on safe ground saying it. It was about as likely that Sandra would give up her foundation garments as that the cardinal would stop wearing a hat.

"Well," she said, and left it at that. Turning half profile, she appraised her chest with that amazing dispassion women can muster when looking at their bodies. When Joey looked in the mirror, he tended to see muscle definition that wasn't quite there, tended not to notice the merest beginnings of a tummy. But Sandra duly recorded every crease and flaw, pitilessly noted every lack or excess. Humbled by such realism, Joey changed the subject.

"So the potatoes are in, the lettuce is washed. What else?"

"I wish the plates matched."

"It's a rented place. Bert'll understand."

The evening, even by Key West's relentless standards, was beautiful. A slow and undramatic sunset had left the sky pale yellow in the west, lavender backed by pearl gray at the zenith, velvety blue like the inside of a jewel box in the east. The air was the temperature of lips and there was just enough breeze to lift the smell of jasmine from the hedge. The compound was given over to uncomplicated pleasures. Wendy was sitting chin-deep in the hot tub while

Marsha massaged the tension out of her shoulders. Luke the musician and Lucy the mailman dangled their feet in the still blue pool, their twin headsets plugged into a single Walkman. Steve the naked landlord, draped now in a towel against the relative chill of dusk, had dozed off in a lounge chair, a paperback about clones rising and falling on his ample stomach.

Joey ushered in Bert the Shirt just as Peter and Claude, dressed in peppermint-stripe tunics, were heading off to work. He introduced them.

"And who's this little fur-face?" cooed Claude.

Joey could not help cringing a little. Fur-face?

But the retired mobster held his chihuahua forward in the palm of his hand so Claude could pet him. "This useless thing? This is Don Giovanni."

"Like the opera," Peter said, and he burst into a scrap of tune.

The tune sounded vaguely familiar to Bert, though since he'd died notes all sounded more or less the same to him. Still, the episode put him in a buoyant mood. It reminded him somehow of his wife. "Joey," he said, gesturing around him as they approached the cottage, "ain't this paradise?"

Sandra had come to meet them. "In paradise," she said, "the plates match."

She held out her hand to shake. But Bert had the dog in his right hand, and so took her fingers in his left, raised them to his lips, and kissed her on the knuckles. "You're as lovely as Joey says you are."

"Joey who? If Joey paid me a compliment, I think I'd plotz." She wagged her finger at Bert, admiring his perfectly draped shirt of midnight-blue voile. "But you're as sly as Joey says you are, and that's the truth."

"So Bert," said Joey, "glassa wine? We'll sit out by the pool awhile."

He brought a tray and put it on a small wooden table just outside the sliding door of their cottage. The wine seemed to draw into itself the last rays of dim light, and glowed a shimmering garnet.

"*Salud,*" said Bert the Shirt, and Joey could not help noticing that the word made Sandra wince. The Italian sound, the Italian wine in stubby glasses, a certain old-fashioned and very appealing swagger in the way Bert lifted his drink to toast—these things, to Sandra, were a threat, unintentional but real. They were the old ways, the family ways; their warmth and comfort bound a person to the neighborhood as much as did the promise of easy earnings, maybe more so, and made it hard to change. At any moment a gesture or a word could pull a person back to the small, sad, cozy place he'd come from.

"And how do *you* like it down here?"

Sandra barely heard the question. "Me? Oh, I like it fine. The weather's great, the girls at the bank are nice."

She stopped talking, but Bert just looked at her. It was a simple trick he'd developed decades before to get people to go a little farther.

"But ya know," Sandra obliged, "for me, it's not that big a change. A bank's a bank. Money's money. I mean, if you think about it, money's the least interesting thing there is. There's no variety about it, you know what I mean? Seen one dollar, you've seen 'em all."

"Yeah," said Bert, "but until you've seen a helluva lot of 'em, it doesn't really seem that way."

"I guess," she said. "But people. That's what's interesting. Now, with Joey's job . . ."

Joey looked down at the wooden table and gave his head a modest shake. This job. It was confusing, this job. He couldn't decide whether to be proud of it or embarrassed. It was like the time he painted some autumn trees and won an art contest in grade school. He was happy to win, happy to see his mother flush with satisfaction, but at the same time felt that making pictures was for girls. Of course, with the job, it had a lot to do with who was asking. With Sandra, yeah, he was proud, he could tell it made her happy. Around Bert, well, it wasn't like Bert was putting it down, it was just that, let's face it, Bert had a different sense of what a man should be. Joey wondered if he'd ever have a more firmly held opinion of his own. He had to believe that life would be easier if he did.

"Anybody hungry?" he said. "If I can figure out how to work the stupid grill, we can eat sometime tonight."

The hiss and pop of propane being lit reminded Joey how quiet the compound had become. The women from the antique store had abandoned the hot tub and gone inside; Luke and Lucy had disappeared into the thickening dark; Steve, under his towel, seemed down for the count. Joey looked at the blue flame of the grill, felt, rather to his own surprise, the prideful contentment of being the host, then went inside to get the steaks. Walking past the wooden table, he saw that Bert the Shirt was now holding Don Giovanni on his lap. All that was visible of the tiny dog was the thin silver spikes of its whiskers and a morbid gleam from its oversized eyes.

"You really love that little dog, don't you?" Sandra was saying.

"The dog? I hate the dog. The dog is like a rock I

can't get outta my shoe. You ever heard of a dog being, whaddyacallit, not a kleptomaniac, a hypochondriac?"

Joey slapped the steaks onto the grill, then poured himself another glass of wine. Standing there above his hard-earned dinner, holding a giant fork in a fireproof mitt, he had to laugh at himself: a citizen having a cookout. What would come next in this groping toward respectability, a goddamn sing-along?

The filets were delicious.

They had moved into the Florida room to eat them, at a table covered with a plastic cloth, knives and forks of random pattern, and unmatched plates whose stripes and borders had been scratched and nicked by many hungry renters.

"Joey," said Bert the Shirt as the younger man refilled his glass, "this is more like it, huh? This is what I been tellin' ya. Come to Florida, take it easy, enjoy what there is to be enjoyed. Look at him, Sandra—nice and relaxed. Joey, the other week when we talked, jeez—"

"I'm more relaxed 'cause I'm makin' some money," Joey said, gesturing with his fork. "But it hasn't been that easy, Bert. I mean, my feet hurt. Besides, the little I'm making—"

"It's not bad money," said Sandra. "Especially for right at the beginning."

"It's O.K.," Joey said with a shrug. "But it's all according to how ya measure. Bert, you know what I mean. Our friends in New York, one night out, they spread around in tips what I make in a week."

Sandra dabbed her lips. "So they're big shots," she could not resist saying. "Real sports. I'm impressed. But Joey, let's keep things in proportion. It's not like you were in that league when we were up there anyway."

Joey started to protest, then chewed some steak instead and realized he had nothing to protest about. "It just makes ya wonder. That's all I'm saying. Am I better off doing what I'm doing, or am I better off doing what I was tryin' to do before?"

"There's no comparison, Joey," Sandra said.

"Excuse me, Sandra," said Bert the Shirt, putting down his wineglass. "I'm a guest in your house, I don't wanna get in the middle of a disagreement or anything. But I think there *is* a comparison. The comparison is called money. Legit, not legit, that's not the point. Results is the point. Lookit the guys I play gin with." He counted them off on his long yellowish fingers. "A retired judge. A guy who ran a big Buick dealership. A doctor. Why are we all of a sudden inna same club? Not becausa what we did. Because we all got the same kinda results. We all ended up to where we could buy condos onna beach. That makes us equals, friends almost. Legit, not legit, that isn't how people add it up. You wanna end up respected, you gotta go where your best shot is."

"But that's just it," said Joey. "I don't know where my best shot is."

Bert neatly laid his knife and fork across his plate as Joey poured more wine. "Well, kid, there's nobody that can tell you that. That you hafta decide for yourself."

Sandra had her hands in her lap and was making a point of looking past Joey, through the louvered windows at the empty night. "Well, I've had enough," she said, referring to her dinner. "Bert, how 'bout some steak for the dog?"

"No, Sandra, no thanks. Dog's a vegetarian."

"A dog vegetarian?" said Joey. "This I never heard of, a dog vegetarian."

"Not by choice. Meat don't agree with 'im. Kinda clogs 'im up. You don't wanna hear about it, believe me."

Then the telephone rang.

This was a rather rare event, as the only people who ever called were tellers from the bank who wanted Sandra to take a shift for them, or avid young men looking for a former tenant named Pippy. Joey got up. In his concern to be a gracious host, he'd been pouring wine at a brisk clip, and was a shade unsteady on his legs. The bedroom phone was on its fifth ring when he reached it.

By the time he returned to the Florida room, the table was cleared and coffee cups had been placed around a tray of pignolia nut cookies. "That was my brother Gino," Joey announced. "He's here. In town."

The news was sufficient to spoil the evening. Gino Delgatto had a gift for that kind of thing. Every face clouded over, although each for a somewhat different reason.

"Why's 'e here?" asked Bert, wondering how much, if anything, Joey had told Sandra of the family business that was, strictly speaking, none of her business at all.

"He says he's on vacation." Joey had had just enough to drink so that he heard his own voice from the inside of his eardrums, and he didn't like the steely sound of it. "Says he figured he might as well come down and pay a visit."

"You believe that?" Sandra asked.

Joey took a heavy breath that had a tough time

coming in and going out again around a bellyful of steak. "Yeah, right. I believe it. He's here to fuck things up for me."

"Joey, don't—"

He cut her off quick and hard. "And don't tell me not to curse."

"That isn't what I was gonna say," she came right back. "Don't fucking let him, Joey. That's what I was gonna say."

Part II

16

The first thing Joey noticed about his half brother Gino Delgatto—noticed from thirty feet away—was that his new girlfriend had enormous breasts. They started about three inches below her shoulders, then billowed out and down but mostly out, tapering only slightly as they went, with the jolly, bouncy, cozy taper of small blimps. You could have run raft trips down her cleavage. Measured against these monumental bosoms, the girlfriend's features could only appear ungenerous and pinched, the eyes smallish in spite of all the tricks to make them bigger, the narrow nose barely equal to the job of sucking in air, the mouth, for all its caked-on lipstick, as austere as a mail slot. Gino did not think to introduce her. He would as soon have introduced a new settee. Instead, he watched Joey approach their booth at the Eclipse Saloon, and when he was still far enough away so that the remark needed almost to be shouted, said "What's with the pink shirt, Joey? Ya look like some kinda fairy."

Joey walked faster toward his brother's table, not because he was eager to get there, but because he wanted to close the space between them before Gino could fill it with any more embarrassments. "That's not the kinda thing ya say down here," he said.

Gino didn't seem to notice he'd been scolded. In his world, there were people above you and people below you. If someone above you set you right on something, your whole soul immediately changed to accommodate the advice. This was education of a profound but brittle sort. If someone below you made bold to criticize, you could shrug it off or hit him, but usually neither was necessary. Opinions from below just didn't register.

"And the pink shirt," Joey went on, "is what I work in."

"Oh yeah," said Gino. "You work." To show that the idea amused him, Gino smiled. It was an odd, abrupt smile that squeezed his eyes and stretched his mouth so wide that the flesh of his cheeks piled up like drifted snow. But there was no humor whatsoever in the smile, and it seemed like Gino struck the expression only because he'd seen it on other people. "Well, siddown, siddown."

He motioned Joey into the booth next to the girlfriend, and still he didn't introduce her, so Joey introduced himself. He would be sitting thigh to thigh with her, breathing in her perfume that smelled like a rose garden on a very humid day. He ought to know her name at least.

"I'm Vicki," she said, and she held out a hand whose long red fingernails jabbed into Joey's wrist as they shook. Hearing the name, he could not help taking a quick confirming glance at this Vicki's semicredible boobs. Their top acre jiggled as she slid across the booth, and he felt reassured that they were made of flesh.

"Had lunch?" asked Gino. He had a frozen daiquiri in front of him and a menu at his elbow.

"Don't have time," said Joey. "Gotta get back soon."

"My brother the executive," said Gino.

"Someday, maybe. Or maybe not. So what's up with you?"

Gino shrugged. His elbows were on the table and his beefy forearms framed a triangle of his wide and powerful chest. There was a definite resemblance between the two half brothers, but everything about Gino was thicker, coarser, more rough-hewn, as if he'd been sprung from the mold and sent on his way while Joey had continued to be carved and whittled, losing in strength what he gained in elegance. Where Joey's neck was thin but graceful, Gino's was sturdy but squat. Where Joey's gait was modest but springy, Gino's was imposing but earthbound. And while Gino had a handsome face, it was a handsomeness that existed on the very edge of the ugly. His black eyes were bright and hard, but at moments they fell into a beady stare that suggested a birdlike unintelligence. His strong square nose, with its ample nostrils, could have been lifted directly from a Roman statue yet was only a hair's breadth away from being hoggish. His mouth was as lippy and sensual as his girlfriend's was unpromising, yet sometimes in the effort of forming words it appeared blubbery and almost lewd. "Things are pretty much status quo with me," he said. "But hey kid, I got a bone to pick with you. How come you didn't come see me before you left New York?"

Now it was Joey's turn to shrug. To answer the question properly would have taken a lot more time than he had, probably the rest of his life in fact, and Gino wouldn't get it anyway. "Lot to do," he said. "And you know how it is, once you decide to go somewhere, ya just wanna get onna road. But how'd you decide to come to Key West?"

"Like I said, just a vacation. As good a place as any to catch a tan, and this way I get to see you."

Joey pulled his eyes away from his half brother and looked around the Eclipse on the pretext of scouting up a waitress. He found one and ordered a club soda. But all the while, he was reflecting on what a lousy liar Gino was. Or rather, Gino was a barely adequate liar, given the very low ambitions of his lying. A topnotch liar was satisfied with nothing short of convincing. An imaginative liar could spin out a story whose amusingness made up at least in part for the fact that you were being jerked around. But Gino didn't have enough imagination to make up a good story, or enough shame to give a damn if you knew he was lying in your face. It was just his way—one of his ways—of letting you know you would get nothing from him.

"Well, it's nice you came," said Joey, deciding to answer lie with lie. "So what'll you do while you're here?"

"Ya know," said Gino. "Hang around. Eat. Do some shopping."

The word galvanized Vicki like a pinch on the nipple. "Shopping's lousy here," she suddenly piped up.

"I never seen a town where all they got is T-shirts. All up and downa street."

"So you'll buy T-shirts," Gino said.

Vicki pulled her thin mouth into a pout. "Inna Bahamas, at least there's duty-free. Ya know, like perfume, jewelry—"

"Shut up," said Gino. "We ain't inna Bahamas."

"You could take a tour of the condo," Joey said, and regretted it before the words were out of his mouth. But he had a long history of misspeaking around Gino, out of discomfort. Besides, it was already getting to be a salesman's reflex with him to tell people they should have a look at Parrot Beach.

"That might be fun," said Vicki.

Gino didn't look like he thought so. He had no interest in Florida real estate. Or maybe what he had no interest in was what his kid brother was doing with his time.

So Joey backpedaled. "Nah, forget about it. It's not that inneresting, and besides, you hafta qualify."

"Whaddya mean, qualify? What kinda bullshit is qualify?" As a great sprinter comes to full speed in a single stride, so Gino Delgatto had the knack of coming to full belligerence in a single word. He was always ready to take umbrage at the merest suggestion that he might not be good enough for something.

"Like, for one thing," Joey said, "you need a credit card. You got a credit card, Gino?"

"Course I got a credit card. What kinda jerk travels these days widdout a credit card? I got a Gold Card. Dr. somebody. From Westchester, I think." And Gino smiled, not the stiff, forced grin but an easy smile of true delight. He was stealing. He was happy.

"And a license," Joey said.

"I got Bald Benny's old license," Gino said. "You know that."

Joey sipped his club soda. He was almost enjoying the conversation now. Should he point out that it might be awkward when Gino was asked to show both IDs, or should he leave his big brother with the mental challenge of figuring it out for himself? In the meantime he glanced at Vicki. Not much of a vacation for her, he figured. No shopping, no condo tour, no casinos with big-name entertainment. Did she withhold sexual favors when she was ticked off? Joey hoped so.

Gino at length came to the end of his analysis. "Yeah, I guess it would look, like, strange."

"Too bad," said Joey. "I coulda made forty bucks offa you guys."

"Hey, you strapped?" said Gino, and predictably, he reached into his pants pocket. Joey had seen him do it hundreds of times. He did it as naturally as other guys took their dicks out to pee. A single motion, the fat, spiraled wad of bills appeared, and Gino was once more master of the situation.

But this time Joey waved him off. "No, thanks, Gino. I'm not strapped. Besides, it wouldn't be the same, taking the money from you. It's a game, getting people to take the tour. The kick, that comes from figuring the game out, playing it good, and winning. Winning—you can understand that, can't ya, Gino?"

Rockaway, or Coney Island. It was made of old coral, the bigger pieces resembling knucklebones, the smaller ones looking like shards and ribs from a well-picked chicken. Over the coral was a layer of imported sand that the town fathers had decided would be good for tourism. Where did it come from, this yellow-brown sand that looked like nothing else in the lower Keys? Or, for that matter, where did it go? Joey had no idea. But from day to day, and even from hour to hour, the sand seemed to sift downward through the coral, gradually disappearing into the bowels of the earth. What didn't fall through the cracks in the limestone blew unpredictably on every changing wind. One day it seemed that every grain of sand had decided to congregate up near the airport; next day the yellow-brown mass had migrated three quarters of a mile and was leaning against the fence that enclosed the private beach of the Flagler House hotel. There was only one thing you could count on about this sand: it would not be where your next footstep fell. No, your next footstep would carry you to an exposed and upturned knuckle of coral, a piece of ancient Florida history that would stab you in the arch.

But for Joey, wearing new tennis shoes purchased with his own earned money, the torturing surface of Smathers Beach was no more a problem than the hot sidewalks of Duval Street. His feet were comfy. His feet had adapted to where he was. Too bad it wasn't as easy for the rest of him.

He scanned the beach, looking for his friend. The sun was low, and the western horizon had taken on that perfectly neutral color where you can no longer tell if it's cloudy or clear, whether the sun will douse itself in the ocean or vanish in midsky, slipping into haze as modestly as a letter slides into an envelope. Joey saw no one except one guy with a metal detector and another flying a kite.

Then, finally, he spotted Bert. Bert was sitting in a beach chair, far out on a finger of crumbly gray rock that jutted into the green ocean. His back was to the land, and he was recognizable only by his bronze-white hair; that, and the canary-yellow polka-dotted silk of his shirt.

"Hello, Joey," Bert said when the younger man was still half a dozen steps behind him.

"How'd ya know it's me?"

"Dog twitched," said the Shirt, turning slowly, "so I knew it was someone. That it was you, that was a percentage play. Ya know, kid, it's not like I'm really that popular. But how are ya?"

"Not bad, considering I saw my asshole brother today."

Bert shook his head slowly. Family feuds saddened him, but not because he regarded them as unnatural. Just the opposite. What was more natural than that disappointment, rage, and the sense that you were being gypped should start at home? The family was where you really took a beating. You looked to the outside world for comfort not because the outside world was kinder but because it mattered so much less, it couldn't get under your fingernails. "Joey," Bert said, "lemme ask you a question. Is he really an asshole, or does it just look that way to you because of, ya know, the situation?"

Joey looked at Bert, and at Don Giovanni nestled in his lap. The dog really did seem to be savoring the sunset. Twin orange disks were reflected in its glassy, oversized eyes, making it look like some diminutive species of hellhound. "Bert, I've had a lot of time to think it over. As God is my witness, he's really an asshole."

Bert just nodded and never took his eyes off the sky. The sun was almost on the horizon now, at the point where its reflection seemed to jump out of the ocean to rejoin it, making it look not like a sphere but a cylinder, a giant candle slipping away.

"And what's going on," Joey resumed, "I really don't like it. It's the exact same bullshit as in New York. The lying. The hiding things. All the time having to wonder who said what to who. Who's clued in, who ain't. It's like ya can't open your goddamn mouth without worrying ten different ways if you're gonna say somethin' ya shouldn't say. I mean, Bert, life shouldn't be that fucking complicated."

Bert the Shirt, his long face rosy in the last red rays, smiled the inward smile of a patient teacher whose lesson is at last getting through. "No, it shouldn't be." He didn't want to say I-told-you-so to Joey, so he spoke to his dog instead. "Ya see, Giovanni, now he's starting to talk like Florida."

"Yeah," said Joey, "but now I got my brother here, and he talks like the gutters of Astoria."

"That's a problem," the old man conceded. He lifted the chihuahua off his lap and gently placed it on the warm gray rock. Then he plucked a real or imaginary dog hair from the belly of his splendid yellow shirt. "So kid, let's think this through. First off, why do you really think your brother is here?"

Joey gave a mirthless snort of a laugh that had to do only with what he saw as the ridiculous obviousness of the question. "Bert, lemme put it this way. I can't think of one fucking time my brother ever crossed the street to say hello to me, let alone went fifteen hundred miles. So it ain't a social call. Vacation? Nah. He hates gays, he's with a broad who all she wants to do is shop—he wouldn't come to Key West for vacation. It's gotta be this bullshit with Charlie Ponte."

"Awright," said Bert. "We agree. Now, does he know you know about Ponte, about the emeralds?"

"No."

"You sure?"

Joey glanced off toward the west, at the underlit pink clouds whose edges were already dimming out to purple. "Yeah, I'm sure."

"You tell anybody in New York?" Bert pressed.

"One guy. My buddy Sal."

A look of concern flickered across the old man's face, and the look triggered in Joey an instant of doubt followed by a moment of anger toward Bert for being the agent of suspicion. Mistrusting Sal would be about as painful as any possible consequence of being let down by Sal. If you couldn't rely on your family, then you could not afford to doubt your friends. "Sal's solid," Joey said, and there was defiance in his voice.

"O.K., O.K." The Shirt raised a pacifying palm. "So what're you gonna do, kid?"

"About Gino? I'm gonna do what I always do with Gino. I'm gonna try to stay outta his way and hope I don't get steamrolled."

Bert reached down and absently stroked Don Giovanni behind the ears. "Well, your brother knows who I am. He knows I'm here. Maybe he'll look me up, maybe he won't. I hope he doesn't."

Joey could not help laughing. "Ain't it great what a popular guy my brother is, the way he's always spreading sunshine?"

"Yeah, it's great," said Bert. "But listen, kid, if you want my advice, or even if you don't, play as dumb as you can for as long as you can."

Joey looked down at his feet and kicked lightly at a knuckle of coral. "That'll be easy. I mean, that'll just be acting like he expects me to act."

"And Sandra? What'll you say to Sandra?"

"As little as I can," said Joey. He hadn't really thought about it, but he knew the answer that was expected of him. "I don't want her involved."

The old man nodded his approval. "Best that way," he said.

Joey nodded back, glanced briefly at the vacant western sky, and for just an instant felt as empty as the place the sun had been. "Best that way."

"So how'd it go with Gino?"

Sandra was standing at the stove, watching macaroni boil. She wasn't a bad cook, just a nervous one, an Irish girl making Italian food for a half-Jewish boyfriend who'd grown up with the finest pork products Queens had to offer. In her efforts to be organized, precise, she meddled too much with the food. She was always poking at cutlets, stirring things that didn't need stirring. She memorized recipes and timed things on her watch.

"Went O.K.," Joey said. He was looking for some orange juice and his head was in the fridge. "He's got a new girlfriend with him."

"What's she like?" Sandra bothered the broccoli.

By way of answer, Joey held his hands about a foot and a half out from his chest.

"He's consistent," said Sandra.

"Give him that," said Joey.

There was a pause. A lid lifted softly from a sauce-pan, then settled back down. Sandra had an instant's panic that the red sauce was scorching. It was not. She stirred it anyway. "Joey, why's he here?"

He leaned against the sink and hid his face in his glass of orange juice. His answer, when it came, sounded harsher than he meant it to be. "Sandra, get real, willya. You think my big shot brother tells me why he does things?"

Or maybe Joey meant the answer to be harsh. Maybe he wanted to goad Sandra into pressing him. If she pressed, maybe he would tell her more, and could persuade himself he wasn't violating the code that made him wrestle with things alone but was only giving in to a woman's nagging. But Sandra didn't nag. She had her code too.

"I didn't even know your brother was such a big shot," she said.

"Well, he is," said Joey, and even as he was mum-bling out the words, he was thinking how ridiculous it was: standing up for Gino practically in the same breath he was saying what a louse he was, still trying to make him a big brother instead of a big pain in the ass. Ridiculous. This whole business with family was ridiculous, and to stop himself from saying anything more, Joey filled his mouth with orange juice and walked out of the kitchen.

18

"Hello, folks, how ya doin'? Crummy day, ain't it? Barely eighty-one degrees, I'd say, and hey, where'd that one little cloud come from, Cuba? Yeah, that's some kinda Commie cloud. Havana's only ninety miles away, ya know, twice as close as Miami. Yeah. Think about it. We're practically, ya know, in South America. And this beautiful condo, Parrot Beach, it looks right at downtown Havana. You think I'm kidding? Hey, get a good pair of binocs, you can watch Castro trim his beard inna morning. Really, take a tour. Takes an hour or so, and we give ya champagne, free food, a paira passes to . . ."

Joey was having a good day. He'd chalked up two commissions and it wasn't even noon. Moreover, he was gradually discovering what tens of millions of working people already knew but would not publicly admit: that going to your job was a great way to forget about your life. Patrolling his street corner, giving his

spiel, he didn't have to think about the dinner he and
Sandra would be having with Gino and Vicki that evening. He didn't have to worry about why Gino was in
town. He could imagine himself beyond the long
reach of circumstance. On these few squares of sidewalk, he was in control of things. He was confident,
and more so all the time. He knew how people would
react to him, knew how to play off the drunks and
the yogurt eaters and the kids. Like anyone who's any
good at anything, he could at moments drop out of
time and move into the blessed and utterly private
realm of his skill.

He was in that realm when the dark blue Lincoln
pulled up.

It had come down Duval Street slow and heavy, as
if it were leading a funeral, overflowing its fair share
of the pavement like a fat man in an airplane seat.
The car stopped in front of a fire hydrant, its tires
squeaking against the curb. Two men got out. They
exuded menace like a bad smell, and an open space
instantly appeared around them on the crowded
street. They wore blue suits that almost matched the
car and almost matched each other. They were beefy
in a way that made them walk with their feet wide
apart because their thighs rubbed together, making
wrinkles in their groins and shiny places on their
pants.

"Yo, fuckface," the taller of the two said to Joey.
He had the pink upturned nostrils of a pig, and his
hair was raked, swirled, and peaked like something
you'd see in the window of a fancy bakery.

"Me?" Joey found himself strangely unsurprised to
be confronted by these thugs, who, he realized in an
instant, worked for Charlie Ponte. But unsurprised is

not the same as not terrified. The bone seemed to
melt out of his knees and he wanted to sit on the
john. Having grown up with thugs, he was both more
and less afraid of them than the average person.
More, because he knew they were killers. Not by ru-
mor, not from the movies; he *knew* it. Less, because
he also knew what fakers they were. They had to act
scary like doctors had to act concerned. It went with
the job. It didn't mean they meant it.

"Yeah, you, dickhead," said the thug. "We wanna
talk to you."

"So talk."

"Take your sunglasses off," said the shorter thug.
His lower lip was creased by a deep off-center scar,
and he wore a very bad toupee. It was the color of a
wet brown dog, and where it was parted there was a
fissure as between two strips of badly laid sod. "So we
can see if you're lying."

"They're prescription," Joey lied.

"I should give a fuck they're prescription?" said the
shorter goon. "I don't give a fuck if you're blind. Take
'em off."

"Go fuck yourself."

Joey had only an instant to savor this flash of bravado. The shorter goon stepped behind him with the
practiced quickness of a high school wrestler and pin-
ioned his arms. The taller goon reached out and
plucked the sunglasses off his face. In a moment of
excruciatingly slowed-down time, Joey watched them
tumble to the sidewalk. They landed eyebrow-side
down, bounced once, and did not break. They cast
twin blue shadows onto the pebbled sidewalk. Then
the taller goon lifted his foot. His shoe was shiny and
tapered like a missile, and it came down heel first on

the sunglasses Sal Giordano had given him. The
lenses were reduced to tiny blue beads as from a
thrown bottle.

"So now, douchebag," said the taller thug, "we talk.
You in on this with your brother?"

"In on what?" said Joey. He tried to look past the
two sets of massive shoulders to remind himself there
was still a world beyond the blue suits. Traffic continued going by on Duval Street, bending around the
parked Lincoln. Pedestrians gave wide berth, as they
might around someone throwing up, but showed no
particular interest.

"Don't be cute, shitbird," said the goon with the
terrible rug. "You know what we're talking about."

"Sorry, guys, but I really don't." As if to prove his
innocence, his uninvolvement with anything rough
and dangerous, he gestured delicately toward his own
pink shirt and down at his wholesome tennis shoes.
"I live here. I got a job. My brother's here on vacation. I really don't know what you want from me."

The two goons glanced at each other. They seemed
to be straining to maintain their aspect of menace,
but mostly they just looked confused. They were not
long on ideas, and they had come to the end of their
morning's worth. If Joey had given them one single
thing to grab on to, they could have clubbed him with
it. But he hadn't. *Play as dumb as you can for as long
as you can.*

"You gonna be seeing your brother?" asked the
taller thug.

"Course. He's my brother."

The thug wagged a thick forefinger under Joey's
chin, but it was an unimpressive gesture, a shot in the
air by an army in retreat. "Tell him to watch his ass."

The thugs stepped around the ruins of Joey's sunglasses, got into the Lincoln, and drove away. Almost immediately the life of Key West surged back into the space they'd emptied, the way water finds the only dry spot on a piece of cloth. Joey bent down and picked up his shades as one would an injured bird. The frames at least seemed more or less intact. He put them in his pocket. Then he walked gingerly into the Parrot Beach office to use the bathroom.

"Did I ask you if they were worth fixing? I mean, did I come in here and ask your expert opinion, or did I just say I'd like 'em fixed?"

The young woman behind the optician's counter was wearing tinted contacts in a startling shade of copper. She leaned back slightly in the face of Joey's vehemence, but held on to her pleasant and relentlessly helpful tone. "It's just that, with the cheaper frames—"

"Did I ask if they were cheap frames? Did I ask what any of this costs?"

Zack Davidson, his sandy hair falling in a perfect arc across his forehead, his pink shirt immaculately draped, intervened. "He's a little upset. The glasses have sentimental value. So if you could just fit them with new lenses . . ."

The woman behind the counter lifted the frames, wiggled the loosened hinges of the earpieces, and said, "Sure. O.K. What color?"

"Blue," said Joey. He said it like a little boy who's fallen down, is being bribed into feeling comforted, but owes it to himself not to come around too soon.

"O.K.," said the woman behind the counter. "Blue. They'll be ready by five."

On the short walk back to the Parrot Beach office, Zack regarded Joey from under his reddish eyebrows. "You wanna tell me what that was all about?"

"Nothing," said Joey. "It was about nothing. These two guys thought I was needling them, I guess."

Zack frowned. From his office window, he'd noticed the Lincoln pull up and the two men approach. He didn't hear what was said, but the two beefy fellows hadn't waited to be needled, that much was clear. "You in trouble, Joey?"

"No."

"Debts?"

"No."

"Drugs?"

"No."

"You want me to call the police?"

"No."

For a minute they walked in silence among the characters of Duval Street. A fellow in a torn undershirt with a green parrot on his shoulder. A woman with a small monkey in a diaper. Then Zack said, "You know, Claire and Sandra, they're getting to be good friends."

The remark seemed to connect with nothing, and Joey turned it this way and that in his mind, trying to see where it fit. It didn't at first dawn on him that maybe it was a backdoor kind of offer, an offer of confidence, of alliance. Joey wasn't used to offers like that. He was isolated, and isolation made people suspicious, and suspicion kept them isolated. "That's nice," said Joey. "I been hoping Sandra would make some friends."

Zack looked as if he might speak again, but didn't. He turned up the pathway to the Parrot Beach office,

19

Gino Delgatto, whatever else he was or was not, was a true sport as a host.

When Joey and Sandra arrived in the grand columned dining room of the Flagler House, a magnum of Dom Perignon had already been placed tableside in a silver bucket, canapés of caviar and salmon had been arrayed on triangles of toast, and the staff had fallen into the somewhat ironic deference that accrues to the big spender. On the presentation plates of the expected guests lay pink hibiscus flowers. Gino had moved his to his bread-and-butter plate, and Vicki had placed hers between her alpine breasts, where its pistil had at first quivered then begun to droop from the excessive heat.

Gino, on best behavior, stood up as the maître d' ushered Joey and Sandra to the table. He gave Sandra a quick hug, deciding in the first glance that, in her cream-colored slacks and cardigan, she was, as usual, not dressed up enough. Gino had known Sandra for over three years now, and had never yet managed to pin down what he thought of her. He supposed she was pretty in her way, but her way was so unshowy, so unglamorous, that Gino really couldn't tell. Sandra was practically flat-chested. Her nails were short and she didn't do much with her hair. She wore makeup but, as Gino saw it, not enough. As to her personality, she seemed to have some brains, give her that. Now and then she could be pretty funny, in a dry kind of way. But fun-loving she was not. Had Gino ever seen her have more than two, three drinks? Had he ever seen her really drop her guard and laugh? He didn't think so. In fact, she usually seemed to be the one who decided when the party was over. Probably she was good for Joey, who, after all, didn't have much going for him and wasn't likely to attract the really super babes, but still, she was a little bland, a little dull.

It did not occur to Gino that Sandra was subdued around him because she loathed him to the marrow of her bones.

But he was family, and so she returned his hug and answered his kiss on the cheek with one of her own. She shook the red-taloned hand that Vicki presented with the weirdly arched wrist of a great lady from some previous century. Then everyone sat down and started sipping champagne.

"Cheers," said Gino.

"Cheers," said Joey.

"You having a good time here?" Sandra asked Vicki.

Vicki reached toward her cleavage on the pretext of toying with the flower that was wilting there, and twisted her thin mouth into an expression of mixed feelings. "Pretty good. Weather's great. But the shopping—" She made a dismissive sound that was something like *dyukh,* then leaned close to Sandra as though sharing a deep and shameful secret. "It's like junky stuff. Homemade. No brand names. No designers. It's not like, ya know, elegant."

Gino emptied his glass and gave his head an indulgent shake. Like sugar daddies everywhere, he felt truly secure only when his mistress was either spending his money or talking about it. "Vicki thinks 'elegant' is a whaddyacallit, a pseudonym for 'expensive.'"

"Synonym," said Sandra.

"What the hell," said Gino. "Anyway, she don't like cheap stuff. Do ya, baby?"

Vicki shrugged her shoulders with an effect that was seismic. "Who does? I mean, if people liked it, it wouldn't be cheap no more."

"Hey, that's good," said Gino. He said it looking at Joey and pointing a thick finger at Vicki. "Well, hey, anybody hungry?"

They looked at menus and decided to order lobsters from Maine.

"Seems crazy," Vicki said, when the waiter had refilled the champagne glasses and vanished. "I mean, here we are right by this ocean just full of a zillion kinds of fish, and we have lobsters flown in from Maine."

"There's nothing like Maine lobster," said Gino with finality, and Joey realized, in spite of himself, something he admired or at least envied about his half brother. Gino knew what he liked. He enjoyed things. For him, everything fell into a list, and you went for the things at the top. Drinks, that was champagne.

Champagne, that was Dom Perignon. Food, it was lobster. Women, big tits and high hair. Shoes, suits, cars, watches, hair tonic, olive oil, whatever. There was always something that was the best, and if you could have that thing, you knew you were doing good.

Then, too, lobster was a great equalizer. Everybody was a slob eating lobster, and so Gino, who was a slob eating almost anything, didn't especially stand out. Or rather, he stood out unmistakably as the leader in a ritual of gusto. Too strong, with not enough grace, he crushed shells so that juice went squirting out of every crevice, hitting his waxed bib with a sound like soft rain on a tin roof. Vicki, hampered by her long nails, plucked at her lobster with the patient murderousness of a gull. Sandra was, as ever, methodical, her small neat hands coaxing out the flesh as efficiently as if she were counting out twenties at the bank. And Joey, who was perhaps too tentative at many things, was tentative as well in his attack on his dinner. He didn't get all the meat out, for fear of twanging a sinew and having it fly off, for fear of flicking a speck of lobster at a tablemate—for fear of being like Gino.

"More champagne?" the older brother asked.

"Not for me," said Sandra.

"Maybe one glass," said Joey.

Gino summoned the captain with a wave of a hand covered in lobster slime and ordered up another magnum.

"So Gino," Sandra said, "all the time I've known you, I've never once heard of you taking a vacation. How come all of a sudden you are?"

Did Gino flinch at the question, or was he just yanking off a stubborn lobster leg? "Just due for a break, that's all. Besides, Vicki here, she's been such a good kid, I thought it would be nice to take a trip with her."

"I wanted to go to Aruba," Vicki said. "Ya know, where there's duty-free. But no. Gino says he's got some business down here anyway."

"Shut up, Vicki. What she means is I wanted to visit you guys."

Sandra dabbed her mouth on her napkin. Around the dining room, plates clattered and corks popped.

They finished the lobsters, had mango ice cream and coffee, and the captain brought the check nestled in a leather sleeve on a silver tray. "I trust everything was satisfactory, Dr. Greenbaum?"

"Yeah, terrific," said Gino, signing. "Here's a little something for you." The captain retreated, backing and bobbing, and Gino dropped his napkin onto the table. "Walk onna beach?"

Outside, a yellow half-moon was perched over the Florida Straits, and a light south breeze that smelled of dry shells and seaweed was just barely rustling the palms. Underfoot, the trucked-in sand felt cakey with the moisture of the evening. Gino handed Joey a cigar and unwrapped one for himself. The gesture was enough to make Sandra and Vicki fall in side by side, leaving the men to trail behind, wreathed in their blue and nasty smoke.

For a couple of minutes they walked in silence, and Joey, to his own surprise, found himself slipping into a state of mysterious contentment. To walk next to a bigger, older, stronger brother was a comfort. It almost didn't matter what you thought of him, it only mattered that he was there, like a roof, like a wall, like anything big and solid that protected you or surrounded you.

"I'm sorry I didn't come see ya before I left," said Joey. "I shoulda."

"Don't matter," said Gino, waving the apology away with a red flash of his cigar. "But kid, ya shoulda gone to see Pop. I think ya hurt his feelings."

"Maybe I wanted to."

"Hey, ya wanted to, ya wanted to. But that don't make it right."

And they walked. Gino's shoes plowed over the sand with the heavy assurance of wide tires. His thick chest blacked out a broad swath of the Atlantic. The women, walking with the grim purpose of after-dinner exercise, had gotten almost out of sight.

"Ya know," said Joey, gesturing back toward the twinkling bulk of the Flagler House, "I been wanting to see this place since the first day I got here."

Gino exhaled some smoke and said nothing.

"I think Pop used to come here with my mother."

Gino stiffened and bit down on his cigar, but Joey didn't notice. The younger brother was drifting into memory and into trust, two places he didn't often visit.

"Yeah," he went on, "I'm pretty sure this is the place. I don't remember the name, but my mother useta describe it to me. Said it had the big dining room with the hanging-over porch. Said it had its own beach, private from the others—"

Gino stopped walking and stood with the yellow moonlight on his shiny dark hair. "Joey, I don't really wanna hear where my father went to catch some pussy."

Joey did not know he was about to hit his brother. He didn't notice that the cigar had dropped out of his hand and was glowing dull red on the beach, and he didn't feel his arm draw back, coiling to throw a punch. He was about as surprised as Gino when his fist slammed into the stronger man's gut, finding the soft triangle at the bottom of the ribs.

The air came out of Gino as from a ruptured football, a popping whoosh followed by a long wheeze. Helplessly, he doubled up and stayed that way for the endless moment of wondering if his lungs would ever again remember how to breathe. He struggled to lift his head, and strained his eyeballs upward to look at Joey with the befuddlement of a bystander who finds himself winged.

Joey stared down at him and felt no remorse, only fear. Gino could beat the hell out of him, easily. He'd seen Gino fight, with his fists and his feet and his elbows, he'd seen him use the top of his head to knock out other men's teeth, and the thought of it gave Joey a sickening awareness of cigar smoke turning to brown juice at the back of his throat.

But Gino didn't go for him. He straightened up slowly, arched his back, and threw his arms behind him to stretch his chest. "Fuck you do that for?"

"You don't talk about my mother that way."

"Talk about your mother? What is this, Joey, the fucking schoolyard? *Talk about my mother.* What are you, a fucking baby?"

Joey locked onto Gino's hard narrow eyes, and Gino was the first to quit the stare. "Awright," he said. "Awright. I shouldn'ta said it. But Joey, let's you and me decide on something right now. We don't talk about my father and your mother, O.K.? We just don't talk about it."

Joey shifted his feet in the caked sand and nodded. He couldn't have said why he'd raised the subject any-

20

Just before five the next day, Bert d'Ambrosia came walking down Duval Street in a seersucker shirt of mint-green and cobalt-blue stripes, colors that vibrated in the orange light of late afternoon. Unseen, and with his nervous chihuahua quivering against his chest, he watched Joey from half a block away, saw him dance toward his prospects, lean toward them as if he could somehow stretch his being to surround them, smile the salesman's hungry smile, and launch into his pitch. Eight hours of that, Bert thought. It must take a hell of a lot of energy. You had to show a lot of animation. That's what people responded to, animation. Like show biz. You wanted to get people on your side, you had to put out for them. And the street was hot. As March advanced, the sun climbed higher in the sky and sliced more relentlessly between the shimmering roofs. The cars and the scooters shot their hot blue puffs at sidewalk level, you felt them on your shins.

"Joey, why don't you wear shorts at least?"

"Oh, hi, Bert," Joey said. He swept off his repaired sunglasses and raked a forearm across his sweaty brow.

"No, I'm serious," said the old man, as if Joey had suggested he wasn't. "You'd be a lot more comfortable."

Joey gave a noncommittal shrug. He felt he'd given in enough already. He had the pink shirt, the sneakers. He'd broken down and bought a smugly cheap plastic watchband like Zack Davidson's. But shorts, that was where he drew the line. Where he came from, only dorks wore shorts. He could picture them. Dorks in shorts waiting for the bus on Astoria Boulevard. Dorks in shorts collecting deposit bottles in shopping carts. Dorks in shorts, with baseball caps, lumbering in overweight packs toward Shea Stadium. Nah, forget about it. These were losers with hairy knees and goofy socks. Even Bert— Joey didn't like to think anything bad about Bert, but face it, Bert looked a little dorky in his shorts. Too much empty space around his shrunken thighs. Too much skin for the amount of meat that was left. But O.K., with old guys it didn't matter as much. Old guys deserved some extra slack, they could look a little dorky without totally giving up their dignity.

"Got time for a quick one?" Bert asked.

"Sure," said Joey, and they crossed Duval Street, heading for the Eclipse Saloon.

The tavern was cool and dim, dim enough so that Don Giovanni's oversized pupils opened wide and gleamed with a morbid mauve glow. The bar was just starting to fill up with that select group of Key Westers who actually worked and therefore had a set time to begin their drinking. Cliff the bartender had daydreamed his way through the sluggish hours and now he greeted them with the distracted gentleness of a man just waking up from a nap. " 'Lo, Bert. The usual? Joey?"

Cliff started in on Bert's whiskey sour while listening for Joey's order. As far as Cliff could remember, he never asked for the same thing twice. And the fact was that while Joey enjoyed the ritual of the cocktail, the shapes of the glasses, the sound of shaken ice, the sheen of frothy liquor cascading out of stainless steel, and yes, the feel of alcohol trickling into his bloodstream, he'd never yet found a drink he liked more than other drinks. Which is to say, he hadn't found the drink that fit his image, because he hadn't found his image. "Gimme a gin and tonic."

"*Salud*," said Bert.

"*Salud*," said Joey.

The old man took a sip of foam, then wiped his loose mouth on his cocktail napkin. "Your brother came to see me this morning."

"Really? What for?"

Bert rested his elbows on the thick padding at the edge of the bar and shrugged. "I'm not really sure. It was a strange kinda visit. Like, formal. Not the kinda thing I expect from young guys anymore. He said he was coming to pay his respects and to bring regards from your father. And that's really all he said."

"Hm," said Joey. He sucked in an ice cube and let it melt on his tongue. "Was Vicki with him?"

This made Bert lean back on his barstool. "Why the fuck would Vicki be with him? Vicki the transvestite?"

"No," said Joey. "Vicki the bimbo. This broad he has with him."

Bert looked relieved. "No, he was alone. Very alone, if ya know what I mean. Like, the feeling I had, he's down here all by himself, there's more goin' on than he can handle, and he can't talk to anybody. He needs some answers but he can't ask the questions. Ya know what I mean?"

"Yeah, Bert, I know whatcha mean. He tell ya about last night?"

"No. What about last night?"

So Joey told him about the lobster dinner and the walk on the beach. Bert threw his head back in a horsey but silent laugh and slapped the edge of the bar.

"You hit 'im? You hit 'im, Joey?"

Joey couldn't help smiling. "Yup. It was a sucker punch, but I caught him a good one."

"Jesus." Bert absently reached down and tickled Don Giovanni behind the ears. "*Guyones*," he said to the chihuahua. "The kid ain't bright, but he's got *guyones.*" And now he leaned close to Joey and dropped his voice. "But hey, you know the rules about hitting a made guy, brother or otherwise. I mean, that shit can get dangerous."

"I know. I know. But it's not like I had it planned. It just happened. A guy's gotta do what he's gotta do, am I right?"

Bert sipped his sour and his expression turned thoughtful. "Yeah, Joey, you're right. Only problem, though, is that one guy does what he's gotta do, and it gets inna face of another guy doin' what *he's* gotta do. Ya hear what I'm sayin'? Like, especially with families. So O.K., Gino makes some stupid crack about your mother. Ya gotta slug 'im. Ya gotta. But look at it from his side. What about *his* mother? Ya can't just forget about her. She's left at home with the pots and pans and the babies and the stringsa garlic hanging from the ceiling. She goes to church while your father goes to hotels. She worries when he don't come home. If she bothers to think about it, she's gotta know there's another woman and the other woman is younger and prettier and has a better shape than her. I mean, it's no picnic for the wife."

Joey had put his hands flat on the bar and was looking down at them as though in shame. He was starting to feel like he hadn't knocked the wind out of Gino but out of the little old Italian mama who was Gino's mother.

"Hey," Bert resumed, "I ain't sayin' this to make you feel bad. It's just that, ya know, it's complicated. Ya can't ask someone not to be a little crazy where his mother is concerned. But Joey, your mother, you should only be proud of her. She was a remarkable person, an artist. Yeah. That's why she went to work at the funeral parlor. You know that?"

Joey didn't know it. In fact, he knew very little about his mother's working life. If your job was beautifying corpses, you didn't come home and describe it in detail to your kid.

"It's true," said Bert. "She tol' me. Before she worked inna funeral home, she useta work inna beauty parlor. It drove her nuts, she said, to work so hard on these ladies, get 'em looking just right, then they'd walk out the door and immediately screw it up. She'd get their nails perfect, they'd put on lipstick that didn't match. She'd get their hair just so, they'd pull a slip on and knock it down. Or the wind would blow.

Or they'd wear an ugly dress. Or crappy jewelry. Ya know what she said to me one time, your mother? She said, 'Bert, it's like painting a picture and then watching the paint wash off inna rain.' Isn't that a sad thing? I remember it all these years. So that's why she switched over to corpses. Do the job once, the job stays done. Family, friends, they get their viewing, then, boom, the lid comes down and it's straight off to God. She was, like, a perfectionist, your mother. I got a lotta respect for that."

Joey squeezed his glass and tried to smile. The bar had filled up, and he felt the nearness of bodies at his back. Cliff had sloughed off his grogginess and was rattling two cocktail shakers like a pair of maracas, taking another order at the same time, and giving off the animal contentment of the fully occupied man. Joey took a momentary vacation in the rattle of the ice and the mounting buzz of saloon noise, gave himself a respite from having either to talk or to listen. When he returned, he was able to put his hand on the old man's shoulder. "Thanks, Bert. It's nice of you to tell me that."

"Sure, kid," said the Shirt. "But now I gotta tell ya somethin' that ain't so nice." He took the orange slice out of his drink, nibbled the flesh from the skin, and, from long habit, glanced over his shoulder to see who might be listening. But in Key West no one ever was.

"After your brother left this morning, I didn't have a good feeling about things. So I made some calls. Coupla days ago there was a sit-down. In Brooklyn. Charlie Ponte, your father, coupla other big guys. Ponte says he's running outta patience about this bullshit with the emeralds. He says it to your father. Your father says whaddya want from me? Ponte flat

out accuses him of being involved. Your old man de-
nies it and gets very hot. Ponte says, 'O.K., if you're
onna level and wanna avoid a lotta headaches, you got
no reason not to make a deal with me.' 'What's the
deal?' your old man asks. 'The deal is this,' says Ponte.
'I find the guys who have my stones, I whack 'em. No
questions asked, and no retaliation.' And your father
agrees."

"He agrees?" Joey repeated. It was all he could
think of to say.

Bert raised a qualifying finger. "The guy I got my
information from, it's, like, secondhand. I don't know
if he agreed 'cause he couldn't go back on what he'd
already said. Or if he's got something up his sleeve.
Or if he really believes his crew is clean. I don't know
any of that. But yeah, he agreed. They kissed on it.
It's settled."

The noise of the bar seemed suddenly to rise up
like a wave, and as if from underneath it Joey heard
himself mumbling dully. "So if it's Gino, he ain't even
protected."

"Nope."

"And if he ends up gettin' clipped, the old man's
gonna feel responsible."

Bert just shrugged.

"Does Gino know about the sit-down?"

"I'm not sure," said Bert the Shirt. "But I sorta
doubt it. I mean, the way he seems to be doing everything by himself, I think he's stayin' outta touch."

"Maybe I oughta tell 'im."

Bert reached down and rubbed Don Giovanni's
chin. The gesture seemed to help him think. "Well, I
don't know. Maybe. But how could you tell 'im without openin' a whole canna worms? Like, how much

else d'ya know? Like how come ya didn't let on before? And besides, Joey, once ya get involved, your
ass is inna same sling his is."

"But Jesus, Bert, if Ponte has a green light to clip
'im—"

The Shirt held a big, wrinkled hand in the younger
man's face. "Joey, lissena me. A lotta what we're talking here, it's guesswork. Ya know, we're assumin'
Gino's involved. Maybe he ain't. Maybe he's a lot
smarter than we give 'im credit for. Maybe everything'll be fine. But if it turns out he's in this kinda
trouble, don't imagine for a second you can help 'im.
You can't. So don't be a schmuck."

"Bert, hey, he's my brother."

"Joey, brothers die too, what can I tell ya? If your
brother Gino has the stones, make your peace with it
and write 'im off. I'm telling you like a father."

21

"I mean, really, Sandra, how does it look? They're here, what, more than a week already, and we haven't had 'em over. It's not right."

"You *want* to have 'em over?" Sandra asked.

They were lying side by side on lounges near the pool. It was Sunday afternoon, the only time of week that all the compound residents tended to be at home. Steve the naked landlord was waist-deep in the water. Peter and Claude were sitting at their little table, having herb tea and scones in their undies. Wendy and Marsha, chaste, fuzzy, and bookish in one-piece bathing suits, traded sections of the *New York Times*. Luke, in deference to the sociable Sunday gathering, had taken his headphones off his ears and looped them around his neck. Lucy the beautiful Fed was quietly swimming laps in a pair of boxer shorts.

"What's *want* gotta do with it?" Joey asked. He tried to keep his voice low, so as not to make the conversation communal property. But on certain subjects he could not keep himself from becoming emphatic. "This is family, Sandra. Want's not the issue here."

"Then what is?" She pushed herself up on her elbows. In keeping with the compound's blithe attitude toward the exposure of skin, she'd bought a two-piece bathing suit. Not a bikini but a squared-off baby-blue top and bottom reminiscent of the *Gidget* movies. The panties went full down to the little arc where the leg joins the buttock; the bra had sturdy-looking straps and built-in cups that left Sandra plenty of room to breathe. Still, a two-piece it was, and Sandra felt pleasantly risqué in it.

"Obligation," Claude piped in. "That's the issue."

Joey, whose back was to the bartenders, rolled his eyes.

"I don't agree," said Peter. He wiped a crumb of scone from the corner of his mouth. "I mean, it *starts* as obligation, sure, but then as you get older, as people accept each other more, you realize you can really enjoy seeing family."

Joey turned over on his lounge. In the languor of afternoon, with the sun beating down through the palm fronds, the act took considerable effort. "Guys, listen, you can have your opinions and all, but with my family, things are, like, a little different."

"Honey," said Claude, "what about with ours?" He widened his eyes as if posing for the cover of *Vogue*. "My father's career air force. You don't think that makes things a little weird?"

Marsha shook the Arts and Leisure section, then peeked out over the top of it and over the top of her reading glasses. "All families are weird," she pronounced. "Don't claim it as a special privilege, Joey."

Was this meant to be comforting, or was he under attack? It often happened that Joey wasn't sure. "Privilege?" he said. "The aggravation I have with my family, you think I think it's a privilege?"

"You'd think so if you didn't have any family," said Steve. He waited his usual beat, then started to smile; the smile was half formed when he seemed to realize it didn't go with what he'd said.

"My family, when I see 'em, it's a treat." This was Luke talking. It was so rare that Luke spoke that everyone looked twice to make sure of where the sound was coming from. "They're way up in Rochester. It's always snowing when I see 'em. I love 'em, my folks, but it's like I can't picture 'em without shivering."

"Shuddering?" said Wendy. She was doing the crossword puzzle, making associations.

"Speak for yourself, babe," Peter said, and everybody chuckled.

"Well, look," said Joey from behind his sunglasses, "all I know is that where I come from, there's like certain things you do, and one of 'em is that ya live somewhere, ya show your family where ya live. Ya have 'em over, ya give 'em food, ya show 'em. It's, like, expected. Am I wrong?"

No one could say he was, and Joey, encouraged by the tacit and unaccustomed approval, lifted himself onto an elbow and went on, getting more emphatic as he went.

"So like, with my brother, my half brother really, I mean, I know up front he isn't gonna be crazy about this place. For him, it isn't fancy enough. I mean, ya know, fancy. Like, sharing the pool, that kinda thing.

And another thing, I don't know exactly how to put it, but my brother, he's like, well, he's a fucking bigot, pardon my French. So like, if he met you guys, he wouldn't like ya. Any of ya. He'd have like, ya know, things to say. Now, only fair, you wouldn't like him either. But like, what I'm saying, whether he likes it or not, I should have him over. Am I wrong?"

No one said he was wrong. No one said he was right. Peter and Claude went back to their scones. Marsha snapped her paper and returned to Arts and Leisure. Lucy the beautiful Fed stopped swimming. She lifted her bare brown shoulders above the edge of the pool and blinked chlorine from her enormous black eyes. "Got so quiet all of a sudden," she said, "I could hear it underwater."

Later, when they were alone in the cottage, Sandra said, "Joey, you wanna have your brother over, of course we'll have him over. But while we're at it, ya know what I wish?" She looked at him hard and tried to push her gaze through his eyeballs and into his brain. "I wish we had some friends."

They were sitting in the Florida room, drinking iced tea out of gigantic glasses that dribbled condensation. Joey could not help sounding a little bit affronted. "We got friends."

"Yeah? Who?"

He threw his head back on the settee and looked upward through the louvered windows. "Bert."

"Come on, Joey. I'm not gonna say anything against Bert. He's a sweet old guy. But really. He's three times our age. He's your friend, not mine. And he's not really the kind of people I have in mind."

"No? what kinda people you have in mind, Sandra?

My kinda people aren't good enough to be our friends all of a sudden?"

Sandra leaned forward in her chair and hugged her knees. She was still wearing her bathing suit and Joey admired her midriff. It was one of the prettiest parts of Sandra, lean enough to show the arc of her ribs, the skin as smooth as if it were powdered. "Don't start in on that, Joey. You know that's not what I'm saying."

"But Sandra, the way you make it sound—"

"Joey, all I'm saying is I think it would be nice to have some regular friends. Some normal, ordinary people. That's nothing for you to get offended about."

"You got friends at the bank, right?"

"Yeah," said Sandra, "the girls at the bank are terrific. But Joey, this is exactly my point. Do I ever see them outsida the bank? No. And why not? 'Cause you don't seem to have any interest. The other girls, they see each other. Claire and Zack, they have dinner with Tina and Mike. Betsy, they invite her to the movies, they try to line her up with guys sometimes. But, ya know, they do things as a couple. Me, I get left out 'cause the guy I'm a couple with couldn't care less."

Joey crossed his arms and listened to the palm fronds scratching against the roof. He was very tempted to flat out agree with Sandra and leave it at that: he *couldn't* care less. But he wasn't quite sure that was so. Was he thrilled at the idea of sitting in the movies and eating popcorn with these citizens? Was he all excited at the thought of hanging around their backyards and shooting the breeze over a bowl of potato chips? No. But at the same time, he had to admit that maybe he shied away from these ordinary, casual friendships for the same reason he'd shied away from the idea of a job: he just didn't know how they

worked. Joey's own kind of friendship—that, he understood. It came from the neighborhood, it was like
an outgrowth of family. It came from crime. Crime
told you right away who your friends were because it
made it so clear who your enemies were. But without
family, without enemies, what reason did you have to
fall in with this guy rather than that guy? Where was
the glue to hold that kind of friendship together? And
what did you do—like call up somebody you hardly
knew and say, hey, you wanna go bowling or something? It was a mystery. But Joey wasn't ready to admit that out loud.

"Ya know, Sandra, it's not exactly like all these terrific people have been rolling out the welcome wagon
for us."

Sandra shook her head and flicked cold water off
her glass. "Joey, I'll tell you the truth, I don't think
you'd notice if the welcome wagon pulled up right in
front of you with bells on. You just don't pay attention. Besides, that isn't how it works. It's give-and-
take. Ya gotta make an effort."

"Sandra, I'll be honest with ya." Joey rubbed his
chin and ran a hand through his moist hair. "I'm just
not sure I see the point. I mean, there's this stuff ya
don't especially wanna do with people ya don't especially wanna know, you're pretty sure you're gonna be
bored stiff, but still, you're supposed to make an extra
effort to have it happen. Why?"

"Why?" said Sandra. "Why? Because, Joey, it's one
of the things ya do to make a life. It's *nice* to have
friends. And it might help you at work—you ever
even think of that?"

He hadn't.

"Besides," Sandra went on, "you don't know for

sure you're gonna be bored. These people do nice things. They go boating. They go snorkeling. They look at fish. Don't laugh, Joey, you might even like it."

Joey squinted backward through the louvers. The palm fronds looked feathery against the sky. He still wasn't convinced, but he was willing to take Sandra's word that maybe making some local friends was worth the trouble. Only not right now. He reached across and put his hand on her knee. "After Gino leaves."

"After Gino leaves, what?"

"After Gino leaves, we'll see, maybe we'll decide to make some friends."

22

That Wednesday evening, Gino, Vicki, and Bert were invited to the compound for dinner. Joey bought stone crab claws because they were the only thing he could find that was more expensive than lobster, and besides, he wanted to give his brother something he could crush. But when he got the claws home, Sandra pointed out a problem.

"Joey, ya need, ya know, those squeezie things to break the shells. The crackers."

"We don't have any?"

"Joey, you know we don't."

"Hm." He put the white paper bag on the counter, sniffed his fingers, and washed his hands with dish soap. "Well, we got a hammer and some pliers."

Sandra put one hand on a hip and held the other out with the goofy grace of a charm school headmistress. "Vicki won't find that very elegant."

"You give a crap how Vicki finds it?"

"I don't if you don't."

"And I don't if Gino doesn't. Which means that no one does. Wine inna fridge?"

At a few minutes after the appointed time of seven-thirty, Bert arrived, resplendent in a big shirt of nubbly lavender linen, monogrammed over the left breast pocket in navy-blue silk. Don Giovanni was twitching in his hand, and as soon as the old man put him down, the dog ran stiffly toward the shrubbery, lifted a leg as scrawny as a chicken wing, and deposited a few drops of urine on a coleus. "Is that rude or what?" said Bert, but he could not quite disguise an expression of wonderment and admiration, as if life with the chihuahua were an unending discovery of the creature's profundity. "Most places he won't do that. I guess he's really getting to feel at home here."

"We're so flattered," said Sandra. She approached Bert with a plate of olives in her hand, and kissed him on the cheek.

"Come on," said Joey, "we'll have a glassa wine."

They sat by the pool and made chitchat amid the faint smell of chlorine and damp towels. Overhead, the leaves shook in the light breeze with a raspy sound like a broom on a sidewalk. After ten minutes or so, Joey got up and fetched more wine; after ten minutes more, the small talk was wearing thin, the way it does when people are afraid they'll use up all their stories before the party actually gets going. By eight o'clock, Bert was sneaking glances at his watch. By ten after, Sandra was wrestling with the impulse to point out that Gino was being extremely inconsiderate, and Joey was secretly depressed at the realization that lateness had long been one of his half brother's many ways of insulting him.

At eight twenty-five the telephone rang.

Joey jogged into the cottage, sat down on the edge of the bed, and took a deep breath to collect himself before he picked up the receiver. "Hello."

"Joey."

"Gino. Where the hell are you?"

"I'm inna hospital."

Joey's sweet and righteous irritation soured instantly to guilt and made the wine go rancid in his belly. "Jesus, Gino, wha' happened? You O.K.?"

"Me?" He sounded surprised at the question. "I'm fine. It's Vicki."

Joey knew it was a lousy thing to feel, but he felt relief. "Wha' happened to Vicki?"

Gino blew some air into the telephone, and Joey could picture him shaking his head and puffing out his heavy purplish lips. "Crazy fuckin' thing, Joey. Just before we're gonna come to your place, she goes out for a walk, ya know, to do some window-shopping. She's standin' there, lookin' inna window, fuckin' moped goes outta control, clips 'er behind the knees, knocks 'er right tru the fuckin' glass."

"Holy shit. How bad is it?"

"Bad enough. Not that bad. I mean, she's kinda cut up, took a lotta stitches. And she got a little hysterical, ya know, worryin' about her looks and all. So they give 'er a sedative, put her out for a while. But listen, kid, I gotta ask a favor."

"Name it," said Joey.

"Well, I rode out here inna cop car," Gino said.

"So you want me to come get you? No problem."

"Nah, I think I oughta be here when she comes around. But I need ya to bring my car out here for me. I got some extra clothes in it so, like, if I spend the night, ya know."

Joey paused. He was touched that Gino would give up the comforts of the Flagler House to be at the bedside of a girl like Vicki. Now and then, not often, his half brother surprised him. "Sure, Gino, sure. I'll work it out. I'll be there right away."

"Thanks, kid," said Gino. "Listen, I'm sorry to fuck up your dinner."

"Hey," said Joey.

"And remember, tell the valet the car's for Dr. Greenbaum."

"Goddamn mopeds," said Bert the Shirt. "I wish they'd ban 'em."

"Treacherous," said Sandra. "And the noise."

"Hey," said Joey, "I don't even know where the hospital is."

"It's out on Stock Island," said the Shirt. "By the dump." He gathered up Don Giovanni and rose. The kind of guy Bert was, he didn't wait to be asked to help. "Come on."

Sandra glanced through the sliding doors into the cottage, where the table had been set for five. It looked pretty festive, with a big mound of crab claws, a large hammer, a small hammer, two pairs of pliers, and an ice pick. "Come back for dinner, Bert," she said. "At least there's nothing to get cold."

23

Bert d'Ambrosia gently placed his dog in the passenger-side bucket of Gino's rented T-Bird, then snapped on his seat belt and fussed with the mirrors and the tilt on the steering wheel. Joey Goldman looked on through the smashed window of his rusting Cadillac and squirmed. Usually he didn't think of Bert as old. But now, when Joey was in a hurry, he noticed the fidgetiness, the excessive caution, the extra thought and care that went into an old man's preparation for almost any action. Now he tested the emergency brake. Now he clicked the car into gear, and double-checked that the shifter was firmly set in drive. Finally he inched forward through the parking lot of the Flagler House.

Joey followed him through the narrow streets of Old Town. Bert came to a dead halt at every stop sign and waited a full five seconds before crawling on again. Joey looked out through the top of his roofless car, squeezed his steering wheel, and tried to talk himself out of his antsiness. There was no real reason to hurry. Vicki was asleep; Gino was probably watching television in a waiting room. Was his brother going to be impressed if he got there thirty seconds sooner? Besides, hadn't Joey had enough of the eager-beaver errand-boy routine, wasn't he a little tired of being the guy who arrives panting and sweaty so maybe he'll get a pat on the cheek for trying so hard? Screw it.

At White Street, Bert turned onto U.S. 1, and Key West instantly stopped being a place and rejoined America. Franchise restaurants and chain motels lined the highway; stacked traffic lights said whose turn it was to pull into the six-plex movies and the supermarket that never closed. License plates from everywhere made it plain that you were nowhere in particular. Bert stayed in the right lane and braked every time someone pulled off the road for a doughnut or a hamburger.

Key West is separated from Stock Island by the Cow Key Channel, such a narrow cut between the Atlantic and the Gulf that Joey barely noticed he'd gone over a bridge to cross it. Land is cheap on Stock Island; it is Secaucus, New Jersey, to Key West's Manhattan. The help lives there, in trailer parks and in half-painted cinder-block shacks that would not look out of place in the deep Caribbean. People get knifed in bars there, crack is sold on street corners, battered women now and then shoot the hearts out of their boyfriends. The parts of Stock Island not given over to squalor are given over to the public good. There is a junior college at which one can study the repair of outboard engines and get credit for scuba diving. There is the dump, Mount Trashmore, whose incal-

culable tons of garbage have been heaped into a
weirdly splendid pyramid, the summit of which is the
highest point in all the Florida Keys. Along the same
road that skirts Mount Trashmore is the hospital complex, generously endowed by Key West's most prom-
inent families, the proud descendants of pirates.

Bert the Shirt turned down this road, and Joey followed. In the dim glow of headlamps and moonlight,
he noticed how the old man held his thin neck perfectly still, as though driving a car at thirty miles an
hour required his most ferocious attention. Maybe it
was this recognition of Bert's frailty that gave Joey a
sudden queasy recollection of his mother dying and
the smell of the hospital she died in. It was a smell
at once overscrubbed and putrid, bracing as ammonia
yet stained with the stench of unspeakable fluids and
vomit. Please, Joey thought, don't let this hospital
smell that way; give it a different brand of floor
cleaner at least. Then he wondered if he'd actually
see Vicki, and then he was assaulted by a lewdly grue-
some image of Vicki's body going through the plate-
glass window, and her wrecked and bloody clothes
being peeled off her . . .

Then, in the shadow of Mount Trashmore and for
no apparent reason, Bert the Shirt jammed on the
brake, went into a tiny skid, and stopped just a few
inches too short for Joey to avoid hitting him. Fenders
collided, made a surprisingly soft sound, like the
crumpling up of foil, and came away not destroyed
but dimpled. The impact was not painful, just rude
and startling, as when an unseen and unwelcome
friend comes up and slaps you on the back. Joey
barely had time to say What the fuck? and to put the
Caddy in reverse, before he realized that he could not

back up because a dark blue Lincoln had pulled
snugly in behind him.

A big guy in a blue suit was standing next to Joey,
and he held a gun that glinted dully in the moonlight.
"Get out and hug the fucking car," he said.

Joey found he couldn't move, and so the big guy
helped him. He yanked open the door of the Caddy,
grabbed Joey by the front of his shirt, and pulled him
up into the street. He turned him with a slap of the
gun muzzle across the ribs, then pushed him down
across the hood of the car and ran his hand along his
sides and up his crotch to check for weapons. Joey
just lay there. He supposed he was terrified, but
mostly he was confused. The car engine was hot under his chest, and he found this strangely comforting.
Lying there, his cheek against the warm gritty steel,
he could see another dark blue Lincoln pulled across
the road in front of Gino's rented T-Bird, and he
could see that Bert the Shirt was also being frisked.
Yes, it was very confusing, and all the while Bert's
chihuahua was baying and howling like a very small
and very shrill coyote.

24

The equipment shed did not smell like garbage, exactly. It smelled worse than that. It smelled like what garbage is on its way to becoming as it rots, as the brown bags soak through with the ooze of putrefying vegetables, as gristle falls off meat bones and turns to a yellowish paste, as bacteria eat through the membranes that have been holding the stink inside of things, letting the foulness into the air like a filthy secret. Added to the humid fumes of decay were the bitter tang of gull shit and the chicken coop reek that came from the riled and oily feathers of the carrion birds. Joey glanced around the room and tried to figure out if anyone else was on the verge of gagging.

They were seven altogether: Joey and Bert; the two toughs from Duval Street and two of their sturdy colleagues, all of whom, like players in a second-rate orchestra, had suits that almost matched, but not quite; and a small neat man who was clearly the guy in charge. He sat on a scratched metal desk in the middle of the shed. Above him was a single yellow bulb tucked into a dented metal cone, and at his back a frame without a door outlined part of the slope of Mount Trashmore. He wore a pale gray suit over a white silk turtleneck, and even in the feeble light his patent leather pumps could be seen to gleam. His feet were very small, and the shoes' tall heels made his arches look impossibly dainty and high, like the arches of a leprechaun. His black hair was swept straight back on the sides and stood in ridges like the gunwales of a boat; on top his hair was thinner and less perfectly trained. His face was unlined but his eyes looked tired; under them, there were sacs the color of raw liver and the texture of poultry skin.

" 'Lo, Bert," he said. He said it almost fondly but distractedly, like someone running into an old acquaintance at the racetrack.

"Charlie," said Bert the Shirt, "where's my dog?"

"Your dog? Your fucking dog?" Charlie Ponte glanced at his crew as if to say, *Didn't I tell ya?* "Jesus Christ, Bert, you really have become a fucking old lady."

"You're right, Charlie. I'm a fucking old lady. But please, do me a favor, have my dog brought in."

Ponte shrugged and nodded to one of his flunkies, who vanished through the doorless frame. "And you're Joey Delgatto."

"Joey Goldman."

Ponte shrugged again. It was his most characteristic gesture, but it didn't mean for him what it meant for most people. For most people, a shrug suggested a kind of helplessness, a lack of knowledge or clarity that stymied them. For Ponte, the shrug meant simply that he didn't know, he didn't care, it made no difference, he would do what he felt like. "I know who you are," he said.

The flunky returned, carrying Don Giovanni at arm's length, as though he feared some exotic Mexican disease. At a nod from Ponte, he passed the quivering dog to Bert, and Joey could see that the old man's fingers were trembling. He hugged the animal to his belly, and the chihuahua flicked out a white-coated tongue and lapped at his wrist. Now that he had his dog back, Bert was bolder. "Charlie, what the fuck is this all about?"

Ponte, the only one sitting, settled himself more comfortably on the metal desk, crossed his ankles, and said, "Bert, I called the meeting, I'll ask the fucking questions. For starters, Joey whatever the fuck your name is, whyn't you tell me what the fuck you're doin' out heah, with your brother's car, going to the dump when the fucking dump ain't even open?"

Joey took a deep breath. He shouldn't have. The smell of rotting garbage became as solid as a piece of half-chewed steak sitting on top of his windpipe. "I wasn't going to the dump," he managed to say. "I was going to the hospital."

"The hospital," said Charlie Ponte. He mugged toward his crew. "O.K., let's try that one. Why were you going to the hospital?"

"Because my brother's there. His girlfriend got knocked through a window."

Ponte folded his arms across his chest and turned a perfect deadpan toward his boys. They grinned on cue, four white Rochesters to his Jack Benny. "Come on, kid, you're Vinnie Delgatto's son, you can do better than that."

"Charlie, listen," said Bert the Shirt. "I was there when Gino called."

"So now the old lady's chimin' in," said Ponte. "Shut up, Bert. And stop insultin' my intelligence, the both of ya. Gino's been in his hotel room all fucking day, that much I know. You think he's glued to the Weather Channel? I think he's hosing that top-heavy bim he's with. Either way, he ain't inna fucking hospital, and as for her, she's probably been gettin' knocked around all right, but not tru any windows. So cut the bullshit before I get annoyed."

Joey gazed blankly at the dim yellow light bulb and tried to ignore the way the stench of garbage was poisoning his saliva. He tried to find a way to believe that his brother hadn't set him up. He couldn't.

Ponte drummed his fingers on the metal desk. The only other sound was the deranged laugh of a gull at the top of the pyramid of trash. "Gino came outside exactly once today," the Boss resumed. "Around six-thirty. Just when it was getting dark. He comes out with a little suitcase. He looks around. He puts the bag inna trunk. He looks around again, and goes back inna hotel. Coupla hours later, you guys show up. Ya take the car, come riding out here in the middle of fucking nowhere. I mean, really, gents, how does it look?"

The neat little man sprang down from the desk and his dainty shoes clicked dryly on the cement floor. He walked to the empty rectangle of the doorframe and motioned for Joey and Bert to follow. They stood close together and looked out at the alp of garbage. It had weird floodlights on it and gleamed an unearthly pinkish orange. At half a dozen random places along the slope, parked bulldozers looked like yellow toys. Most of the mountain was not exposed but had been covered over with a heavy plastic seal. Here and there, the seal was slit by long obscene gashes oozing rot.

"Ain't it amazing," Charlie Ponte said, "the advances that have been made in gahbidge? Ya see the way they cram it in those seams there? It's like stuffing a quilt. Deep, those slits. Fresh gahbidge, it gets squeezed in there and that's the end of it."

Joey did not like the way Charlie Ponte looked at him while saying this. He could handle being called fresh garbage. But he didn't relish the thought of spending eternity with other people's coffee grounds in his ears, the rank oil from other people's tuna fish sliming through his hair. "Hey, Charlie," he croaked, "we ain't involved in this."

Ponte turned toward him, in no particular hurry and without even a hint of malice on his face, and slapped him hard across the cheek. "You don't call me Charlie. Only my old friends call me Charlie, and kid, I got my doubts about whether you and me are gonna know each other that long." He gestured toward the largest of his goons. "Bruno, bring that fucking bag in heah."

In a moment Bruno was back, carrying a small, square case covered in turquoise vinyl. He put it on the desk under the cone of yellow light.

Charlie Ponte approached it slowly and critically. "Lookit this piece a shit," he said, flicking the case's plastic handle. "No class, your brother. It don't even lock. This fucking guy don't care how he treats my stuff."

He undid the two brass clasps and opened the case. It was lined with fake turquoise silk and had a small mirror built into the top. Slowly, with the salacious care of a man nibbling his way around a piece of wedding cake but saving the flower for last, Ponte started removing items from the bag. Lipsticks. Powder. A bottle of Nair. A box of tampons. An atomizer of perfume. He even took time to have a whiff of it. "Chanel number sixty-nine," he pronounced, and his goons obediently chuckled. Then he removed deodorant, tweezers, an eyelash curler. Mascara, eyeshadow, a disposable douche. "I love messin' around a woman's things," he said. " 'Zis givin' anybody a hard-on?"

Joey, had he been able to speak, would have answered an emphatic no. His knees were weak and he was tasting garbage-tainted snot from when Ponte's slap had set his sinuses running. Bert the Shirt had turned gray as his dog but seemed oddly at ease with the idea of being dead. He'd been there, after all; for him it wasn't that big a deal.

Ponte looked happy. Even as he got near the bottom of Vicki's cosmetics kit, he seemed to have no doubt that his emeralds were inside. Finally things were falling right for him. He'd get his stones back, kill Joey and Bert, bulldoze their corpses through a gash in the mountain of garbage, then bump off Gino when the occasion offered. Only when the turquoise case was totally empty did he begin to show some slight concern. But only slight. He took a penknife from his suit pocket, slit the fake silk lining, and pried off the little mirror. Finding nothing underneath, he became just one small notch more agitated. "Bruno," he said, "smash the fucking thing."

In a single motion, Bruno crossed the reeking shed, turned the empty case upside down, and clobbered it with his gun butt. The vinyl tore, and underneath it were thin layers of Styrofoam, cardboard, and Chinese newspaper. The goon dug his fingers between the layers and tore them apart, but there were no hollow places and no emeralds. Then he splintered the plastic handle, but it contained nothing. Having reduced the case to a heap of rubble, he dropped his hands and looked at his boss as if to ask, *What do I rip apart next?*

Charlie Ponte crossed his arms and seemed to be considering. Then, for the first time all evening, he looked angry. The skin moved on his forehead, his black eyes seemed to pull in closer toward his nose, and one side of his upper lip lifted as if he were sucking something out of his teeth. He put his forearm on the desk and brushed it clean with a vicious sweep. Vicki's jars and bottles smashed against the cinderblock wall, and far from masking the vile stink of garbage, her scents blended in to make it still more foul, adding the cloy of carnal cheapness to the general corruption and making the shed smell like a whorehouse on the lowest rung of hell. "Fucking shit," said Charlie Ponte. "Enough cockin' around. Now I want some fucking answers."

He slapped the desk, walked up close to Joey, and spit in his face. The warm saliva trickled down his cheek and Joey was sure he would vomit if he didn't wipe it off before it reached the corner of his mouth. He started to lift his hand. "Touch your face and I'll break your fucking arm," said Ponte. "Now talk. What the fuck you doin' with your brother's car, and where's my fucking emeralds?"

Joey tried to speak but couldn't, and Ponte nodded at Bruno. Bruno grabbed Joey by the hair and pulled back as if to yank off his scalp. Then he put the muzzle of his gun in the soft hollow behind Joey's ear. Joey tried desperately to say something, and when he heard a voice he thought he had succeeded, but in fact it was Bert who was talking.

"Come on, Charlie, the kid don't know shit. He don't know nothin'. He's a loser. He's a nobody."

"Yeah?" said Ponte. "Well then, what about you, old lady? You ain't a nobody. A fucking limp-dick has-been maybe, but not a nobody. You got connections. So what the fuck is what?"

Bert cradled his dog and shook his head. "Charlie, I swear on my mother, we ain't involved. I don't know any more than what we already told ya."

"I think ya do," said Ponte. "And I ain't got all fucking night." He glanced over at his troops. "Tony, take his fucking dog."

"No," said Bert.

"Shut up, old woman. Tony, take his fucking dog, put it onna desk, and get ready to blow its fucking brains out. Enougha this shit."

Almost apologetically, the thug with the scarred lip and bad toupee approached Bert and held his hands out to take the dog. The Shirt held his ground. "I'll fucking kill ya, Charlie. I swear I'll fucking kill ya."

Ponte snorted. "That's good, Bert. Very brave. But you're still an old lady, so shut the fuck up and give 'im the dog."

Bert stood there. Ponte nodded for reinforcements. Another goon came up behind the old man and jerked back hard on his arms.

The tiny dog flew out of his hands and seemed to hover in the dimness, its legs splayed out like the limbs of a defrosting chicken, its paws kicking as though trying to climb the empty air. Tony caught the animal and put it on the desk. Quivering and all alone in the circle of yellow light, the chihuahua looked like it was about to be the victim of some unspeakable experiment in a Nazi operating room. It whined and its whiskers twitched like the antennae of a dying insect. Tony cocked his gun and pointed it between the animal's bulging glassy eyes.

"Charlie, for Christ's sake," said Bert, and he started to cry. Two hot tears, no more, squeezed out of his rheumy eyes and ran down his gray cheeks.

"Look at 'im," said Charlie Ponte, pointing at Bert with his chin. "Look at 'im. Bert, you look like a fucking fool. If I wasn't so pissed off, I'd be embarrassed for you."

"Be embarrassed for yourself, ya stupid dago. Be embarrassed that a fuckin' idiot like Gino Delgatto is less of an idiot than you are."

"Ah," said Ponte, "you trying to insult me? A pathetic old fuck like you, trying to insult me? Well, you know what, Bert, I ain't insulted. At least now you're saying something. Tony, get ready to splatter the dog. Dog brains all over the place, then he goes inna gahbidge. So come on, old lady, insult me some more. Come on."

Tony's trigger hand poked obscenely into the cone of yellow light, and Don Giovanni looked up curiously at the muzzle of the gun. Joey had gone limp in Bruno's murderous embrace. The fumes from Vicki's toiletries were winding through the air in almost visible curls of sickening sweetness.

"Charlie," Bert said, "ain't it fucking obvious? He decoyed you, man. He's makin' you look stupid. You're out here fuckin' around with a nobody, an old man, and a dog, and he's getting away with your emeralds."

Ponte put his hands into the pockets of his pale gray suit jacket, and considered. Then he took them out again and tugged an earlobe. The thug called Tony took the opportunity to turn a queasy glance on his employer. "Boss, I ain't never shot a dog before. A dog, it's, like, different. I kinda like dogs."

"Fucking stinks in here," said Ponte, as if he'd just now noticed.

"Charlie, lissena me," Bert pressed. "I don't give a fuck if you get your stones back or not. But if I was you, I'd be wondering where Gino is right now."

Ponte shuffled his dainty shoes on the cement floor, then absently kicked at a scrap of the cosmetics case. Chinese newspaper came out.

"So really, boss," said Tony, "I gotta shoot the fucking dog, or what? Come on, it's making me, like, uncomfortable."

25

"You O.K.?" asked Bert the Shirt.

Joey straightened up slowly and tried to work a kink out of his neck. His right ear was ringing from the press of the gun muzzle behind it, and his scalp felt as if he were wearing a very tight hat. He found a handkerchief and wiped his face. That was the only part of the episode that would really stay with him and rankle: that he'd been spit on. Pain, people didn't remember, not really; humiliation, they did. Humiliation changed people, for better or for worse. Either it beat them down so that they stayed down, pathetic but weirdly grateful to have their spirits killed and their hopes ended, or it whipped them into a froth of defiance, sent them skittering into realms of resource they didn't know they had. "Me, I'm all right," said Joey. "How 'bout you?"

Bert was sitting on the desk. He'd half walked to it, half collapsed on it when Charlie Ponte, shrugging, had decided it would be beside the point to kill his captives just then, and the thugs had left the shed. Outside, the big tires of their two dark Lincolns had churned loose garbage; then they were gone. Now Bert was holding Don Giovanni in his lap. The dog was licking his hands and doing pirouettes around his thighs, looking for the most comfortable place to settle in. "I ain't been so worked up since the day I died," the old man said. "I almost forgot what it was like to get that tunnel vision, to feel that pounding inna neck. But I think I'm all right now."

"Then let's get the fuck outta heah," said Joey. "One more minute and I swear I'm gonna puke."

They stepped over the remains of Vicki's beauty aids and went through the doorless frame into the orange-pink light of the dump. Overhead, cackling gulls wheeled, sharply silhouetted against the sky. A whiff of salt from the Gulf sliced through the stink of trash. Some twenty yards away on the flank of the garbage mountain, Joey's Caddy and Gino's T-Bird were parked side by side. The dented, rusted Eldorado, with its smashed windshield, corroded roof springs, cracked upholstery, and dimpled fender, looked like it had reached its consummation on the trash heap.

"Come on," said Joey, "I'll drive you home."

"What about Gino's car?"

Joey, insanely glad to have some small outlet for his disgust, approached the Thunderbird and spat on its hood. "Fuck Gino," he said. "And fuck Gino's car. Let Gino tell Hertz how their new T-Bird ended up inna gahbidge."

Then he remembered that it was probably Dr.

Greenbaum who would have to do the explaining. Getting even with Gino had never been easy.

On the ride back to Key West, Joey and Bert craned their necks toward the open top of the Caddy, trying to breathe in the night air rather than their clothes. When Joey turned off U.S. 1 and onto A1A, Bert worked his loose lips for a few seconds before he managed to form some words. Then he said, "Joey, I'm, like, ashamed."

"Wha' for?"

The old man rested his long hands on his bony knees, and his dog propped its chin on the inside of his elbow. "Ya know," he began. "That I broke down, that I cried." But then he changed his mind. "Nah, fuck it, not that I cried. But that I was, like, selfish. Like, I made it sound like I care more about my dog than about your brother."

"Well, you do, Bert. I don't blame you for that."

"Yeah, but it ain't right. I mean, a human being, a relative."

"He ain't your relative," Joey said.

"Even so," said Bert. "Taunting Ponte like that. O.K., our ass was in a sling, it was a gamble. You and me, we ain't inna gahbidge. But I feel like I sold Gino out."

"Bert, hey, let's keep things like in proportion heah. Gino sold us out. Besides, he has any brains, he's half-way back to New York by now."

The retired mobster absently stroked his dog and looked out the window at the Florida Straits. There was just enough doubt in his face so that Joey said, "You think he *isn't* halfway to New York?"

Bert shrugged. He was barely equal to the effort of

lifting his shoulders. "Me, I'm too tired to figure. My nerves are shot and I wanna go to bed."

Joey drove. A line of mild moonlight tracked the Caddy as it lumbered along the water's edge, but Joey was damned if it seemed to him that the moon was picking him out for anything special. "Shit," he muttered. Then he pushed out a furious breath. "Goddammit, Bert. I'm like finally gettin' my legs under me heah, finally gettin' a little bit comfortable—"

He shook his head, slapped the steering wheel, and left it at that.

At the front gate of the Paradiso condominium, Bert the Shirt got slowly out of the car, his dog nestled in the crook of his arm. "Joey," he said, "what's goin' on, it's all fucked up, but it ain't your problem, don't let it poison your life. And another thing—I swear to God I hope I'm wrong, but I'm apologizing in advance. If your brother Gino gets whacked tonight, I'm really, really sorry."

26

But Gino Delgatto did not in fact get whacked that night, nor did he head back to New York.

By the time Charlie Ponte and his boys retraced their steps from Mount Trashmore, Gino, for reasons known only to himself, was back at the Flagler House hotel. He'd let the valet park his second rented car, and had locked himself in his room, where he remained effectively barricaded for the next week. He saw no visitors and took no calls. He ordered room service meals three times a day, and kept his hand on his pistol in the pocket of his bathrobe when they were delivered. With dinner came a bottle of Jack Daniel's. He slept with the gun under his pillow, and kept a small revolver near the toilet.

After three days of nonstop television, paranoia, drunkenness, and Gino's increasingly perfunctory embraces, Vicki announced that she'd had enough and was going back to Queens. She did not believe Gino when he told her that she would surely be kidnapped on the way to the airport, and that, at the very least, she would be strip-searched by a rough-fingered bunch who would diligently probe every orifice where emeralds could possibly be hidden, and would detain her until, with the help of strong laxatives, her lovely young innards had been purged of all precious stones.

"They'll make you shit in a strainer, Vicki. You wanna shit in a strainer with five guys watching?"

"This is some vacation, Gino," she groused. "I shoulda stood in Queens."

He swilled whiskey and didn't answer.

"They wouldn't do that," she resumed after a moment's pondering. "You're just trying to get me to stay."

"No I'm not," said Gino. He was unshaven, jowly, his color was bad, his eyes were bloodshot, and he gave off the yellow smell of bourbon filtered through an overtaxed liver. "I'm fuckin' sick of ya, ya want the truth. Ya wanna go, go."

She got as far as the swath of shade thrown by the hotel awning. Then she saw the dark blue Lincoln. It was parked not more than thirty yards from her taxi. Ponte's crew wasn't even bothering to be stealthy anymore; in Key West, where private life was public and strange behavior was the norm, they didn't need to be. They were just waiting, and they had the whole world to wait in. Gino and Vicki had their hotel room, a cubicle maybe twenty feet square, with a rumpled bed, a television set, a chair that skin stuck to when sweaty, and a tiny balcony that Gino was now afraid to go out on. Vicki went back upstairs, stopping only at the hotel pharmacy to buy some fresh cosmetics and a stack of magazines.

By day five Gino was drinking bourbon with his breakfast grapefruit and talking back to game-show hosts. He could barely bring himself to touch his girl-friend, and she could barely stand to be touched, but there was nothing else to do. Outside, the sun moved across the sky, glared through the windows, turned the walls orange at sunset. Food arrived. Sleep came fitfully.

"Gino, this is really fucking crazy," Vicki said, lying naked and bored after a passionless poke. "I mean, like psychotic. When can we get outta here?"

He lifted himself on an elbow, scratched his hairy belly, and swirled his Jack Daniel's in the smudged glass. He couldn't bring himself to say so, but he didn't think they'd ever get out of there, unless he came up with a plan. And after a week of thinking about it night and day, while drinking, while screwing, while dreaming frenzied and terrifying dreams, he didn't have so much as a shred of an idea.

"So Joey," Sandra asked, "what's really going on with Gino?"

They were in bed at the compound. A light breeze puffed out the curtains and a waning moon threw just enough light so that dim stripes were cast across the quilt by the slatted blinds.

"You really wanna know?"

A week before, she hadn't wanted to, or maybe it had just seemed to her that Joey didn't want to tell her. Couples must conspire to hide things from one another; it's too difficult for either party to do alone. Joey had come home clearly shaken and reeking of garbage. Sandra said she'd been worried, had called the hospital, didn't know Vicki's last name, asked

about a young woman who'd been knocked through
a window by a moped; the emergency room had handled no such case, and Sandra had felt like a fool.
Joey said that Gino had lied, it was one of Gino's crazy
schemes. And that was all he said. Sandra, as happened not infrequently, was faced with the choice of
pressing or changing the subject. But where was the
line between pressing and nagging? So she asked him
if he wanted some crab claws. He wasn't hungry. He'd
put his clothes in the trash, taken a long shower, and
sat up drinking the wine meant for dinner while Sandra had gone to sleep.

"You really wanna know?" Joey asked again now. It
seemed to Sandra that this time there was more hope
than hesitation in his voice.

"Is it bad?"

"It's really bad."

"Are you involved, Joey?"

"Not by choice—hell no."

"Then tell me."

So he did. He propped himself up on pillows and
absently smoothed the creases in the quilt as he
talked. The breeze coming through the window was
cool and made him grateful for the warmth of Sandra's body next to him. She gave off a nice smell of
talcum powder and hand cream.

"So now he's holed up in his room," Joey concluded, "and Ponte is just waiting for a chance to kill
'im. Where the emeralds are, if he's got 'em, I haven't
got a clue. What he was up to while me and Bert
were kidnapped, why he didn't just blow town, I got
no waya knowin'. I've tried calling him like a dozen
times already. The switchboard just takes messages.
I've gone past the hotel, just to scope it out. The Lin-

colns are always there. Ponte's goons wave at me and laugh, like it's a big goddamn joke. I don't go inna hotel, of course. I mean, that crazy I'm not."

"Joey," Sandra said, "there's nothing you can do."

But he went on as if he hadn't heard. "Ya know what gets me, Sandra? What gets me is that, for all these years, Gino passed for smart. I mean, I believed it. Sure, I bitched, I argued, but basically I bought it. Gino, the guy with big ideas. Gino, the guy who gets things done. Is that pathetic or what? I mean, look at this guy. What the hell was on his mind? And selfish. Jesus Christ Almighty, is he selfish. I mean, he coulda got me killed. He coulda got Bert killed. And what if you came along, Sandra? I mean, you coulda come for the ride." Joey slapped at the quilt and exhaled ferociously, as if trying to dig some family germ out of the very bottom of his lungs. "The fucking guy thinks of no one but himself."

Sandra snuggled closer to him and put a hand on his shoulder. "Joey, those are all the reasons why you have to wash your hands of this."

He pulled away, not in anger but only because her touch was too much a threat to his resolve. "No, Sandra, those are all the reasons I can't wash my handsa this. I walk away, and what happens? Gino gets killed. So now he's dead, but he's still the guy who had the big ideas, the guy who was doing things. And me, what am I? I'm still little Joey, the nobody, the guy who don't know nothin', can't do nothin', and sits by like a jerk, like a worm, while his brother gets whacked."

"But Joey, you didn't make the problem."

"Sandra, that's true, and it means nothing. Listen, I been thinkin' about this all week. If Gino gets killed, it's like the clock stops, nothing can change no more. To my old man he's still the golden boy. In his own mind he's still the big shot."

"But Joey, if he's dead—"

"The only way I can ever get rid of the fucking guy, the only way I can really be done with him, is to save his life. You see what I'm saying, Sandra? I wanna be able to say to him, 'Gino, you fucked up, I saved your ass. You were dead, I brought you back to life. So here, schmuck, here's your life. Take it and get outta my face.' Sandra, ya can't say that to a dead man, can ya?"

Part III

27

"Joey," said Zack Davidson, "we gotta talk."

It was nine o'clock on a bright blue morning on Duval Street, and Joey Goldman was not surprised. In fact, the only thing he found surprising about his job these days was that he still had one. If he'd been running Parrot Beach, he'd have fired himself some weeks before.

He followed Zack up the shady pathway to the office. *Study up*, his colleague had told him at their first meeting. Learn to read people, to recognize the subtle signs by which they identify their peers, their social equals. Learn how to look in order to get the ones who could help you on your side. This was a fundamental requirement of salesmanship, by which Zack Davidson meant survival. So now, as Zack strolled ahead of him, Joey studied his smugly casual khaki shorts and had to acknowledge that in picking out the ones he himself was wearing, he'd overlooked certain details, missed certain nuances. Zack's shorts were of a dull twill with no sheen whatsoever; Joey's were polished in a manner that suggested too much processing. Zack's were not rumpled, exactly, but just mussed enough to create the impression that they had never seen the inside of a closet and spent their off-hours on the back of a bedroom chair; Joey's had a crisp crease that made them look less like *shorts*, pure and simple, and more like an amputated pair of chinos. So O.K., Joey admitted, he didn't yet have the act down perfectly, but he was getting there, he was learning. He wondered how much of it he'd remember, or what good it could possibly do him, now that he was about to get canned.

Inside, the two men skirted the scale model of the condo complex. Joey glanced at it with a pained fondness, as if it were the shrunken but living embodiment of a memory. The sweet little buildings with their tiny pastel shutters; the plastic windblown palms and the swimming pool whose blue Saran Wrap shimmered like real water; the happy owners, littler than Barbies and Kens, laid out on their lounges or standing at the painted edge of the ocean: these things, for Joey, had come to seem the perfect picture of the easy life of Florida, the life whose private, uneventful, and unspectacular appeal was daily getting through to him, and which was being royally screwed up for him by Gino and the long reach of the old neighborhood. He was almost beyond feeling angry about it. Almost. At least he was not surprised. Joey tries to do something on his own; Gino undoes it, basically by declining to notice that it might by some chance matter, and by dwarfing it with something so much bigger, flashier, and more urgent. To a kid brother, a bastard no less, this was not news.

"Siddown," said Zack, motioning Joey into a slatted wooden chair next to his desk. Zack himself plopped down into his rolling, swiveling seat, rocked once so that the tilting back gave a homey squeak, then came forward and put his chin on his interlaced fingers. "Joey," he began, "some jobs, ya know, you do with your brain, right? Other jobs you do with your hands, or your back, or just by getting yourself into a certain kind of mood. Those jobs call for *parts* of you. You see what I'm saying, Joey?"

Joey crossed his knees and hugged the top one. He didn't know exactly how to answer. Getting fired, he imagined, had its protocols and customs just like other parts of having a job, and Joey had never been fired before.

"What I'm saying," Zack resumed, "is that this is a job you do with your whole person, every part of yourself. Sizing people up, that's brainwork, right? But standing out there on the hot sidewalk for eight hours a day, that's hard physical labor, no shit. As to how you actually approach people, that has a lot to do with the mood you're in, right? Whether you use humor, push the freebies, go for sympathy, whatever. And how the people respond to you, well, that's beyond mood, that's a mystery, like religious almost. Are you in the zone? In a state of grace? At one? Ya know, there's all different ways of describing that frame of mind where everything just falls right and people can't resist you. You know what I'm saying?"

Joey thought he did, but he found himself increasingly impatient with Zack's analyses of effectiveness in sales and life. When Joey still had his job, he'd thirsted after Zack's advice, thought about it long and hard. But now it no longer seemed worth the effort. "You're saying I've been all fucked up lately, and you're right."

Zack waved the comment away. It was far too negative for him. "No, Joey, no. That's not what I'm saying." He flipped open a manila folder and removed a piece of paper. On it was a week-by-week graph of Joey's performance on the job. The graph went up, up, up, hit a plateau, then came down, down, down, tracing out a pattern not unlike the pyramidal slope of Mount Trashmore.

"Joey, look at this. The first week you were here, you made a hundred twenty dollars. That's not much money for forty hours of busting your butt and having people turn you down all day, but hey, you hung in, you stayed with it. Second week, you doubled. Third week, you jumped to four eighty. Fourth week, four eighty again. Now that's pretty damn good, Joey. For a guy still learning the ropes, that's excellent. But what happens after that? Three twenty. Two eighty. Two hundred even. Joey, these aren't just numbers. These are like a map of what's going on with you. You wanna talk to me, Joey?"

Joey looked out the window, glanced at the Parrot Beach model under its perfect sky of Plexiglas. The graph depressed him. He was no stranger to lack of success, but this was different, this was active failure, failure clearly drawn and pushed in his face, and Joey didn't like it at all. Nor did he enjoy the bitterness that came with losing something he was just barely ready to admit he cared about losing. "Zack, if you're gonna fire me, can't we just please get it over with."

Zack Davidson sat back and ran a hand through his sandy hair; it fell back exactly where it had been. "Who said anything about firing you?"

Joey tried to say something but all that came out was a kind of blubbing sound, a sound from underwater.

The other man spread his arms out wide and hugged the edges of his desk. "Joey, this isn't about firing you. This is about getting you back on the street so you can make some fucking money. Listen to me, Joey. There's some things you oughta know, and apparently you don't. You're very well thought of here. People like you. They like how hard you try, that you don't make excuses. They like that you don't bitch and moan, that you're not a prima donna. They like it that the people you send, they're almost always in a good mood. They don't feel like they've been jerked around. They feel like they've been dealing with a human being. You've got this warmth, Joey, this... I don't know what to call it. Life, call it life. People deal with you, they feel like they're dealing with someone with some blood in his veins and some thoughts in his head, some curiosity. That works for you. So let it work."

To someone unaccustomed to receiving compliments, Zack's words were as intoxicating and unsettling as empty-stomach cocktails. Joey squirmed, as he generally did when wrestling with the question of thankfulness. He knew he should be grateful to Zack for saying what he'd said, but gratitude was a risky matter. As soon as you acknowledged that someone had done something for you, you opened up the chance that you'd look to them again and they could let you down. If they weren't family, if they weren't neighborhood, what assurance did you have? "Zack," he admitted, "I don't know what to say."

"Don't say anything. But Joey, listen, I don't wanna pry, but it's real obvious that some strange shit is going on. Guys like outta the movies climb out of a Lincoln and rough you up on the sidewalk. Your brother comes to town and your commissions take a nosedive. Now this woman I know, she works at Flagler House, tells me there's some weird guy who hasn't been out of his room all week, there's *two* Lincolns camped in front of the hotel, and for some strange reason the cops won't go near them. Joey, is it me, or does all of this look a little strange?"

Joey fiddled with a sneaker lace to stall for time. Why was everyone always asking him to spill his guts? Then again, what a giddy pleasure it might be if he could spill them. He'd laid it all out for Sandra, a woman. Why not tell it all to Zack, this curious outsider who for some odd reason seemed to want to be his friend? Why not tell everyone and have it the hell over with? Unloading his secrets—what a notion. It was dizzying. It was impossible. "Yeah, Zack," he said, "it looks strange. In fact, it is strange. But it's got nothin' to do with the job."

Joey volunteered nothing further, and Zack put up his hands in surrender. "O.K., Joey, if ya can't talk about it, ya can't talk about it. But listen, if there's some way I can help, I'm here."

Joey hesitated. He hesitated for so long that Zack began to fidget, putting paper clips on things, squaring the edges of stacked stationery. Hot shafts of sun streamed in the office window and glinted off the Plexiglas model. Joey was oblivious. He was wading through thoughts as through limestone muck, and while his preoccupations were the same as they had been for weeks, he was suddenly taking a very different course through the morass. He had two lives, Joey did, and until this moment he'd been trying his damnedest to keep them separate, to preserve the new from contamination by the old. Now he realized that the collision had already taken place—in fact, there had never been a time when the two lives weren't one. So he found a new idea: If the new life couldn't be quarantined from the old, maybe the old life could be solved, settled, and laid to rest by the resources of the new. When Joey finally spoke, his words seemed to Zack a bizarre departure from what they had been talking about. To Joey, however, the question was a perfectly logical and even inevitable conclusion to a rigorous line of reasoning.

"Hey Zack," he said, "you got a boat?"

28

Along about the first of April, the weather changes in Key West. The daytime temperature jumps one day from eighty-two to eighty-five, and there it stays for six weeks or so, until a similar increment signals the setting in of summer. The evenings suddenly no longer call for sweaters; the light cotton quilts are kicked down to the feet of beds, and even top sheets are likely to be bunched around waists but pulled no higher. The east wind, which had been rock-steady at twelve to fourteen knots all winter, becomes fitful, moves toward the south, loads up with salt, and blows moist enough to make cars wet. These changes, by the standards of the temperate zone, are so subtle as to seem insignificant. In the subtropics, however, people grow spoiled; the range of perfect comfort shrinks for them as it does, say, for the very rich, whose standards of acceptable luxury become so crazily refined that they can hardly ever be satisfied. So, while eighty-two degrees with a twelve-knot wind seems sublime, eighty-five with an eight-knot wind seems sultry, and people alter their routines accordingly.

At the compound, Peter and Claude put aside their silk sarongs and seldom wore anything more confining than the lightest of seersucker robes. Wendy and Marsha decided that the hot tub was too hot, and were more likely to stand chest-deep in the pool while discussing modern sculpture and rubbing the stress out of each other's shoulders. Luke and Lucy spent a lot of time in their outdoor shower and never quite looked dry. And Steve the naked landlord, to fend off dehydration, carried four beers rather than three to the pool with him at ten A.M.

"Whatcha reading, Steve?" Joey asked him as he went to hand over Sandra's check for the April rent.

Steve turned the damp paperback over and looked at the green flying saucer on the cover. "Aliens," he said. "Germ warfare from space." Then he smiled.

As for Sandra, she had finally broken down and done some shopping, finally put aside her fuzzy cardigans and long-sleeved business blouses with the built-in shoulders that made even Joey forget how radically compact she was. Now, for work, she wore pale blue cotton knits that nicely set off her version of a tan. Her skin, it seemed, had not changed color, but the tiny hairs on her arms had been bleached an almost tinsel silver, which offered much the same effect. Also, Sandra had greeted the warmer weather by going on a salad binge, a veritable orgy of roughage. Joey would open the refrigerator door and be confronted by a jungle of romaine, an impenetrable forest of spinach, watercress, endive. "Sandra," he'd say, "how come there ain't no food in heah?" And Sandra would smile. The heat made her softer-spoken but no less immovable. "There's a steak in the back somewhere. Probably behind the cottage cheese."

Certain other routines were also changing around Key West, although for different reasons. Bert the Shirt d'Ambrosia, for example, no longer took Don Giovanni to the beach across from the Paradiso condominium to watch the sun go down, but had moved a third of a mile or so down the shoreline, closer to the Flagler House. He brought with him on these excursions his wife's old opera glasses, ladylike things encased in mother-of-pearl and trimmed in silver, and he looked quite eccentric if not perverted, fondling the chihuahua as he peeked through the oleanders and buttonwoods that fringed the beach. Joey had asked him to study up on the habits of Charlie Ponte's thugs, and Bert, while he hemmed and hawed at getting involved in any way, was still pissed off enough at Charlie Ponte to do it. As far as the old man could tell, two guys in one Lincoln were always stationed at the near end of the self-parking area, with a clear view of the hotel entrance. At around seven o'clock this watch was relieved by the two soldiers in the other car. The second car would take over the same parking space as the first one drove away. It didn't appear that all four thugs were ever employed at once. And it didn't seem that Charlie Ponte had thought to place a lookout on the ocean side.

"So Joey," said Zack Davidson, "you ever run a boat before?"

Joey looked down at the water, wiggled the ear-pieces of his shades, and tried to choke back his long-standing impulse to bullshit, to make it sound like he'd done more than he had and knew more than he knew. "Well, uh," he began, "this one time, up at Montauk, well, uh. No."

It was after work, around five-thirty, and they were at City Marina, a decidedly no-frills establishment for people with yacht club tastes and a rubber ducky budget. A very democratic place, City Marina was. Very Key West. Clunky houseboats with vinyl siding and TV antennas lay in berths next to dainty sloops whose polished hulls reflected every glint in the water, and also next to the staunch craft of working fishermen, where razor-beaked gulls scraped slime off moldy planking. The marina was nestled in a well-protected cove known as Garrison Bight, whose location underscored Key West's status as an intersection at the end of the world. On its south end, the Bight lapped quietly against the embankment of Highway 1. To the west, narrow channels wound through mangrove flats toward the open Gulf of Mexico; to the north and east, the long arced chain of the Keys stretched away under its freight of bridges and pylons.

"No." Zack repeated the single syllable, briefly puffed his cheeks out like a trumpeter, and ran a hand through his unvarying hair. He looked down at his little boat, which had never before appeared so frail. It was an eighteen-foot fiberglass skiff with a dark blue Bimini top. A perfect flats boat, it did less well in the ocean swells, where it bounced from wave to wave like a skipping stone and skidded down following seas like a riderless surfboard. The skiff had a sixty-horsepower outboard and an eight-horse auxiliary that was propped next to it on the transom, seeming to nestle up like a duckling to its mother.

"What's the little motor for?" Joey asked.

"Emergencies," said Zack. His mouth twisted up as if the word tasted bad. "But hey, first things first. You know how to tie up?"

Joey gave a nonchalant shrug. He told himself that, in his pink shirt and khaki shorts, he at least looked like he belonged at a marina. "Sure," he said. "I mean, I guess so. Well, not really."

Zack showed Joey how to make a clove hitch around a post, while pelicans banked by and cormorants dried their spread wings on top of pilings. On board, he showed him how to tilt the engine down, hook up the extra gas tank, and close the choke. "You know what the buoys mean, right, the green and the red?"

"Yeah, sure," said Joey. "It's, like, the red ones are stop and the green ones are go."

Zack leaned back against the gunwale and played with an ear. His boat was insured, but only for liability, not for being totally trashed by a guy who had no idea what he was doing.

"Joey, you sure there's no way I can go with you?"

The novice looked down at the fiberglass floor of the cockpit, toyed with his sunglasses, and shook his head. "Zack, listen, if you're having second thoughts, I understand. I really do. But like I said, this is something I hafta do alone. Believe me, it's not fair to involve anybody else."

Zack hesitated, though there was really nothing to hesitate about. He'd offered Joey the use of the boat, no strings attached, no explanations demanded, and it would be too undignified to back out now. "Well, let's take 'er out for a test drive, at least. Ya know, once you're away from the dock, it's mostly just like driving a car."

"Yeah," said Joey, "that's what I figured, like driving a car. That I can do."

"And swim," said Zack. "You can swim, right?"

Joey choked back his impulse to bullshit, but not quite soon enough. "Sure," he said. "I can swim. Sort of. Like, a little. Not really. Nuh-uh."

29

Zack told Joey many things, but he failed to get across how different water looks at night. Mainly, it disappears.

Joey realized this while edging the skiff out of Garrison Bight, just after ten P.M. on an evening without a moon. The shadings and dapplings had vanished from the surface, and all that remained was a featureless blackness shot through here and there with green flashes of phosphorescence. Was Joey even *seeing* those green flashes? He couldn't be sure, because they looked so much like what happened inside your head when you pressed on your eyeballs. Another thing Joey couldn't be sure of was where the coastline was. In daylight it had been so clear; now the boundary where land met water seemed unhealthily approximate. That flasher over there—was it a buoy or a traffic light? That dark bulk getting closer to him—was it another boat or a stray shred of North America?

Joey Goldman squinted, leaned so far forward that his head was almost caught between the top of the windshield and the front edge of the Bimini, and squeezed the steering wheel in his sweaty palms. *Go under the bridge and hang a left,* Zack had told him. It sounded so easy, as easy as driving the Caddy to the grocery store for a carton of milk. But Joey hadn't figured on the eddies that formed near the bridge, the swirling rushes that rendered the wheel almost as useless as if it had come off in his hands, and that spat him broadside, as though in distaste, between the stanchions.

Stay between the red and green markers, Zack had instructed, but Joey hadn't realized that at night, with only starlight on them, red and green channel markers look very much alike. Joey had expected two ranks of beacons, pointing the way as clearly as the reflectors on the Brooklyn-Queens Expressway. What he found was a seemingly random array of unlit pilings hammered into muck, winding through grass flats and scattered coral heads. He throttled back, rubbed his eyes, and took a thin comfort from the sound of his engine. The motor noise sounded a lot like a car; it had become the only thing still linking him to the world of the familiar.

He picked his way to the mouth of the harbor, where the vast Atlantic collides with the huge gyre of the Gulf, and the clapping currents raise ripples whose foamy tops stand in the air like cake frosting. Joey didn't understand why the boat was bouncing so much all of a sudden, why every instant his knees had to find a different angle to stand at. He didn't grasp why he was going more sidewise than forward. He fed more gas to plow through the rip; warm spray hit him in the eye and a big splash soaked his sneaker.

Then he was past the harbor entrance and out into the Florida Straits.

Here the water was empty and the shoreline black with the drooping shapes of the Australian pines. Small waves were pushed toward Joey by the breeze, and the boat did belly flops over them, the hull taking off like a low-launched rocket, then smacking back down with a spanking sound, the engine whining as the prop lifted into the foam, then stabbed back into the solider water below.

For some minutes Joey sliced ahead through the sameness of the waves, and from moment to moment a change was coming over him. There is a wide-awake drunkenness that comes from doing something new and finding that it is not impossible. In the grip of that brave giddiness, nothing seems impossible, and people look for ways to prove this joyful lunacy to themselves. They take dares, jump from rooftop to rooftop, surpass themselves and usually survive but sometimes die excited. Joey suddenly remembered a conversation he'd had up north, sitting over an espresso with his buddy Sal. *Joey, you're gonna be like all alone down there,* Sal had warned. *Maybe I like that idea,* Joey had said, with swagger, but in his own mind the accent was on the maybe. But here he was, in a boat, in the ocean, at night, without even experience for company, about as alone as a person can be, and whaddya know, he did like it. He liked it the way some people like icy showers or large amounts of hot sauce. It set him up. It got him ready. Ready for what? He couldn't have said and it didn't matter. Just ready. Ready was enough.

◇ ◇ ◇

A few minutes before eleven o'clock, Joey climbed onto the private dock of the Flagler House with two lines in his hand, and tied four different attempts at knots in each of them. Then he took a moment to get his land legs back and look at the hotel. The building was long, squat, and heavy, a checkerboard of lights turned on and lights turned off. A cool blue glow hovered over the swimming pool, and on the palm-strewn beach torches were still burning, the remnants of a Caribbean Night cookout or some such entertainment. Joey did not yet have a plan of approach. Something inside him knew that in a place where most people arrive by car, rented cars no less, the man who arrives by boat is marked as special and should stroll in like he owns the joint. But he could not be sure that Charlie Ponte had not put a lookout in the lobby; or that his thugs outside didn't have a sight line to the elevators, or that Ponte hadn't bribed someone on the staff to do his watching for him. Getting caught consorting with Gino—with Dr. Greenbaum—would no doubt win him another and final trip to Mount Trashmore.

So Joey slowly and vigilantly walked the length of the pier. On the beach, busboys were still clearing chafing dishes from long tables whose cloths were splattered with barbecue grease and melted sherbet. Their soiled uniforms tinged orange by torchlight, they loaded the glinting pans onto trolleys and wheeled them away. Joey watched where they went: along a narrow concrete path that lost itself in a clutch of palms, then reappeared at the back end of the poolside bar and curved off again toward what seemed to be a descending ramp near the far end of the building.

Discreetly, trying to look like any other tourist who hoped not to appear lost, bored, or caged, Joey meandered toward the ramp. Skirting the pool, he heard vapid hotel lounge music filtering through beaded curtains; under the thatched roof of the poolside bar, a blender, sounding very much like a tiny, frenzied outboard, was frothing up some dubious milk shake of a cocktail for what seemed to be the only couple left outside. The bartender gave Joey a friendly nod, an offer of conviviality in sympathy for his being all alone. Joey smiled the shy smile of a passerby who knows that he will be forgotten the moment he has passed.

At the head of the ramp, there was a pair of ocher-painted limestone posts, and on the right-hand post was a sign that said Staff Only. Joey paused. His pants legs were damp from the ocean spray; his left sneaker was wet. His thick black hair had been blown tautly back by the wind and was coarsened by the airborne salt. His hands still tingled from the vibration of the boat's wheel, and he still didn't know what he'd say to his brother.

He started down the incline.

At the base of it was a set of swinging doors, their brushed-steel surface marred from the push of trolleys and the banging of trays. Joey went through and found himself in a long narrow hallway lit by bare bulbs in yellow wire baskets. On the left, through a broad open doorway, was the kitchen; above the din of pans and dishes clattering, the singsong of Spanish banter rang between the cinder-block walls. Joey slipped past, walking quick and silent to where the corridor turned right and led to a bank of elevators. Unfortunately, a room service waiter was already there. He was thin and blond, had a cart in front of him with a champagne bucket on it, and was dressed, absurdly, in a tuxedo. Joey caught him picking his nose, which seemed to make the waiter feel defensive.

"May I help you?" he asked accusingly.

Joey opened his mouth well before an idea had sparked. But he was cruising on that insane and blessed sense of readiness, and he said the first thing that came into his mind. "Mafia."

"Excuse me?" said the waiter. His pale eyebrows lifted, he swallowed so that his bow tie did a little dance, and he seemed by reflex to be wiping his thumb on the satin stripe of his pants leg.

"The linens, the labor situation," Joey said. "It's like, ya know, a spot check. They treatin' ya right, or what?"

"Oh, fine," said the waiter. "Fine." He looked down at the napkins on his cart. He hoped he hadn't grabbed a frayed one.

The elevator arrived. The employee stood aside for Joey to enter first, though it was unclear whether he did this out of protocol or to avoid showing his back. He rolled his cart out, very quickly, at the second floor, and Joey continued to the fourth, the top. Gino had a list for hotel rooms, as he had for everything. Top floor, water side—that was the best, and so that, of course, was what Gino had bragged he had. Only the best for Joey's older brother. The best of everything, so he could remind himself that he was doing good.

30

"Who is it?" said Gino Delgatto, in the rough yet somehow mousy voice of a man who has his door double-locked, with the night chain on, and his sweaty hand wrapped around the warm butt of a gun he clutches by habit but in whose power to protect him he has stopped believing.

"It's me. It's Joey."

There was a long pause. Gino had now been holed up in his room for almost two full weeks, and his life had become so radically uneventful, his mind and body so muddily torpid, that the channels in his brain had silted over. Any piece of information now struck him as dauntingly new; any decision, such as when and for whom to open his door, required all the concentration he could possibly muster.

"Whaddya want?" he said at last.

"I wanna save your sorry ass. Lemme in."

Again there was a pause.

"You alone?"

"Totally."

There was a sound like surrender in the dry slide of the dead bolt, the cheerless tinkle of the night chain. Gino opened the door just wide enough for a man to slip through, and stood there framed for a moment in the slice of yellow light. He was wearing a hotel bathrobe and he looked like hell. He'd put on ten pounds during his days of doing nothing but eating and drinking, and the increment was enough to push his barely handsome features over the border into brutishness. His fattened cheeks rose into little pads that accentuated the piggishness of his eyes. His nose seemed somehow to have softened and broadened, and was spreading across his face like melting clay. Deep lines at the edges of his mouth gave his jaw the slightly spooky, hinged look of a puppet's, and his skin had the stretched oiliness of someone who is thoroughly constipated. But he was still strong. He grabbed Joey by the arm and yanked him into the room so that the two men were standing chest to chest. Was Gino giving his half brother a hug, or just trying to get the door shut and double-locked as fast as possible?

"Anyone see you?" he asked. Their faces were close and Joey smelled the bourbon.

"No one that matters."

"How'd ya manage?"

"I came by boat."

Gino stepped back and took a moment to process this new fact. He seemed to see in it an opportunity to get on top of the situation by his time-honored tactic of patronizing Joey. But for this he needed an ally, so he shot a facetious glance at Vicki. She was lying in bed, the sheet pulled up so that only the top acre of her chest was exposed. She'd been leafing through a fashion magazine, which she now placed facedown on top of her boobs; the bent spine made a kind of tent for her cleavage. Gino's glance was meant to say, *Ain't he clever—for a nobody?* and while he was flashing that look at Vicki, he said to Joey, "Fuck you know about driving a boat?"

"Enough to get heah. It needed doing and I did it, didn't I, Gino?"

Gino sat slowly on the edge of the bed, as if something in Joey's tone had grabbed him by the shoulders and pushed him down. Absently, he noticed that his gun was still in his hand. He slid it along the sheet and tucked it under a pillow. "Drink, Joey?" He motioned toward a low table where the dirty dinner dishes were scattered and a two-thirds empty bottle of Jack Daniel's was standing like a monument. On the dresser next to the table, the television flashed the eleven o'clock news with the sound turned off.

Joey shook his head, settled into a vinyl chair, and took a moment to rearrange his damp trouser leg so the wet part wouldn't lie against his thigh. "You're a selfish prick, you know that, Gino?"

Gino absorbed the comment like an exhausted heavyweight eating one more jab. "You come here just to tell me that?"

"I come here to get you outta my town and outta my life. But first, we talk. You coulda got me killed the other week. You even give a shit about that?"

Gino wrapped his meaty hands around the edge of the mattress and looked down between his knees. "I'm sorry, kid. I was in a bind."

"In a bind?" Joey pulled himself forward by the

arms of his chair. "In a bind? You fucking jerk. You're in a bind, so the whole resta the world can go to hell? What if Bert dropped dead? What if Sandra was with me?"

Gino took a deep breath that seemed to cost him a lot of effort. He couldn't help looking back over his shoulder at Vicki. Girlfriends were not supposed to hear this kind of thing. It messed with their respect. "Listen, kid, I'm sorry. I fucked up. 'Zat what you wanna hear me say?"

"Yeah, Gino, that's exactly what I wanna hear you say. And now that you've said it, I want some explanations. Like why the fuck are you still here? You almost get me killed so you can run away, then you don't even manage to run away."

"Joey, Joey," said Gino, in a tone the younger brother knew well. It was the tone he used when he wanted to make it clear that he, Gino, was the planner, the thinker, and Joey, like an army grunt, had neither reason nor right to ask the why of things. "There's more to it than you know about."

"Wanna bet?" Joey snapped. "It's about three million dollars in Colombian emeralds that disappeared from Coconut Grove."

A wave of slow surprise moved across Gino's swollen face. It pulled at his mouth and made him mumble. "Ponte tell ya that? Bert tell ya?"

"Never mind. But now I want your side of it. From the top."

Gino crossed his legs, uncrossed them, slapped his knee, and grunted. "Sure you don't want a drink?"

"You have one, Gino. You need it. I don't."

The older brother got up and lumbered toward the bourbon bottle. Joey looked at Vicki, lying just at the fringe of a yellow pool of lamplight. In some ways, oddly, she looked better than she had before. She'd washed the tease out of her hair, and while it was now lank, thin, and coarse as straw, at least it looked like part of her. Without the foot-high helmet on her head, her features looked less pinched, and without their labored paint job, her eyes even had a kind of softness. Her mouth seemed calm, though Joey could not tell if she had broken through to some extreme form of patience or had become quietly deranged.

Gino returned with three fingers of Jack Daniel's in a smudged glass and sat down heavily on the bed. Either he sighed or some air came out of the mattress. "Awright, Joey," he began. "Awright. Now the first thing ya gotta know is that nunna this was my idea." He swigged half his drink. "But O.K. There were these two guys, Vinnie Fish and Frankie Bread. They were, like, a little bit attached to my crew, a little bit attached to Ponte, but it was, ya know, a vague kinda thing, nothing really solid. Ya follow?"

"Yeah, Gino. I follow."

"Well," Gino continued, "these guys knew about the stones, they knew about the drop. So they come to me, they wanna be partners, and Joey, I swear to God, I tell 'em it is a very fucked-up idea. I tell 'em no way. But these guys, Vinnie and Frank, they're like very persuasive guys. They say, look, who's Ponte gonna suspect—his own *paisans* or the fucking spicks? It's a piece a cake, they say. Lift the stones, Ponte decides the Colombians fucked him, and that's the end of it."

Dried salt made Joey's scalp itch and he gave it a luxurious scratch. "Then wha'd they need you for?"

Gino drank. "They figured they'd walk away with like a million and a half each. How can they spend that kinda money without it lookin', ya know...? So the deal was this: They cut me in, I get them made, so then it looks like they're earning good with us, and that's where the cash is coming from."

Joey tapped his fingers on the blond wood arms of his chair. "Except Ponte doesn't believe it was the Colombians."

Gino tugged at the lapel of his bathrobe and gave a bitter laugh. "Ain't that fucking sad? I mean, what's the fucking world coming to when a guy would trust the spicks before his own friends? Who knows, maybe Vinnie and Frank fucked up. Maybe they left a trace, maybe they acted guilty. I dunno. I wasn't in on that part of it." He lifted his glass and, unwilling to admit it was empty, turned it upward until he was looking through the bottom of it as if it were a telescope. Then he got up and plodded toward the table.

Vicki looked at his wide back and spoke for the first time. It was not the voice of someone who had found the key to perfect patience. "Bring the bottle, Gino, you'll save steps."

"Shut up, Vicki," he said without turning around. But he took her advice.

"So what part *are* you in on, Gino?"

Gino sat down and poured himself another bourbon before he answered. He stashed the bottle between his thighs, and the neck protruded unattractively. "Vinnie and Frank got whacked. You know that, right?"

Joey nodded.

"Well, before they did, we made up a place where they would leave the emeralds. My part of the job was to pick 'em up, bring 'em to New York, and get 'em sold."

Joey realized quite suddenly that the flickering, voiceless images from the television were driving him nuts. He got up, turned the set off, and paced the room. "Gino, lemme make sure I got this right. Your partners get clipped. Which obviously means that Ponte knows what's what. And you still come down here to cop the stones? You gotta be a total asshole."

The older brother hunched forward, looking more than ever like a tired fighter who puts his head down and bulls off the ropes for one last and desperate offensive flurry. "Joey, tree million bucks, and no one left to split it with—could you just walk away and leave that sittin' onna table? Huh?" He sipped bourbon. "So O.K., things ain't workin' out so good, now I gotta sit here and get insulted. All of a sudden it's O.K., it's safe to dump on Gino. Even you, Joey, you're the big man all of a sudden. But what if it worked? Would I be an asshole then? Bullshit. I'd be a hero."

"Some hero," said Vicki. It didn't seem like she'd meant to speak. It just came out like an ill-timed fart.

"Shut up, you bitch. Yeah Joey, I'd be a hero, and we both know it. I'd lay some money on Pop, I'd spread some around, I'd take on some new guys, and even if, sometime downa road, Ponte figured things out, you think he'd have the balls to touch me? Nah. I'd be too big by then."

Joey reached out and grabbed his brother by the arms. "Gino, there ain't gonna be no *then*. Can't you see that?" He gave Gino a shake, but the bigger man seemed to have gone limp; it was like shaking a bag of cotton. "So where're the emeralds now?"

Gino looked down and said nothing. Vicki cracked the silence with a tittering and demented little laugh. "He don't know," she said.

Joey was not aware of starting to pace again but found himself treading the narrow runway between the dresser and the foot of the bed. "You don't know?"

"I do know," Gino protested. He half swiveled and looked at Vicki with a face full of loathing. Then he added, in a softer voice, "I just couldn't find 'em."

"Couldn't find 'em *when?*"

Gino was seeking distraction in the bourbon bottle between his thighs, toying with it like a masturbating chimp. "The night I set up you and Bert," he said. "This is what I'm tryin' to tell ya, Joey. I didn't do it so I could run, I did it so I could cop the stones."

"But you didn't cop the stones."

Gino shook his head forlornly and came as close as Joey had ever seen to looking embarrassed. "I couldn't find the fucking place. Then I ran outta time. I barely made it back here aheada Ponte. Maybe I shoulda just said the hell with it and bolted. But tree million dollars! I wasn't ready to walk away."

Joey suddenly felt very tired. It was the kind of melting fatigue in which the most familiar things no longer seem familiar. Was this fat drunk guy in the bathrobe a relative of his, someone he was supposed to care about? This woman under the sheet—who the hell was she? "So Gino," he said very slowly, "where —are—the emeralds?"

Gino opened his mouth, then abruptly stopped himself, like a card player who realizes he is on the brink of throwing in what could yet be a winning hand. "Joey, I ain't sure I oughta tell ya."

Joey sucked his teeth, crossed his arms, and leaned back against the dresser. "Gino, asshole, you're a walking dead man because of those fucking emeralds. You don't see that?"

"What kinda split you looking for, Joey?"

"Split? Split? You think this is about a split? Jesus Christ, Gino, you really are a putz." Joey looked at his watch on its arrogantly inexpensive plastic band. "Look, it's late. I don't need this shit. Either you tell me what I need to know in the next thirty seconds, or I'm outta here and you're on your own."

Gino stared at the carpet but found no answers there. Vicki's foot moved under the sheet and kicked him in the kidney. "Awright, awright. Supposedly the stones are stashed at this place called Sand Key Marina. It's about ten, twelve miles up, and that's all I know about it. Drove me bullshit tryin' to find it. There's no signs, no streetlights, you like go down these tiny roads that turn into gravel and then dead-end at these swamps. Over and over again, fucking swamps. Mosquitoes. Fireflies. Things croaking. Anyway, there's an old wreck of a fishing boat at this marina. Just, like, tied up there, ya know, it can't be used no more. It's called the *Osprey*. So Vinnie and Frank, they scoped it out, and they put the stones in this wreck, under a plank inside with like a little X marked on it. And that's as much as I know, I swear to God."

Joey nibbled a thumbnail and glanced at the dirty dinner dishes. "You got cash?"

Gino nodded.

"Gimme a thousand."

"Wha' for?"

"I don't know yet," Joey said. "I gotta think."

Gino leaned over, put the Jack Daniel's on a night

table, took a wad of bills out of a drawer, and gave his kid brother some money.

"Tomorrow at midnight," Joey said, "go down to the basement, up the service ramp, around the pool, and out to the dock. No luggage, no nothing."

"What about my stuff?" said Vicki.

"Shut up," said Gino.

And Joey left. He saw no one in the elevator or in the basement kitchen, and when he encountered a security guard on the private beach, he just walked past him like he owned the joint and went out to his boat.

31

There is a kind of preoccupation that makes people muddled, absentminded, out of rhythm, but there is also a kind that hones them, makes them as taut yet supple as a child gymnast. The next day Joey was riding the crest of this second kind of preoccupation. He had a golden day at work. No one could say no to him. He patrolled his corner of Duval Street with the loose-limbed confidence of a great outfielder, and with similarly uncanny anticipation. He just knew what people needed to hear. One couple he won over with a winged spiel about award-winning resort design. Another couple—how could he tell they were starving?—signed on at the promise of a meal voucher for an oyster brunch. Then there was the older gent with the gold chains, the silver belt buckle, and the pebbled ring. This was a man who liked shiny things, an easy mark for the free passes to the Treasure Museum. By noon Joey had made half as much money as he had the entire week before.

Yet never for a moment was the Gino situation off his mind. It kept nagging at him like a bad but catchy tune replayed in a dozen different versions, and every time Joey ushered customers into the Parrot Beach office, he took the opportunity to pick Zack Davidson's brain.

"Hey, Zack," he asked at around nine-thirty, "they got this thing, right, like a mappa the water?"

Zack looked up from some papers on his desk. "Yeah, Joey, it's called a chart."

"Like, whadda they put on it?"

Zack shrugged. "Depths, buoys, lighthouses, landmarks—"

"Marinas?"

"Not usually. Not unless there's a big tower or water tank or something. Why?" Zack laughed at himself for asking this. He seemed to know by now that Joey wasn't going to tell him why.

"Just curious," said Joey. He put his sunglasses back on, let the earpieces slide through his hair with a feeling smooth as sex, and returned to his post on the sidewalk.

At around ten-fifteen he shepherded in another couple, deposited them in the waiting room, and was ready to resume the conversation exactly where he'd left off. Time was running on two tracks for Joey. There was the thick, slow time of his salesman's skill, then there was the urgent yet strangely serene countdown toward his midnight date with Gino. At moments the two times ran parallel, but then one would stop, freeze, wait for the other to have its say. "So, like, if you're looking for a marina and it ain't onna map—"

"Chart," corrected Zack.

"Whatever. How d'ya find it?"

Zack ran a hand through his sandy hair. "Well, there's gotta be a channel to get to the marina. So if you know roughly where it is—"

"Ah," said Joey, and hit the street again.

At midday he jogged to the Habaneras Marine Supply store and bought a nautical chart of the lower Keys. He brought it back to the office, unfurled it on top of the Plexiglas case of the Parrot Beach scale model, examined it with frank befuddlement, and experienced an emotion he couldn't quite place. It was humility. Bafflement, helplessness, littleness, shame —all of those he'd felt before. But this was different, rounder. Humility required a certain amount of confidence, a little bit of knowledge and pride, to give it a place to nest, and these parts of the mix were new. "*Marrone*," he said, "what is all this shit?"

Zack Davidson leaned over the chart and pointed with a pencil. "Latitude. Longitude. Loran lines. Compass rose. Shoaling. Harbor ranges . . ."

Joey scanned the paper for an easy place where his eyes could rest. "And what's this blank part over here?"

Zack was momentarily thrown by the question and shook his wrist to rearrange his watch. "That? That's the land."

For some reason this struck Joey funny: a map where all the important stuff was in the water and the nothing part was the land. This he'd never heard of in Queens. The idea pried open his imagination, turned everything superbly upside down. He scratched his head, dashed outside, and within an hour had chalked up two more commissions.

"Reefs?" he said when he came back into the office. "They put reefs onna chart?"

"Sure," said Zack. "This parta the world, that's like the most important thing on there."

"Right," said Joey. "And onna land part, they show where the bridges are, right?"

"Yeah," said Zack. "With the clearances."

"Right."

He returned to his post and realized for the first time that it was an extremely hot afternoon. The breeze had stalled and the palms, so lazily efficient at husbanding their strength, let their fronds hang as limp and seemingly weightless as flags. The yogurt eaters bent their necks to lick drippings from their cones, and young women in undershirts had beads of sweat at their hairlines. Joey sold one last tour with a heartfelt pitch about the gorgeous pool at Parrot Beach.

"Hey Zack," he said, " 'zere an airport between here and Miami?"

"Yeah," he said, "at Marathon. Fifty miles up."

"Great. And what's a rowboat cost?"

Zack Davidson folded his hands on top of his blotter, unfolded them, tugged an ear, and yawned. The heat and his younger colleague were making him tired. "Joey, you're awful hyper today."

"Yeah, I guess I am. Sorry."

"Hey," said Zack, gesturing toward the stack of tour chits Joey had amassed, "don't be sorry. It works. But Joey, man, aren't you getting exhausted?"

He let the question slide. "Zack, listen. I need your boat again tonight. I gotta keep it overnight, and I need tomorrow off. I know it's a lot to ask, but after this, I'm through with this craziness, I swear to God."

Zack shrugged. If Joey didn't wreck his boat the first time, odds were he wouldn't wreck it the second. Besides, the kid was on a salesman's roll, in that zone where no one could say no to him. Far be it from his boss to break the trance. "O.K.," he said, "you got it."

"And there's one other thing," Joey said. He leaned across Zack's desk and wagged a finger under his chin. "You gotta promise you're gonna lemme make this up to you sometime."

"Joey, hey, it's no big deal."

"It is to me. Come on, Zack, I'm serious. Don't insult me."

Zack looked at the younger man and blinked his sandy eyelashes. Skeptical crinkles bunched up at the corners of his hazel eyes, as if he had a tough time imagining Joey in a strong enough position to do much of anything for anybody else. "Whatever, Joey. When you can. If you can. No pressure."

"Soon," said Joey. "It's gonna be soon. And if things go right, Zack, you're gonna see that I'm a guy who knows how to return a favor."

32

In the screened gazebo at the Paradiso condominium, the late afternoon gin game was just breaking up, the players about to go their separate ways for the rituals of cocktail hour and sunset. When Joey arrived, Bert d'Ambrosia was gesturing through a final kibitz with the retired judge, his colleague in age, assets, and the respect accorded to each. Bert wore a pale yellow shirt whose weave was almost as thin and open as cheesecloth; the fabric nearly disappeared against his bronze, stretched skin. Don Giovanni perched on his forearm like an acrobat, seeming to use his whiskers as a kind of balance pole.

"Hi, Bert. Got a minute?"

The old man flashed him a wry look that said that was exactly what he had. Minutes. Hours. Days. Maybe even a few years yet.

Joey motioned him outside, and the two men sat down under one of the steel umbrellas by the pool.

Bert put his dog on the table, and although Joey didn't
say a word about it, the old gangster seemed to feel
called upon to explain. "The other owners don't like
it," he said, "and I don't blame 'em. A dog onna table—it ain't, like, whatchacallit, sanitary. But this dog,
ever since the night with the gahbidge, he don't like
to be out of my sight. Like, under the chair, that's too
far away now. Fucking dog's a royal pain innee ass.
Ain't you a pain innee ass, Giovanni? I shoulda let
that little sear-faced fucker blow your brains out."

Joey looked through his blue lenses at the blue
shimmer of the pool. "Yeah, Bert," he said. "Well,
speakin'a pains innee ass, I took a boat, slipped inta
the Flagler House, and wenta see Gino last night."

The Shirt took the news in stride. "And how's he
doin'?"

"He's fallin' apart," said Joey. The statement came
out oddly neutral because in it sympathy was balanced
with rage, letdown canceled out vindication.

"Figures," said Bert. "Soft inna middle, Gino is.
If things don't fall his way, if he can't play the big
shot—"

"Well, I'm gettin' him outta town tonight. I got it
mostly figured and I think it's gonna work."

The old man reached up and stroked the strands
of flesh that were like the rigging for a double chin
that wasn't there. "You *think* it's gonna work?"

"It'll work," Joey said softly. He looked out through
the open side of the Paradiso quadrangle, across the
bustle of A1A to the imported sand of Smathers
Beach and the green Atlantic beyond. "But I'm gonna
need some help."

"Like?"

"Like I need you to drive about twelve miles up

the Keys and meet me at dawn at this little bridge between Big Coppitt and Saddlebunch."

"That I can do," Bert said. "It's not like I sleep good anyway."

"Then I need you to take Gino and Vicki to Marathon airport and get 'em onna first flight out. But not to Miami. I think it'd be better to avoid Miami. Where else they fly to outta there?"

"Prob'ly West Palm, Tampa."

"Yeah," said Joey, "someplace like that. Soon as possible. Then fuck it, we're done."

Bert scratched his chest through his cheesecloth shirt, and with his other hand he scratched the dog's. "Joey, ain'tcha forgettin' something?"

"Whassat?"

"What about the emeralds, Joey? Gino have the emeralds?"

Joey drummed his fingertips on the white enamel table and slowly shook his head. "The two guys that got whacked? They stashed 'em. And my genius brother, the night he almost got us killed, he went to cop 'em and couldn't find 'em."

"So that's that?" said Bert the Shirt. He was retired, more than comfortable, he had no use or even desire for extra money, but still, the idea of three million dollars going unexploited seemed to offend him profoundly. "So the stones'll just sit somewhere and rot?"

"Emeralds don't rot," said Joey. "That's the beauty part."

Bert paused. Back when he was active in the business, he'd been one of the better pausers in New York. He'd squint, toy with his collar, reach ever so slowly into his monogrammed pocket for a smoke. So supple were his pauses that they were equally suited to exuding menace or concealing knowledge or simply shaving parts of beats off the rough jazz of his speech. "Giovanni," he said at last to the dog, "you think this kid's holdin' out on us?"

Joey patted the chihuahua's head as a way of placating its master. "Bert, I ain't said one thing that isn't true. But hey, listen, coupla other things. Ya know where I can get a sleeping bag?"

"Sleeping bag? Joey, what're you runnin' here, a fucking Boy Scout camp? There's an army surplus on Stock Island."

"Great. And I need a rowboat. You got any idea where I can get a rowboat?"

"Prob'ly right in Garrison Bight," said Bert the Shirt. "Along the embankment there. There's always some winos, they sit in these old boats, sleep in 'em, I guess. Offer 'em twenty bucks. They'll take it, get drunk, and steal the boat back tomorrow."

Joey nodded, rapped the metal table with his knuckles, and started to get up. "Sounds easy enough. But ain't that what you tol' me, Bert, that in Florida everything should be easy?"

The Shirt nodded, a little bit uncertainly. He hated getting tripped up on what he did or did not remember saying.

"And money comes outta the water here," said Joey, pressing the old man's bony shoulder. "You tol' me that, too, didn't ya, Bert?"

Here Bert felt himself more firmly in the grip of recollection, and he smiled his loose-lipped long-toothed smile. "Always has," he said. "It's, like, tradition."

Sandra was in the pool.

Now that the evenings were staying hot, this was

her favorite time at the compound. Steve the naked landlord had disappeared, taking his beers, his ashtray, and his nakedness with him. Peter and Claude had left for work; Wendy and Marsha had gone inside to eat either brown rice or pepperoni pizza; Luke was off playing music somewhere, and Lucy the mailman was in front of television with her feet up. Sandra had the place to herself, under a dimming sky that was still greenish yellow at the western fringe, with the palms and poincianas losing the last of their daylight color and turning black and flat as etchings overhead. She stood midriff-deep in her chaste two-piece and breathed in the jasmine and the chlorine.

Then she grabbed on to the edge of the pool and started doing her kicking exercises.

That was when Joey came through the gate. Sandra was facing away from him, and he watched her as he approached. She craned her neck to keep her pale short hair out of the water. She pointed her toes, probably the way she'd once seen in a magazine. And while she was kicking furiously, she barely made a splash or a sound. Sandra, Joey thought. This is Sandra. Quiet, private, disciplined, precise. The little kid who would always find something worth doing if stuck in her room, who would always have a project for a weekful of rain. He watched her firm and narrow back, her skinny and determined shoulders, and a strange thing happened: he realized he truly was in love with her. He did not prime himself to feel this, and there was no such thing as readiness for the feeling when it came. It started at his feet and swelled upward as pure, sore, and irresistible as a sudden welling of graveside grief, and it left him with a closed throat and a milky feeling at the backs of his knees.

He walked lightly around the pool's damp apron and crouched low in front of her. "Hello, baby."

"Hi, Joey," she said, still kicking. "Thirty more makes four hundred."

"I love you," he said.

Sandra, the banker, had never before lost count. But now her scissoring legs fell out of their forced march and fluttered softly downward until her feet found the bottom. Joey, kneeling on the wet tiles, kissed her and tasted chlorine.

"I mean, Sandra, I think you're terrific. The best. The way you are. The way you've stuck with me. Hey, Sandra, you want friends? We're gonna have friends, Sandra. I promise. Lotsa friends. And salads. Friends and salads, all you want. And, like, we'll do stuff. I don't know what, whatever you like. Ya know, regular stuff that people do. Movies, picnics, I dunno. But we'll like go out, we'll have, like, a life. You and me. O.K.?"

sion. Outside, orange floodlights collided with the
blue shimmer of the pool and gave a mottled desert
aspect to the beach. On the far side of the building,
Charlie Ponte's thugs sat in their Lincoln scratching
their bellies, yawning, talking about Italian food and
parts of the female body. Their landlocked brains
traveled predictably down marked roads; they could
not conceive of a getaway on the wide, dark, and lane-
less water. Joey idled at the end of the pier and
waited.

His view to the top of the service ramp was blocked
by the shaggy thatch of the poolside bar, and by the
time he saw the silhouettes of Gino and Vicki, they
were winding their way through the ranks of vacant
lounge chairs near the beach. Gino had his hand in
the small of Vicki's back, a gesture not of gallantry
but of bullying. Shadowy and forward-leaning, the
couple bore, for all their attempted nonchalance, the
unmistakable stamp of people fleeing, and when Gino
stepped onto the thick boards of the dock, his heavy
tread seemed to pass along an edginess that shuddered through the nails and down the pilings until it
was smothered by the muck at the bottom of the sea.
Halfway along the pier, one of Vicki's high heels
caught between two planks; she took her shoes off
and scurried the rest of the way with mincing steps.

"So you made it," Gino said. He managed to muster some of his former high-spirited sarcasm, maybe
because Joey was now literally beneath him, hugging
a piling to keep the boat close and not looking especially dignified. But it was also true that Gino had
made a brave attempt to pull out of his nosedive on
this, his last evening in Florida. He'd eased off on the
bourbon and just let Dr. Greenbaum buy him one

final bottle of champagne with dinner. He'd shaved, cut his toenails, and even managed to find a clean shirt and a silk sports jacket. Like many people who have been humiliated in a strange and distant place, he seemed to imagine that going home would be sufficient to erase the episode, that since none of the neighborhood guys had witnessed his shame and the baring of his weakness, it hadn't really happened.

"Come on," said Joey, "get in. Step inna middle of the boat."

Vicki's behind was in his face as she lowered herself down the wooden ladder. Her butt was clothed in mauve-colored capri pants and seemed to be perfumed. Vicki had tried to fix her hair in honor of her reemergence into the world, but she couldn't duplicate the skill, patience, and apparatus of the beauty parlor. Like a failed soufflé, the rough teased do held its own around the edges but caved in in the center; in silhouette it was as if her scalp had been cleft by a hatchet. She lurched around the cockpit until she managed to grab a rail. Then Joey stepped well back as Gino lumbered in. The skiff rocked under his weight, and once he was safely in the boat he cast a sneering glance back through the hotel to where his colleagues were intently but stupidly waiting to kill him. "Assholes," he said.

Joey pushed off, took the wheel, turned the boat toward open water, and jammed the throttle forward.

The breeze was light, the water only slightly rippled like a washboard, and no one spoke until the skiff was half a mile out from land. Then Joey slowed the engine and said to Gino, "Gimme your guns."

A late half-moon was just coming up. Its dim reddish glow mixed with the silver blue of starlight to make a spectral gleam that seemed good for telling lies. "I didn't bring 'em," Gino said. "I mean, Christ, we're goin' to the airport, ain't we?"

Joey turned off the motor. It was a gesture intended to remind his passengers of their essential status as captives. Amid the violent silence of the ocean, the only sound was the lapping of water against their hull; it was a noise at once delicate and full of threat, like a lion licking its chops. "Gino, I known you a long time. Gimme the fucking guns."

Gino seemed to be considering, though in an eighteen-foot boat a person does not have a lot of options as to where to go or what to do. He reached into his jacket pocket, pulled out his pistol, and with a resentful pout on his jowly mouth handed it to Joey. Then he pulled his second gun out of his pants at the small of his back and surrendered that one, too. Joey glanced at the weapons for just a second, and tossed them over his shoulder into the Florida Straits. They somersaulted through the red moonlight then landed with a slap-slap followed by a baritone kerplunk as they broke the skin of the water and dove pinwheeling toward the bottom.

"Fuck you do that for?" Gino asked.

Joey restarted the engine. " 'Sgonna be a long night, Gino. It could get, like, emotional."

At the eastern end of Key West, the airport beacon raked the water, and through the cut of Cow Key Channel, the weird mass of Mount Trashmore could momentarily be seen. Then came the low, dark sweep of Stock Island, with its trailer parks and oil tanks, then the barricaded expanse of Boca Chica, where navy pilots learned to fly. The skiff planed along the ripples, two miles out from shore; the towed rowboat sledded along in the flat water between the rays of the wake.

"This is *nice*," Vicki yelled over the roar of the motor. She sounded surprised, innocent, and girlish, as if the salt air had blown away her years of bimbohood, swept her back to the younger verge of an adolescence marked by wonder at the mystery of ballooning breasts and their hypnotic effect on certain sorts of men. The wind had yanked her hair straight up and back and made her look unprecedentedly stylish. "Gino, how come *you* never took me boating?"

"Shut up, Vicki," he shouted. Was he still sulking over the loss of his gun, or was he just that thoroughly sick of her?

"No, *you* shut up, Gino," she yelled back. Then she started cackling. Had she truly lost her mind, or was she just so tickled to be standing up to him? "I'm sicka you bossin' me around."

"Shut up the botha yuhs," said Joey. "I gotta find the spot."

He slowed the boat and peered toward shore, wondering if the contour of the land would look anything like the image he'd carried away from the nautical chart. He was looking for the place where the bulge of Big Coppitt gave onto the cluster of mangrove outcrops called the Saddlebunch Keys, where Highway 1 hopped and curved from one dry place to another over a series of short low bridges. Turning landward, he rode the current that was streaming toward the Gulf, filtering through the islands and the trestles as through a giant sieve, and when he could just make out the hum of traffic from the pavement, he cut back to idle speed and drifted. The raised road loomed ahead like a low black rainbow. Widely spaced streetlights lit up globes of vapory air; the occasional car pushed its meager beams straight in front of it.

"We gettin' off here?" Vicki asked as they floated toward the stanchions.

"You are," Joey said. He didn't look at her but kept his eyes on the bow of the boat.

Vicki swallowed, blinked, licked her thin dry lips. She'd thought the kid brother was her ally. That made it O.K. to stand up to Gino. But would an ally drop her off all by herself in the middle of nowhere with lizards and bugs and maybe even alligators all over the place? She pointed her chest toward Joey and inhaled. "Hey," she purred.

By way of answer, Joey reached down and handed her a neatly bundled sleeping bag. "Ever been camping, Vicki?"

She looked at the quilted parcel like it came from Mars. "You gotta be crazy," she said. "I'll get raped. I'll get murdered."

Joey maneuvered the skiff so that it was drifting broadside toward the bridge. Current parted around the concrete pillars; the pavement sang under the weight of a truck. Off to the left, the land was low, dark, and overhung with tangled trees. "Vicki, this ain't New York. The worst that's gonna happen is you'll get mosquito-bit. Gino, get onna side and get ready to grab the bridge."

Gino Delgatto compressed like a squeezed beach ball as he absorbed the impact between fiberglass and concrete. He held the skiff fast while Joey hoisted Vicki onto the small front deck. The roadbed was just at the level of her face, and under it was an I-beam that was pocked with rust and had the texture of a nutmeg grater. Vicki grabbed it and leaped about six inches into the air. "Hold on, now," Joey said. "Lift. Come on, lift."

The boat was rocking, current was slapping against it, and Vicki was trying her damnedest to pull herself onto the bridge. In her mauve capri pants, her long legs kicked and jerked like those of a hanged man. Finally Joey put his hands on her perfumed backside and shoved for all he was worth. It was satisfying, this vigorous handling of his brother's girlfriend's ass, and it propelled her to where she could swing a leg onto the pavement and scrabble up to the shoulder of the road. She stood, monumental from the perspective of the men below, and glared down at them accusingly. Joey tossed the sleeping bag up to her, and she clutched it to her bosom as though it were her last friend in the world.

"Go over by the trees there," Joey said. "We'll be back around dawn."

She looked down at Gino, who was still hugging the bridge stanchion, and for a moment it appeared she might spit on him or burst into tears. Instead, she just walked away. After a few steps she turned around. "Some vacation, Gino," she hissed. "I shoulda stood in Queens."

34

"So Gino, it's just you and me."

Joey Goldman had turned seaward again, and was a mile offshore by the time he spoke, or rather, yelled over the grind of the engine and the hiss of water shooting past the hull. The moon had gone from red to yellow to eggshell white, and spilled an endless beam that glinted over the water and seemed to single out the little skiff.

"Yup," yelled Gino. He was suddenly rather giddy, made so by too much freedom and too little control. Being sprung from his hotel room was about as invigorating and disconcerting as getting out of jail. Being rid of Vicki felt, for the moment at least, as good as waking up to find that a throbbing boil had vanished in the night. But then again, he had no gun, no car, no crew, no plan, and no idea what Joey had in mind. "So kid, what the hell we doin' now?"

Joey smiled without parting his lips. His thick hair

had been pressed back by the wind, his eyes were
narrowed against the spray, his forearms were ropy
from clutching the wheel. Gino almost noticed that
his bastard half brother had become a grown man.
"We're gonna find your fucking emeralds," Joey hollered. "What else?"

"You can do that?" Gino screamed.

Joey did not immediately answer but gave himself
a moment to savor the hope, need, and doubt in Gino's tone. He thought he could do it. He'd studied
his chart. It seemed to him there was only one place
Sand Key Marina could be. Straight out from a radio
tower, behind the arc of a narrow peninsula that
curved away like the bone on a lamb chop, there
should be a narrow channel marked by unlit buoys.
If there wasn't, well, that was that.

"I can find 'em," Joey yelled.

Gino suddenly felt tears of greed welling in his
windblown eyes—greed and amazement, as if he'd
stopped believing he would ever see the three million
dollars' worth of Colombian stones. "Great, kid," he
screamed. "We'll go partners." Then he realized that
the word implied a fifty-fifty split, and he quickly re-
covered from his spasm of generosity. "I mean, I'll
cut you in."

Joey let that slide, and continued with his own line
of thought. "But Gino, ya gotta do everything I tell
you."

"Sure, kid, sure," Gino shouted.

"Before, during, and after," Joey pressed.

"Whatever."

"Swear on your mother, Gino. Whatever I say, you
do."

Gino looked away. Water was flying off the side of

the boat like it was shot from a fire hose. "Christ, Joey. We gotta start with this mother shit again?"

"Yeah, Gino, we do. Swear."

He did, and Joey eased back on the throttle. He scanned the shore for the radio tower. There seemed to be lots of radio towers, but most of them were probably electrical pylons. From a mile away, by moonlight, it was hard to tell. Joey steered closer to land, waiting for the low shapeless ribbon of limestone and shrubs to show some useful feature. For some minutes no such feature appeared; the land showed blank as an oil slick, and Joey choked down the thought that he might yet have to admit to Gino and himself that once again he'd failed, that just like the jerks from the neighborhood, he'd talked big and could not deliver.

Then, finally, he spotted what seemed to be the peninsula shaped like a lamb chop bone. It was nothing more than a finger of mangrove and showed only as a brief interruption in the gleam of moonlight. He made toward it. Gino started pawing around like a dog that hears its food bowl being filled.

" 'Zat it?" he asked. " 'Zat it?"

Joey just shrugged. Then, a couple of hundred yards off the tip of the peninsula, he thought he saw a channel marker. It was unlit, stood crooked in the water, but was dabbed with a reflective paint, and for just an instant it caught the moonlight and sent back an improbably bright flash. Joey realized that his heart was pounding. This had nothing to do with emeralds, but with finding what he was looking for, studying a picture that stood for the world and discovering that the pieces fit, that both the picture and his ability to read it could be trusted. The radio tower was dead ahead. Joey idled forward.

Now, what passes for a harbor in the Florida Keys would not be called a harbor most other places. There is no deep water, not much shelter, just skinny passages where the limestone muck has been dredged away and boats have a reasonable chance of making it to shore. The channel that Joey hoped he was following soon narrowed to a swath of flat water barely wider than the skiff. On either side, little tepees of mangrove popped out, their greedy roots already capturing nests of land. Mosquitoes swarmed and buzzed at the nearness of fresh meat. Toads croaked, night herons screamed out their ugly clicking screech. The moonlight was swallowed up as the foliage closed in, and something that sounded like giant crickets made a noise like sandpaper scratching bone.

Gino fanned invisible bugs from in front of his face. "Joey, man, this can't be right. It's like we're halfway inna fucking jungle." Black leaves and low branches drank up the sound of the engine.

Ahead, on a nubbly, tilted wooden stake, was what might have been another marker. Joey edged toward it. Behind it loomed a seemingly endless wall of mangrove that gave off a smell of sulfur and anchovies kept too long in tin. But at this second stake, the channel took a sudden dogleg left, and the new angle revealed an overhung cut between two islets. The cut was so narrow that waxy mangrove leaves scratched against the skiff's hull as the little craft slipped through.

Then there was a clearing in which the still water gleamed black and flat as a lake.

At the edge of this cove was a falling-down dock.

Its outermost pilings had crumpled like the forelegs of a crippled horse, and its planks had come unhinged like the keys of a broken xylophone. On shore, half grown over with vines and shrubs, was the rotting structure of what once had been an office or store; next to it was a gas pump with no paint left on it, then, propped on cinder blocks, a rusty mobile home with smashed windows and a guano-caked TV antenna.

"Here's your marina," Joey said. "Don't feel bad you couldn't find it. And there's your boat."

He pointed to a black hulk tied up to the far side of the dock. Made of ancient planking, with thick sides and a small, square pilothouse that had lost both its windshield and its roof, it seemed to be floating only out of habit. Joey pulled the skiff closer. In small flecks of brittle paint caught between splinters of wood, he could just make out the vessel's name: *Osprey*.

If Gino Delgatto had had a tail, it would have been slapping wildly against his buttocks. As it was, he paced the skiff with avid steps, making it rock as though in a gale. "Holy shit, Joey! Tree million bucks. There it is! It's mine! Oh baby, I can taste it! Come on, willya, move the boat closer, lemme get on there and grab the fucking stones."

Joey didn't. He idled some twenty feet away and held steady at that tantalizing distance while a cloud of mosquitoes formed around them and his brother tried to jerk the skiff closer with body english. "Hol' on a second, Gino. We're not just grabbin' the emeralds. We're takin' the whole boat."

On Gino's red and beefy face, the features all pushed forward, as if his mouth and nose were racing to the stones. The more his blood rushed to the surface, the better the mosquitoes liked it. "Joey, what I want with the fucking boat? Just lemme get the emeralds and let's get the fuck outta here."

Joey crossed his arms. "Gino, did you or did you not just swear we're doing things my way?"

"Sure, kid, yeah. But I don't see the fucking point—"

"Gino, use your head. The guys that got whacked— you got no waya knowing what Ponte got out of 'em before he clipped 'em. Am I right? Ya gotta figure he squeezed 'em pretty good. So maybe they gave it up that the stones are on a boat. Maybe they even tol' 'im where, and Ponte couldn't find it, just like you couldn't."

"So?" Gino crushed a mosquito that had landed in his ear; it squirted some of his blood. He never once took his eyes off the junked fishing boat.

"So, what if sometime Ponte *does* find the boat, and the stones ain't on it? Who's he gonna figure got there first? You, Gino. So you'll be fucked all over again. This way, we take the whole boat, there's nothin' to find, it's done with."

Gino scratched, thought, and let out a deep breath that blew some bugs around. "O.K., kid," he said. "You're right."

"I know I'm right," Joey pressed. "I been thinkin' this through for weeks. So Gino, willya do me a favor? Stop questioning every little goddamn thing and do like I tell ya."

Gino nodded through a faceful of mosquitoes. Anything to get his hands on the emeralds. Besides, what did it cost him to take orders from Joey in a place where no one could see and no one would ever know?

"Awright," Joey resumed as he clicked the engine

into gear and edged closer. "So here's what we're gonna do. The skiff, we're gonna leave it here. We're gonna take the little motor off the back, put it on the junker, and use it to get the junker outta heah. We're gonna tow the rowboat, then put the little motor onna rowboat to get back, then pick up the skiff. Got it?"

Gino hadn't got it. He wasn't listening. He was thinking about emeralds and swatting mosquitoes, and had no attention left for other things.

Joey mustered a tone of command. "So Gino, don't just fucking stand there. Take the little motor off."

Gino unclamped the auxiliary engine and hoisted it over the *Osprey*'s splintery gunwales as Joey softly clunked the skiff against its side. But once Gino actually reached the treasure boat, his fragile patience let go all at once and he went blind with lust for the emeralds. He leaped out of the skiff, sending it scudding sideways, and clambered onto the *Osprey*'s damp and spongy deck. His soft imported loafers skidded on the slimy planks and he dove obliviously toward the roofless pilothouse. By the pale but steady light of the moon, he searched out the board on which an X had supposedly been marked. For some moments he couldn't find it, and seemed inclined to rip out his eyes for their failure.

Then he spotted a smudge as of damp powder. He fell to his knees in front of it and tried to pry up the plank with his fingernails. A soft unwholesome grit of moldy wood and the remains of ancient ants and spiders covered his fingers. Then, from a hole at the base of the steering console, not two feet from where Gino knelt, there emerged a rat the size of a dachshund. For an unspeakable moment the rodent's beady red eyes met those of the mafioso from New York. Gino could see the gleam of mucus on its pointy black nose, which was twitching in terror. The rat scratched at the floor, hunkered low as a snake, then, with desperate courage, it charged along the only escape route it had. It darted over Gino's hands, its damp, rank fur obscenely tickling his wrists. Gino, recoiling, flicked his arms and caught the rodent in the underbelly. It rose in a macabre claws-out somersault, landed on Gino's Achilles tendon, and scampered away. Gino went back to pawing at the plank.

Finally it lifted. Nothing was visible in the dark, narrow gap, but far down in the bilges, fetid water was dully gleaming. Gino plunged his hand in, and slime stretched out along the sleeve of his silk jacket. The slime had a skin on it like burned milk, it clung to his wrist like a condom. His fingers found a small burlap sack, and squeezed it hard.

Still kneeling, his pulse throbbing in his mosquito-covered neck and his lips stretched tight across his teeth, he tugged at the sack's drawstring, then poured into his palm a sampling of uncut, unpolished Colombian emeralds.

They didn't look like much, just green rocks that didn't shine, and were coated with a rough white dust that seemed to have bubbled out from inside them. They varied in size, the biggest like brazil nuts, but nubbly as potatoes. Gino closed his hand around them and shook them softly like a favorite set of dice.

"You happy now?"

Joey was standing on the deck, leaning against the rickety frame of the pilothouse. He'd secured the skiff and put the small outboard on the *Osprey*'s rotting transom. "You got your stones. You happy?"

The words seemed to bring Gino out of his trance

of avarice. He glanced up over his shoulder, and for an instant he seemed abashed, as if it had dawned on him that he must look like a real horse's ass, kneeling like in church, slime all over his hands, elbow-deep in crud. Only now did it register that a rat had run on him, that he had touched its fur and felt the yielding of its gut, and he choked back a sudden nausea. But what the hell, he had the emeralds, it was worth it, worth everything. He grinned. "Fuck yeah, Joey. Hell yeah."

"Good," the younger brother said. "Now put 'em back, and put the plank back on."

Gino swiveled on his knees. "Fuck for?"

Joey showed him the tired look of a teacher stuck for too many years with the dumb kids. "Coast guard, Gino. They patrol. For drugs. But a bagga emeralds on a crummy old fishing boat—Gino, how's it gonna look?"

35

"So Joey, wha'?"

The sodden hulk of the *Osprey* had scratched its way through the narrow cut and lumbered out of the Sand Key channel, Zack Davidson's little eight-horse motor laboring mightily to push it through the lapping water and pull the paintless rowboat behind. It was two A.M. The Big Dipper, dimmed by a bright moon, loomed in the spring sky. It was the only constellation Joey recognized because it was the only one piercing enough to have occasionally penetrated the gummy and overlit summer air of Queens. He and Sandra used to go up on the roof sometimes to look at it and neck.

" 'Bout five miles out," Joey said, "there's a little island. We're gonna ditch the boat there, scrape the name off, bust it up as good as we can. Then we come back and you're outta heah."

Gino nodded, though he was paying only half-attention. His body was on deck but his brain was in the bilges. He tried to recapture the feel of wet emeralds in his palm.

For some minutes they didn't speak, then Gino asked absently, "How you know that?"

"It's onna chart." Joey was leaning against the *Osprey*'s stern, steering with the stem of the engine.

Gino made no response. He didn't much care what a chart was and he didn't want to give Joey a chance to show off what he knew. So he kept quiet and fantasized. He pictured what a sport he'd be when he cashed in his three million dollars' worth of rocks. He saw himself in an immaculate mohair suit, spreading smiles and fifties around crowded restaurants and nightclubs. He'd buy Vicki something nice. Discreetly, he'd lay some money on the widows of Vinnie Fish and Frankie Bread.

Joey steered the boat and watched his half brother swelling into the role of big shot.

Gino gave a self-contented little smile. He seemed to be imagining the pride and affection he'd bask in when he presented some of the stolen money to his father. He liked money, Vincente Delgatto did; he liked the rituals of people forking it over. And Gino liked when his father patted his cheek.

But then Gino frowned. With a flash of secret shame such as assails a person who has somehow forgotten a dear old friend at Christmas and knows deep down there's a reason why, he realized he had left out Joey. Jesus. Without Joey, he'd still be in his hotel room with his gums wrapped around a bourbon bottle; the emeralds would still be sitting at that falling-down dock with nothing but mosquitoes and rats for company.

"Kid," he began. After the long interval of silence
but for the whine of the motor, the sound seemed out
of place, intrusive. "Listen, I gotta give credit where
credit is due. Ya did good, Joey. The way ya thought
things through, I got a lotta respect for that. And I
wanna show my appreciation."

Joey looked off at the glinting water, the steady
stars. Gino didn't exactly sound like his old self, and
Joey figured he was rehearsing his role as the bigger
cheese he was about to become. But now Gino had
put himself in a position where he had to name a
number. A guy like Gino, if he talked about appreciation, gratitude, he couldn't just leave it vague like
that, he had to make it a specific amount. And this
was difficult. It wasn't that Gino was cheap. It was
more complicated than that. Whatever he gave to
Joey didn't only mean there was less for himself; it
also meant that Joey would be a little bit of a big shot
on his own, and the real question was, how much of
a big shot could Gino stand for him to be?

The older brother cleared his throat and ran a hand
over his chin. Then, in a gesture he'd seen his father
make in similar situations, he yanked down on the
collar of his shirt as if to give it a military straightness.
"Ten thousand, Joey. For you. For helpin' out.
Howzat sound?"

Some questions just cannot be answered, and this
was one of them. Besides, Gino wasn't asking it to
open a discussion but only as a setup to be thanked.
Joey was not inclined to thank him. He was neither
surprised nor unsurprised by the paltriness of his
brother's offer, and he decided he would not regard
it as an insult, just as a matter of bookkeeping. That's
what it came down to with Gino, after all—book-

keeping, the totting up of gyps and bonuses, the usual disappointments and very occasional windfalls of regard. "That's fine, Gino. Whatever you think."

Gino started to speak again, but just as the air was pushing past his throat, he realized he had nothing to say. In some dark recess of his mind he suspected he was being a cheap and jealous son of a bitch. He filtered this suspicion through his well-developed machinery for making himself seem right, and it came out looking like Joey was being very ungrateful in the face of his largess. But then, Joey had always been like that—grumpy even, or especially, when Gino was trying to help him out. The kid just couldn't accept generosity.

The *Osprey* plowed on slowly through the Florida Straits. Behind it, the land had fallen away until the mangroves looked like nothing more than dead spots on the ocean, and the dim lights of U.S. 1 appeared as stars bellied down to the horizon. The moon was nearing its zenith and its light was now a stark white that seemed to throw a sphere of steam around it. The breeze came in soft warm puffs from the south; ahead, the water was nearly flat, and then, perhaps a half mile away, just beyond a buoy that blinked a mesmerizing red, it broke into curious moonlit ripples, as if whipped by some unfelt freshening wind. Gino yawned. Joey dodged the contagiousness of it by looking away and taking a big breath of salty air.

Now, it has often been observed that in the midst of a terrible accident, time slows down and disaster unfolds with an almost pornographically explicit sense of close-up detail. When a boat runs up on coral, just the opposite is true. Everything that has been quietly humming along to the languid rhythm of calm water is instantly, bafflingly accelerated, as if the entire racing violence of the ocean were sluicing through the crazy currents in the shallows.

The *Osprey* was laboring along at a three-knot crawl when she first hit bottom.

Even so, her momentum carried her forward so that the stern came up like the backside of a bucking horse and the suddenly airborne propeller revved like a jet. When the creaking hull came back down, it listed to starboard, took a groaning bump, then turned its nose broadside to the chop.

"What the fuck?" screamed Gino, spreading out his arms and trying desperately to hold on to a gunwale.

"Fuck," said Joey. He was still trying to steer, but his efforts counted for nothing. The eddies carried the soft wooden boat from one coral head to another. The doomed craft slammed, caromed, and flew on helplessly toward the next blow; it was as if giant, stone-hard hands were playing volleyball with it. Overhead, the stars wheeled as the boat was tossed. Gino's thin shoes gave him no purchase on the slimy boards, and he slid around the deck as if on skates. The *Osprey* reared up, dove nose first, then, on the return bounce, slammed the shaft of the little outboard into unyielding coral. The force cracked the already rotten transom; it sheared off like wet cardboard. The motor, still attached, still running, dove backward like a scuba diver, punched a hole in the water, and vanished.

"Gino, man, we're fucked."

"My stones," he yelled. "Jesus Christ, my stones."

The older brother scrambled forward toward the pilothouse. A vicious, twisting collision with the bottom sent him sprawling, his face against the slimy planks, his ribs compressed against the side. He took a breath that burned, then got up on his hands and knees and tried crawling toward his fortune. He was halfway over the threshold of the roofless cabin when the *Osprey* came crashing down onto a spike of coral that poked into it like a drill. Water came spraying up through the pierced deck like oil from a gusher. Gino crawled over the rupture, and the hissing water seared his skin. He groped toward the loose plank, and a head-on crash sent him skidding face first into the base of the console where the rat had nested. Lying there, smelling brine and rodent, Gino heard or rather felt a profound and ungodly noise. It was a slow but all-encompassing vibration, a loose rumble as from the bowels of the earth. The boat was breaking in half.

Still pinned on his belly, Gino strained to look back over his shoulder. Through the pilothouse doorway, he could see that the back half of the *Osprey* was at a different angle. The craft was folding, like it was on a hinge. He pushed off with all his strength and scuttled backward like a crab. He made one last desperate grope toward the plank that hid his millions, but came away with nothing except a pencil-size splinter that tore through a waterlogged finger. Then he felt his ankles being grabbed. Joey pulled him backward, yanked his rigid body over a widening fissure in the middle of the boat and launched him toward the stern, where warm salt water was already pooling, welcoming the *Osprey* to the bottom of the sea.

"Quick," said Joey. "Inna rowboat."

Without quite knowing how he got there, Gino Delgatto found himself over the side, his hands clinging to the sundering timbers, his feet groping for the dry boards of the dinghy. A moment later, Joey followed. He took the oars just as the *Osprey* was going down. The bow went first. Like a dying animal, it seemed to give its head one final shake of defiance or supplication, then slid silently into the deep water at the far side of the coral canyon. Somewhat anticlimactically, the stern had yet to follow. Thinly attached by the few boards still intact, it had to be pulled down like a ham actor reluctant to leave the stage, and gave off an unseemly sucking sound as it finally submerged.

Joey needed to row only a couple hundred yards to escape the ferocious turbulence of the reef, and the instant he'd done so, the water was again so placid, the night air so still and coddling that it would have been easy to imagine that the wreck of the *Osprey* was only a quick nightmare, a hellish vision from a brief and otherwise pleasant nap.

Except the boat was gone. The motor was gone. The emeralds were gone.

Joey rowed in silence past the buoy blinking red.

Gino looked back in disbelief toward the empty place where his fortune had been. Moonlight twinkled on the ripples, and that was it. He pulled in a deep breath that added weight to the unhappy suspicion that he had cracked some ribs. Then he grabbed his hair and pulled. "Ah fuck, Joey," he said. "Fuck, fuck, fuck."

Joey put his back into his rowing. He hadn't wanted to thank Gino for his offer of a measly ten grand, and he didn't want to apologize now. He shrugged as well as he could shrug while handling the oars. "Gino, hey," he said. "I'm new at this. I tried."

36

"You tried. You tried? You *tried*?! Joey, you fucking little halfass loser pissant twerp, tree million dollars onna table, and you tried? That kinda money, Joey, ya don't *try*. A boy tries, Joey. A man *does*."

Gino Delgatto sat in the stern of the rowboat and screamed. Salt water squished through his nylon socks and out through the seams of his soft, ruined loafers. His silk jacket was full of slime and splinters. He was bleeding freely from his sliced-open finger and didn't notice until after he'd run that hand through his hair.

"I shoulda known you'd fuck it up," he went on. "Ha!" He slapped himself on the forehead. "Where was my fucking brain? What was going on in my fucking head that I would leave anything up to you? I must be crazy. How long I known you always fuck things up? Always. Shit, don't I know that's why you come down here inna first place? You couldn't cut it in New York, Joey, so here you are in this pissant little nothing place."

Gino enjoyed screaming. He had a voice that razzed like a trombone as it got louder, and it could fill a room, a house; sometimes it seemed like it could shout down everything for a city block. But it couldn't fill the ocean at four A.M., and this was a little frustrating. Also, to really crank up the volume, he had to squeeze from the gut, and this made his ribs burn as if touched with lit cigarettes. Well, tough, thought Gino. Let it hurt. His emeralds were at the bottom of the ocean and, goddammit, somebody, everybody, was going to pay.

"Yeah," he resumed, agreeing with himself. "You come down here because up there ya gotta do things right, and you never did. Ya couldn't even handle a bagga money without fucking it up somehow. Rough a guy up? Forget about it. You got no nerve, Joey. No balls. And everybody knows it, don't kid yourself. Pop, your so-called buddies—they all know you're worthless." He slapped himself in the head again. "Me, I know it. So why the fuck did I listen to you? Did I figure, O.K., I'm on your turf, maybe you're less of a fuckup here? Did I figure, hey, give the kid a chance, maybe by some miracle he ain't such a total loser anymore?"

Rowing is a very serene activity, private, repetitive, with constant evidence of slow but uncomplicated progress. So Joey rowed. He'd never done it before, and he didn't do it well, but he did it. He'd kicked off his wet sneakers, rolled up his wet pants legs, and was almost comfortable. He answered his brother softly. "Gino, come on, you listened to me 'cause you were desperate. You were drunk as a skunk, scared shitless, and you didn't know what to do next."

To Gino, this version of events already sounded wildly false, and if he didn't yet have a more satisfactory tale to tell himself, he'd construct one on the fly. "That's where you're wrong, kid," he razzed, wagging a bleeding finger in Joey's face. "Very wrong. I woulda come up with a plan. I was already workin' on it. And it wouldn'ta been so fucking halfass like yours. Mine woulda worked. I got impatient. That was my mistake." He slapped his head. "I got impatient, and yeah, I let my confidence get shook, that much I admit. So I depend on a little shitass nobody like you to pull me through. So O.K., I deserve what I got. Nothin'."

Joey rowed. Emerald-green flashes of phosphorescence streamed out from the blades of his oars, and the whole world seemed to exhale with relief at the pause in Gino's tantrum. The stars appeared to be receding with the prospect of the end of night. When Gino spoke again, he was not yelling but seemed to be thinking aloud.

"Nothin'. No money. No stones. All I got for my trouble is this big fucking problem with Charlie Ponte."

"Yup," said Joey, "ya still got that."

Gino said nothing. He shifted on the cracked stern seat of the rowboat and watched blood congeal on his finger. Somehow the zest went out of his rage when he remembered he was scheduled to be rubbed out.

"So what ya gonna do about it?" Joey resumed.

Again Gino made no answer, and Joey, between strokes of the oars, could not resist adding, "I mean, you said you had a plan and all."

"I do have a plan," Gino said by reflex. In the old days Joey might have believed him.

"Want my advice?"

Gino snorted. "Yeah, Joey, like I want a root canal."

"Just lay low for a while. Not long. A week, tops. Don't get antsy. 'Cause I got a feeling that things can still work out."

Gino considered this a moment, then his temper kicked in again. "Yeah? Like as good as they been workin' out so far?" His blood pressure rose so that his cut finger spat out its half-formed scab. His side throbbed like a drum. "Joey, man, I cannot fucking believe you are still giving me advice and I'm sittin' heah like almost half taking you seriously. After what you did to me, you dumb twat." He gestured off in the general direction of land. "Joey, the fucking stones were in my hand. *In my hand!* Why couldn't you just leave well enough alone? I coulda been halfway to New York by now. But no, you gotta get fancy. You gotta play the smart guy. And I listen." He smacked himself in the head. "Joey, do me a favor, don't fucking talk to me no more."

Joey shrugged and rowed. For a long time the only sound was the soft splash of the oars, a noise that was companionable and oddly domestic, like a cat lapping milk in the kitchen. Off in the east, in a colorless and utterly undramatic way, the sky was just barely beginning to lighten. Low stars were doused and two different shades of black were sandwiched at the horizon.

"Gino, man," Joey said at last, "I got, like, a suggestion I wanna make."

He paused, waiting to see if Gino would shut him up. He didn't. It was one thing to sulk, but with two guys in an eight-foot rowboat, silences could turn truly psychotic.

"So listen," Joey went on. "I realize maybe this isn't the best time to bring this up, I know you're a little upset and all. But Gino, I been thinkin'. I been thinkin' it would be a good thing if like you and me could just forgive each other."

Gino Delgatto looked at his half brother as if he'd never seen him before, as if he'd just that minute dropped from the sky and landed in the rowboat. "Fuck you talking about?"

Joey breathed deeply but kept rowing. "Gino, I just lost you a fortune. You were gonna be a big man, set for life, and I fucked it up for you. I could say I'm sorry, but you know what? I'm not sorry. I'm glad."

Gino stared at Joey. He had a thought to lunge forward and strangle him but was held back by stupefaction and the fear of falling overboard and drowning.

"All my life you been makin' me feel bad, Gino. It's like either you use me or ignore me. When I was a little kid, you didn't protect me, you lemme get beat up. When I dropped outta school—"

"Joey, what is this bullshit? We're gonna sit here inna middle of the fucking ocean and drag out grudges from a million years ago?"

"Not from a million years ago," said Joey. "From now. 'Cause it's never changed, Gino. You don't take me serious. I leave New York. Does it ever dawn on you to wonder how I'm doin', what I'm doin'? No. When *you* get involved in somethin' down heah, then you're innerested 'cause then you can use me. You can take it for granted that I'll drop everything to help you out. You see what I'm sayin', Gino? You don't treat me right, but you don't lemme get away either."

"You wanna get away, get away," said Gino. "Who's stoppin' ya?"

"Who am I chauffeurin' around inna fucking rowboat? But O.K., say I really do break away. Gino, my mother's dead. Your mother's a little old lady. Pop, you look at 'im close, he don't look great. He can still keep his tie straight and his shoulders back, but he's an old man. What happens when they're all dead, Gino? Are we still brothers then? Why, what for? Are we even gonna talk?"

"Sure we are, kid. Sure."

"I'm not so sure," said Joey. "Why should we? I'm not gonna run errands for you. I'm not gonna make you any money. That's over. And I know you, Gino. A guy doesn't do exactly what you want, right away he's disloyal, he's ungrateful, he's an enemy. So that's how you're gonna thinka me. And that's just gonna get me more pissed at you for all the time you held me down."

Gino slapped his knees so hard the rowboat bucked, and gave a grunt that mingled with a bitter laugh. "Joey, this is fucking rich. You drop tree million dollars a mine inna fucking water, now you try to make it sound like I'm inna fucking wrong and that's why it happened?"

"Gino, this is the whole point. I'm not talking right and I'm not talking wrong. I'm saying that what goes on between the two of us, the way we're always busting each other's balls, it's like a, whaddyacallit, a vicious cycle, circle, whatever, and the only way it's gonna stop is if we both stop. That's why I'm saying, hey, let it go, we gotta forgive each other."

Gino hesitated, maybe even wavered. Then he remembered the feel of the emeralds in his hand. They were solid, cool, he knew their price, he had a vivid idea of what they could have done for him. "Nah, Joey, save it. Ya sound like a goddamn priest. I'm pissed about the fucking stones. You wanna be pissed too, that's your business."

Joey looked down at the water. There was enough light now to blot out the phosphorescence streaming from the oars. He noticed suddenly that he'd raised blisters on both palms. "O.K.," he said, "I tried."

"And there you go again," razzed Gino, revving up for one more spasm of exasperation, "with that *I tried* bullshit. Joey, you're givin' me advice, lemme give you advice. No one gives a fuck *you tried*. Do something right, and do it to the end. Cut this bullshit with *I tried*. It just makes you look like a horse's ass."

Joey rowed in silence through the Sand Key Channel. By the first light of morning, the derelict marina was even more forlorn than it had been at night. Lizards darted in and out of the windows of the abandoned trailer. Pieces of forgotten boats lay stranded on the shore like dead animals. Joey Goldman and Gino Delgatto, their backs stiff and their feet wrinkled with wetness, climbed out of the twelve-dollar dinghy and left it to rot with the others. Then they stepped into Zack Davidson's skiff and motored off.

Beyond the dimness of the cove, the sun was already glaring across the water, going from orange to yellow and from warm to searing hot. It was not yet six-thirty.

Bert the Shirt was waiting at the bridge, standing against the early traffic of fishermen and truckers. A stickler for grooming, he was already shaved, his cheeks pink from freshly slapped-on bay rum, his white hair with its tinge of bronze still damp from the shower. He was wearing a sea-green pullover of knitted silk, and he had Don Giovanni in the crook of his arm. The chihuahua, rousted out of its velvet dog bed before the accustomed time, looked grouchy; its huge black eyes refused to open all the way, its whiskers hung down in a sour are. Vicki didn't look too chipper either. She'd dozed but hadn't slept, yanked back from the brink by visions of snakes and spiders and by the infernal buzzing of mosquitoes in her ears. Her thin blond hair was matted on one side and electrified on the other; her neck and forehead were dotted with bug bites as closely arrayed as chicken pox.

The goodbyes were brief, almost nonexistent. Nobody thanked anybody. Nobody apologized. Joey held the skiff against a bridge stanchion while Gino, his ribs on fire, slime on his clothes, dried blood matted in his hair, clambered up and out.

"Jesus, Gino," Vicki said to him, "they gonna let you onna plane like that?"

"Shut up, Vicki."

They climbed into Bert's car and slammed the doors behind them. Joey had almost forgotten there could be so dry a sound as a car door clicking shut.

He pushed off and headed for home. He suddenly realized he was exhausted. His hands were swollen, his eyes were crusty, and he'd forgotten to bring along his sunglasses. But all in all, he felt O.K. He'd gotten his brother out alive and thought he had a reasonable chance of keeping him that way. He didn't have the emeralds but he knew where the emeralds were. He figured he had enough of Gino's thousand

Part IV

37

He slept till four, and woke up feeling the dryness and dislocation that are the price of daytime sleep. His eyes itched, his arms hurt, he smelled his own sweat on the pillow. Gradually he remembered where he was: not just in Key West but in a Key West that was free of Gino. A pleasant place, an easy place, a place he had chosen for himself. He rolled over, stretched, and slowly started noticing things he'd been too nervous to notice for the past few put-upon weeks: the smell of the air that was sometimes dusty, sometimes flowery, depending on how humid it was and where the wind was coming from; the way the curtain fluttered over the louvered window, like the skirt of a woman walking. His eyes half open, he groped on the nightstand for his sunglasses.

He pulled on a bathing suit, threw a towel around his neck, and went outside. No one was around, and Joey jumped feet first into the pool. Waves rolled from his body, collided with the sides, and started back again, converging at a dozen angles like the roiled water over a coral reef. He threw himself backward and tried to float. For a few seconds the water held him; then, as if overburdened by the added weight of his doubt, it sagged and let him sink. One of these days, he told himself, he'd learn to swim. To live in Florida and not know how was crazy.

He toweled off and settled into a lounge chair under a palm tree. He was looking up absently through the interlaced fronds when Sandra came through the wooden gate of the compound. She was wearing a straight white skirt with a zipper on the side, white shoes with low heels, and a short-sleeved pink blouse whose shoulders stuck out an inch or two beyond her own. She walked with quick, compact steps around the hot tub and sat down next to Joey on the lounge—sat with her usual precision so that she was as close as she could be without putting her skirt against his wet bathing suit. "You're back," she said.

"Sure I'm back. You worried?"

"A little, yeah," she said. "It's been a long time since we spent a night apart, Joey. Besides, I'm always worried when you're with Gino." She reached out and touched Joey's hair, brushing it back from his forehead. Her fingertips felt good against his scalp, and he surprised himself by clutching her wrist and kissing it.

"Well, Gino's gone," he said. "He's back in New York by now."

Sandra said nothing, and Joey was grateful for her restraint. If she'd come out with too much relief, he would have had to take Gino's side somehow because he was family. That's just how it was. But she kept

still and looked down at the blue shimmer of the
pool.

"Yup," Joey resumed, "he's history. So, Sandra, now
I can start making good on some a the promises I
been making."

"Promises?" said Sandra. "You, Joey? You've been
making promises?"

"Yeah, ya know, like having friends and all, doing
stuff. I'm ready."

"Just like that?" said Sandra. "Ready for *what*,
exactly?"

"I don't know. Ya know, like life. Hey, what day is
it?"

"It's Thursday, Joey."

"Right. Well, like, on Saturday. Zack and Claire,
let's have 'em over to dinner. And Bert."

Sandra started to smile but could not help letting
a quick flinch tighten the corners of her mouth. Joey,
just then discovering the comfort of small affections,
put a cool hand on her knee.

"Sandra, hey, I know what you're thinking: Bert isn't
gonna fit in, it's gonna be, like, awkward. But ya know
what I think, Sandra? I think the more ya try to keep one
part of your life over heah, and another part over theah,
the more it doesn't work. I've tried it, believe me. You're
embarrassed, ya try to keep things separate, they just get
more bollixed up together. Ya can't go around feeling
like ya all the time gotta apologize for where ya came
from, who ya came from. Ya gotta, like, trust that people
are gonna adjust, adopt, adapt, whatever. Ya know, like
lighten up and get along."

Midway through dinner, Joey started yawning, and af-
terward, when he and Sandra made love, it had some

of the floating bafflement and tender discontinuity of
sex in dreams. He did not feel her slip out of bed to
straighten up the kitchen.

But by three A.M. he was all slept out. His eyes
popped open, and the moonlight filtering through the
curtains was more than bright enough to guide him
to the stove to put up coffee. He pulled on his bathrobe and took a cup out by the pool.

The night was just barely cool enough for the coffee to steam. Overhead, the palm fronds rustled
dryly; the sound was almost like brushes on a snare
drum. The closed flowers had lost their individual
perfumes and gave off a generic sweetness like that
of wet paper. Joey sipped from his mug and thought
about the last time he'd been out by the pool at
three A.M. It was only ten weeks or so ago. His
prospects had been zero and a sense of failure was
keeping him awake as stubbornly as a toothache.
He'd had no job and he was running out of money.
Sandra was getting fed up and the one person he
could talk to was a resurrected mafioso who talked
to his neurotic dog. He was trying to concoct a way
to pull a living out of Florida, and all he could think
of was baby alligators, suntan lotion, pencil sharpeners in the shape of oranges.

He shook his head and laughed softly into the
night. From baby alligators and pencil sharpeners to
real estate and emeralds. O.K., Joey admitted, he
wasn't home free yet, not every last piece was in
place. Still, at three A.M., everyone deserves the benefit of the doubt, and Joey indulged in the rare pleasure of paying himself a compliment. It was an
unusual compliment for Joey in that it was not
bullshit, it was not bragging, it was not meant to im-

press anybody. He took a sip of his coffee, put his head back against the hard webbing of the lounge, and basked in the belief that, for a kid from the neighborhood, he wasn't doing too bad down here in Florida.

38

At 8:55 A.M., which felt to Joey like the middle of the afternoon, he walked into the Parrot Beach sales office, wearing his pink shirt, his by now broken-in khaki shorts, and his confident watchband that told the world he frowned on flash. When Zack Davidson showed up a few minutes later, Joey handed him nine hundred and seventy-three dollars in cash. It was what was left from Gino's thousand after the rowboat and the nautical chart had been paid for.

For Zack, however, nine A.M. was not afternoon, it was first thing in the morning. His sandy hair was still damp from the shower, he hadn't even had his second cup of coffee, and he glanced down at the wad of bills as if they were a face that looked familiar, but only somewhat. "What's this about?"

"The little motor?" Joey said.

Zack tilted his head expectantly. Yes, he knew the little motor.

"I lost it."

Zack sat down in his desk chair and drummed his fingers on the blotter. He had a fair amount of experience with outboard engines. Many things went wrong with them. Their spark plugs got gummed up. Their water pumps crapped out. Their propellers fell off, their starter ropes came away in your hand, their shifters jammed so you could only go backward. Outboards were a plague, an affliction. But how did you lose one?

"You lost it," he said, plucking a dark thread from the sleeve of his pink shirt. It was not a question. He just needed to hear it in his own voice.

Joey nodded.

"I don't imagine you wanna tell me how it happened."

Joey shook his head. "Sometime maybe. Zack, I don't know what they cost. If that isn't enough . . ."

Zack waved away the offer. Nine hundred and seventy-three dollars was in fact more than the old motor was worth, less than a new one would cost— in that gray area where insurance adjusters quibble and gentlemen do not. "You get done what you needed to do?"

"Yeah, I did," said Joey, and though he hadn't meant to smile so soon after telling Zack of the loss of the motor, he couldn't help it.

Zack slipped into sales manager mode. It was something he could comfortably do while half asleep. "So the cockin' around is over? You're gonna get out there now and sell some goddamn real estate?"

"Bet your ass. Tons. But Zack, listen, Sandra and me, we'd like you and Claire to come over for dinner on Saturday night. Can ya do that?"

Zack hesitated just an instant, and Joey felt suddenly shy. A strange and basic thing, the courting stage of friendship. The offers of alliance and the gestures of warmth got passed back and forth like wampum. "Pretty sure we can," Zack said. He hoped it didn't sound like he was reserving himself an out. "Sounds real nice."

"Florida," said Joey. "Sounds like Florida. Grilling steaks. Eating outside with shorts on. How sweet it is, huh, Zack?"

Zack rubbed his reddish eyebrows, and Joey headed out, pausing for a second to contemplate the Parrot Beach scale model with its Saran Wrap pool and miniature residents on beach chairs. Boating, barbecues, company—his life was getting to where it could almost fit right in with that ideal of ease under sunny skies and Plexiglas.

At around eleven, with two commissions in the bag, Joey took a break and called Perretti's luncheonette on Astoria Boulevard in Queens. He could picture the old maroon phone booth at the back of the green-painted store, with the pebbled metal walls that were always cold to the touch and the accordion door that always fooled you about whether you should push or pull. Joey asked for Sal Giordano, but his buddy wasn't there. He said he would call back in a couple of hours, and if Sal came in, he should leave a number and a time he could be reached. This meant that Sal would organize his afternoon around getting down Northern Boulevard or over the Gowanus Bridge in a timely fashion, before rush hour if possible, and hoping that when he got there, his public telephone had not had its coin box chiseled out by a crack addict or its metal-sheathed wires yanked apart by an aggravated pa-tron who had lost his quarter.

When Joey called back at two he was given a num-ber where Sal could be reached at four, and when he called at four Sal picked up almost before the phone had rung. The first thing Joey heard sounded like the screaming whine of jet engines close enough to blow your hat off. "So Sal," he screamed, "you're at the Airline Diner?"

"Nah," Sal shouted. "Outside the Midtown Tunnel. That's buses. Airline Diner, some dumb fuck in a U-Haul backed up and crushed the booth. How the hell are you, man?"

"Good," yelled Joey, "real good. How are things up there?"

"Quiet," hollered Sal. "Makin' a living. With Gino gone, ya know, it's pretty much business as usual."

"Well," Joey hollered back, "Gino ain't gone no more. This is why I'm calling, Sal. He should be in New York by now."

There was a pause, and Joey heard a truck laboring through its gears as it lumbered out of the toll booth and started up the incline on the Queens side of the tunnel, the Empire State Building in its side-view mirrors. "He's back?" Sal shouted, and Joey had the feeling that maybe he was a little bit surprised that Gino was still alive. "What's with Ponte? What's with the stones?"

Joey was speaking from the far end of the lunch counter near the Parrot Beach office, the place where short-order cooks with shaved heads whipped up mango smoothies for young women in undershirts to suck through straws. This was not New York, where you couldn't even talk on your own phone for fear of being listened in on. This was Key West, where you could scream about gangsters and emeralds in a public place and no one bothered to turn around. "The stones are innee ocean," he shouted. "And Ponte, well, I'm like tryin' to work out a way to smooth things over with him."

"You?"

"Whaddya sound so fucking surprised for, Sal? Ya sound like my goddamn brother."

Sal waited for an ambulance to go careening past. "Hey, Joey man, don't get touchy. I didn't know you were involved, is all."

"Well, I am. Didn't wanna be, but there it is. But Sal, here's the thing. Right now I'm playing for some time. Ponte's goons, I don't think they know it yet that Gino slipped 'em. If they find out before I get things organized—"

Some jerk burned rubber coming out of the toll booth, and Sal Giordano interrupted through the screech. "Joey, whoa, I don't like the sounda this. I don't like you fucking with these guys."

"Sal, man, who's fucking? I'm just tryin' to straighten things out. You worry too much."

Sal considered this. He was a street guy from New York; of course he worried. "O.K., Joey, maybe you're right, maybe I do. But maybe you worry too little. Warm weather, sunshine—maybe it's makin' you calmer than is good for you."

Joey yanked his mind away from that possibility like a hand from a hot stove. "Sal, listen, right now there's nothin' I can do but what I'm doin'. So do me a favor. If Gino's dumb enough to show his face up there, tell him to hide it again. Can ya do that for me?"

"Sure, kid, sure." Joey didn't like the flat way he said it.

"And if he starts tellin' ya how brave and clever he was down here, don't believe a fucking word."

Sal laughed over the roar of an ancient Pontiac without a muffler. "I haven't for years," he screamed.

"Well, you're smarter than I am, Sal. Me, I only caught on inna last coupla weeks. How's my old man doing?"

There was a pause, and Joey could picture Sal shrugging, the way some of the flesh of his thick neck crinkled up and almost touched his earlobes. "Doin' O.K. He's under some strain, but hey, he's used to that."

"Tell him I said hello."

"O.K."

"Ya know, Sal, I been thinking. The way I left without seeing him, that was wrong. It was, like, small. You can tell him I said that if you want to. Or I'll talk to him myself one a these days."

Joey's friend said nothing. A cement mixer came galumphing into Queens. At the Key West lunch counter, a cook dropped a scoopful of shrimp salad into the hollow of an avocado.

"And what about you, Sal?" Joey resumed. "When you gonna get your pale ass down here?"

"One a these days," Sal said. It was that flat tone again, the tone that neighborhood guys used with people they couldn't protect, and Joey tried not to notice that it scared him.

"Those sunglasses ya gave me, Sal, I wear 'em every day."

"Every day?" shouted Sal. He sounded skeptical. "How' bout when it rains?"

"It don't, Sal. This is what I'm tellin' ya. It's fucking unbelievable down here."

39

Saturday evening was particularly warm, with a yellow sky smeared with wisps of unmoving purple cloud. Steve the naked landlord, his ashtrays and his beers in front of him, his shriveled genitals nested under the cliff of his belly, lingered especially late in the pool. He was standing there bare-assed when Zack and Claire arrived, and Joey had no choice but to introduce him.

"Hi, Steve," Zack said. "Whatcha reading?"

Steve turned the damp paperback over and looked at the cover to remind himself. The cover showed a large city breaking in half. "Earthquake," he said. "Los Angeles." Then he smiled.

Joey steered his guests toward a big bowl of raw vegetables on the outdoor table, and as he did so he studied Claire. Claire did not look like Joey expected. She was pretty enough, with tightly curled brown hair and hazel eyes, but she didn't have Zack's knack of looking just so without seeming to be trying. She appeared to be the type for whom blouses would not stay tucked in, for whom tabs on zippers would not lie flat. When she dressed up, the effort showed, kind of like a painting that had looked better as a sketch.

She plunged a celery stalk into a bowl of dip, and Joey watched with interest because he'd voted against the vegetables. "Sandra," he'd said, "isn't it a little much? I mean, we're gonna have that gigantic salad and all."

"Joey," she'd said, "women like that stuff. Just pour the drinks, grill the steaks, and let me plan the rest, O.K.?"

He'd shrugged. Giving a dinner party, like having a job, like reading a nautical chart, had its own rules, its own logic. If women liked raw vegetables on top of raw salad on top of cooked broccoli on top of melon balls for dessert, so be it.

Sandra had also lobbied for some dishes and some silverware that matched.

"It's a waste, Sandra. We're moving soon."

That was the first she'd heard about moving, and Joey let it slip as casually as if he'd said he was going out to gas up the car. Sandra didn't believe it, and besides, she hadn't had time to make it a discussion just then. "So we'll take them with us," she said. Practical, precise, and forward-looking as always, she added, "I'll save the boxes."

Again Joey had shrugged, and Sandra bought a set of plain white plates and some stainless with blue plastic handles. The matching stuff did make the table look better. Joey had to admit it.

Now he was asking Zack and Claire what they wanted to drink. They both said wine, and Joey wondered why he'd bothered buying all those different-shaped bottles of liquor.

When Bert the Shirt arrived, the two couples were sitting on the edges of lounge chairs, Claire with her feet dangling in the pool. The sky had faded, the palm fronds were drooping limp as flags. From halfway down the gravel path, Bert was motioning to Joey that he shouldn't bother getting up.

He looked splendid, Bert did. His white hair was combed back tight, and aside from the nicotine-bronze tinge in it, there was almost, in the dimming light, a suggestion of pink. His shirt was the purplish black of ripe olives, with bone buttons and pale blue piping the same color as the monogram. He held his chihuahua in the crook of his arm, and gave a stately little nod of his head when Joey introduced him.

Claire, a lover of all small animals, reached up to pet the pooch. "What a cute little dog," she said.

"He's not cute," said Bert the Shirt. "He looks ridiculous, he's a hypochondriac, and he's got a lousy—"

"Don Giovanni?" came a caressing voice from the far side of the pool. "He's *very* cute." The voice was Claude's. He and Peter had just emerged from their cottage. It was Dress-Up Night at Cheeks, and the bartenders wore lamé. Peter's was silver, Claude's was gold.

"Oh, hi, fellas," said Bert. "Youse look terrific." Then he turned his attention back to Claire and back to the subject of the chihuahua. "This dog," he said, "this dog is the bane a my life, a stone around my neck. Joey, I tell ya the latest about this dog? The latest aggravation? Dog needs sunglasses."

"Come on," said Joey.

"Yeah," said Bert. He held the chihuahua forward like a loaf of bread. "His eyes heah? The whaddya-callit, the pupils, they don't close right. See all that black? That shouldn't be. The light shoots straight inta his brain. He needs shades, I'm tellin' ya."

"Maybe a visor?" offered Zack.

Bert shrugged. "What the hell, I just keep him dim places. He don't like the heat anyway. Heat like de-hydrates him, gives him kidney stones. The way he whimpers when he passes one . . ." Bert shuddered. "But hey, enough about the stupid dog. Joey, you gonna gimme a glassa wine or what?"

Joey stalled an extra few seconds getting the Shirt his drink. He wasn't used to parties, to so many people at once, so much to figure out. It made him a little dizzy.

When he came back, he noticed something different about Sandra. She was smiling a more thorough smile than he usually saw. Her green eyes crinkled at the corners, it was like enjoyment was seeping in everywhere. It seemed to Joey that she had never looked prettier or happier. She had friends, vegetables, plates that matched; the man she loved was not off doing something shady or dangerous; she was at ease.

Joey studied. He wanted to see how people acted at a dinner party, what they talked about, if there was a code for what you did or didn't say. The women talked about the bank, about some new system for closing out the cash count at the end of the day. Zack asked Bert about the Paradiso; he was interested in the real estate angle.

There was a sound of cascading water as Steve the naked landlord got out of the pool. People tried not to notice the flash of crotch before he wrapped his towel around him and said goodnight. Joey went inside to fetch more drinks.

When he returned, Bert was holding forth about the old days in New York. "Fifty-second Street," he was saying. "The jazz clubs. Beautiful. Three, four inna morning you could walk downa street. There was no drugs, no crime. It was perfectly safe."

As if conjured up by the mention of music, Luke the reggae player at that moment stepped out of his front door. He'd put his hair in dreadlocks, and his guitar was strapped across his back. Lucy the beautiful Fed followed him out. She'd done her eyes up big and looked like Cleopatra.

After they had passed, Claire said, "Jeez, you guys live, like, an interesting lifestyle here."

Joey hadn't thought about it quite that way before, but now that she mentioned it, he supposed they did. Very Key West. Extremely Key West. Feeling proud, he got up and lit the gas grill, then took a moment to look at the first star that had popped through the deepening sky. He filled glasses one more time, then went to the kitchen for the mountain of steaks.

Zack Davidson, who knew the protocol of cookouts, joined him at the grill. It was part of a guest's responsibility, part of the ceremony, this manly convocation around the fire and the meat. "This is nice," Zack said, with a small but enveloping gesture that took in the compound, the weather, the heavens.

Joey nodded. "Nice we're getting together outsida work."

"Away from Duval Street. The fucking zoo."

Joey stabbed a filet mignon, slapped it onto the grill, then realized, a beat later than a more practiced host would have, that he now had the opportunity he

was waiting for, the opening that the whole evening
had been set up to afford. It was strange, he reflected.
He used to imagine that crime was easy and legitimate enterprise was hard. But just the opposite was
true, because the whole world was set up to thwart
the one and lubricate the other. Joey used to have to
slip twenties, sometimes hundreds, to limping cross-
eyed numbers runners from Catholic school to set up
meetings that might advance his criminal career; but
here in the legit world such meetings simply happened, around the barbecue, around the table, even,
no doubt, around urinals at the office.

"Zack," he said, above the companionable crackle
of burning fat, "I wantcha to know I really appreciate
the way ya hung in there with me when I had, ya
know, this personal bullshit that needed taking care
of."

Zack waved the gratitude away, but Joey continued
without a pause.

"And I remember you promised that you'd let me
make it up to ya."

Zack said nothing, as if he assumed that Joey meant
the dinner party was by way of thank-you.

Joey fiddled with the steaks. "So Zack, I'd like to
give you a quarter-million dollars."

Zack was swallowing some wine, and he took an
extra second to make sure it went down. Joey did not
sound like he was kidding. He did not sound like he
was drunk. Zack couldn't even stammer, but just
stood there with his throat closed tight, Valpolicella
pooling on either side of the constriction.

"There's just one more little thing I need you to do
for me," Joey resumed, "and if that works out, we're
in."

Zack still could not speak, and there was growing in him the heady and not totally unpleasant conviction that whatever Joey was talking about, it could not possibly be legal. The odd satisfaction Zack took from this made him wonder if maybe *he* was drunk; it made him wonder, too, if maybe he'd known all along that Joey was a desperado, and if it was this whiff of the outlaw that had drawn Zack to him.

"You're serious?" Zack choked out at last.

"Serious as diabetes," said Joey.

"Wha'do I gotta do?" As Joey had been groping for a toehold in normalcy, so Zack in that moment was getting on terms with the possibility of crime, and it was as if the boundary between their two positions was nothing more dramatic than a faint chalk line dabbed on rotting boards.

Joey poked a filet. "Set up a meeting with Clem Sanders and, ya know, sort of ease the way with him."

Zack shifted his feet, looked up at the sky. He was relieved yet somehow let down that he was not being asked to drive a getaway car or carry a satchel through a border check. "That's all?"

Joey flipped a steak, admired the grill lines etched across it, and nodded.

"Joey," said Zack, "I talk to Clem all the time. You don't have to pay me to talk to Clem."

"This is business."

Zack sipped some wine and found himself at a loss once more. Unlike Joey, he was unaccustomed to feeling out of his depth. He didn't improvise as well, couldn't fall in with a new cadence quite as readily.

Joey peeked at the underside of a filet, then looked toward the little group sitting by the pool. Bert, he noticed, had given Claire the high honor of holding

Don Giovanni in her lap. "Sandra," Joey hollered over, "you ready with the salad and the broccoli?"

She waved yes, and jogged with her small neat steps toward the kitchen.

Zack cleared his throat. "This thing you wanna talk to Clem about," he said. "Is it, ya know, against the law?"

"I'm not really sure," said Joey, heaping the steaks onto the platter. Zack could only admire his blitheness, his certainty that it was not worth overcooking a filet mignon to discuss a mere question of legality. "That's one of the things we have to talk to him about."

Zack nodded, and Sandra bustled by with a salad bowl you could've bathed a baby in. Then she made a second pass with an avalanche of broccoli. Joey turned off the grill. "So you'll do it?" he said to Zack.

"Sure," Zack said. "But it's really not worth—"

Joey dropped his voice another notch to cut him off. "And lemme ask ya one more thing, while we're here, ya know, the two of us. In your experience with women, are they all such nuts about salad, about vegetables?"

40

"I get half," said Clem Sanders.

It was Monday lunchtime, and they were sitting in his office at the Treasure Museum. The office was a big room with barred windows, lined with glass display cases filled with old coins, ancient jewelry, corroded pistols, pieces of silver robbed of their luster and fused together by salt water and time so that they resembled crude models of the atom. Behind Clem Sanders's chair was a wall covered with photographs of himself outsmiling various dignitaries and local celebrities, none of whom Joey recognized.

"Come on, Clem," said Zack Davidson, "take a quarter. It's not like you really have to go hunting. Joey here can pretty much pinpoint the spot for you."

Sanders folded his hands as if in prayer and cocked his head at the sympathetic angle an undertaker or a southern politician strikes when he is about to tell you he wishes to God there were more he could do for you, but there isn't. His face was deeply lined and seemed sunburned right down to the bone, just slightly redder than the color of dark-meat chicken. The pigment seemed to have been bleached out of his blue eyes, leaving them pale as hospital paint. He wore a green jumpsuit open at the neck, and nestled in his gray chest hair was a Spanish doubloon on a leather string. His hands were huge and crinkled, his voice a honeyed drawl fashioned for coaxing funds out of greedy but skeptical investors. " 'Taint the huntin' that's involved," he said gently. "It's the precedent."

Joey spoke not to him but to Zack. "It's too much. I wanted to keep it local, but we're gonna hafta shop it in Miami."

He started to rise, and as he did so, the neatly rolled nautical chart that had been laid across his lap rustled with a crisp sound like new-printed money. Clem Sanders could not pull his eyes away from the precious tube of paper. He squinted as if trying to pierce it with his gaze, to locate the treasure that, in his view and under the law, was as much his as anybody else's. "Now hol' on a minute," he purred. "I didn't say we couldn't negotiate."

"So negotiate," said Joey. He sat back down but stayed near the edge of the seat.

Sanders tugged absently at the doubloon around his neck. "If it's like you say, if you've got the location, then I s'pose I could live with sixty-forty."

Joey frowned. "Clem, you know what I do for a living, right? I stand out onna street corner and I give people a pitch to go see Parrot Beach. One a the things I tell 'em, I say, *free passes to the Treasure*

Museum, Clem Sanders, greatest treasure hunter of all time."

"Thank you kindly."

"Yeah, well, I'm not sayin' I believe it, I'm sayin' it's parta my pitch. But hey, if it's true, it's gonna take you half a day to do this job. Maybe less. Are you gonna tell me you won't take a million dollars for three, four hours' work? I'm willing to cut you in for a third, no more."

Sanders looked at the ceiling, then exhaled past lips that were permanently cracked and crevassed by the sun. He glanced at Zack, fingered his doubloon, then lightly slapped his desk. "Shoot—why not? You got a deal."

Now, Joey had been an observer at certain low-level sit-downs in New York. The people running those meetings had been observers at midlevel sit-downs, and the people running the midlevel gatherings had been present at certain congresses of the big boys. What filtered down from the top was a style based on rigorous restraint. One did not show emotion at the striking of a bargain. It was unmanly to smile, dangerous to gloat. So Joey kept his face and voice as neutral as he could.

"Good," he said, watching light stream through the barred windows of the treasure room. "Now there's just a couple other things. We're partners, I'm gonna be totally up front, 'cause I don't want any headaches after. These emeralds, the way they got there, it's not, like, totally—"

Clem Sanders held an enormous pink palm in Joey's face as if fending off the evil eye or some terrible contagion, and at the same time he let out a deep defensive noise: *Bup, bup, bup, BUPPPP.*

"Hol' on," he said. "I don' need to know, I don' wanna know, and besides, hit don't make no difference. No difference a'tall."

"None?" asked Zack, with a lifted eyebrow. Still hovering between salesmanship and crime, his voice hinted at a secret disappointment that he wasn't well on his way to outlawhood.

"None," purred Clem. "By law. The ocean, gents, it's like a baptism. Cleans away everything. Old secrets, old errors, old sins. All gone. Stick somethin' in the ocean"—he cupped his hands, then slowly lifted them in a sacramental gesture as of rising from murky depths into the virginal light of day—"it comes out reborn."

At this, despite his best efforts to remain becomingly stone-faced, Joey could not help smiling. Innocent emeralds. Free of the taint of Gino. Cleansed of the reek of Mount Trashmore. Redeemed from the horror of fleeing rodents and the threat of getting whacked. Or so he needed to believe.

"That's terrific," Joey said. "But listen. You don't wanna know the reasons why, that's fine. But ya gotta understand it's very important that everything is out innee open heah. Ya know, like public, so people can see it's onnee up and up."

Now it was Clem Sanders's turn to blow the stoic act. He grinned and in fact could not help chuckling. Not for nothing was he widely regarded as Key West's most undaunted self-promoter. "Son," he said, "this is gonna be the most public damn thing you ever saw. Everything I *do* is public. First off, if I'm goin' out, I call the papers, tease 'em along. Then I get the cable people. Plus I got friends at the networks. They'll send crews down from Miami

'cause they know I'll deliver, I'll come cruisin' in in
time for the midday news, twelve o'clock local edi-
tion. If there's a find, I radio right away, the coast
guard sends boats, sometimes helicopters, guardian
angels like, to hover over us. Every cop in Key West
meets us at the dock. City cops. County cops. State
cops. Marine cops. Fuckin' IRS is there. The mayor
shows up to get his picture taken with me. Then we
all hop into armored cars and ride in a televised
motorcade straight into the bank vault. That public
enough for you?"

Joey nodded, savoring a moment of perfect contentment as he imagined Charlie Ponte's thugs, their
almost matching blue suits soaked with sweat, their
hemorrhoids on fire from endless weeks of sitting in
the car, leaning against the hoods of their Lincolns
and watching helplessly as an army of police brought
their boss's emeralds to the bank.

"Sounds fine," he said. "But me, ya know, I wanna
be left out of the public part."

Sanders gave a worldly shrug. He'd seen it all.
Some people craved the spotlight, some had compelling reasons for staying out of sight. "We can set it up
any way you like. Basically, it's a legal partnership.
With shares. You pay in a certain amount to under-
write the costs, then you get your split. I'll retain a
third, the rest is up to you."

"And the costs?" Zack Davidson asked.

Clem Sanders toyed with his doubloon and picked
an easy number. "If it's as quick and dirty as you say,
call it fifteen thousand. Five thou a share up front."

Joey had already decided. "Fine. I want it one third
in Zack's name and one third in my brother's. Gino
Delgatto."

The world's greatest treasure hunter smiled past cracked lips. "I'll have the papers drawn up." His bleached eyes had once again become glued to the tube of paper on Joey's lap.

"How long does it take?" asked Joey.

"The papers?" said Sanders. "About a week."

"No good," said Joey. Ponte's goons might be dumb, but how much longer would they stake out a hotel that Gino had already escaped from? "How 'bout you get the stones tomorrow?"

Sanders let out a slow whistle. Young guys, northerners especially, always seemed in such a hurry. Sanders usually was not. Most of the stuff he went after had been lying on the bottom of the ocean for two, three hundred years—what was the rush? "We are hot to trot, ain't we?"

"Yeah, we are," said Joey. "By noon tomorrow—yes or no?"

Sanders cocked his head, toyed with his doubloon. "Well, the boats are ready, I can raise a crew. I s'pose we could go out tomorrow, weather permitting. But you know, boys, nothing happens till I get the ten thousand for two thirds of the shares."

"No problem," said Joey, and Zack could not help flashing him the kind of look that partners in a negotiation should not flash each other while talks are under way. "Get the papers drawn up, I'll be back with the cash in a coupla hours."

"Cash," said Sanders. The word brought forth a most benevolent expression. "O.K. Dawn tomorrow, calm seas, we hunt."

Joey and Zack got up to leave. Sanders pointed to the rolled-up nautical chart in Joey's hand.

"May as well leave that here so's I can study up," he said.

Joey sent back a smile every bit as trustworthy as the treasure hunter's own. "Study it later, Clem. After the papers are signed."

41

Hot April sunshine poured in through the open top of the old Caddy, shafts of it splattering into rainbows as they sliced through the facets of the spiderweb windshield. Joey was buoyant as he drove away from Clem Sanders's office and out toward the weird migrant sand of Smathers Beach. He gingerly fondled his hot steering wheel, he tapped his left foot as he drove. He felt like he finally had the different pieces of his life perfectly lined up. The new part, the Florida part, that was right where it should be: he was wheeling and dealing in a way that fit the climate, he was about to pull his fortune, or at least the start of it, out of the water. The old part, the neighborhood part, well, he was on his way to dip one last time into its deep pockets and to use the proceeds to put it behind him once and for all.

The legit world—Joey Goldman thought as he turned onto A1A and wove through its wobbly traffic of bicycles and mopeds—it really had its advantages. Like the way it was so neatly set up to lubricate the making of money, like how easily guys with angles on the right side of the chalk line could operate. Still, the old neighborhood way had its advantages too. For instance, in the borrowing of funds. In the neighborhood way, you didn't fill out forms, you didn't mortgage your house, you didn't wait. You told someone what you needed, and either he peeled off the bills or he told you forget about it. But Bert wouldn't tell him forget about it. Of this Joey was sure. He was on a salesman's roll and no one was going to say no to him.

He drove through the gate of the Paradiso condominium like he owned a triplex there. He looked for his friend around the pool, he looked for him in the screened gazebo where the old men played gin. Only as an afterthought did it occur to Joey that maybe Bert was in his apartment. In Key West on a sunny afternoon, you just didn't expect to find anyone inside.

But sure enough the old mafioso was at home. He came to the door dressed in a subdued shirt of maroon silk, no piping, no monogram, and it took Joey a few seconds to realize it was pajamas. "Hey, Bert, you O.K.?"

"Whaddya mean? I'm fine. Guy can't stay in his fucking apartment without it's, like, a problem? Dog ain't feelin' so great, is all. Come on in."

He led the way under a crystal chandelier and into a living room that had too much furniture and too little blank space. The place seemed like an old lady still lived there. There were clocks on pedestals, lamps like statues. The drapes had loops in them so you couldn't tell if they slid sideways or up and down.

Don Giovanni's dog bed was a kingly purple velvet, and it lay on the carpet next to Bert's well-rubbed recliner. Bert sat, motioning Joey onto a brocade sofa, and Joey wasted no time on chitchat.

"Ten grand," he said. "In a week, maybe less, I'll give ya back fifteen."

Bert did one of his better pauses, his eyes exploring the edges of the room, his soft mouth flubbering around between amusement and offense. When he finally spoke, it wasn't to Joey but to the dog. "You hear this, Giovanni? At my age, now he's makin' me a fucking shylock. Joey, what is this bullshit? I lend ya ten, ya gimme back ten."

"Bert, hey, this is business."

"For you maybe. Me, I ain't got no business, and I don't want any."

Joey tried a different tack, a tack that made him smile in spite of himself. "Bert, what the fuck, the money that comes back is gonna be Gino's money anyway."

The old man rubbed the arms of his chair and checked to see that his dog was still in place. "You wanna explain that?"

"Not now. I ain't got time."

Bert sighed. Then he spilled himself out of the recliner and walked toward the bedroom. Don Giovanni struggled up out of the velvet bed and followed. The dog was brittle, its knees were shot; it bounced along like a car with no shocks. Joey saw Bert walk around a neatly made bed covered with a fancy gold and white spread. He came back with a bundle of hundreds thick as a steak and handed it to Joey. "Here ya go, kid," he said. "Give it back when ya can."

Joey took the money and flushed. Bert's trust excited him and he could barely squeeze out a thank-you.

The old man stood over him and waved away the attempt. "The money, kid, fuck the money, it's nothin', it's shit. I ain't worried about the money. But I gotta tell ya, Joey, I'm a little worried about you. Ya sure ya know what you're doin' heah?"

Joey was sitting on the very edge of the brocade sofa, his shins against a marble coffee table. He was leaning forward, and he was pumped with a heat that the Paradiso's central air-conditioning couldn't quite siphon off. He didn't want to hear about Bert's concern, just like he hadn't wanted to hear about Sal's. They meant well, sure, but what good did it do? "Bert, listen," he said, "I appreciate—"

"Ya know what worries me?" Bert interrupted. "It's like in a checkers game, a guy gets so fuckin' happy he sees a chance to double-jump that he don't notice he's gonna get triple-jumped right back. Ya hear what I'm sayin', Joey? You're a little too happy as far as I'm concerned."

Joey's head suddenly felt very heavy, and for a couple of seconds he let it dangle buzzardlike between his shoulders. "Bert, what can I tell ya? I've thought this through the best I can."

The old man went back to his recliner, but didn't settle in, just perched on the front of it. The dog went back to its velvet bed and collapsed, exhausted from its jaunt to the bedroom. "Okay, Joey, okay. But listen, there's somethin' you oughta know. Maybe it means somethin', maybe it don't. I went by the Flagler House last night for sunset. No Lincolns."

Joey pursed his lips and tried to figure out if he was

surprised to hear this. Usually when something went wrong, he more or less expected it. "You sure?"

Bert stroked the soft placket of his pajama top. "I watched for half, three quarters of an hour. They're gone, Joey."

Joey said nothing, and Bert went on as if thinking aloud. "They gotta know by now that Gino got away. It's been, what, four days, five?"

Joey propped his elbows on his knees and looked around for an empty place where he could rest his eyes and think. But everywhere he looked, there was a candy dish, a figurine, a souvenir ashtray. "Maybe this means, like, they're backin' off."

"Could be," said Bert. The comment wasn't meant to be convincing.

Joey looked down at the marble coffee table. The grain running through it reminded him of bloodshot eyes. "I mean," he said, "they probably went up to Miami, ya know, to sit down and decide their next move."

Bert folded his hands.

"Or maybe they flew to New York. I mean, they'd figure that's where Gino was."

Bert shrugged.

"You know what, Bert?" Joey said, "I just can't fucking worry about it." His nerves rather than his muscles propelled him to his feet, and he stood with his shins against the marble table. "I mean, I'm so goddamn close to having this bullshit solved. I gotta do like I'm doin', and after that, what happens, happens. Am I right?"

Bert the Shirt reached down and petted his exhausted dog. "You're right, Joey, you're right. What happens, happens. Who can argue?"

42

"Hi, Steve," Joey said. "Whatcha reading?"

After leaving Bert, he'd driven back to the Parrot Beach office. He'd picked up Zack, who was duly titillated when he saw the illicit-looking stack of hundreds. Together, they'd returned to the Treasure Museum to sign papers. Smiling like a senator, Clem Sanders accepted the cash and the nautical chart. He was on the phone to the media before his two young partners had made it through the door.

It had been blisteringly hot downtown, asphalt softening and harsh light glinting painfully off tin roofs. Doing business in this weather was a sweaty affair and stank of nerves; driving around in the mufflerless Eldorado entailed a lot of grit, noise, and the reek of half-combusted gasoline. After the errands, the compound had never seemed more of a haven. It was quiet. It smelled good. The greenery ate up the worst of the heat. Steve the naked landlord stood waist-deep in the cool water, a monument to ease. He was on his fourth beer, his ashtray was full, his second pack of cigarettes lay crumpled on the wet blue tiles. He glanced up at Joey, then turned his paperback over to remind himself what he'd been reading. The cover showed a big black car and some guys with guns giving off red flashes for bullets. "Mafia," said Steve. "Rubouts." Then he smiled.

Joey smiled back.

Then Steve added, "Oh, your friends from Miami are here. I let 'em in." He waited a beat and smiled again.

"Friends from Miami?" said Joey.

The words seemed to rise up like a puff of steam. Then they solidified and took on a sickening weight, and Joey ran out from under them as one would from a falling rock. He skirted the pool, skidded on the tiles, and reached for the sliding door of his cottage, knowing in that moment that everything was over, everything was fucked, he'd come up short as usual, he'd blown it, the old neighborhood was not about to let him get away, and he'd been a loser and a fool ever to imagine for an instant that it might be otherwise.

He yanked open the door. He saw no one, heard nothing, only vaguely noticed that the bungalow was darker than usual. It was darker because Charlie Ponte's thugs had closed the louvered windows in the Florida room, and they had closed the louvered windows because that's where they were keeping Sandra.

They had her tied up in a chair.

Her ankles were bound with a dirty gray rope. Big loops of a different line ran around her midriff and her arms and kept her pinned back in her seat. She was wearing her work clothes, a neat cream-colored skirt and a plain beige blouse, and across her mouth was a wide piece of shiny silver duct tape, frayed where it had been torn from the roll. Her short blond hair, usually faultless, was frazzled now, clumps of it hanging onto her forehead. She looked up at Joey, and in her pale green eyes there was terror but no blame, rather a kind of silent, desperate wisecrack—*You spring this on me now? Just when things are going right for me?*—and it raced through Joey's mind that what he and Sandra really shared were their crazy gropings toward optimism and their ability to meet disaster, if not with courage exactly, then at least with a lack of complaint and a lack of surprise. Ponte's thugs did not prevent Joey from going to Sandra and putting his arm around her. The only thing she could move was her face. She turned it into his stomach, and only then did she start to cry. The tears went right through Joey's shirt.

"Hello, shitbird," said one of the thugs. It was Tony, the short one with the scarred lip and the bad toupee, the one who'd been squeamish about splattering a dog. But now he was holding a gun on Sandra and seemed to feel no discomfort at all. "We had a really shitty few weeks 'causa you, scumbag. We ain't in a good mood."

Joey squeezed the knob of Sandra's shoulder and reminded himself how slight she was inside her oversized shirt.

"Stop hangin' on to your girlfriend, faggot," said the other thug. It was Bruno, the huge one who liked to rip things apart. He was standing in the dimness between a bad painting of birds and a bad painting of seashells. He'd taken off his blue suit jacket and he looked even bigger without it. "Come ova heah," he said, pointing down at the sisal rug.

Joey went. He knew the rituals. He knew he was going to get hit, he just wondered whether it would be face or gut. His blood turned thin and sour and he stood at loose attention like a tired soldier. Bruno took a moment to size him up, then slugged him in the belly. Joey doubled over, his empty chest folded down across his trembling thighs. His eyes were open but everything was black, with streaks of phosphorescent green. He thought he heard a little shriek but couldn't tell if it was Sandra giving a sympathetic wince through her duct tape, or his own wheezing as he struggled for air. Before he could straighten up, Bruno grabbed him by the head and pushed him backward onto the settee. "Where's your fucking brother?" he asked.

Joey couldn't answer because he couldn't breathe. He tried to use the time to think, but he found he couldn't do that either. "Fuck should I know?" he finally managed.

"You helped him get away, ya little cocksucker," Tony said.

"I don't know nothin' about it," Joey said.

There was a pause. The two thugs looked at each other. Sandra squirmed. Outside, there was a splash from the pool. The motor of the hot tub clicked on and hummed. The easy life of Florida was proceeding. Tony reached slowly into his jacket pocket and pulled out a silencer. Very deliberately, he fitted it onto the muzzle of his gun.

"You and your girlfriend, kid," said Tony. "You're nine-tenths dead."

He leaned over Sandra and tucked the gun under

her chin, pushing it into the soft place between her jawbone and her throat. Her head was rigid against the back of her chair and she tried not to go cross-eyed staring down at the threatening hand.

"Don't fucking touch her," Joey said. He found himself getting to his feet.

"Ain't he brave?" said Bruno. As he said it, he bashed Joey across the ribs with his forearm. Joey's chest rattled, his heart seemed to shake off some juice, like a thrown sponge. He sat back down.

"Mr. Ponte wants his emeralds," Tony said. He hadn't moved the gun away from Sandra's chin. His finger was on the trigger and he didn't seem to be paying very close attention to whether or not he was squeezing. "He's tired of waiting and he's tired of being dicked around by little shitasses like you."

Joey looked at Sandra and suddenly he wanted to cry. It was less out of fear than out of frustration and remorse. He wanted to crawl across the floor and tell Sandra he was sorry. Sorry he'd taken her away from Queens, sorry he couldn't really take her away from Queens, sorry that Queens seemed to inhabit his life like a virus.

"So where's the fucking stones, kid?" Tony went on.

Joey said nothing. Bruno leaned down and smacked him hard with the back of his hand. The pain went from Joey's cheek to his gums, then lodged behind his eardrum.

"Kid," the shorter goon resumed, "I gotta tell ya somethin', no offense. Your brother Gino, he's a cunt. He's a dumb twat who don't know what he's doin'."

"You hear me disagreeing?" Joey said.

"Then why the fuck are you protecting him?"

"I'm not."

Tony seemed to consider this. The effort made him cranky, and he tapped the silencer against the underside of Sandra's chin. It made a morbid sound, not quite a slap and not quite a click. A vein was pulsing in Sandra's neck. "Awright, kid, you're not protecting your brother. So maybe you'd like to protect your pretty little girlfriend heah." He pulled back the hammer. "I'm gonna ask ya one more time: Where's the fucking emeralds?" He was dimpling Sandra's neck with the gun.

"They're innee ocean," Joey heard himself say.

Tony and Bruno consulted with their eyes. They didn't seem to like the answer. It struck them as an insult and a lie.

Bruno bent down and stuck his face in Joey's. His eyes were like puddles of oil and his breath smelled of old seafood. He butted Joey's forehead with his own, and Joey's skull rang like a Chinese gong. The shock wave ran from the bridge of his nose to the top of his spine and back again, it felt like his brain was being sliced with a serrated knife. But the thing about pain is that beyond a certain point it stays the same, it lodges just this side of insanity, and the thing about fear is that after a while a person's terror glands get all wrung out, and panic levels off to a kind of jungle alertness. Through his dizziness, Joey felt the old lunatic readiness returning, felt it filling him the way air pumps up a tire.

He heard Tony saying, "I cannot believe you are still givin' us bullshit."

"It isn't bullshit."

Tony ignored him. "We could blow you away right heah. We could take you to the gahbidge. We can do anything. You know that, right?"

Joey nodded. He grew up with it, he knew it. "Wha' does it getcha?"

Bruno bent low and hissed in his face. "Satisfaction."

"Four million dollars' worth?"

"Fuck you talkin' about?" said Tony.

Joey just sat. If he knew anything about staying alive, it was that your chances were better if you made people curious.

"Fuck you talkin', four million?" Tony pressed. Absently, he moved the gun an inch or two from Sandra's throat. It was enough space for idiot hope to inhabit.

"I'll tell Mr. Ponte all about it," Joey said.

The remark offended Bruno, who reached down and pressed his thumbs hard on the soft place under Joey's collarbones. A sharp pain arced down clear to the bottom of his lungs. "You ain't in no position to tell Mr. Ponte nothin'. Got that?"

Joey stayed silent and the silence caromed off the walls. Outside, there were water sounds, breeze sounds. Out there the air was the temperature of skin, and life, sweet life, felt good.

Tony and Bruno consulted with their eyes again. Bruno scratched an armpit. "We could bring 'em to Miami," he said. "We gotta ice 'em, we could ice 'em just as good up there."

Tony frowned, his scarred lip puckered. "But if the stones are down heah . . ."

Another pause. Joey tried to decide if saying something more would get him slugged again. He tried to decide if it mattered if he got slugged again.

"Guys," he ventured, "I'm telling you, I got a way to work this out. Whyn't ya call Mr. Ponte? Tell 'im if he'll come down heah, he'll see his stones tomorrow."

Tony and Bruno locked eyes. Then, oddly, Bruno broke into a crooked and horrific smile. "No phone," he said. "I yanked it outta the wall."

"Little, like, precaution," said Tony.

Joey pointed out toward the compound. "So use a different phone. We'll borrow one."

Bruno and Tony considered.

"Look," Joey said, "the naked guy, the landlord, you told 'im you were friends a mine from Miami, right? So that's the story. I'll play along."

"We got the broad," Tony reasoned. "He don't want we should hurt the broad."

As a reminder, he stroked Sandra's neck with the silencer and a sound came out of her like the squeaking of kittens in a cardboard box.

"No," said Joey. "I don't."

"And," said Tony, "we gotta ice 'em, what the fuck if it's tomorrow or today?"

"Yeah," said Bruno. "Tomorrow, what the fuck. Just as dead as like today."

43

It was dusk when Joey and Bruno emerged through the sliding door of the cottage.

The western sky was green and mauve, the trees had already gone black. A light breeze barely rattled the palm fronds, and there was a sense, as always at the close of a hot south Florida day, of the world exhaling a clenched and overfull breath and deflating slowly into a grateful languor. Luke the reggae musician was sitting at the far edge of the pool, his Walkman on and his feet in the water. Lucy the beautiful Fed was swimming silent laps in a flowing pair of boxer shorts. Steve had finished his beers and vanished. Wendy and Marsha passed by arm in arm, walking their cat on a leash.

Joey's head throbbed and his knees were stiff with fear. Bruno loomed over him like a building, and he tried to hold his face together as he nodded his hellos. He felt a rush of weird affection for these neighbors he barely knew, a flash of ferocious nostalgia for this life that seemed to be receding from him as fast and unstoppable as a comet. He could not help wondering if Tony was sitting close to Sandra, breathing on her, and the thought made him nauseous. He led Bruno across the damp tiles toward Peter and Claude's bungalow. Lights shone through the bougainvillea on the trellis. The front door was open, opera was playing. Joey poked his head in. "Anybody home?"

Claude came around from the kitchen. He walked toward them like he was modeling a mink, though in fact all he was wearing was a tiny pair of pink bikini briefs that stopped around three inches below his navel. "Oh, hi, Joey," he sang out above the music.

"Hi, Claude, how ya doin'?" Joey's voice sounded metallic and false behind his ringing ears. The whole world felt suddenly foreign to him and he wondered if he could possibly be fooling anyone. "I want ya to meet a buddy a mine from Miami. Claude, Bruno. Bruno, Claude."

The two men regarded each other like ambassadors from countries fourteen time zones apart. They nodded. It was impossible to figure which one decided they would not shake hands.

"Claude," said Joey, "my phone's onna fritz and Bruno needs to make a call. Any chance—"

"Come on in," Claude said. "We're just making some eggs before work."

He led the way back to the kitchen. Unlike Joey and Sandra's, the bartenders' kitchen didn't look rented, transient. It had white tile, plants, copper pots, and Joey felt a pang at such settled domesticity. Peter was hunkered over the counter, neatly dicing scallions. He was wearing briefs exactly like Claude's, except his were lime green. Joey introduced Bruno. Claude pointed to the wall phone. Then he broke eggs and hummed along with the music.

" 'Scuse me," Bruno said, in a voice surprising by its bashfulness, "is there a phone that's, like, more private?"

"Sorry," Claude said. "That's the only one."

Peter stopped his dicing and looked up from under his eyebrows to flirt. "No secrets in this house," he said.

Bruno tried a smile that didn't quite work. Teeth came out, but more like he was going to bite. He dialed Charlie Ponte's Miami club and tried to figure out a coded way of telling his boss the situation. This messed with Bruno's confidence. Talking was not what he was best at.

A flunky answered the phone in Miami. Ponte was in but of course he wouldn't take the call. No self-respecting mobster ever took a call the first time. Bruno was given another number and told to call it in ten minutes.

"Hope that's not a problem," Bruno bashfully announced.

"Don't be silly," said Claude. "Want some eggs?"

Bruno in fact looked hungry.

"No, Claude, no thanks," said Joey.

There was a silence, a long one. Joey stood in the foreign fluorescent light of the kitchen and watched Claude whipping eggs, Peter slicing mushrooms. He couldn't shake off the image of Sandra tied up in the chair, her pretty midriff ringed with rope, her mouth taped like a tear in the upholstery. And it was gnawing at him that there was nothing more he could do. He couldn't accept that.

"That opera you got on?" he said at last. " 'Zat *Don Giovanni?*"

Peter and Claude glanced at each other and seemed to be deciding whether they should laugh. Like a lot of people Joey had met in Florida, they sometimes couldn't tell when he was kidding.

"It's *Porgy and Bess,*" Peter said.

"Ah," said Joey, "I thought it was *Don Giovanni.* That's my favorite, *Don Giovanni* is."

Peter and Claude shared a wry look along the countertop. A funny kid, this Joey. Claimed to love opera, but couldn't tell Gershwin from Mozart. Or Italian from English.

"Bruno," said Claude, "how's the opera up in Miami?"

Bruno's mouth moved but nothing came out. He fumbled for a place he could put his giant hands without smashing something.

"Miami," Joey cut in dismissively. "Miami's nothin'. For opera, theater, New York is the place. Paradise. Paradiso." He reached for the bartenders' eyes the way a drowning man reaches for a log. But their attention was riveted on the omelette. Claude handed Peter the bowl of eggs. Peter poured them into the frying pan on top of the scallions and mushrooms. They gave a homey sizzle and started immediately to blister at the edges.

Joey went on, casual as cotton. "Yup, for all that culture stuff, paradise. Course, this is paradise too, but down here paradise is different, right? It's onna beach, by the water. Hey, when you guys go to work, you drive up along Smathers?"

It was a screwball segue, but not screwball enough to tear Peter and Claude away from their bubbling eggs. Bruno brought his eyebrows a quarter inch closer together, and Joey wondered if that quarter inch of displeasure meant that he'd get beat up some more.

"Usually we cut through town," Peter said blandly. He gave the frying pan a gentle shake. "It's shorter."

"Yeah," said Joey, "but if you're talkin' paradise, that ride up A1A, along the water . . ."

Peter reached for a spatula. Claude stretched toward a high cabinet where there was a big stack of plates. Maybe a dozen, all of them matching, enough for lots of friends. The plates broke Joey's heart.

"Sure you won't have some?" Peter offered one last time.

"Nah," said Bruno. "But lemme try this call again."

Joey shuffled his feet. Peter coaxed the omelette out of the pan. *Porgy and Bess* kept playing.

"Mr. Ponte," Bruno said. "Yeah, we hooked up O.K. . . . Nah, we're at a neighbor's. His phone, it like stopped workin'. . . . Well, here's the thing, the present you wanted, he says it's innee ocean. . . . Yeah, I know that sounds, like, crazy, but that's what he says. He says he can get it, though. Tomorrow—"

"Mind if we start eating?" Claude whispered.

Joey made a maternal sort of gesture, like motioning food into their mouths. He shot them a pleading look and he knew it went unnoticed.

"And another thing," Bruno said into the phone, "he says it's like worth more than we figured. . . . Nah, I don't know why. . . . Nah, it can't be in Miami, 'cause the present is down heah, ya know, like inna water. . . . Tomorrow, yeah, he promises. . . . Sure he invited us to spend the night. . . . Don't worry, Mr. Ponte, nobody ain't goin' anywhere. . . . Yeah, O.K., see ya tomorrow, bright and early."

———————— 44 ————————

"Ya think ya could maybe, like, untie her now?"

It was full dark outside and Tony had switched on the lamps in the Florida room. In their pools of thick yellow light, the scene appeared not merely squalid but lewd. By daylight, Sandra had seemed just one more bargaining chip, the handiest object of value to grab. With the onset of night, it moved to the forefront that she was also a woman. The fact of sex came out like a red star and colored the room in the nastiest way. Brute impulses hung in the air and everybody squirmed as if under a swarm of gnats. Sandra struggled to keep her posture. She wanted to believe that as long as she kept her shoulders back, her tummy in, as long as she stayed within her own crisp outline, she would be inviolable. Joey was less sure. The surrounding darkness made a sort of firefly glow come out of Sandra, and it seemed to Joey that with every nighttime moment

314

she was bound, the greater the chance that Tony and Bruno might get really crazy.

"Come on," he coaxed, "you got no reason to keep her like that."

"Fuck you, jerk-off," Tony said. "We don't need a reason."

He said it mildly, offhandedly, balancing his gun on his thigh. But now, suddenly, it was Bruno who seemed short-fused, exasperated. Maybe it was the strain of having to speak in front of strangers that had gotten him wound up. He stood over Joey and grabbed his hair. Then he yanked as if pulling up a weed.

"Kid," he said through clenched teeth, "I am really sicka hearin' your mouth. Ya talk too fucking much. In theah"—he pointed vaguely across the compound—"in heah, all ya do, ya talk, talk, talk. Like ya got somethin' to say, somethin' to bargain. But ya know what, kid? You ain't got shit to say, and you ain't got shit to bargain. No leverage. Zero. You're fucked. Understand that. Tony, where's that goddamn tape? I'm gonna shut this motherfucker's mouth so's I can have some peace and quiet heah."

Tony gave a little shrug; it was all the same to him. He reached into his jacket pocket and threw Bruno the roll of duct tape. The big thug tore a length of it off the roll; it came away with a sound like a ripping parachute. He slapped it on hard enough to make Joey's teeth hurt, and Joey, though his hands were free, didn't dare to reach up toward his face. The adhesive had a vile taste, it was like eating a fistful of stamps.

Bruno stepped back like a painter admiring his work. The silver slash where Joey's mouth used to be gave him satisfaction. But he wasn't quite ready to calm down yet. "Talk, talk, talk," he muttered. "With this fucking jerk, everything is talk, talk, talk."

Tony smiled at his colleague's little tantrum, and the smile tortured his dented lip. The gun was across his thigh, and he leaned a shade closer to Sandra, who glowed like a firefly in the nasty light.

"Now who could that be?" said Bert the Shirt d'Ambrosia to his dog.

It was twenty minutes before ten, not a time when visitors often called. The old man zapped the volume on the television, slowly got up out of his recliner. His chihuahua struggled out of its velvet bed and rattled along behind. "Who is it?"

"It's Peter and Claude. From Joey's compound."

Bert felt a quick clutch of dread, a feeling he remembered too well from his working years. It grabbed at his windpipe and made his rib cage squeeze down on his heart. He opened the door.

The bartenders stood close together in the bright light of the hallway. It was Leather Night at Cheeks, and they were wearing matched calfskin vests fastened in front with links of chain. "Hi, fellas," said Bert the Shirt. "Come on in."

"Just for a sec," said Claude. "What beautiful pajamas." They were plum-colored satin, piped with sky blue, and the buttons were made of shell.

"My wife bought 'em. Used to pick out all my clothes. Except shirts. Shirts, I had made. So what is this, guys, a social call?"

Peter and Claude stood there in the dim foyer and looked down at their feet. They'd argued a little about whether they should stop by at all. They had a certain tendency, they knew, to blow things out of proportion, to take a scrap of gossip and raise it to the level of tragedy. That happened in Key West, where life could be so placid, so restful, that people imagined upheavals, disasters, just to exercise their nerves.

"Bert," said Claude, "did you know Joey has friends down from Miami?"

Bert bent down and picked up Don Giovanni. "Why would I know that?" he said, and the bartenders had to start over.

"He came to use our phone before," said Peter. "Said his was on the blink. He had this guy with him—"

"Wha'd he look like?" asked the Shirt.

"Big, with 1950s hair," said Claude.

That described most of the people Bert knew. "He have a name, this guy?"

"Bruno," Peter said.

"Marrone," said Bert the Shirt.

"So Bruno used the phone," said Claude, "and Joey, well, from some things Joey was saying, we sort of got the feeling, we could be wrong, it might just be our imagination—"

"Spit it out," said Bert.

"We thought maybe he's in trouble and he wanted us to let you know," said Peter.

Bert absently stroked Don Giovanni and the dog put its cool nose between the buttons of his pajamas. "Well, ya did right comin' to tell me. I appreciate it."

The bartenders had expected more of a response. "Is there something we should do?" Claude asked. "Should we call the police?"

"No."

Bert volunteered nothing further, and now Peter

and Claude couldn't help feeling gypped. It seemed only fair to them that they should be given some information in exchange for theirs.

"Maybe we shouldn't ask this," Claude said at last, "but Bert, is this, like, Mafia?"

The Shirt launched into a mellifluous pause. He glanced from Claude to Peter, up at the crystal chandelier, down at the rug. He petted his dog, started to smile, erased the smile and put on a look that used to carry menace but had now become an expression of gentle warning. "You're right," he said softly. "Ya shouldn't ask."

It was midnight. Tony and Bruno had taken out huge black cigars and the Florida room was wreathed in smoke. Joey and Sandra faced each other across the width of the sisal rug and struggled not to gag on the stink of tobacco and the taste of tape. Outside, the air was heavy, moist, the palm fronds barely scratched against each other. Good conditions, if they held, for Clem Sanders to make his dawn departure. If they didn't hold? Joey chased the thought from his head. He was out of chances. Either the emeralds appeared tomorrow or everything was over.

Tony yawned. It was a profound yawn that twisted his scarred lip until it was almost folded double.

A moment passed, then Bruno caught the contagion. He stretched like a grizzly bear and gave off a sound like some large thing mating in the jungle. "Fuck I'm tired."

"Take a nap," said Tony. He was showing off, like he had better stamina. But then he yawned again.

"What about duh lovebirds heah?" Bruno gestured

vaguely toward Joey and Sandra, and in the gesture it was terrifyingly clear that the captives had stopped being human in his eyes. They were freight, furniture, mute parcels that needed guarding and were keeping him awake.

"Duh lovebirds," Tony echoed. He was getting slaphappy with fatigue, and the word tickled him. "Duh lovebirds, fuck 'em, whyn't we just tie 'em up together inna sack. Good and tight. Pack 'em away, forget about it, you and me can take turns sleeping."

Bruno took a puff of his cigar, then nodded agreement. He went to untie Sandra just long enough to move her into the bedroom and truss her up again. He got down on one knee like a grotesque troubadour and fiddled with the knots at her ankles. Then he muttered a curse, pulled a knife out of his sock, and cut the ropes. He did the same with the loops around her midriff, and the sight of his meaty hand against her body made Joey feel faint with rage.

For a moment Sandra sat as rigid as she'd been before she was unbound. Tony leaned over her and looked at her hard, the way a referee looks at a beaten fighter to see if there are any brain connections left, any sanity. "Listen, lady," he said, "you want I should untape your mouth?"

Sandra was afraid to nod. She felt that anything she did would be the wrong thing, would lead to some horrendous and perverse response. She just sat.

Tony wagged a warning finger in her face. "Any noise, any trouble, you're in deep shit, lady. You got that?"

He grabbed a corner of the duct tape and ripped it away. The skin around Sandra's mouth seemed to draw into itself like the foot of a probed clam. She licked her lips and felt a rough white residue of glue. "I have to pee," she said.

Tony followed her to the bathroom and guarded the door.

"And you, peckerhead," Bruno said to Joey. "You gonna be quiet, or do I gotta cut your fucking tongue out?"

Joey stayed still. It had worked for Sandra. Bruno grabbed the tape and yanked like he was starting a lawn mower. Joey's lips felt gone, his teeth felt suddenly as naked as those of a skeleton. Bruno stared at him with his oil-puddle eyes and seemed to be daring him to speak. He didn't.

"Get inna bedroom, Romeo."

"Lay down," Tony ordered when they were all assembled.

Joey and Sandra got into bed, and the thugs stood over them in some hell-born parody of putting the kids to sleep. Bruno had loops and scraps of rope slung over his shoulder like a cowboy. Tony slipped his gun in his pocket to free up his hands. He tied their outside ankles to the legs of the bed and their outside wrists to the corners of the headboard. Their inside wrists he tied together.

Then he brandished the gun. "Listen, you pains innee ass. One of us is gonna be sittin' right outside heah. Any noise, any aggravation, we break heads. Got it?"

The thugs turned off the bedroom light, and half closed the door behind them as they left.

For a few moments Joey and Sandra lay silent, trying to let some of the fear seep out of them. It was a moonless night and dim suggestions of starlight came in blue slices through the louvered windows.

"I hate sleeping on my back," Sandra whispered.

"Baby, I'm so, so sorry," Joey said. "I never meant—"

"I know you didn't."

She rubbed the back of her hand against his. It was almost the only thing she could move. There was love and forgiveness in the gesture and it put a lump in Joey's throat.

"If they killed us," Sandra went on, "they'd get away with it, wouldn't they?"

Joey nodded.

"Will they? Will they kill us, Joey?"

"I don't know."

"Why? It's not gonna get them their money, their jewels, whatever."

"It's not about that, Sandra. It's about not being made a fool of. It's about winning. They wanna win."

Sandra considered this, then tried without success to turn onto her side. "And you, Joey, whadda you want?"

He looked up toward the ceiling. It seemed very far away. He felt the back of his hand tied against Sandra's. It was hard to tell whose veins, whose pulse, was whose. What did he want? He wanted an honorable truce with his old life, and something like a fair start in the new one. He wanted a kitchen like Peter and Claude's, one that didn't look like the last tenants had bolted an hour ago leaving their dishes still in the sink. He wanted, he admitted now, a normal job, some normal friends who did normal things. He lay there trying to figure out how to explain all this to himself, how to sum it up to Sandra, and suddenly the thread, the cord that held the whole package together, seemed utterly clear to him. "I want you to marry me," he said.

For a while Sandra said nothing. She was not the type who fantasized about marriage proposals, and if she had been, she would not have fantasized being proposed to while her limbs were tied to bedposts and her free hand was bound with a greasy rope to that of her betrothed. Besides, was Joey full of love or just remorse? Maybe, for him, a proposal stood mainly as the biggest apology he could think of.

"Joey," she finally said, "I've been waiting a long time to hear you say that."

He gave a little laugh that was full of sad, sudden, and useless knowledge. "I been waiting a long time to get ready to say it."

"But listen," said Sandra. "Not tonight. Not with the state we're in. I'm not gonna hold you to what you say tonight."

"Hold me to it, Sandra," he said, and there was a note of pleading in his voice. "I wanna be held to it. This is what I'm telling you. For once I wanna be held to it."

At two A.M. Bert the Shirt d'Ambrosia was still sitting in his recliner sporadically looking at television with the sound turned off. But mostly he was thinking out loud, talking to his dog. "This is not good, Giovanni. Not good at all."

The chihuahua did a little pirouette on its velvet bed. The flickering TV picture made kaleidoscopes in its stuck-open pupils.

"Fucking Gino gets away clean, Joey gets grabbed. Ponte's gotta be very frustrated, very pissed."

The dog lay down and licked its private parts.

"Ya know what bothers me, Giovanni, what gets to me? In like the backa my mind, I can't help wondering if maybe it's my fault."

The dog gave a little whine of disagreement, or maybe it was in pain.

"Maybe I gave some bad advice," the Shirt went on. "Did I? I really can't remember. Sometimes, I'll tell ya the truth, Giovanni, I don't even notice I'm givin' advice. That's the scary part, huh? Sometimes I'm just yakkin' away, and a kid like Joey, he sees the white hair, he figures, hey, this old guy must know somethin'. Ha. Fuck do I know? Poor kid, he listens to me."

The old man shook his head. The chihuahua shook its whiskers. Then Bert spent a long moment climbing out of his recliner and the two of them walked stiffly to the bedroom.

45

Joey did not think he'd slept. He was too scared, too uncomfortable, too weirdly proud of himself for proposing marriage, and besides, he'd been keeping a weather vigil. He wanted to believe that by paying close attention, he could usher in a calm dawn, could keep away the winds or squalls that would prevent Clem Sanders from going to the reef. He lay still and silent, sniffing for airborne salt and iodine. The back of Sandra's hand was against his, his left ankle was chafed from the rope that held him down. Over and over again, he'd rehearsed what he would say to Charlie Ponte, how he would explain his plan for turning three million dollars into four. For what seemed like many hours he stared at the grooves in the louvered windows, searching for the first pale slices of saving light.

But he must have dozed at least, because suddenly the objects in the room had sharp outlines, people

were talking on the other side of the half-closed bedroom door, and he was extremely confused. He gave
an involuntary yank of the wrist that was bound to his
fiancée's. Sandra let out a little grunt of protest. Then
they both blinked themselves more or less awake.

"Lazy sacka shit," came a voice from the other side
of the door. It was followed by some slaps. "I pay you
to sleep, or what? Stupid fucking dagos I got heah.
Where's the fucking kid? I want my stones."

There was a scuffling of chairs being pushed away,
sounds of big bodies springing out of furniture, and
within a couple of seconds Joey and Sandra's bedroom
was invaded. Charlie Ponte himself led the charge.
He was wearing a silver jacket, his eyes were wild
above their liverish sacs, and the little man did not
look as faultlessly neat as Joey remembered. It was
the hair, which was now windblown, almost spiked,
peaked a little like a crown around the balding place
on top. Ponte was full of a manic, savage cheer that
was first cousin to blood-lust. He circled the bed and
grabbed Joey by the front of his pink shirt. "Rise and
shine, scumbag," he said. "Today's the day I get my
emeralds."

He seemed not to notice that Joey was tied, and he
started slapping him for not getting up fast enough.
The slaps made the bed bounce and Sandra started
to cry.

"Shit," said Ponte. "Shit. I ain't heah to deal with
assholes, and I ain't heah to deal with crying broads."
Only then did he see the ropes. "O.K., O.K.," he said
over his shoulder to the two thugs who'd accompanied
him from Miami. "Untie these losers and let's get out
onna fuckin' water."

On the water? The two goons leaned over the bed

and started wrestling with Tony's bizarre knots. The mattress rocked, Sandra whimpered. On the water? The new thugs took out knives. The steel got hot against Joey's ankle as they sawed away. He tried to think but things were moving way too fast for him. His eyes were crusty. He had to piss. He hadn't so much as yawned and already he'd been smacked across the face, pummeled around the nose. This wasn't the way it was supposed to happen. He'd rehearsed his pitch to Ponte; he'd thought the whole thing through. It was supposed to be civilized, a sit-down where people could work things out. This was just mayhem. One of the new thugs slipped with his knife and poked Joey in the calf. He started to bleed on the sheet. *On the water?*

"Mr. Ponte," Joey blurted, "wait a—"

By now Bruno had blustered into the bedroom. His boss had caught him napping and Bruno wanted to make amends by being extra ugly. "Can it, mouth," he said. He reached for Joey and held him by the throat while the other two finished unbinding him.

"But—" Joey squeezed out. Bruno backhanded him across the cheek.

The thugs yanked Sandra and Joey to their feet and pushed them out of the crowded bedroom. There was no air left in their bungalow, it was all dark suits that swallowed the light, black shoes that freighted the earth so it seemed to tip. "Lemme take a piss at least," Joey said as he was being bundled through the kitchen.

"Piss off duh backa duh boat," one of the goons advised him.

"What boat?" Joey was looking down at the black and white linoleum squares, they swam at his feet and made him dizzy. He spotted his sunglasses on the kitchen table and just managed to grab them as he was being swept along.

"What boat?" mimicked Charlie Ponte. Joey's bafflement amused him and he spat out a derisive laugh. "Asshole."

The goons obediently cackled along with their boss as they herded their captives out through the sliding door and into the compound. The morning was dead still, a pillow of mist sat on the flat water of the hot tub. The sky was halfway bright but even through shades it had no color, and Joey, who had little experience with dawns, guessed that the sun had been up for maybe fifteen minutes, half an hour. He wished he could stop being so confused and wished he could walk closer to Sandra, could push aside the two thugs who loomed between them as they crunched along the gravel path.

Bruno and Tony's dark blue Lincoln was parked between some garbage cans around the corner. There was no other car.

One of the new goons opened a back door and stuffed Sandra and Joey through it. He climbed in after them, his colleague sandwiching the captives from the other side. Bruno got in the driver's seat, Tony squeezed in the middle, and Charlie Ponte rode shotgun.

"Where are you taking us?" Sandra asked.

Bruno pulled away from the curb.

Ponte didn't bother to turn around. He didn't see the point of talking to hostages. But he was in high spirits and he did like talking to his boys, liked to show them how smart he was. "Broad wants to know where we're takin' 'er. Kid wants to know what boat." He shook his head. "Ya know what's wrong with this fuckin' country? People are stupid, they can't figure nothin' out. Fuck she think we're takin' 'er? To the emeralds, honey! Inna boat we come down from Miami in. Guy tells us the stones are inna water. Fuck's he think—we're gonna fetch 'em with a Lincoln?"

The goons laughed.

"But Mr. Ponte—"

"*But Mr. Ponte,*" mimicked the Miami Boss. "Asshole's a broken record with this Mr. Ponte shit. Smack 'im for me, will ya." One of the backseat thugs obliged, but he couldn't get much leverage in the packed car and the blow did nothing more than make Joey's sunglasses rattle on his nose. "And tell 'im he ain't heah to talk, he's heah to bring us to the stones." Ponte paused as the Lincoln slunk through the narrow empty streets. "And if he don't bring us to the stones, he better not waste his fucking breath yammering, 'cause he's gonna have a long swim home."

46

The cigarette boat was cobalt blue and shaped like a shark. It sat perfectly still in the celery-green water at the end of the Flagler House dock. Two guys had stayed on board. Divers. They had stubble beards, crinkled eyes, and wore wet-suit tops unzipped to the solar plexus. One of them reached up to help Sandra into the open cockpit. The other started the twin engines; they fired into life with a roar that shook the ocean. Joey was pushed into the boat, then he was pushed up against a gunwale as Ponte's goons piled in behind him. He just had time for one quick look at the sleeping hotel, early light throwing triangle shadows across its balconies. Then the cigarette spun seaward. In three seconds the hull was up on plane, shushing over the slashed water of the Florida Straits with a sound like a million skis on icy snow.

Charlie Ponte crab-walked across the tilted cockpit

and screamed in Joey's face: "So, asshole, where we goin'?"

White-knuckled, Joey squeezed the gunwale and willed his brain to think of something clever. Through the wildly vibrating air he glanced back at Sandra; she was pressed between two goons on a little wraparound settee at the stern, and her eyes did not look good, they looked forlorn as candles whose wicks had gotten buried in wax. Joey was still stalling even as he watched Charlie Ponte's small neat fist coming toward his chin, and the instant before the blow was one of stunning clarity in which Joey realized there was no lie that would save him and the truth probably wouldn't help much either.

Now, what the hell, he was ready to talk, but his mouth wasn't quite right after getting hit, and all that came out was a mumble.

"What, asshole?"

"Like twelve miles up," he shouted. "There's a piece a land shaped like a lamb chop bone. Then it's about five miles out from there. But listen—"

Charlie Ponte didn't want to listen. He had what he needed, and he turned his back on Joey. He shot a look at the guy at the wheel. The guy nodded. Then Ponte smiled. It was a big smile of genuine contentment. Finally he was winning, and winning was what he liked.

Joey leaned back against the gunwale and watched Key West whiz by. Smathers Beach and the open U of the Paradiso condo. The airport with its faceted weather bubble like the eye of a bug. Cow Key Channel, and beyond it, the gross pyramid of Mount Trashmore. Joey gave a bitter silent laugh. Gahbidge, he said to himself. Nice try at a life, kid, but it's all coming down to gahbidge.

He turned around and looked out at the blank green water of the Straits. Here and there it was blotched purple with coral heads or under the ragged shadows of the few small clouds. Joey scanned the horizon, wondering if he'd be able to spot Clem Sanders's salvage boat, wondering if Clem Sanders had even made it out there. He took big gulps of salt air, and each breath carried a different mix of fear and acceptance. He'd had his plan, his plan had been short-circuited, and now what happened would happen. Like Bert said, who could argue with that?

The boat roared on. Sometimes its noise was a featureless rumble; then at moments its engines would sync a certain way and there'd be piston beats like drumrolls. The sun was flame white by now and they slammed straight toward it. Tiny pellets of spray screamed past the boat and pebbled Joey's glasses. Up ahead, maybe half a mile landward, was the promontory that led into the channel for the Sand Key Marina. A low line of mangrove arced around like a rib. The boat driver pointed to it, Joey nodded, and the cigarette banked steeply and headed south.

Joey searched the horizon. But his shades were bouncing on his nose, his eyeballs were rattling in their sockets, and he couldn't see much of anything.

The driver abruptly cut back on the engines.

The deafening noise softened to a rhythmically popping clatter, the spray stopped slicing past. Then the water caved in like a disappointed dream and the blue boat came off of plane and settled down heavy and dead. The driver pointed past the bow. "We got company out there, Mr. Ponte."

Ponte moved his mouth but no sound came out.

The driver reached into a small compartment underneath the steering wheel and produced a pair of binoculars. " 'Bout two miles off," he said. "Could be a shrimper, but I don't think so. Looks to be anchored."

"Gimme the fucking glasses," Charlie Ponte said. He pressed them to his eyes and Joey could see his hands were trembling. Unconsciously, his thugs moved closer around the Boss, as if they could somehow all see through the binoculars at once. With the boat stopped, the morning sun was brutal, and everybody started to sweat. "What you know about this, kid?"

Joey took an instant to look at Sandra. His expression was wry, flat, and fatal, the same expression he'd worn when he asked her to drop everything and move to Florida with him. "It's a salvage boat, Mr. Ponte. I been tryin' to tell ya this all morning."

No one moved, no one breathed. Ponte's face crawled, his upper lip pulled back from his teeth. He wanted to claw at Joey's eyes, wanted him held down so he could kick him around the cockpit. The only thing that stayed his fury was that he couldn't spare the time.

"How the fuck you know about it?"

Joey leaned back against the gunwale and exhaled loudly. He shifted his weight, looked down at his feet. A man with a tortured conscience, with a terrible confession to make. "Gino," he softly said.

Ponte went toward him and hit him with both hands on the chest, as if he were trying to beat open a door. "Gino, *what? What*, Gino?"

Joey looked off to the side. "Gino put the stones

there, ya know, to hide 'em. He's got a piece of the salvage job. That's all I know about it."

Ponte stepped back, rubbed his chin. There were nine of them baking in the boat, they could smell each other through the salt and iodine, but Charlie Ponte was a guy with a knack for making himself a hole in space and disappearing into it all by himself. He thought a few seconds. Then he came up with a way to make himself look at least a little bit smart. "Ya see?" he said to no one in particular. "Ya see? I knew he was protecting his twat of a brother." He paused, tapped his foot. "How many people they got on that boat?" He said it to his two divers.

The divers shrugged so that their wet suits squeaked. "Couple guys to go down probably," said the one who hadn't been driving. "Couple guys to work the winches. Maybe a guy to navigate."

"Armed?"

The divers looked at each other. "Not usually. One gun, maybe, for sharks or whatever."

Ponte went to the edge of the boat and spat thickly in the green water. Then he reached inside his silver jacket and came out with a dainty little pistol. "Fuck it, let's take 'em."

"But Mr. Ponte—"

"Shut your fuckin' mouth. Bruno, smack this fuckin' kid for me, willya? Smack 'im one like it was Gino too. Fucking family. This whole fuckin' family, I'm sick of 'em."

47

The loud blue boat lifted its nose from the water and hurtled forward. Ponte's troops spread their feet like sumo wrestlers to keep their balance while they readied their guns. Sandra sat alone now on the stern settee, and Joey sidled back to her. No one bothered to stop him. He took Sandra's hand and squeezed it between both of his.

Up ahead, like a small pillar of flame in the ferocious light, was the red buoy that Joey had used as a signpost for the place to scuttle the *Osprey*. Beyond the marker, the water roiled and bounced, curled like cake frosting and twinkled like smashed crystal. A third of a mile shy, the driver geared down into neutral and again peered through the binoculars. "They're anchored on the far side of the reef," he announced.

"So wha' does that mean?" Ponte growled.

"It means we have to go in real slow, pick our way across."

Ponte pulled back his lip. He had by far the faster boat and it killed him to give up an advantage. Joey looked across at the salvage craft. It was a tub, maybe forty feet long, painted battleship gray. It sat high and graceless in the water, top-heavy with smokestacks, cranes, a pilothouse. "Fuck," said Ponte. "We can't just make a run at it?"

"Not unless you wanna rip the bottom outta this baby."

"They see us yet?"

The driver shrugged. "If they're lookin' this way, sure. If they got divers down—"

"And my stones? They find my stones?"

The driver was sweating rivulets inside his wet suit and gave in to an instant's exasperation. "Fuck should I know, Mr. Ponte? They got their anchor down, they're probably still looking."

Ponte stiffened at his tone, then decided to let it slide. The cigarette was a valuable thing. He needed this guy to keep it that way.

The driver shifted into forward. But now he didn't push the boat onto plane. He went slow, the engines sounded constipated, like a Porsche in second gear. The blue hull pulled even with the red buoy and suddenly the water went crazy all around it. It streamed in tiny rapids, sucked itself into hollowing whirlpools. Ponte's thugs lurched around like drunk men dancing, their guns held gingerly in front of them like cocktails they were trying not to spill. In the heightening sunlight, the reef shimmered as through aquarium glass. Brain coral sprouted like astonishing broccoli. Fan coral waved with the currents, bright yellow fish swam between its magenta fronds. Fascinated, Sandra leaned over the side.

"I'm glad I'm getting to see this," she said, in a tone of deathbed gratitude that made Joey want to bite his own face off with remorse. "The girls at the bank, they said it was beautiful."

The gray salvage boat was not more than a few hundred yards beyond them now, but it inhabited a realm of flat, calm sea that seemed a universe away. The men looked up at the sunstruck pilothouse. Only Sandra watched the water.

She elbowed Joey in the ribs.

He didn't react and she elbowed him again. She pointed with her eyes toward a small bright something that had just poked through the surface, maybe twenty yards beyond Clem Sanders's boat. Joey trained his gaze that way and squinted through his blue-lensed sunglasses. Searing light glinted off the green ocean, and in the center of his view there was a brighter glint, a blinding, intermittent flash. It was the reflection off a diver's mask. There was a person in the water. He had something in his gloved hand, and he was waving it toward his comrades on the slow gray boat.

There was movement on the deck of the salvage craft and in an instant it was clear to everyone what had happened.

"Shit. Balls. Fuck," said Charlie Ponte. "Get after those bastards."

The driver accelerated and the blue boat started cutting a lunatic slalom course through the coral. The twin props clattered and complained as they bit through the shallow, viscous water, the cockpit leaned steep as a butte as it banked left, cut right, and zigzagged back again. Immaculate cobalt fiberglass scratched here and there against the lacerating reef; the sound was like giant cat claws ripping at silk.

And on the gray salvage boat, Clem Sanders and crew looked up from their triumph and realized they were under siege.

The diver with the emeralds bolted for home as though a shark was nosing his flippers. The engines were started, they belched wet black smoke through their rusty stacks. The windlass creaked, yanking up the anchor with Clem Sanders already on the fly. Joey tried to peer through the sun-shocked windows of the pilothouse, to see if the treasure hunter had yet managed to get on the radio to his promised allies.

The cigarette boat pivoted and splashed, its freight of dark suits and gunmetal bouncing like loose boxes in the back of a truck. The salvage boat, as if in mockery, had turned its wide gray ass on them and was heading out to sea. Charlie Ponte's silver jacket was soaking through with sweat. He believed in going in straight lines toward what he wanted, knocking over whatever was in the way. It pushed him toward utter madness to have to zig and zag, shuck and jive, dodge like some *melanzane* halfback while his quarry receded in plain view. "Come on, come on," he screamed at the driver. The voice was not quite human, and the driver ignored him. He wrenched the wheel and scudded past a coral head that poked up like a murderous cauliflower, he skated through a school of indifferent parrot fish. Joey and Sandra huddled on the settee, their ears assaulted by the screams and rumbles of the tormented motors.

The salvage boat was escaping, but it was not escaping fast. It furrowed through the deepening water as if it were planting corn, its ancient diesels laboring like a tractor in soft dirt. It was maybe half a mile off by the time the cigarette had danced and capered to the far fringe of the reef. The boatload of gangsters did a final series of dips and curls, endured a last set of scrapes and dings, then finally broke free of the killing shallows. The driver jerked the throttle, the cigarette took off like a goosed horse, and Charlie Ponte's thugs were pressed backward like astronauts on takeoff.

The white sun shone fiercely on the torn-up water, and every instant the gap between the two boats narrowed. Sandra and Joey had their elbows locked like kids on a roller coaster. Off the wide transom of the salvage craft fanned a peacock's tail of flattened wake, and the cigarette homed in like a missile on that swath. Ponte was grinning now. He held up his dainty gun and yelped. His goons smiled. Victory was on the horizon and the horizon was scudding toward them. They were so close that they could see the rust bubbles in the salvage craft's gray paint, could see the lumps in the old boat's imperfect welds. They were almost ready to start shooting. The engines of the blue boat sounded full of steely joy.

There was no way, above that potent motor noise and the glad hissing of the water, that the thugs could hear the coast guard helicopter approaching from behind, coming at them low and hard, its rotor blades pitched frantically forward, a machine gun poking out of its bulletproof belly at a jaunty angle like the dick of a dog.

Nor did they yet see the two marine patrol cutters closing in from seaward in a neat V.

They saw only the lumbering craft ahead of them.

There was something pathetic in its attempt to outrun them, pathetic like a hobbled cow trying to escape a lion. Through the glare of the pilothouse windows, they could see the silhouettes of Clem Sanders and his crew. Either they would surrender the emeralds or they would die.

Then the driver of the cigarette noticed the circle of dented water where it was beaten down by the force of the chopper's blades. He looked over his shoulder, the others followed his eyes. There the helicopter was, not more than fifty feet above the water, not more than a hundred yards behind them and closing fast.

"Ditch the guns," the driver screamed. "Drop 'em low over the side, right now."

He said it in such a knowing panic that no one hesitated a second. Five firearms of assorted make and caliber were jettisoned, adding to the untold number of weapons scuttled in the Florida Straits. In another fifteen seconds the aircraft was directly over them, hovering in the hot sky like an apocalyptic bug, and a stern voice bizarrely amplified was ordering them to halt their vessel and stop their engines. The driver throttled back and looked at Charlie Ponte. Ponte stood numbly by, sweat-soaked and bewildered. The salvage craft slowed and began to circle, came back as if to gloat. From over the horizon came the twin wakes of the converging cutters, completing the elegant geometry of a capture at sea.

Joey squeezed Sandra's knee. Then, as the chopper was descending, bringing its pontoons close to the water, he got up and walked over to Ponte. The Boss was so boggled that Joey had to tap him on the shoulder. "Mr. Ponte," he shouted above the whooshing clatter, "we're fucked heah. Attempted piracy. You know that, right?"

Ponte didn't answer. He looked straight ahead; his goons milled stupidly around the cockpit.

"Well, lissena me," Joey continued. "I can take care of it."

The little mobster glared at the kid, his glance emerging from under one eyebrow. The chopper had set down, its slowing rotors still churning the water like a blender.

"I can't fight you, Mr. Ponte. I can't run away. I know that. You wanna kill me, kill my brother, sooner or later you will. But inna meantime I can get us outta this. Now here's the deal."

Ponte's lip pulled back as if to protest. Who was this fucking nobody to tell him what the deal was? But he looked down at his dainty feet and let Joey continue.

"You lemme handle this. I get us off, you gimme ten minutes to explain things. That's all I'm asking. After that, you do what you want."

Ponte said nothing. Joey pressed. "Gimme your hand on it." Grudgingly, the little gangster held out a damp and slippery mitt. But the eyes were unyielding, they promised revenge.

Three guardsmen were standing on the pontoons of the chopper. They had repeating rifles. The cutters had closed in. Clem Sanders was edging his slow boat nearer. And it was hot as hell in the merciless sun.

48

"What the hayle—" said Clem Sanders, leaning on the railing of his old gray salvage boat. His bleached blue eyes were narrowed against the glare and he was trying to act like he hadn't almost wet his jumpsuit while the cigarette was pursuing him.

The salvage craft was tied up to one of the patrol cutters. Ponte's blue boat was tied up to the other. The helicopter sat between them like a dragonfly on a swimming pool.

"Hi, Clem," Joey said. "Sorry for all the, like, commotion."

The coast guard guys from the chopper hadn't lowered their rifles. One of the men from the marine patrol, a beefy guy with a crew cut and Ray-Bans, said in a surprisingly squeaky voice, "You wanna tell us what this is all about?"

"Just wanted to see how the search was going," Joey said. "My brother's one a the investors."

The marine patrolman looked dubiously at the boatload of thugs, sizing them up while they fried in the sun. Charlie Ponte with his soaked silver jacket and hair spiked around his bald spot like a crown. Tony with his evil lip, his toupee blown cockeyed; Bruno with the blank dumb gaze of the enforcer; the two from Miami dressed in blue suits and shiny black shoes in the middle of the Atlantic Ocean. " 'Zat so, Clem?" he asked.

The treasure hunter shot a hard look at Joey before he answered. " 'Tis," he said.

The cop frowned down at his fingernails. The boats and the chopper rocked lightly together in the morning's weak breeze. "Then why the hell'd ya call us?"

For an instant Sanders looked almost sheepish. "Didn't know they'd be here," the salvor said. "Didn't recognize the craft."

"It's my fault," Joey offered. "I shoulda let 'im know. But it was like, ya know, a whim."

"A whim," the cop with the Ray-Bans repeated. The boatload of thugs did not strike him as a whimsical group, and he managed to look skeptical behind his opaque glasses. But no crime had been committed as far as he could tell. "So Clem, whaddya want us to do?"

Clem Sanders savored the moment. His boat was taller than the others, and he loomed on the deck like a preacher casting his blessing across the waters. He didn't need to look down to know that the desperadoes in the cigarette were going through a purgatory of helplessness: the ocean revealed guilt even as it offered absolution, and Sanders let the guilty squirm. He cleared his throat, scanned the sky. To the north, the low land of the Keys was just barely visible, a smudge on the horizon. To the south was the indigo ribbon of the Gulf Stream, winding its way to the ends of the earth.

"No need to trouble about these people," he said at last. "But if you'd be so kind as to cruise on in with us—"

Sandra suddenly got up from the stern settee. Her hair was mussed, her pale skin was splotched pink with sun and fear, but she managed to sound calm and self-contained, poised within her own crisp outline. "Mr. Sanders, would it be O.K. if Joey and I rode in with you?"

The little flotilla bobbed in the water, the guardsmen finally brought their rifles to their sides, and Clem Sanders smiled like a politician pinching babies. "Well, of course, little lady. If you like."

Sandra smiled as one of the marine cops reached a hand to help her over the gunwale. Joey followed. But if he felt relief, Charlie Ponte squelched it in a second.

"See ya later," the little mobster said. He tried to make it sound casual and friendly. It didn't. "We got a date."

Joey just nodded, then trailed Sandra as she climbed a rusty ladder that brought them to Clem Sanders's side. Lines were uncleated, fenders brought in. Above the noise of starting engines, the treasure hunter said to Joey, "Kid, what the hayle you doin' here? You said you wanted to stay outta the public part."

"Those guys," said Joey, by way of answer, "they like persuaded me to change my mind."

◦   ◦   ◦

Very Key West. The scene at Mallory Dock was very Key West.

As the crew was tying up, Joey looked out from the deck of the salvage craft. Pier bums, their beards stiff with salt and old food, were milling around, sucking their gums. Aging hippies with gray feet swarmed toward the spectacle like pigeons to a tower. But mostly Joey saw cameras. Local cable crews, network gangs from Miami, tourists with video zooms—they were all there to document this old Key West tradition, this miracle of money coming out of the water.

A line of city cops had cordoned off the gangway. County sheriffs made a gauntlet to the armored car. Highway cops on Harleys sat in a chevron formation in front of the mayor's ancient but gleaming Imperial convertible. Meek visitors edged cautiously closer, not sure where they were allowed to stand, not sure if what they were gawking at was interesting. Key West—a town of people passing through, looking around, waiting, hoping for something special to happen, then not having a clue what was going on when it did.

Clem Sanders, his sun-crevassed lips spread into his best television smile, his gold doubloon flashing on its leather necklace, led the triumphant procession down the ramp. He waved, shook hands, tantalizingly dangled the burlap pouch full of Colombian emeralds. The treasure hunter's ego swelled to fill the moment the way bread rises to fill a pan. Joey felt himself squeezed to the edge of the occasion, the fringe of events, he felt himself disappearing, and he was glad for that. He was suddenly very tired. Emeralds, brothers, ropes, speedboats; gangsters, helicopters, blows to the head, threats against his life. It was extremely draining, disorienting almost to the point of madness. He suddenly felt like a loose wire, limp, frayed, power oozing away like blood. He put his hand in the small of Sandra's back. He badly needed to touch her, to ground himself, to remind himself how compact she was, how neat and taut the little humps of muscle on either side of her spine.

They followed in Clem Sanders's wake, down the gangway and across the concrete pier. Through the tumult, they only half heard the salvor's quick sly comments to reporters, only half noticed the clicking cameras, the helmeted police. Then a familiar voice broke free of the crowd's buzz from behind the saw-horse barricades.

"Joey, hey, Joey."

It was Zack Davidson. He was wearing his pink shirt, his khaki shorts. His collar was turned up perfectly but not too perfectly, his sandy hair fell as if by chance into an inevitable arc over his forehead. "We got it, huh, we got it!"

"Hm?" was the best Joey could manage.

"Joey," said Zack, reaching over the barricade to punch him lightly on the shoulder. "We just got a little bit rich. For a guy that just got rich, you don't look that happy."

Joey smiled, but his cheeks felt weary, bruised, and sunburned as they bunched up around the corners of his mouth. He toyed with his sunglasses, slid the earpieces through his hair. "I guess I'm getting ready to be happy, Zack," he said. "I'm not quite there yet, but I'm getting ready."

Numbly, his hand on Sandra's slender back, he followed the course of Clem Sanders's small parade. It was just after they'd passed the armored car and were standing in line for handshakes from the mayor that Joey saw the dark blue Lincoln waiting for him across the street. Sandra saw it too.

"Whyn't you go inna motorcade with Clem," Joey said to her.

Sandra said nothing and didn't budge from Joey's side. Together, they inched down the receiving line. Twenty yards away was a rank of cops, and beyond that was a wide world where there was no one to protect them from Charlie Ponte and from the long reach of the old neighborhood.

"Really, Sandra," Joey whispered. TV cameras were on them, local big shots were slapping backs. "These guys are killers. They're really pissed, their patience is used up. There's no reason for you—"

"There is a reason, Joey," Sandra interrupted. "You asked me to marry you, remember? You said I should hold you to it. So I am. I'm going with you. It's part of the deal."

"Sandra—" he began, and then he realized it was useless to protest. He took a deep breath, cast a foreigner's glance at the cameras and the gawking tourists, then steered his fiancée out of the receiving line. "Awright," he said, "we can't dodge no more. Let's go and get it over with."

They walked with neither haste nor hesitation through the line of cops and toward the waiting Lincoln. Tony shot them a malicious scar-lipped smile from behind the wheel, and Bruno held a back door open for them with the grim solicitousness of an usher at a funeral.

49

Steve the naked landlord was on his second beer and had just lit a fresh cigarette from a butt still smoldering in the ashtray. He watched Joey and Sandra approach along the white gravel walkway, Tony and Bruno trudging along behind them. Then he turned his paperback facedown on the damp tiles. "Joey," he said, motioning him over, "can I talk to you a sec?"

Joey crouched down on the pool's cool apron.

"Joey," Steve said. "All these houseguests, these parties. Is this gonna be like a regular thing?"

Joey waited the usual beat, but Steve's smile did not appear. Naked, working on his morning buzz, he was still the landlord. "I wouldn't call 'em parties," Joey said softly.

"No?" said Steve. He lifted an eyebrow toward their bungalow, and in that instant the house appeared not just small but miniature, a scale model of a place where people could maybe make a life. "Joey,

every time I turn around, you got more people
crammed in there."

"We do?"

Steve just dragged on his cigarette and blew smoke
out his nose. "Come on, Joey, let's be fair."

"Fair," said Joey. "O.K." He straightened up, then
sucked in a deep breath scented with jasmine and
chlorine. He reached for Sandra, touched her arm to
stop the electricity from oozing out his fingertips, and
walked with her between the pool and the hot tub,
Tony and Bruno following behind. Palm fronds
scratched lightly overhead, the high sun slashed
through in punishing slices. Joey's stomach didn't feel
right, it felt like stale but icy air was swirling around
inside it.

The sliding door to their bungalow was open wide,
and through it came a sort of cool dim humming
threat, a threat like that of a too quiet jungle. Joey
swept off his sunglasses as he crossed the threshold.
There were more people than he expected, more
faces than he could process at once.

Charlie Ponte's Miami thugs and divers were glut-
ting up the living room. Thick thighs were thrown
over the arms of chairs, big white shirts with dark
stains in the armpits were arrayed next to wet suits
against the walls. There was a stink of clashing after-
shaves and dry-cleaning fluid being sweated out of
fabric too long in contact with damp skin. The thugs
regarded Joey with an indifference more wilting than
active menace.

In the Florida room, the louvered windows were
still cranked shut, and a furtive, illicit twilight was being enforced against the day. Charlie Ponte, his silver
jacket splotched with moisture, his hair restored to its

usual neatness, was perched in the wicker seat where
Sandra had been tied. Bert the Shirt d'Ambrosia,
dressed for the occasion in nubbly black linen, a bur-
gundy monogram on his breast pocket, rested on the
settee, his chihuahua serene yet vigilant in his lap.

Next to him sat Gino Delgatto, nervously crossing
and uncrossing his legs. Joey's half brother did not
look healthy. His skin was yellowish and he hadn't
dropped the weight he'd put on while holed up at the
Flagler House. His eyes were gradually disappearing
under pads of excess skin, his fatty chin had lost the
squareness that brought him to the brink of being
handsome.

You had to look beneath the fat to see how he resembled his and Joey's father.

Vincente Delgatto was sitting with a perfect still-
ness that was the emblem of his dignity and his au-
thority. He was lean, dry, with a long crescent face
and a crinkled stringy neck that no longer filled his
stiff collar. He wasn't dressed for Florida. He wore a
gray pinstripe suit and a red silk tie with a massive
double Windsor knot. He had a broad straight nose
that came down directly from his forehead, and his
teeth were long and veined with brown, stained by
half a century of cigars, espresso, and red wine.

Joey stared at him through the strange striped dimness cast by the louvered windows. His legs felt dis-
connected from him, he wondered if his brain had
come unmoored from getting hit too many times then
being cast out in the throbbing sun. He didn't quite
recognize his own voice. "Pop?"

Bert the Shirt, a man who had been dead, seemed
to recognize the moment after which a person could
not be pulled back from oblivion, helplessness, or par-

alyzing confusion. "I called him, Joey," he blurted. "Last night."

"The fucking old lady," Charlie Ponte grumbled. "He's always in my face down heah, always stickin' his nose in."

"What could I tell ya?" Bert stroked his dog and addressed this to the room at large. "I tried to do the right thing."

"Pop," said Joey.

The old man gave the smallest nod, the smallest lift to his thick brows, whose tangled black and silver strands gave a look of stark realism to his deep but filmy eyes.

"Awright, awright. I ain't got all day," said Charlie Ponte. "I'm givin' the kid a chance t'explain things. So go 'head, let 'im explain."

Joey was still standing numbly in the archway. He looked down and saw that Sandra, silent, alert, practical Sandra, had slid a kitchen chair in next to him. He sat.

But Charlie Ponte, having ordered Joey to speak, now decided he wasn't quite ready to give up the floor. He ignored Joey, ignored Gino, ignored Bert, and spoke only to the patriarch. "But Vincent, remember, you and me, we got an agreement. We can sit here and make nice, but if I don't get satisfaction from this meeting—"

Ponte stopped talking because it was one of those statements that could not be finished. But then the Miami Boss made the mistake of thinking back over the whole story of the heisted emeralds, the irritating trips down the Keys, the waiting, the disappointments, the manpower wasted, the putrid and futile evening with the garbage, and he launched into a slow burn.

"Because I'm tellin' you, Vincent, the aggravation I been getting, the bullshit I been putting up with, and for what? From who? From this nobody, this jerk, this little faggot with a pink shirt on, this fucking clown—"

"Cholly, he's my son."

The short and simple words, the way the old man said them, stopped Charlie Ponte cold. Acknowledging the bastard, proclaiming the tie. This changed things. Kinship. It was in the blood, sure, but that was only half of it. It also hinged on what people said to each other, or didn't say, what they were proud of and what they kept buried. All of a sudden Ponte was less sure he knew who he was dealing with.

"The agreement," Delgatto senior went on, in a voice that was low but carried, that seemed to be everywhere at once, like a rumble underground, "it stands. Ya don't get satisfaction, ya do what ya gotta do. No retaliation. I shouldn't've agreed, but I did. I didn't know. My son Gino, he fucked up bad. Didn't ya, Gino?"

Gino nodded miserably. His fat chin was down on his chest, and his shirt was stretching open between the buttons.

"Only thing I ask," the patriarch concluded, "is ya give Joey a fair shot at workin' things out."

Ponte pursed his lips and nodded. Joey swallowed, looked at his father. The old man met his gaze and Joey took away from the exchange a hit of that undaunted readiness, the anyplace, anytime preparedness he'd felt that first time alone in a boat, alone on the ocean, alone in the night. His head cleared, the situation was clean as a razor. Either he would save himself or he would not.

"O.K.," he began. "O.K."

But immediately he stopped. He swiveled on the plastic seat of his kitchen chair and looked back over his shoulder. "Sandra. Where's Sandra? I want you here, baby."

In the Florida room there was a shuffling of feet, a disapproving rearrangement of limbs. You didn't invite broads to a sit-down. But it was Joey's meeting now, it made his hair itch to realize he could do what he wanted. Bruno carried a chair for Sandra. She made no sound as she sat. Her hands were motionless in her lap and her posture was breathtaking.

"Right," said Joey. "O.K. Yeah. . . . Now, Mr. Ponte, your emeralds are gone, you saw that for yourself. They're inna vault by now, there's nothing to be done." It was a dicey opening, it already cast the Miami Boss in the role of the guy who'd lost. Ponte looked down between his knees and tugged at a thumbnail. "So let's like go over how it got to that.

"The two guys that ain't around no more," Joey went on, "Vinnie Fish and Frankie Bread—they grabbed the stones from Coconut Grove, and my brother Gino was in with them. Weren't ya, Gino?"

Gino looked down and nodded, his fat chin coming up like a high collar as he did so.

"So the deal was this," Joey said. "Vinnie and Frankie, they stashed the stones on a junky old fishing boat, then they took the boat out and sank it. The idea, ya know, was to let some time pass, let things cool off some, then the three of them would salvage the wreck and walk away with the money. Ain't that right, Gino?"

The older brother looked at Joey from under the fat pads of his eyebrows. Gino didn't mind lying to

Ponte, not at all, but he wanted to be in control of
the story. His bastard kid brother was now asking him
to drive blind, let go, bend over and leave it all to
him. The idea rankled almost as much as it terrified.
But Gino had no plan of his own and it seemed he
had finally realized he had nothing more to lose. He
nodded.

Vincente Delgatto moved forward an inch in his
chair and folded his lean and papery hands.

"So O.K.," Joey resumed. "Frankie and Vinnie disappear. For Gino, this is good news, bad news. He's
got nobody to split the money with. That's good. He's
got no one to help him salvage the boat. That's bad.
So the night your boys grabbed me and Bert and took
us to the gahbidge—Gino set that up so he could run
up the Keys to scope things out. Bert knows that too.
Don'tcha, Bert?"

The Shirt petted his chihuahua, scratched it behind
the ears. "He used us. As decoys. No hard feelings,
Gino, but that wasn't right. Someone coulda gotten
hurt. Sandra here, she coulda been with us."

Joey's fiancée gave a small nod of gratitude for
Bert's concern. The nod stretched but did not violate
her crisp outline.

Then a low rumble seemed to ripple the striped
dimness of the Florida room. It was Joey and Gino's
father starting to speak. The voice was very sad. "To
your own brother you do this, Gino?"

"Pop, hey, it's history," said Joey. "Besides, Gino
and me, we forgive each other, don't we, Gino? Life,
ya can't get through it without ya forgive people, ya
drown in bullshit otherwise. I mean, forgiveness,
that's really what this meeting is about."

"Bullshit," put in Charlie Ponte. "This fucking

meeting is about what happened to my fucking emeralds."

"Right, Mr. Ponte. You're right. But forgiveness, the stones, it all comes together. 'Cause here's what happens. Gino realizes there's no way he can salvage the wreck alone. So he goes to a pro—that's Clem Sanders, the salvage guy. He reaches him through me, 'cause, hey, this is my town now, I know who to go to. This much, Mr. Ponte, I'm involved"—he lifted his hands in a gesture of surrender—"and this is why, me too, I'm asking your forgiveness.

"But this Sanders, he's a businessman, he's legit, he's got a certain way he does things. An expedition, he sells shares. He keeps a third, he keeps the right to sell a third, the third third he sells to the guy who proposes the search. So now Gino is back to being a one-third partner. You follow?"

Charlie Ponte propped his elbows on his knees and rested his chin on his crisscrossed fingers. "So you're telling me that Gino owns a one-third share a my fucking emeralds?"

"This is exactly what I'm telling you, Mr. Ponte. It's in the public papers, you can check for—"

"Now wait a—" Gino interrupted.

His father cut him off in turn. "You done enough, Gino. Your brother's talkin' now."

Joey hesitated. He glanced at Bert, pulled in a chestful of air, and continued. "Now here's where the forgiveness comes in. The shares that Gino bought, they cost ten thousand dollars. Bert fronted the cash for 'em, didn't ya, Bert?"

The old mobster nodded, his chihuahua twitched.

"So Gino is gonna pay that money, outta pocket,

that's gonna be, like, his cost for forgiveness, his penalty for fucking with you."

For an instant Gino froze like a skunk in headlights. Then he pitched thickly forward on the settee. "Joey, hey—"

His father raised a single gnarled finger. "Zippuh your fucking mouth shut, Gino. You'll pay the money."

"And of course," Joey resumed, "his third of the emeralds, that goes right to you."

He fell silent, as though his pitch was over. Outside, the pool pump switched on and hummed, the palm fronds rustled dryly. Don Giovanni stood up and did an impatient pirouette in his master's lap. Sandra smoothed her cream-colored skirt across her thighs. Joey glanced at her pink neck and wondered how many years in Florida it would take for her to get a tan.

Charlie Ponte's mouth was moving as he worked out some arithmetic, but the numbers didn't solve his problem. When he finally spoke, it was not to Joey but to Vincente Delgatto, and his tone was oddly calm. It was the tone of a general who'd endured the charade of diplomacy and could now move joyously into war.

"Vincent," he said, "outta respect for you I'm sittin' heah quiet, I'm listening, I'm giving these boysa yours every chance. Joey heah, what he says, a lot of it makes sense. I give 'im credit. But Vincent, his bottom line, it fucking stinks. I lost tree million dollars in emeralds. He's telling me he can get me back one million, and he's makin' it sound like a big fucking favor. Come on, Vincent, you know it as well as I do—

the numbers don't add up. Whaddya want from me? I got no choice."

Vincente Delgatto sat still as a parked truck. But there was an admission in his posture.

Even Bert the Shirt could not deny the numbers. "Don't come out right," he muttered, like he was checking over a grocery receipt.

Sandra, who never fidgeted, started fretting with her fingertips.

"Wait a second, Mr. Ponte," Joey said. "Who said anything about one million dollars? I'm talking four million. This is what I was tryin' to tell ya all morning. Since last night I been tryin' to tell ya this."

Everybody sat. Everybody waited. There was a lull in the breeze and the air smelled like scorched sand.

"Mr. Ponte, lemme ask you something. The Coombians—you ever tell 'em about the missing stones?"

The Miami Boss could not help snorting. "Right," he said. "And look like a horse's ass? Like I can't control my own people?"

Joey raised a pacifying palm. "Who's gotta know it was your own people that heisted 'em? You never got 'em. End of story."

Ponte pursed his lips and considered.

"Now tell me if I'm wrong," Joey continued, "but these emeralds, they were, like, a goodwill gesture, like to make it up to you for some other business they screwed up, right?"

Ponte gave a grudging nod.

"Well, they screwed up again. I mean, hey, what kinda goodwill gesture is it if you never got the stones? The way I see it, they still owe you."

The Miami Boss threw a sideways look at Vincente

Delgatto. The patriarch sat still, his expression blank as the ground.

"They're gonna believe me," Ponte said, "I tell 'em the stones never got to me?"

Joey leaned forward over his knees and put a conspiratorial rasp into his voice. "Mr. Ponte, this is the beauty part—they don't hafta believe you." He gestured past the louvered windows at the world. "They're probably watching it on television right now. It's gonna be in all the papers. Headlines. Pictures. *Three million in mystery gems*—this is a big deal down heah, you know that. Your stones ended up innee ocean, you have no idea how. This is what you tell the Colombians. Shit, what's three million to them? They wanna keep you happy, they'll give ya three million more. Three, plus the one ya got from Gino. That makes four, am I right?"

Ponte tugged an ear, looked down at the sisal rug striped with filtered sunlight. Then he shrugged. Then he almost smiled. Then he said to Joey's father, "Vincent, where you been hiding this boy?"

The patriarch moved his lips a fraction of an inch and his filmy eyes darkly gleamed with something like pride.

"So Mr. Ponte," Joey said, "we have an understanding here?"

"Enough with the Mr. Ponte shit," said the little mobster from Miami. "Call me Charlie, kid."

50

"Come on, Pop," Joey Goldman said. "This is Florida, we'll sit out by the pool."

It was midafternoon, the sun was fierce though the breeze was freshening, and Joey slid the outdoor table into a patch of shade. The compound had grown weirdly, blessedly quiet. Gino Delgatto, fat, oily, and ashen, had bolted immediately at the conclusion of the sit-down. Bert the Shirt, using his frail dog as an excuse, had gone home to take a nap. Charlie Ponte had kissed his older colleague from New York, given Joey an avuncular pat on the cheek, gathered up his sweaty minions, and headed for Miami. Sandra had excused herself to take a long hot bath, to try to soak the terror and the memory of captivity out of her sun-burned skin. Only Steve the naked landlord was about, and he turned his bare backside on his newly troublesome tenant, this quiet guy who all of a sudden was always entertaining.

"A swim or something, Pop? I'll lend ya some trunks."

Vincente Delgatto hadn't even taken off his dark gray suit jacket, and he seemed to find something droll in being invited to go for a swim. He gave a small smile, strong, veiny teeth flashing for just an instant between his thin dry lips. Then he waved the suggestion away. "No, Joey, no thanks."

They fell silent and for a moment the father and the son enjoyed the air that was the temperature of skin and carried the pleasantly rank sweetness of wet cardboard. "Joey," Vincente Delgatto said at last. "Joey. The way you handled that, it was beautiful. Beautiful." He sounded transported, as though by an aria perfectly sung. "I never realized, Joey. What you could do, I never realized."

Joey Goldman toyed with the ribbing on the sleeve of his pink knit shirt, slid the earpieces of his sunglasses through his hair. "There was nothin' to realize, Pop. Up in New York, when I lived up there, hey, let's face it, I couldn't get outta my own way, I couldn't do nothin'."

His father shook his head, which wobbled slightly on his shrunken neck. An old man's errors mattered both more and less than a young man's. More because there was less time to undo them; less because there was less time to endure their consequences. "You coulda done plenty, Joey. I never gave you a chance."

Joey just shrugged. The palm fronds scratched like brushes on a snare drum, the little wavelets in the pool traced a bright pattern on the bottom. The silence went on a beat too long, and Joey fiddled with his glasses. "Sal gave me these shades, ya know. Like a going-away—"

"You hate me, Joey?"

The son hesitated. It was not so much that he was in doubt about his answer as that he was taken aback at being asked the question. His father was not a man to make a habit of offering his upturned throat.

"Nah, Pop," Joey said at last. "I don't hate ya. I wish some things were different, but hey."

"Things could be different, Joey." Vincente Delgatto reached up to straighten his already perfect tie. This was still, as it had been for as long as Joey could remember, the signal that the Don was about to offer the benefits of his influence. "I could set you up good. You wanna come back to the city, I could set you up very nice."

"Nah, Pop, that's not what I mean. I don't want that anymore. I'm over it. What you do, what Gino does, it's not for me. I know that now." Joey paused, tapped his fingers on the table, and gave a little laugh. "I ain't a tough guy, Pop. Never was. I useta try to be, and let's face it, it was fucking ridiculous.

"Besides, New York? Nuh-uh. Pop, my life's in Florida now. I like it here. It's easy. Palm trees. Sunsets. And I'm gonna tell ya somethin', it's gonna sound, like, sarcastic, but I don't mean it that way. You did me a big favor, not takin' better care a me before. I mean, if things weren't so, so frustrating up there, I never woulda left. I wouldn'ta thought of it. I mean, how many guys even think of it?"

It was not a question meant to be answered, but Vincente Delgatto raised a finger as though he might try. Then he dropped his hand into his lap and a faraway look came into his deep but filmy eyes. His lips pushed slightly forward toward what might have been a pout but looked, oddly, almost like the preparation for a kiss, and suddenly, for the first time ever, it occurred to Joey to wonder if his father had sometime thought of leaving, of changing, of turning his back on the neighborhood and his place within it to live a life he'd chosen for himself.

"Pop," said Joey, "can I ask you something?"

The old man simply cocked his head to listen.

"Did you love my mother?"

For some moments Vincente Delgatto did not answer. He stared down at the damp tiles around the pool, at his polished shoes. He was still a married man. It was not proper to discuss such things. But Joey had received so little and was asking for so little now.

"Yes," the father said. "I loved her very much."

Joey nodded. "I'm glad. She loved you too. You ever think of being with her? I mean, really being with her?"

The old man retreated behind his filmy eyes and scudded backward through the decades, back to the times when, just as now, his errors had both mattered more and mattered less. "Often," he said, in that voice that was like a rumble underground. "Every time we could get away, ya know, to someplace peaceful. Every time I held her in my arms. But Joey, I couldn't do it. I couldn't."

"I know you couldn't, Pop," said Joey Goldman. He reached out and put a hand on his father's. From inside the bungalow, he faintly heard the whoosh and plunk of Sandra getting out of the bathtub. She was so neat, Sandra was, so precise. By now she'd have a towel tucked under her arms, she'd be wiping the steam off the mirror to brush her hair. "I'm glad you thought of it at least, Pop, I really am. I'm glad you were, like, romantic."

──Epilogue──

Charlie Ponte's emeralds were appraised at three million two hundred and ten thousand dollars. But Joey was mistaken in imagining that his one-third share, discreetly registered under the name Zack Davidson, would break out at seven figures. In his newfound enthusiasm for all things legitimate, he'd overlooked the one great disincentive to doing things the lawful way: taxes. The disbursed funds were just under eight hundred thousand per partner.

Charlie Ponte took this graciously. He could afford to. The Colombians seemed mainly amused that he'd gotten his stones heisted; they seemed, as well, reassured at the disorganized state of the Italian-American mafia. They added three million dollars' worth of free cocaine to Ponte's next shipment and told him not to lose it.

Zack himself, ever the gentleman, insisted on giving

up a proportionate fraction of the quarter-million Joey had promised him.

Joey brought home something shy of six hundred thousand, and tried without success to give part of it away. Bert the Shirt d'Ambrosia would not accept a penny beyond Gino's repayment of his ten-thousand-dollar loan. "But Bert," Joey had argued, "nunna this coulda happened without you. It was you that started me thinkin' about a scam that fits the climate. You helped with—"

The old man had stopped him with a wave of his elegant, long-fingered hand. "Joey, I got what I need." Then he paused. "You wanna do something for me?"

"Yeah, Bert. This is what I'm saying."

"Here's what you can do." He held Don Giovanni in his palm and lifted the tiny animal toward Joey's face. "The fucking dog, if I die again, I mean for good this time, promise me you'll take care a the dog. It's like a curse from my wife, I'm passing it along."

Vincente Delgatto gave an admiring chortle when Joey confessed to him how he'd finagled a third of the treasure, but he also declined to share in his younger son's windfall. "No, Joey," he'd said, his profound voice thinned out by the wires of the pay phone a discreet distance from his social club. "From Gino I'd take because to Gino I've given. But from you, no, I'd be ashamed."

The Don, however, did accept a first-class round-trip ticket to Key West to attend Joey and Sandra's wedding. He was accompanied by best man Sal Giordano, to whom Joey had also sent the finest pair of sunglasses he could find. Gino Delgatto was invited but did not attend. Perhaps he did not want to chance being spotted at the reception at the Flagler House, where he—or rather, Dr. Greenbaum—still owed a tab of nearly eleven thousand dollars.

Joey and Sandra were married in a civil ceremony on a blisteringly hot day in the middle of June. Outside the courthouse, the palm trees rustled dryly, sounding like a broom on a sidewalk; smells of jasmine and iodine wafted through the dusty air. The bride wore a cream-colored skirt and a matching blouse with shoulders built in. She'd tried to get tan for her wedding day, but had managed mostly to turn her short hair nearly white. She flushed a becoming pink during the ceremony; her green eyes moistened and shimmered like the calm and prosperous ocean.

Bride and groom held hands as the vows were pronounced, and Joey Goldman made no attempt to choke down the lump in his throat. He took in the grand words pronounced in a somewhat hurried monotone by the judge, and in his own mind he distilled them down to an essence from which he took enormous comfort: "To make, ya know, a life together. Do stuff, look out for each other. It's, like, serious."

Suddenly awash both in romance and funds, Joey had suggested a lavish honeymoon, perhaps in Rio, but Sandra, practical and steady, had argued for postponement. There was, for now, too much to be decided. Joey and Zack had agreed in principle to become partners in business; they had not, however, figured out what kind of business it should be. In the meantime they were keeping their jobs at Parrot Beach, conferring as often as time allowed while leaning on the Plexiglas that covered the pristine and silent model of the perfect life in Florida, the Saran Wrap swimming pool and the tiny people on lounges. Sandra was still working at the bank, but had cut back on her hours so she could begin to shop for a house. She wanted something small, unpretentious, easy to keep clean; Joey lobbied for something grander, hidden behind hedges and banks of bougainvillea, and of course with a pool.

They looked at many places, and after looking they would sit in the old Caddy with the smashed windshield and come up with all sorts of reasons not to buy. The truth was they were looking for excuses not to move just yet. They had come to feel an odd affection for the mismatched furnishings and thrown-together people of the compound. It had been, after all, their first nest in their new life, and the more they thought about it, and the more they understood they would in fact be moving on, the more it seemed to them that they'd been very happy there.

Match wits with the best-selling
MYSTERY WRITERS
in the business!

SUSAN DUNLAP
"Dunlap's police procedurals have the authenticity of telling detail."
—*The Washington Post Book World*

☐	AS A FAVOR	20999-4	$3.99
☐	ROGUE WAVE	21197-2	$4.50
☐	DEATH AND TAXES	21406-8	$4.99

SARA PARETSKY
"Paretsky's name always makes the top of the list when people talk about the new female operatives." —*The New York Times Book Review*

☐	BLOOD SHOT	20420-8	$4.95
☐	BURN MARKS	20845-9	$4.95
☐	INDEMNITY ONLY	21069-0	$4.95
☐	GUARDIAN ANGEL	21399-1	$5.99

SISTER CAROL ANNE O'MARIE
"Move over Miss Marple..." —*San Francisco SundayExaminer & Chronicle*

☐	ADVENT OF DYING	10052-6	$3.99
☐	THE MISSING MADONNA	20473-9	$3.50
☐	A NOVENA FOR MURDER	16469-9	$3.99
☐	MURDER IN ORDINARY TIME	21353-3	$4.99

JONATHAN VALIN
"A superior writer...smart and sophisticated." —*The New York Times Book Review*

☐	LIFE'S WORK	14790-5	$3.50
☐	EXTENUATING CIRCUMSTANCES	20630-8	$3.95
☐	SECOND CHANCE	21222-7	$4.50

ANTHONY BRUNO
"The best fictional cop duo around." —*People*

☐	BAD BLOOD	20705-3	$4.99
☐	BAD BUSINESS	21120-4	$4.99
☐	BAD GUYS	21363-0	$4.99
☐	BAD LUCK	20934-2	$4.99

At your local bookstore or use this handy page for ordering:

DELL READERS SERVICE, DEPT. DGM
2451 South Wolf Rd., Des Plaines, IL. 60018
Please send me the above title(s). I am enclosing $_____.
(Please add $2.50 per order to cover shipping and handling.) Send check or money order—no cash or C.O.D.s please.

Ms./Mrs./Mr. _____

Address _____

City/State _____ Zip _____

DGM-4/93

Prices and availability subject to change without notice. Please allow four to six weeks for delivery.